The

Peculiar Grace

of a

Shaker Chair

a teacher

dreams

of

summer

The Peculiar Grace of a Shaker Chair

a teacher dreams of summer

Ian Ruderman

STAR BELLY BOOKS
ARLINGTON, MASSACHUSETTS

ISBN 9780692209141

To Melanie, Henry and Will

When good is near you, when you have life in yourself, it is not by any known or accustomed way; you shall not discern the foot-prints of any other; you shall not see the face of man; you shall not hear any name; the way, the thought, the good, shall be wholly strange and new.
  -Ralph Waldo Emerson, *Self-Reliance*

[I]n this world you will have to make your own way. To do that you must have friends. You can make friends by being honest, and you can keep them by being steadfast. You must keep in mind that friends worth having will in the long run expect as much from you as they give to you. To forget an obligation or be ungrateful for a kindness is a base crime – not merely a fault or a sin, but an actual crime. Men guilty of it sooner or later must suffer the penalty. In personal conduct be always polite but never obsequious. None will respect you more than you respect yourself. Avoid quarrels as long as you can without yielding to imposition. But sustain your manhood always. Never bring a suit in law for assault and battery or for defamation. The law affords no remedy for such outrages that can satisfy the feelings of a true man. Never wound the feelings of others. Never brook wanton outrage upon your own feelings. If you have to vindicate your feelings or defend your honor, do it calmly. If angry at first, wait till your wrath cools before you proceed.
  -Elizabeth Jackson's dying advice to her son, Andrew

Life and the Party

One

When I crossed the state line into New York, I began to have second thoughts. On the side of the road I saw the flag of late summer: grass browning out, leaves getting darker and thicker. The pavement had become pale and shimmery. The clock on the dash no longer made sense. I was thinking in fifty-minute blocks instead of hours, of lesson plans instead of meals. And when I flicked off the radio and rolled down the windows, there was that smell. Something about the trees in this corner of the world, the already hot morning, the purple wildflowers, the lumber mill, the gravel pit, the whir of my truck's tires, the spot where two years earlier a tornado had torn through the trees and left behind a sea of splinters.

A few minutes later I coasted over a graceful hill and from behind a veil of maples my school emerged. Once The Mount had been the site of an industrious Shaker village and for some years afterward an academy of excellent repute, but two decades of steady decline had almost ruined the place. When I'd arrived eight years earlier, I'd found a school that was little more than a ragged stump in the woods, a lonely child with three minivans, an asthmatic yellow bus, a grimy cafeteria and a collection of dorms that could only be described as fixer-uppers. But hard work over time inspired change, and now the dorms were scrubbed and cheerful, the headmaster's house was freshly white, the Tannery's windows were gleaming in the morning sun, and the library's new metal roof was creaking its tribute to late summer.

I parked outside Wickersham, unfolded from the driver's seat and climbed two flights of dim stairs to the Winter Meeting Room. Pausing in the doorway, I saw Candy Dafoe, wearing red sneakers and a pair of enormous pink and green shorts, merrily shaking her fist at someone foolish enough to smile at her on the first day of school. They all looked quite happy as they jockeyed for pastries and found seats, but there was one couple—a mutual curiosity as to what pastry the other was sniffing gave them away—that stood out. Handsome and pink cheeked, he had a face that would've looked good on a paint can. She, in prim white shorts and a Kelly green polo shirt, made me think of new dishtowels. And when they reached across each other, he for a mug, she for a napkin, I could tell they weren't quite sure where everything belonged.

I stole into the room and poured a glass of cranberry juice. The girl in white shorts lifted her eyes from the bagel she was wrapping in a napkin and I said hello. She stuck out a firm hand and apologized for stealing my breakfast.

'Take anything you want,' I said, 'even the furniture. I'm Jeff.'

She nodded at her guy, who was now by the window working on his cheese danish. 'I had a feeling. I'm The Girlfriend Mary.'

Her comment made me think of mangers and Magi and told me she wasn't working on The Mount. I didn't get to question her though, for as soon as Candy heard my voice, she spun around and put me in a bear hug. Another friend started tickling me, someone messed up my hair, and for a moment I wasn't on the verge of thirty-five. I was ten and doing a football drill, running between two lines as my buddies knocked the stuffing out of me. *Big guy! So nice of you to grace us with your presence! We almost sent out a search party! Check you out!*

When the mugging stopped, our meeting began and The Girlfriend Mary's boyfriend—now sans his better half—started to squirm. Sympathetic, I ventured a smile in his general direction, but the young man kept looking at me funny, as if he had the same shirt or something, maybe with different buttons, and he was too shy to say anything. So I turned my attention to the official introductions, and in time Candy presented the squirmer as 'Sam Iafrati, our new Swiss Army Knife.' Aha, he's a tool, I thought, and I enjoyed my joke for about five minutes until the soporific effect of a guest speaker sucked all the energy out of my body. I think the guy was talking about the plight of adopted middle children, or was it the union of psychopharmacology and pedagogy in community building? No matter, my eyelids slid shut and soon I was back in New Hampshire, hammering nails into my mom's deck. I could've stayed there, too, but the butterflies of July were scared off by the banging chairs of September, and when I sat up, I saw folks heading for the doors. For a second I thought we were done, but then the fog lifted and I realized I was being sent off yet again to write down goals for the year.

Given forty minutes to do the impossible, I drove up to my apartment in Medicine Shop, where I dropped my duffle by the stairs and opened a few windows. Air began moving through my four rooms, stirring dust and alerting a horde of black flies that their long summer vacation was over. Rolling up a magazine, I felt the stir of exhilaration. One or two of the flies noticed and tried to flee, but it was too late. The slaughter was quick and brutal, and once I'd checked to see that the fridge and the television still worked, I swaggered proudly back to the Winter Meeting Room.

When I sat, Candy spotted my foolish pride and asked ever so sweetly if I'd share my goals. I declined, so she smiled wryly and insisted, most likely in retaliation for the note I'd passed earlier, one that asked whether her new hairdo was *The Country Mullet* or *The Northern Belle*. But now that she'd challenged me, I had a choice: I could cower like a rookie or act like the unprepared interim department head that I was. Rising to the occasion—or was it bait?—I cleared my throat and shared that I wanted to go on a real vacation this year, drink better beer, eat less chocolate and, most importantly, find out where Candy got those amazing pink and green shorts she was wearing.

As a few people chuckled, Candy rubbed her nose with her middle finger and I was quite pleased with myself. She'd get me back—she always did—but for the moment I was in stride.

That night the smell of barbecue pulled me across fifty yards of twilight to Art and Goldie Remlap's house. On their patio I found Candy playing quarters with Sam, The Girlfriend Mary and a few others. At the grill our resident mensch, Art, was flipping burgers. His wife, Goldie, who supervising with her hand on her hip, spotted me the second I stepped out of the shadows.

'Hey stranger,' she said, smoothing the front of her skirt.

'Hey yourself,' I said, giving her the quickest hug possible and starting a round of how-was-your-summer with the rest of the gang. Like me, they were sad to be losing the freedom of July and August, but as the first tinges of red and yellow lined the playing fields, they were also excited for the kids to bring order back to our lives. Goldie, my tenacious opponent in the popularity contest that had resulted in my becoming an interim department chair, was by far the most excited, for the each school year brought her not just students to inspire but also a new crop of unwed faculty members to torment.

'You know,' she said, making sure Sam and Mary Katherine were a safe distance away, 'I asked that little Iafrati boy if he'd gotten his marriage license yet, and I swear his face turned white. And that girlfriend of his, she gives you the most innocent smile ever, just what you'd expect from a Catholic school teacher. But I saw the corner of her mouth turn up when I started teasing him, and I knew for sure that when she wants the ring, my word, it is hers.'

Under the guise of grabbing a beer I took refuge at the edge of the party. A few minutes later Candy joined me on the grass and we watched the last glimmer of pink fade above the hills across the valley.

"Goldie's already up to speed," I said.

Candy gave me a shove. 'Proving yet again, how lucky we are to have you as department head.'

'Remember, sister, it's one semester and then it's back to the coal mine.'

'Please, you're the guy who turns kids onto Jane Austen and Isabella Whatshername. When it's time, that chair is yours.'

'And if I don't want it,' I said, risking serious injury, 'I'm sure Goldie will do a great job.'

Candy grabbed the front of my shirt. 'Don't you dare talk like that. Wait, have you been working on your resume?'

'Not yet,' I said, prying her fingers from my lapels, and while I did my best to assuage her fear of Goldie and her vanity, a woman in jeans and a white shirt came out of the house. From her interview five month earlier, I remembered a black leather portfolio, a pale gray resume and a navy suit. But tonight with the porch light behind her she was a silhouette and a halo. Candy and I watched her—her being our new ELL teacher, Kara Calabria—move over to the quarters game and lean against an empty chair.

'I put that girl under the table twice this week,' said Candy, forgetting that she was mad at me. 'But she's got potential.'

'Someone should've warned her about your hollow leg.'

'I did, but she's stubborn.' To illustrate her point, she told me Kara had been cutting her mom's grass ever since her dad died. I didn't see how that was stubborn, but I agreed that she was nice to look at. Candy told me I was a dog and wondered if maybe Kara would like hook up with an interim department head, and if maybe that wouldn't change my mind about leaving.

'So she single?' I asked.

'She told me she's on the fence about some guy. Maybe you could knock her off?'

Of course she had a boyfriend. But considering my less-than-ambitious goals for the year, it was probably better that way. 'You saying I should throw a rock at her?'

'I think charm works better. Do you still remember how?'

I was pretty sure I did, but since I hadn't been on an actual date in close to a year, she had a point.

'How about I follow his lead?' I asked, nodding at Sam Iafrati, who was having a hushed but heated exchange with Mary Katherine. They'd moved to a patch of grass down the road and the shadows hid the exact shape of their words, but you could hear the dread in his voice.

'That'll get you far,' said Candy, and she planted a fat kiss on my cheek. 'Dude, there's something you should know. I thought you might've figured it out by now, but you're obviously too stupid. Anyway, remember those discussions *you* initiated last spring about collaborating and how we do it so poorly? Well, while you were off banging women at fat camp, we decided you'd be the perfect one to show us how to do it.'

'Do what exactly?' I asked.

'We meant to tell you, honest...'

'What am I doing?'

'...but you didn't call us, so we sort of forgot to tell you about your new boy.'

I finally realized that she was exacting her revenge.

'No,' I said. 'Iafrati can't be mine? He can't be English?'

'But he is, and you are going to be so good together. Guy's worked at a newspaper. He's taught summer school. And since you're sharing your sophomores, you can kick back and give him half of everything. I can see you now, fast asleep at your desk while he teaches grammar.'

'Team teaching? No, no, the kid should be an intern, with a mentor who isn't his department chair.'

Candy rubbed my head. 'If you have any complaints, you'll have to take them to the headmaster. You know, come to think of it, he's the one that should've called you, so why the hell am I apologizing?'

'This sucks,' I said, pulling up some of Goldie and Art's lawn, 'I haven't said squat to the guy. No wonder he's so freaked out.'

'He probably thinks you're a giant asshole,' said Candy, 'but, hey, you've got the whole year to make it up to him.'

Two

We had to sit down together, so the morning after I ignored him at the faculty meeting and for most of the party, Sam hiked the lonely road up to my apartment and banged politely on my door. Inviting him in, I apologized for being away all summer and handed him the syllabus I'd sketched out. Nothing was set in stone, I assured him, as he read for thirty seconds, scratched a spot below his left eye and read for thirty more. When we finally started talking about our class, he couldn't keep his eyes off the small hoop in my left ear. Maybe he was trying to figure out whether I was gay. Maybe he thought French presses—I'd been holding mine when I answered the door—and oriental rugs were signs of homosexuality. To confuse me even more, he eyed the bricks over the woodstove and told me I had a lovely apartment. Lovely? Who was this guy? Candy kept insisting he was funny and that he looked like a promising teacher. But as Sam ruminated on my course description, I got the feeling they were both pulling my leg.

When I couldn't take any more, I went to the kitchen and grabbed the muffins I'd bought that morning. Back in the living room I found Sam at the bookcase, eyeing my library of stolen fiction and a few relics from my college days. He grabbed a cranberry muffin and I asked how he'd ended up on The Mount.

'I drove,' he said with an awkward smile, and he confessed he'd more been interested in schools in Virginia and the Carolinas. Being inexperienced, however, he had little choice but to feign excitement when our headmaster called with the prospect of a unique one-year position. When he arrived to find Don DeWillum without a hiring committee or even a real job description, he almost got back in his car. But then Candy Dafoe and Gunnar Davis, my other best friend and our highly-respected Dean of Studies, stepped out of the summer haze, and despite the fact that they were wearing bathing suits and carrying a cooler full of adult beverages, Sam had a real interview.

The quartet sat under a tree, Sam perched atop the cooler so he wouldn't mess up his suit and the others sprawled on beach towels at his feet. As they chatted about the weather, teaching, coaching and the art of raising money, Goldie and Art Remlap passed by on their way to look at puppies. From Goldie, who stayed for the interview, Sam learned that no one in the English Department—except for her, of course—stuck to their syllabus, and we all needed to grade harder. From Gunnar Sam learned that I was nice but ornery. Upping the ante, Candy bragged that I'd qualified for the Summer Olympics in the javelin. To their amazement, Sam didn't bat an eye—a javelin throwing English teacher, why not?—so Gunnar informed him that I'd memorized the entire *Odyssey* and was in the habit of reciting it at parties. That I was six foot nine, tattooed like a pirate and missing teeth were tidbits Candy tossed in to rouse our new headmaster, who'd already met me but had wilted to the point of incoherence in the afternoon heat.

'How drunk were they?' I asked.

'Beats me,' said Sam. 'But they had fun messing with me.'

'And you still took the job?'

To her credit and probably against her will, Goldie pointed out that I was not an evil giant, but Sam still brought a slingshot in the form of Mary Katherine.

As I pondered how I might encourage the rookie to take a red shirt year and let me do all the heavy lifting, he took my copy of *The Scarlet Letter* from the bookcase. A tough novel, I'd taught it to honors classes and one particularly ambitious section of American Literature. Sam closed the book, suggested skipping the introduction, which usually is a wise move, and we got down to the business of fleshing out our course.

When lunchtime rolled around, we strolled down to the cafeteria and ate sandwiches under the pines. Afterward, I took an ice cream sandwich to the classroom I hadn't seen in three months and started pushing desks into place. I'd always taught with them in a circle, but when the custodians vacuumed the ratty green carpet, they left the desks in rows so we'd know they'd been there. Anyway, five minutes after I'd made my circle and cracked a window, the rest of the English Department sauntered into the room.

In the moment before I started talking, just as silence turned into attention, I fantasized about my a speech. I'd start on a personal note: my mother's ashes had been spread along the river she'd loved and I'd already received two offers on her summer house. I still had the Tudor to deal with, but I was ready. I'd connect empty closets to the sense of purpose I felt driving back to The Mount. Then I'd get to my message: how we should talk less in class and trust kids' intentions even when we don't understand their ideas. It's a question of faith, a belief that all will come round right if we just turn to each other for support. It was a principle eight years in the making, no need to explain the allusion or to smile at Goldie. No other olive branch than humility.

Then I welcomed Sam to the Department. Then we gave him overviews of our classes. Then we talked about book orders and field trips. Then we passed around a big bag of M and M's and I handed out an article on teaching poetry, which elicited a few sideways glances because our real chair, ancient Oscar Lazarus, never passed out olive branches or articles about teaching. Looking over my work, someone joked about getting homework before the first day of class. Someone thanked me and asked if she could open another window. By all means I said, and I reminded everyone that I was just keeping Oscar's seat warm while he was away.

Goldie, who'd enough humility for one day, tapped her pencil and stared into space. But when folks started reading my article and making satisfied noises, I thought, maybe, just maybe, she'd would get over whatever was bugging her and keep things civil.

Three

We'd endured orientation, two dorm meetings, an all-school assembly, another cookout, and now the cruel march to enlightenment was beginning, so we introduced ourselves, practiced the kids' names, and Sam, looking very professional in his crisp white shirt and college tie, stepped into the spotlight. The script was simple: give out a poem, explain what we were doing and make a good first impression. Unfortunately, my partner waded into an extended anecdote, swam off on a tangent for a historical reference and crawled back to tread a little water. One by one our students began drowning until a disinterested girl snapped her gum. Without missing a beat, Sam walked to the door, picked up the garbage can and held it under her nose as if it were the solution to all that had gone awry in the last five minutes. The girl spat out her offending gum without protest, but then Sam noticed Joe Causeway, a seventeen-year old sophomore with exceptionally thick and exceptionally dirty glasses, had a finger in his nose. Sam looked the boy square in the eye and said 'we don't do that here.'

That's right, no digging without a permit, and I saw a prodigious shadow hovering outside the door.

'Okay folks,' I announced, as our new headmaster slid into the room, 'in groups of three you're going to read the poem and look for two very specific things that I will now write on the board. Mr. Iafrati will put you in groups.'

Sam read the names aloud and the kids changed seats. Soon they were working earnestly and we were moving from group to group coaching them. For exactly five minutes, Don leaned against the wall at the back of the room; then he slipped out as quietly as he'd slipped in.

'What was that?' asked one little smartass.

'What was what?' asked Joe.

'That shadow, didn't you notice the eclipse?'

'The big guy was here?' asked another student. 'No way.'

I told them to keep working—the headmaster could do whatever the hell he wanted—and after class I apologized to Sam for butting in.

'Maybe I was aiming a little too high,' he said. He glanced at the window. There was a fluffy brown cat on the sill staring back. 'What would you do different?'

I made a few suggestions. Sam said 'got it' three times and went off to tutor somebody. I went off in search of coffee and got found by an attractive woman.

I was in the back of faculty lounge trying to remember which coffee mug was mine when Kara Calabria gave me a little elbow. She was wearing a silk blouse, a dark linen skirt, and calfskin boots, and because we were old friends by now, I told her she cleaned up nice and could pass for a lawyer. We sat in the overstuffed chairs across from the mailboxes cradling some horrible coffee and with a laugh she describe her previous life teaching ELL in New York City. The tips were good—a Swiss watch from a Saudi boy, Broadway tickets from a South American beauty queen—but despite all the perks, she'd maxed out three credit cards.

'I needed a sugar daddy,' she said. 'If I'd only known you, Mr. I'm-selling-a-house.' Candy had obviously been talking me up. I made a note to thank her. I also realized, with no small start, that Kara was flirting with me, for real.

'I would've taken you to a club or something.' I sounded okay, my voice maybe a little higher than normal, but I thought I pulled it off.

'I prefer the theater, thank you,' she said. 'I break toes on the dance floor'

'You really Latina?' I asked.

'My mother's ashamed of me,' she said.

I had dirty thought. The word 'ashamed' just did that to me. She hugged a throw pillow and I started thinking about stuff, like the

Claddagh ring on her finger. I don't remember which way the heart was facing, but I was pretty sure it explained the freckles splashed across her nose.

'I doubt it,' I said.

'So do you do a lot of clubbing in this neck of the woods?'

'My weekends involve drinking with the brain trust, grading until my eyes give out and driving kids to the valley for junk food. But not in that order.'

'Man, that is depressing.'

Yes, it was depressing, and I'm sure there was a clever way to respond. But at that moment an e.e cummings poem popped into my head, something about a pretty girl naked being worth a million statues. It had nothing to do with anything—just part of brain acting up—and when Kara waved her hand in front of my face, I realized I'd already said too much.

'Mister,' she said, checking her watch. 'I have got to get you off of this island before something horrible happens to you. So two weeks from Saturday I got a party with a bunch of idiots and no date. Forty-minute drive max. You in?'

I thought she was teasing me, but then she stuck her nice warm hand into mine and we shook on it.

Feeling confident, but in an anxious kind of way, I sat with Goldie during lunch. I even asked how her first day was going and if she needed anything. With a smile she pushed a little hair behind her ear and told me she had some really sweet students this year. Her 'sweet' made me think of *Hansel and Gretel*, but when I checked the witch's hands, no daggers. I inspected my macaroni and cheese for glass, too. None. And when I peeked in my mailbox that afternoon, no rattlesnakes. Nothing but that gracious, creepy smile and one more thing to be anxious about.

To distract myself, I vacuumed my apartment and went for a run. On the way home, I stopped at the gazebo by the softball field and said hello to some of my favorite teenagers.

Joe Causeway, who was especially happy to see me, threw an arm around my neck and rubbed his fuzzy head into my cheek.

'Greenie, you look different,' he said. 'When did you get all your fat sucked out? That must've cost a fortune?'

'Thanks,' I said, disengaging myself from his tentacles. Still smiling at his own joke, Joe pushed his glasses up his nose. In addition to a slightly asymmetrical head, the young man had nine fingers, one of which seemed to have been relocated from another part of his body. Sometimes they called it 'The Tinger.'

'You buy new clothes, too? For the ladies?' he asked. 'You know, I could buy you a new tie, too, set you up like a pimp. Or some pants that don't fall down in library.'

As Joe tried again to drape his arm around my sweaty shoulder, Per Rothstein threw a pebble at him. Another of my wonderful advisees, Per had once been a shy junior, but the day his skin cleared up, he decided it'd be fun to drop his trousers for his math tutor. Three minutes after he'd desecrated our library, the intern was reevaluating her career choice and Per was heading back to Scarsdale for a week. For the rest of the year he, too, had an appendage with an alias. In his case it was called 'The Hypotenuse.'

'If you flashed us, we'd go blind,' said Per.

'Your mom didn't go blind,' said Joe.

The kids made faces at each other—even Per was grinning—and Joe was proud of himself. He was about to rag on someone else's mother, possibly mine, but Per changed the subject and bet me ten dollars the assembly that night was going to be Don DeWillum talking all about rules. I told him I didn't write the headmaster's speeches, but Per was convinced interim department heads knew everything.

After dinner we assembled in our gray and orange theater, where at seven sharp Don DeWillum materialized right in the middle of the stage. Over six feet tall, wide as a refrigerator and wearing an emerald green tie that ended a good four inches above his belt, he just stepped out from behind a skinny microphone stand and waved at the audience. Despite having seen it before, the kids were still confused. How cold such a large person with such a loud tie and such an unruly head of grayish-blond curls hide in plain sight? Don blew into the microphone. The kids got quiet and he fished an index card out of his breast pocket.

He started with acknowledgments: the Admissions Office for the hard work it had done over the summer and then the kitchen staff for the cookouts we'd enjoyed. While he was speaking, someone swung spotlight toward the stage. Don cowered when the light landed on him, but relaxed as it scanned the audience for those he'd thanked. Unable to locate anyone from the kitchen, the spotlight danced across the back of the stage, painfully close to Don. But it raced back to the seats when he thanked Goldie for the two dozen chocolate chip cookies she'd made for the girls' soccer team's bake sale.

I was used to seeing Goldie in jeans and little red cowboy boots. She also liked wearing corduroy skirts and jewelry made of wood. At my department meeting, she'd worn a pair of Keds and red prairie dress. Today though, as the light found her at the end of a row, we all saw Goldie Remlap in shiny black pumps, a fitted pink skirt that stopped an inch below the knee and a white blouse that looked expensive. She was also carrying a tiny handbag, which if I wasn't mistaken was supposed to be a black and silver ladybug. With all eyes on her, she looked up, made a tentative, somehow dramatic half turn and stuck a shapely leg out into the aisle. And as the room became quiet, the discomfort magically vanished from her face.

'Also,' said Don with a ready smile, 'we need to thank Mrs. Remlap with even more gusto for the countless hours, countless meetings, and countless phone calls she's been making. You see, for some time now we've been talking about a writing lab, a second computer lab if you will, and Mrs. Remlap has helped make that dream a reality. She's secured a substantial gift and now we're ready to start converting the staff lounge in the basement of Wickersham into academic space.'

The spotlight stayed on Goldie as she stood beside her seat. Headmaster DeWillum started clapping. The kids in the front row followed suit and as applause spread throughout the auditorium, a few boys hooted and Goldie demurely mouthed the words 'thank you.'

Countless meetings? Countless phone calls? Don leading the ovation? A hand pressed down on my shoulder and Candy leaned in over the noise. 'Oh look, Patty Hearst is announcing her candidacy. So you going to take her seriously now or what?'

I tried to give her hand a reassuring squeeze, but I barely had the strength.

'Okay, everyone,' muttered Don, tapping the microphone, 'some of you may remember how your former headmaster met with our Board of Trustees last spring. Well, I'm here to share the outcome of those discussions and tell you about a few rule changes. In short, we need to review a few new policies related to excused absences, smoking violations and the taking of rides with classmates.'

Don coughed and quivered. He tugged the bottom of his tie as if it were a stubborn window shade. The kids slumped. Goldie preened. And I vowed then and there that I would never wear pink again.

When I sulked through the Student Center, Per stepped back from the pool table.

'What did I tell you, Greenie? Rules. That's why the handbook's a freakin' Bible. Double D's acting like we're all screw ups.' The boy jiggled his cue for effect.

'Use his name right,' I said. 'And why in God's name are you so hung up on rules all of a sudden?'

'It's just don't want to trip up this year, and my dad told me this place is getting crazy about rules. He also says our reputation sucks because we let anybody in.'

'You're living proof,' I said. 'Now shoot. I got winner.'

Per missed and Kwame Aziz, another of my adorable advisees, eyed the table. The previous spring this young man had been arrested with a .357 Magnum. It wasn't his; he was just posing for a photo with it. Still his mom threatened to make him a ward of the state unless he smartened up. 'He hasn't been himself lately,' she said when we talked, and I wondered whom she was comparing him to, if there was another Kwame I hadn't met.

The scariest thing about the boy, however, was that he often read my mind.

'I don't like having Mrs. Remlap as my English teacher,' he said. 'She's hot and you want her to like you, but she sits at her desk all high and mighty and never lets anyone do anything. No gum, no talking to the person next to you even if you're just asking a question, and she totally favors the girls.'

Per picked up the chalk and started working the tip of his cue. 'I wish she wore that pink skirt when I had her last year.'

'She looks like one of them Japanese tour guides,' said Kwame. 'And that skirt wasn't so short. I bet Cassie got lots of skirts shorter than that.'

'And the biggest closet in school to put them in,' said the girl who'd been watching the game from a nearby couch.

'You're in the morgue this year?' asked Kwame.

It was true. The Mount once had a morgue and, according to legend, it had had an unlikely first guest. In the 1850's, the Shakers had sent a fellow named Barnabus Hinckley to study medicine. Upon returning, this corpulent Shaker began outfitting his infirmary, but while carrying equipment up the stairs, he had a heart attack and became the building's first casualty. Now the building was named after him.

Per thought Cass's attic bedroom room sounded creepy, but the mischievous girl with the long dark hair and the glittery fingernails and the A average didn't care about ghosts, only that the dorm parents never bugged you up there. Kwame muttered some kind of silly remark, but we all knew Cass cared way too much about her GPA to ever get in real trouble.

'What about them babies the Shakers hid in the walls?' asked Per.

'I heard they'd burn you in a pit if you had a baby,' said Kwame.

'They were pacifists,' scoffed Cass.

'My mom told me they were communists,' said Kwame. 'Ann Lee made them give up their stuff when they came here. She made them take a vow that they were now brothers and sisters, so if they did it, it'd be incest.'

I had a laugh—dumb boys are good medicine—and Cass dispelled a few myths about Shakers. Mother Ann Lee, for example, had died in 1784, a year before our site became the center of Shaker Society. Meanwhile Joe Causeway ambled into the Student Center and scanned the balls on the pool table. Joe was a day late picking up social cues and my class would be his personal Everest, but he had a few undeniable talents. In his cranium lurked encyclopedias of trivia, a comprehensive list of colleges with division one basketball programs and, of course, the maiden names of every student's mothers.

'Gimme next,' he said. 'I'll stomp your gay asses.'

I told him I was going to stomp on his rear if he ever said that again. Kwame boasted that he had an extremely heterosexual ass. Per and Cassandra expressed their doubts. And when it was my turn to play, I stopped thinking about Goldie for a few minutes and beat Per. Afterward I fended off Joe, who would've done better blindfolded, and squeaked by Kwame, who talked trash while I lined up the eight ball but shook my hand after I pocketed it.

'You know, Greenie?' said Per, racking up the balls, 'I'm gonna be more serious this year. I may even run for student council.'

'You gonna wear a pink skirt, too?' asked Kwame.

'No, I mean it. I'm gonna run and I'm gonna do most of my homework.'

Cass laughed from the sofa. 'Most of it? You think Mr. Green's going to pat you on the head for that? You'd look good campaigning in a pink skirt though.'

'Shut up, you may be book smart, Cassie, but you ain't that smart. I see you in twenty years still with those hoochie fingernails.'

'And I'm gonna find you pumping gas at the Hess station and pretend I don't even know you.'

'Ma-ay-be,' said Per, hitching his thumbs on his belt and talking out the side of his mouth, 'when you stop in for 100 gallons of diesel for your big rig so you can haul your load of Tater-Tots upstate.'

'And you'll still be flashing women. You gonna embroider the name Wee Willie on your overalls?'

'I can see that, man,' said Kwame, 'but it'll say Little P and you, Cassie, you'll have them bead seat covers and a dancing hulee doll on your dashboard.'

'And a cowboy hat to match your nails and an air mattress for the back of your big rig so you can hook up with all your trucker friends,' added Per, and the boys hooted at the idea of Cass being some kind of nympho trucker.

'And you're gonna have my foot up your ass,' she said.

'That's enough,' I said. 'How about you find something else to talk about?'

Because she got angry it first, Kwame gave Per a high five. Cass stewed for only a nanosecond though before asking what I thought of Missis Calabria. She was implying the obvious: the woman was attractive and I was a fool if I hadn't noticed. She was also suggesting Kara had a husband, but putting 'Mrs.' in front of every woman's name was a habit shared by many of our kids.

'She's dating a cop,' I said.

Cass shared a little dirt. 'He came by last night while she was on duty to bring her a salad and she acted like he was a delivery boy. She wouldn't even let him sit, told him he was distracting us.'

'That tall dude's a cop?' said Kwame. 'Damn, they'll shoot you for looking at their girl and call it self defense.'

'I think Remlap's better looking than Calabria,' said Per. 'And she smells good.'

'I think Iafrati's cute,' said Cass. 'But I haven't smelled him yet.'

Per was incredulous and I couldn't blame him. In less than two days the kids had already given my buddy four names. In the halls he was Iafrati without the mister. In the dorm he had two names: The Turtle because he kept popping out of his tiny apartment to snap at people, and The Kaiser, but in this case the kids were being ironic. Finally, as the assistant soccer coach he was The Asshole With The Whistle.

'That guy should be the cop,' said Per. 'He's already taken two of my water pistols, and he called me a savage for playing hockey in the dorm.'

'Maybe he's right,' I said, and Cassandra waved her fingernails in front of my face. I told her they were glamorous and pointed out that glamour came from the same Latin root as 'grammar.'

'Will you stop being Mr. English for like ten seconds?' she complained, as the mousy new Math intern living in my basement walked into the Student Center. She was about to ask for the next game of pool when Kwame exclaimed, 'Shit, are you really a teacher?' The poor woman didn't know what to say. It didn't help that she had acne and was wearing a baseball cap. I told Kwame to apologize. 'Sorry,' he said, 'that's the way I talk back home. I guess I haven't made my transition yet.'

'You do look young,' said Cass. 'I thought you were a student, too.'

'You should wear a sign that says New Teacher: Beware,' suggested Per.

'I'll get on it right away,' said the intern, her cheeks getting redder.

'Miss, are you dating anyone?' Cass had to ask, and the intern decided she didn't want to play pool after all. I told the kids they were a bunch of idiots and went home, too.

Four

B lame it on James Joyce, the CCD classes that terrorized my schoolmates, or just my own neurotic notions about women, but as a boy I wrestled with the belief that Catholic girls were exotic, dangerous creatures. Soon, as part of a quixotic effort to make peace with my hormones, I began to think of all women—not just cute ones wielding field hockey sticks—as either untouchable saints, who loved God first and wanted no less than five children, or as tantalizing sinners, who might rescue me from a painful adolescence if only I could find one who liked nice Jewish boys.

Now, closing in on thirty-five, I was less delusional but not much wiser.

'Why is it,' asked Kara, turning onto the main road, 'all my Korean boys are fixated on Halloween? I'm trying to teach them about the U. S. government, and all they care about are video games and vampires? And the girls, they just want to know when I'm getting married. They're worse than my mom.'

I put two and two together, came up with five, and asked why she used her mom's name. Kara smiled and said she didn't. Her mom was an Urbina. She was Calabria because she'd been married for about fifteen minutes before she realized she liked the name and not the asshole attached to it. Yes, I was the last person on campus to know Kara was divorced, and, of course, I had to ask if she'd had a honeymoon and everything. Sounding more amused than awkward, she mentioned some towns in Italy I'd never heard of, and I got distracted by the image of her in a condo with skylights, wall-to-wall carpeting and a kitchen full of white appliances. What did she get to keep? What did she have to send back? And the rings? What does a Catholic girl do with those?

'Goldie had a field day when she found out,' said, Kara, then she pointed out that Ms. Remlap had a talent for exposing weaknesses.

'There's not an attractive single person who's safe around her,' I said.

Kara smiled and turned west on Route 20. 'She says the same thing about you.'

'That must be why you invited me out,' I said, wishing I were such a man, and an hour later I was in a living room in Troy, eating chicken wings with an a dozen of Kara's high school friends. The ones I remember most were Sue Me Sue and Rene. Sue Me Sue was a paralegal and an unrepentant Yankees fan. Rene, a six-foot blonde with a pierced navel, was the single lady of the house.

All night they gave me crap for being an English teacher and a Red Sox fan. In their impeccable New York accents words like 'coffee' and 'pork chop' took on new dimensions. They teased Kara, too, calling her K. C. and making fun of her current boyfriend, who was off at some policeman's conference. At one point Rene asked if I was going to be Kara's 'new victim.'

'I'm flattered,' I said, 'but, no, we're still on speaking terms.'

'Ain't that the truth,' laughed Rene, and she told me that one man and only one man was responsible for turning sweet Kara into the tyrant we now saw before us.

'Don't,' said Kara.

'Señor Amor,' said Rene, throwing an arm around her, and Kara had no choice but to tell me how Vincent Calabria quit his job three months after they'd crossed the threshold but conveniently neglected to tell her. Instead, the love of her life waltzed out of their condo in a suit and tie every morning, and every night he'd hang his jacket on a dinning room chair and tell her all about his industrious day.

Kara slipped a hand through my elbow as a Van Halen song started playing.

'Some chick I don't even know ratted him out,' she said. 'Warned me to get my money someplace safe, but it was too late.'

'Fooled us all,' said Sue Me Sue.

'You know, the guy used to hire illegals from Columbia,' said Kara, 'but on invoices he'd refer to them as 'Mexican #1' and

'Mexican #2'? He was a complete fake but still wouldn't admit they were from the same place he was pretending to be from.'

'He was easy on the eyes though,' said Sue Me Sue. 'But then he lost his accent and started sounding like a guy from Ramapo.'

'I introduced them,' added Soupy. 'I kick myself for that.'

'Relationships suck,' said Kara, letting go of my arm and reaching for her drink.

'Only the good ones,' said Rene. 'So, tell me again, baby, why aren't you going out with Jeff here? He seems perfectly decent.'

'Too decent,' said Kara. 'No baggage.'

Rene looked me up and down. 'I find that hard to believe and I'm sure he's got baggage. But if you're not interested in this little snack cake, let me have a taste.'

I offered to meet her in the pantry. Rene said it was a date and someone passed around a high school yearbook to show us a black and white photo of Kara, then Kara Kelly, wearing a tight jean jacket and chewing fiercely on a pencil. Her hair was Joan Jett meets lawnmower and she was skinny as all get out. Rene turned to the Sports section of the yearbook, showed me a picture of my buddy playing field hockey and I started drooling. Rene offered her a pencil to chew on. Kara grabbed the yearbook and jammed it under a cushion. There was some swearing. Steve Miller replaced Van Halen. The New York accents became thicker. More chicken wings came out of the kitchen. Then ice cream. Then shots of Sambuca. At one point, Kara elbowed me. These are my friends, she was saying, what do you think? I snagged that yearbook and took a long last look at Kara Kelly in a plaid skirt and told her they were awesome.

By the end of the party, Kara was drunk, so I got behind the wheel of her car and pointed us home. Settling into the passenger's seat, she kicked off her shoes, thanked me and became quiet. About ten minutes later she started humming. I couldn't place the song—it wasn't the one on the radio—but I liked the tune, seeing her foot on the dash, the soft blue and yellow light dancing over her face.

She stopped humming. 'How do you put up with her?'

'Who?'

'Who else would I be talking about?'

'It's hard to take her seriously,' I said, and I told her that Goldie once decided we needed more overhead projectors, but Oscar Lazarus had spent our last five dollars on DVD players. But she wouldn't accept no for an answer, not when she had contacts at every school in the county and a resourceful husband. So when Simon's Valley tossed a few gently used machines into a dumpster, Art was there to dive in after them. To secure the machines, he had to battle a raccoon, which we're pretty sure wasn't rabid. But, hey, we got four projectors and they didn't cost a dime.

'And that wasn't enough to win hearts and make her interim?' asked Kara.

'I had the protest vote going for me, so I beat her by two. The old headmaster was happy to appoint me. Oscar was so thrilled he gave me the key to his office.'

Kara had heard the rumor that Oscar's sabbatical was a prelude to retirement. And, yes, if the department voted for a new head at the end of the semester, with Sam instead of Oscar, there was a good chance I'd lose my sash. I liked my sash, too. It read *Ms. Teen Interim Department Head, My Word!* Gunnar made it for me, and I wore it for an entire evening while we did shots with Candy and Art.

'Art was there?' she asked. 'Has he gotten laid since?'

'There's a cold breeze on the north end of campus. If you're real quiet, you can hear Art shivering.'

'She's pretty tight with Sammy though.'

'Not that tight, but she's free to get advice anywhere he wants,' I said, and I confessed that when I was a rookie, I was terrified of everything, too, especially the lilac bushes in front of Sisters' Shop.

They were a tangle of flowerless branches and not much to look at, but as the kids in my work crew snipped the September air with their rusty limb loppers, I became anxious. The brats just wanted to hack the old wood out of the bushes and go looking for the hot chocolate truck. What else would they want to do on a chilly morning? But I was convinced killing lilac bushes was a surefire way to lose my job. So I said no, and without blinking they lobbied to cut off the leafy shoots that must've been sucking the life out of the plants. I said no again, and because I couldn't let teenagers push me around, we removed a third of the old and some of the new. I had no clue whether we'd done the right thing, but the next year there were more flowers and more leaves, so again we took out a third of the old and some of the new.

By my third spring all the old branches were gone and we'd had blooms every year. I was elated. We'd saved the patient without ripping out its heart, and I'd found a home. So what if my chinos were covered with chalk dust and the bags under my eyes had become permanent. My girlfriend—a snooty bitch according to Candy—thought I looked weathered, professorial even, and when I confessed that some of the girls made me nervous, she rattled with laughter and almost fell out of bed. She would've been scared of the coyotes that stalked the woods or that load of papers that might break my back. But a do-gooder like me stuttering around teenage girls? Please, it was time to stop worrying and accept my calling.

But then she got quiet, scratched a dry spot on her forehead and shared the one thing that did bother her, a hunch, which soon became a full-blown conviction, that my temple of learning was just a summer camp, a place for overcooked eggs and scrambled hormones, and it certainly wasn't good enough for me. I told her the job wasn't forever, but within ten months my girl was a footnote and I was a master hedge trimmer.

Maybe I was being foolish, but I liked the way Kara looked at me when I finished my sad story. Or maybe it was the just the night teasing, The Milky Way, the smooth ride home turning into a poem. Wheel pen curve enjambment blinking yellow light caesura. Pretty girl chasing away doubt, making me feel I was the right man for the job. Fourteen stoplights door to door. Pretty girl glancing at my profile. Me pulling into her parking spot at Wickersham and enjoying a moment of silence, not wanting to say anything, not until I found a way to thank her for the night.

'Hey, if you're ever available,' I said, 'let's go on a real date. I'll show you my high school yearbook and you can make fun of me.'

'Let's,' she replied, and without thinking she closed her eyes and kissed me, one that tugged at my lips and made my toes curl.

I truly believe that temptation is wonderful, one of the few things that lifts us above the world of bacteria and makes us feel alive, but against my will I said, 'Goodnight, Ms. Calabria,' and reminded myself that she really was seeing someone. Kara flashed a mischievous smile. Then she pushed open the car door, shielded her eyes against the glare of the dome light and tossed out a 'see ya.' I tossed back an optimistic 'definitely' and made the short walk home.

Five

I'd told Oscar to keep it. For my semester at the helm, my classroom would be a fine place to hold meetings. But Oscar was proud of his upholstered chairs and his artfully cluttered bookshelves. He also loathed Goldie, who'd once compared him to an old sock, and on a slightly creepy note I was his boy. So he insisted I take the key, pressed it into my hand and closed my fingers around it.

As a rookie, I used to drop by with questions about Shakespeare and Dickinson. Usually, I'd find him dozing at his desk with a dog-eared novel or a stack of papers that were sure to get inflated grades. Dozing, of course, meant snoring lightly and smelling of fermented fruit. Yes, he was uncouth and occasionally pungent, but the man knew his way around a classroom and he never abused his power.

After opening the door, I held it for Goldie, who marched in and flicked on the lights. For a second I thought I'd chosen the wrong place to have this conversation. I'd thought the office might humble her, but now I realized there were far too many trophies in the room: a first edition of *East of Eden* that belonged to everyone and no one, a framed piece of a quilt that looked Shaker but probably wasn't, heavy slate sills covered with drippy candles, and a row of 150-year old Shaker pegs. Pretending she didn't want any of it, Goldie settled into one of the big chairs by the window and smoothed out the front of her tweed skirt, once again knee-length and businesslike. She looked handsome, put-together, intimidating even, except for the fact that her feet were squeezed into a pair of light blue espadrilles and she was carrying her ladybug purse.

'Thanks for talking,' I said, as a van crunched by outside and momentarily threw us into shadow. 'And congratulations on the writing center. It's a good use of that space.' I asked who donated the money and Goldie's hand closing around the strap of her purse.

'It's anonymous,' she said.

'Well, congratulations again,' I said, wondering why the hell she was being so secretive. 'My only concern is that no one else in our department knew about it. It's not a huge deal, but I'd like it if we were all on the same page. When folks start whining about who's going to staff it, I'd like to have a halfway decent answer.'

'Our plans moved fast,' she said. Her voice quivered and she started blinking. Goldie liked to feign awkwardness—it was part of the routine—but this was real.

'As a department we've got it good,' I said. 'Smaller sections and some nice toys, which I know you helped get. Still, I think a computer center should be more of a school thing than and English thing.'

'Things,' she said with a flutter of eyelashes, 'came together and Don announced them. That's completely transparent. I don't mean to be rude, Greenie, but sometimes you're not aware of what's going on around you. Things do happen when you're out of touch for three months.'

She pulled her handbag into her lap and gripped it tighter. There was more than a grain of truth to what she said, but she was still being rude. And now I was glad I'd brought her to Oscar's office. There, surrounded by soft light and dust motes, I could finally see things. First, that woman wanted my job more than life itself. Second, no matter how nice I acted, she truly thought I was a piece of shit.

That night I stared at the ceiling until the sheets snaked around my legs and I had to turn on the light. I had plenty of things on my mind—classes, Sam, Kara's soon to be ex-boyfriend—but none bigger than Goldie. She was driven and dedicated, possibly even competent. I got aroused when she insulted me, could even imagine sleeping with her, but it was only someone who looked like her, for this woman was the worm in the apple, the black spot on the x-ray, a problem that would not just go away. And while I wrestled, the end of the semester was closing in. Soon Oscar would announce he wasn't coming back and there'd be a new vote. Sam would cast a ballot this time and side with Goldie, and soon she'd be polishing her pretty little tiara in the big chair.

To improve my standing with my young colleague, I gave him lots of gentle feedback, but his performance continued to hover between spotty and just good enough. He came in with clear notes but kept garbling directions and avoiding the kids' confused expressions. Running out of things to say, I suggested he teach as if he had a beer in his hand—boys in particular like teachers who are funny—but the only place he seemed at home was on the soccer field, where he was able to impose order with a loud whistle and a sharp tongue.

I wasn't Sam's biggest critic, however. That honor belonged to Cassandra Diaz, who tracked me down one conference period to share her disdain. The day before, while we teachers were finishing lunch, Cass and few other hooligans marched out to a not-so-secret spot in the woods to smoke and carp about how strict we'd become. Of course, Kwame told everyone I'd caught him with a cigarette behind his ear and all I did was take it away.

'I think it's nice you look out for him,' said Cassandra, who was wearing a long sleeve t-shirt with a pink 47 on it, 'but then some of the guys got everyone thinking about what it would be like if you and Iafrati got into it.'

'Why would we fight?' I asked.

'Because you're super nice and he's the rudest man I've ever met. You know he called me princess when I hurt my elbow in the coatroom? At least that's what I think he said. Anyway, it hurt and all he did was chase me off. I mean, what's with the attitude? And you know what Calabria said when I told her, after she laughed at the book I was reading? She told me to learn the school rules and dress different. Can you believe a woman with three-hundred dollar boots would tell me to put on chinos?'

Thinking Cass would look cute in a pair of chinos, I asked what she was reading.

'Emerson, totally boring, but I like how he tells me to be true to my own genius and ignore the runty people who think they know everything.'

'But there are times when you should listen, right?'

'I know what you're going to say: the rules are for everyone. But you know what, Mr. Green? Even if it's crap, I'm taking Calabria's advice about clothes because I'm sick of not being taken seriously. And you know what else? I think she's mean because of guy trouble. She's worn the same sweater twice this week, and she never inspects rooms, but now she's a Nazi about it and I'm on restriction.'

I figured my precocious messenger would get on restriction for smoking or being out of dorm after ten, not for socks on the floor and an unmade bed.

'Where's the sympathy?' she said when I laughed. 'All I want is just a little sympathy.'

'Okay, okay, sorry,' I said. 'You know, my mom never cared what anyone thought about her. She blurted out whatever popped into her head and wore whatever she wanted. Her attitude used to bug me, but one day she told me men are taught to apologize for their weaknesses, women for their strengths.'

'I'm not apologizing for anything.'

'That's the point,' I said.

Cass scratched the corner of her plum-colored mouth with a plum-colored fingernail and dropped her eyes. 'Oh, right. Well, you might want to know that there was other stuff going on. People making plans for the weekend.'

'What kind of plans?' I asked.

Cass picked up a pen, wrote something on her arm; then she dropped down so I could see only her elbows and her head on my desk.

'Those guys, especially the dumb ones, are not my friends.'

I walked to the bookcase where I kept extra textbooks and novels kids could borrow. 'Cass, if you're really worried about someone...'

'...I know, I know, just don't punk anyone just to make yourself look good. I'm not dumb, Mr. Green.' She eyed the very used copy of *Leaves of Grass* I'd handed her.

'Here's something to contemplate while you're stuck in the dorm.'

'Mr. Green, no matter what Ms. Remlap says, I think you're one of the nicest people at this school. But you have got to work on your pep talks.'

Cass handed me back the book. I was a little hurt until she asked if I was lending it or making a present of it. To clear up any confusion, I wrote the date, the line *Seasons change, grass fades, homework and restriction endure*, and my full name inside the cover.

It was the first book anyone had ever given Cass. Funny, considering she was a kid who enjoyed a book in her lap and who finished most novels in three or four days. 'When I'm with a story, I'm in charge,' she once said. 'I go away and they're gone.' When Sam read a piece of literature, he'd come up with five ways to bring it to a class and usually settle on the worst. He'd realize his mistake while standing at the board. He'd teeter. He beat himself up. The kids would see it all, fill with scorn, and give him only a fraction of their attention. Oh, their eyes may have been facing forward, but more often than not they were glued to the shadow lesson of one Josh Henderson, a little charmer in too big army boots and a *Plan 9 from Outer Space* t-shirt. Josh's lesson, a pithy stream of asides that revealed both insight and a unique talent for subversion. But his talent was a slippery slope, for Sam would pick up on the game, become even more frazzled and I'd have to step in. More than once, I talked to Josh and he always agreed to stop. I talked to the other kids, too, and they tried to behave. But there was mounting proof that Sam was his own worst enemy.

Subbing in a Shaker Utopia class, Sam was reading instructions when an entitled ruffian named Steven Hodge decided it would be more fun to talk to his neighbor. Annoyed that Hodge found Cassandra more interesting than the lesson, Sam directed the boy to another seat. But ten seconds later, Hodge had to go back to his old seat for a pencil. Then he went back for his book. Then he went back for his coat. Sam issued an ultimatum, but the boy, buoyed by his importance to the lacrosse team, began to hum.

The eraser hurled in the Hodge's direction was supposed to hit the wall and startle him. The puff of white powder, the wave of nervous laughter, the obscenity, and the boy storming out of the room with a chalky splotch in the middle of his forehead were not what Sam had expect.

At lunch Kara teased him about assaulting students and throwing like a sissy, but then she pulled out her thumbscrews. The details of the interrogation, shared over ice cream sandwiches that evening, were puzzling. First, Sam claimed not to have known any gay people prior to coming to The Mount. He shared his belief that condoms were a necessary evil—I thought of Thomas Paine meeting Pope John Paul in a motel room. Finally, he confessed that Mary Katherine was the only girl he'd ever slept with and they might be breaking up.

'He turned pink when he told me about his sex life,' said Kara. 'He's proud of it though, kept referring to marriage as a sacrament. I wanted to pop him in the head.'

'Why didn't you? I asked.

'Because we both know love makes you crazy, Greenie.' Sliding behind me, she eased her thumbs into my shoulders. 'And we know what it's like to be a first-year teacher. So give him time and he'll win them over. You can do that, right?'

'I'm made of time,' I said, leaning into her hands and closing my eyes. 'So you available for a real date soon?'

'Sure looks that way,' she said.

Six

I was weaving between the desks, handing back papers, alive with the thought of Kara's fingers on my back and the phrase sure looks that way. Outside the sky had lost its yellow; summer blue had faded into pale autumn. The trees were turning early, too—dingy yellow and red this year, a cold rain away from complete disappointment.

'I got a C,' bragged Josh Henderson, wearing a leisure suit with a pair of ratty Vans. I'd wanted to give his essay on Loki an A, but as expected he'd skipped the outline and handed the work in two days late.

'You tore mine apart, Mr. G,' exclaimed a girl with lips the color of bubble gum and a purple cell phone clipped to her belt. I reminded her that Mother Theresa, while being a wonderful woman, was not a god or a goddess. Then I pointed to her B-minus and told her good research had saved her hide.

Joe Causeway's essay on Bacchus, returned with the request that he learn to type, was nearly impossible to read. I had, however, been able to figure out that he'd spelled 'Roman' R-O-A-M-I-N-G eleven times in four paragraphs.

'Oh my God,' said Josh, 'that looks like one of those heart machine things, like somebody was bugged out on Ritalin.'

The kids gawked at the jagged lines while I secretly agreed with Josh's assessment that it looked like an EKG. Of course, Joe held up the essay so everyone could see his C and Josh muttered an obscenity. I held up one finger. One swear was a warning. Two he was off to see the Dean of Students, a trip that brought a week of restriction: no off-campus or free time at night, weekend check-ins and Sunday work detail. Sadly, Josh had been on restriction for all but two days since the year began.

'What about my report?' asked a boy with dimples and a haystack of blond hair.

'I wasn't able to get to it,' said Sam from the back row, and to everyone's dismay, Miles Twohig's eyes began to tear up. Sam was rattled. He started to roll his eyes but caught himself. By lunchtime he'd graded the paper and apologized to Miles, but a few kids, including Josh, had seen the disgust on Sam's face.

Within a week, they struck back.

I'd just taught a lesson on the beauty of the semicolon, but when it was Sam's turn to dazzle them with a poem by Richard Wilbur, he walked up to me and whispered, 'I didn't think we'd get to it.' Then he retreated to back row and I had no choice but to pull out one of my dustiest files.

'These proofreading symbols,' I said, with as much conviction as I could muster, 'will help you make sense of those hieroglyphics we put on your papers.'

'Hierowhats?' they asked.

'Ancient Egyptian writing that's really hard to read,' I said. 'Okay, check the worksheet and see which symbols are new to you.' Magically, they all looked down, but it didn't seem like anyone was actually reading. Joe and Sam were staring out the window at a cat. Miles was doodling. I asked them a question. Josh tore the corner off his handout and popped it into his mouth and asked why I had an earring.

'Folks,' I begged. 'Any questions about the proofreading symbols?'

'You wear ties and nice shoes, Mr. G. Why the earring?' asked Joe.

'Did you get it for a girl?' asked Josh.

I looked at their cute faces and caved. In the place of a sermon on the importance of writing clearly, I shared my theory that the small hoop in my left ear protected from white supremacists and hardcore Republicans. It connected my college days to the big round number I was fast approaching. I confessed that I'd taken the earring out for job interviews, but once I was hired, it returned. 'And a girlfriend liked it, too,' I added, sitting on a desk and swinging my legs, 'and she was very persuasive.'

After the explanation cum confession, I couldn't get the kids back on track. They were too bored, too excited, too unwilling. All I could do was let them go early, generosity that Josh returned with a cheap shot.

'But I was psyched for Iafrati to teach us a poem. What happened?'

The hair rose on the back of my neck and I pointed to the door. Josh could leave now or come back during conference period to clean the blackboard with his tongue. The other kids made eyes at each other, and when the room was empty, I told Sam I'd talk to the class and that would never happen again.

'I should've had that poem ready,' he said. 'It's just that last night I had this endless thing with Mary Katherine. She wants me to visit Friday for some recital at her school. Then there was poker at Calabria's, which I didn't want to go to, but they coerced me, and then I fell asleep trying to come up with a lesson.'

Sam chewed on his lip. I wanted to remind him that he should do his prep before he went carousing, but I didn't have it in me.

'It's okay,' I said. 'If you need to watch kids sing show tunes or whatever to make your girlfriend happy, go ahead. I can handle class.'

'Thanks,' he said, giving me a puzzled look I hadn't seen since the start of school, 'I owe you. Just let me know when you want me to take the class.'

'Just remember who treats you well,' I said. I went to pat him his arm but came up short. He stared at my hand for a second and we both knew what I was thinking.

Once, because of injuries, suspensions and a looming tournament, Art asked me to practice with the soccer team. Since then I'd been joining them regularly to fall on my ass and head balls with my face. Well, four days and six hours after I'd encouraged Sam to go away for the weekend, I was scrimmaging against my teaching buddy. I'd been running around for a while, not touching the ball, but not making a fool out of myself either. Then a kick squirted off the side of my goalkeeper's foot and bounced toward me. I hoped to corral the ball and send it up the sideline, but at the same time I felt Sam closing on me from the center of the field. I turned my back as both Sam and the ball arrived, and before I knew it, my cleat or shoulder or some other part of my foul anatomy had tripped him. He fell to his knees as if pausing for a mid-game prayer, but somehow his elbow had caught me right below the eye. I apologized up and down and rolled the ball to him for a free kick. A few of my teammates howled that he'd fouled me, but I ignored them, just as I ignored the strangely indignant smile that flashed across Sam's face.

Seven

Gunner Davis sat underneath a saber he'd mounted on the wall of his office. I sat facing him next to a bookcase full of baseball caps. His favorite was a Toledo Mud Hen cap autographed by someone named Jim Weber. I preferred the Houston Astros lid with its big star and bold H. Anyway, as I told my Dean of Studies about Sam's wayward elbow and how I blamed it on Goldie, a mischievous gleam flashed across his face.

'So he's been a real disaster?'

'That might be putting it a little…'

'If we don't think he should be back next year,' said my savvy friend, 'Don should probably know sooner rather than later.'

Teachers that struggled often got their contracts held. We'd string some of them along until the end of the school year to see if they'd get better.

'And when should we tell him?' I asked.

'Before the end of the semester, you know, so he doesn't think we have any ulterior motives.'

'What about his career?'

'He's young. He'll bounce,' said Gunnar. 'Besides, your title's not ceremonial, Jeff. You think it's smart to let him skate this year and vote you out? You know Goldie would dump him? Isn't 'use 'em and lose 'em one of her mottos?'

'She was talking about something else.'

'It's all the same to her. But you, my friend, need to start a paper trail on Sam and write up an improvement plan to show Don. Things he needs to work on it, specific but not too specific.'

'Great,' I said, taking a PawSox cap from the shelf and plopping it onto my head, and I told Gunnar about my chat with Goldie.

'Good grief,' he said when I was done, 'did you really think she'd play nice?'

Gunnar had wispy blind hair and a distant relative who'd come over with John Winthrop, but deep down he wanted to be Jewish. His stories about his overbearing mother and his philandering rug merchant uncle, Steve Shine of Steve's Shine's Wholesale Carpets, were my proof. After my first year on The Mount, the two of us spent a week on Cape Cod at Uncle Steve's cottage, an exquisite hovel lit by a collection of antique kerosene lamps. Every night we grilled fish and played Wiffle Ball until it was too dark to see. One time we got smashed on gin and lemon soda, striped off our clothes and ran down to the beach, where we threw seaweed at each other until there was sand in every crevice of our bodies. When we retreated to the house, we built a fire in the wood stove even thought it was eighty. While he was talking about his love life, Gunnar threw a glass of gin into the fire. Blue flames leapt toward the ceiling and curled their tongues around the wooden beams. His face glowed devilishly and he told me his girlfriend had dumped him to go out with one of his friends.

In his family only two of a dozen marriages had lasted. Bank accounts were divided, houses were sold, and children were relocated. Gunnar had three sets of parents, two sets of half-brothers and sisters, more cousins than he could name, and the burning desire to find another way. But being dumped at twenty-four—just when he'd found a job and paid off one of his student loans—left him bleeding.

I handed gave him more gin. 'Four years is a long time to go out with someone.'

'Longer if you count the time we were friends,' he replied.

We were still naked. The heat was making us sweat. The kerosene lamps were spiraling smoke into the room and a mosquito was biting me between the shoulder blades. Gunnar slapped it, showed me the blood between his fingers and told me he'd almost gotten married in Las Vegas that winter. Despite having bad marriage genes, it was his idea, he'd said, as he rubbed his fingers until the blood disappeared. From then on he focused on his career. He'd be a force on The Mount, a stealth fighter, a bulldozer. I scoffed at the idea. But somehow when I too became single, it really dd help to think of myself as a poised professional with powerful, loyal friends. I wasn't falling into an abyss at all. I was just joining the club that got things done.

When I found my headmaster at his desk, he was typing an email with two fingers and chewing on the inside of his cheek.

'I was an interim once,' he said, leaning back in his leather desk chair and looking over my head as if there were a cue card or a water balloon up there. Today he was wearing a pale green shirt and a pink tie. He was also sporting on his pocket a quarter-sized ink stain, which he was blotting with a paper napkin. He folded the napkin into his pocket when I sat. Now his outfit was cruise ship 1978. If Don could sing, if I could find him a white belt and convince him to grow his blond curls out a little, he could headline.

Gunnar wanted me to be direct, to share my concerns and make it clear Sam wasn't working out. But as I sat there shuffling my landmines, I chickened out and strayed from the script. Before I knew it, I was suggesting not just an improvement plan but that my colleague might benefit from new duties, maybe even his own section. Rope to hang himself with, I thought, no one to blame but Sam.

Don slipped his hands behind his head. 'I'm too new to tinker with the academic core. Why don't you just treat him like an intern? Teach the class your way, break things down for him and let him learn?'

'I'm doing exactly that right now,' I said.

Now Don looked scared.

'I just don't think it's time to make any big changes,' he said. 'Also, I know a lot about Sam and your class. He's told me he's confused in there. Mind you, this is only his perspective so don't take it as criticism, but Sam knows he's missing details. He admires how you engage kids and thinks you're entertaining, but he's hoping for clearer teaching goals and a sense of how he might set up lessons for students who have become used to a more freewheeling experience.'

Don moved his hands on his belly. He liked talking to English teachers, mostly because he thought we had insight into the mysteries of life—such as when to use dashes.

'Freewheeling? Is that Sam's word?' I asked.

'His word, my word, I don't remember. But I'll agree that he needs more structure from you. Don't worry though, there are lots of ways to teach effectively.' Don smile awkwardly, and I know something bad was about to happen. '

'There is a more serious item I'd like to share,' he said. 'It's come to my attention. Actually, I fielded a complaint, and I don't know how to put this delicately other than to just come out and ask. Is it true you told your students you were proud to be a rebel and that you pierced your ear so you might seduce women?'

'Who complained?'

'I can't say. But I want to be clear that there are certain lines we shouldn't cross in conversation with students.'

'First, I did not say that.'

Don opened his desk drawer and peeked at something inside. 'Did you say something to your students about all Republicans being white supremacists?'

'The kids asked about my earring and I joked that it protected me from hardcore Republicans and white supremacists. I laughed. They laughed. They understood what I was saying.'

'Well, sometimes humor, especially political humor, is hard for these kids to understand. So I can see how your statement might be troubling, and I'd like you to a different approach next time students ask a personal question. Jeff, no one at this school is expected to hide or to broadcast their political affiliations or their sexual orientation, but we need to be respectful of our differences. So think of this as a chance to reflect upon your practice. I'm sure it will be a good experience.'

There was nothing I could say that wouldn't sound defensive. I felt like an idiot. Improvement plan. Improvement plan. Why didn't I insist on one and get the ball rolling? In the end, I just smiled at my pink and green boss and resisted the growing urge to tell him he looked like a fucking watermelon.

On Tuesday I told Sam I was taking over the class and I gave him a list of skills to develop. On Wednesday I sat with Kara in the cafeteria. She asked if she was using the right fork—all our forks were the same—and moved to another table. I hoped it would pass, but on Thursday she had an angry lunch and a bitter dinner with Sam. By Friday she was avoiding me, and all I wanted to do was strap a rocket onto Sam's ass.

'Grilled cheese,' he said, looking at the lunch menu posted outside the cafeteria, 'but no tomato soup.' There's apple pie, I thought, and we cut the line of ravenous students and got our grilled cheeses—his with tomato, mine without. At the dessert table, we were greeted by a million bowls of green Jell-O were shimmying in the fluorescent light. Ever hopeful, I spotted a lone piece of pie, but Sam beat me to it. You don't really need dessert, I told myself, and I walked to the faculty dining room, where over the rumble of twenty teachers eating, Don announced that we'd gone over our copy budget and were moving the paper to the business office. He was wearing a white shirt and a honey-colored bowtie. He also had a pair of reading glasses like my late granny's dangling around his neck on a chain.

'I'll have a key if you needed a few sheets on the weekend,' he said. 'Also I wanted everyone to know we're investing in a viewbook: it's a marketing tool. It'll be glossy and expensive, but right now we don't have anything like it to attract students. Anyway, the company we've hired is going to be here soon. They'll take a few candid photos and return for a more elaborate production in the spring.'

Candy asked if it would show the school's diversity. Don put down his coffee. 'We'll make sure the school is fairly depicted.'

'I'd like to piggyback on that,' added Kyle Searcy, our Director of Admissions. 'It's Mommy and Daddy who pay the bills, so we will try to look in some ways like fairly traditional independent school. That stance might anger a few students, but I don't think it's disingenuous at all.'

As he talked, I saw him glance at photogenic Goldie, who glanced at photogenic Kara, who glanced at photogenic Sam, who was taking notes on a napkin. Don reminded us that an attractive school built confidence in parents and ended with the joke: 'How can you tell who the headmaster is? He's the one picking up garbage.'

That said we talked about our image until people began shuffling silverware and slipping cups onto each other's trays. Sam, who had food stuck to his cheek, hadn't touched his pie.

'Folks who ran activities last weekend,' announced Candy, 'I need receipts. I got nothing from the Rockwell Museum trip.'

Roger Day, five years a Biology teacher and the manly leader of the school's work program, spoke up from the back of the room where he was correcting tests.

'We went go-carts instead. Receipt should be in your box.'

'Dude, I offered that trip this week,' she said, jamming a napkin into her glass.

'Do we have time for kids?' asked Kara. 'There is a lot of shady activity going on after study hall.'

'If a kid's out of sorts, give me a call,' said Robert Driscoll, our Dean of Students. Bob, nicknamed 'Ichabob' because of his long-limbs and bouncy Adam's apple, liked talking about kids, but not in the last thirty seconds of a faculty meeting.

'I worry about Miles,' said Sam, and suddenly it was open season on shy Miles Twohig. *He's a sensitive boy. I think he's got some veneer issues going on. His parents are very passive.* Next up was Elizabeth Perkins: straight A's and a spotless room. *Grumpy, but I've got a feeling she's going to have a couple of big enchiladas this year.* Josh Henderson couldn't escape the mill. *Spends half of study hall telling you how much he hates his mother. Let him get a drink and he ends up feeding the fish and making sandwiches.* At some point, Candy pointed out that all those kids studied with me. Don tapped his forehead as if that were part of the equation—insulting even if he was just trying to be in on the joke—and finally, someone brought up a student we should've been talking about.

'Hodge's work is crap,' said Rog. 'Now there's the kid to test for drugs?'

Thinking of the bribe Hodge's parents had given to the school, Goldie and Don snapped to attention.

Ichabob came to their rescue. 'Not if we haven't caught him once, so keep a lookout. But I'm wondering how Cassandra is doing. Her parents are curious because she's not calling home.'

'She's spoiled and the other girls don't like her,' said Kara.

'Could we get her to focus less on boys and more on homework?' asked Don.

'She's got a 3.9,' said Art. 'But last week I did catch her sucking face with Carl.'

'I thought she was going out with Tim,' said Candy.

'Both ancient history,' said Kara. 'Now she doesn't want to date anyone. She did tell me at the beginning of the year, told our whole class actually, that she'd had a boyfriend waxed. And I thought the guy coming up to do her with mom's permission was the showstopper.'

'Does the nurse have any chastity belts?' asked Sam.

I jumped on his comment. 'How about we all show some respect?'

Goldie sneered at me. Candy shot a glance at Art. Don put on his reading glasses for no apparent reason, and Sam, who was pretty sure I'd insulted him again, started looking to friends for confirmation.

'So what are we going to do about the kids and drugs?' said Roger.

'If we think drug use is getting worse,' said Don cautiously, 'maybe we could...I don't know, isn't this the nature of the beast?'

Our headmaster was right. Rural boarding schools attract drugs and kids who want to do them, and despite our vigilance, there was little we could do to change that.

'We should search more rooms,' said Kyle. 'We know where to start.'

'It's time for class,' chimed Art.

'What's our policy, Bob?' asked Rog.

Ichabob pushed his glasses up his nose. 'Officially, two faculty members do it together and the student has to be present, or at least in the hall with the door open. Unofficially, I've always given dorm parents latitude during room inspections.'

Don felt the rift growing and put on a dopey expression I'd never seen before. Taking off his glasses, said, 'Guys, I believe we're moving in the right direction. In fact, judging by the work done here each day, I sense we are articulating core values that could someday become traditions.'

Sam, who was aroused by the words 'values' and 'traditions,' nodded like a bobble-head doll. He still hadn't touched his dessert.

'With community spirit in mind,' announced Kara over the clatter of our departure, 'I'm making a pot of chili tonight. It's BYOB, but I got lots of plastic spoons and paper towels. Everyone's invited, even Greenie.'

'Are Sam and Rog pouring shots?' asked Candy.

Don looked a pale. Sam turned red and told us his girlfriend, Mary Katherine Kimball, was coming. Then he looked right at me and squashed a plastic cup right into the middle of his pie.

Freakishly large snowflakes hung in the air as Art rolled out the soccer balls. Like most of the kids, I was wearing sweat pants, a nylon shell and a pair of gloves. Sam had on tear-away pants with a stripe down the side and a hoodie with the name of his college on it. Because he was a fool, he didn't wear gloves.

'I'm going to split you guys up, so play nice,' said Art, tossing Sam a yellow pinny to wear over his sweatshirt.

The game started out cold and painful, but once the field was covered with a slick layer of white stuff, everyone started falling and laughing.

'Coming through,' shouted Sam, taking choppy steps. He slithered through our defense, but Art dispossessed him with a fifteen-foot slide tackle that caught the ball, then Sam. The two went sprawling across the snowy field. The kids hooted and everyone began to slide. Sam even went to the deck in an effort to get the ball from me. Everyone was having fun and no one was really trying. After a few minutes, my team scored. One of my teammates dropped to his knees, crossed himself and shouted 'Iafrati, got nothin'.'

Sam thrust his hands into his pockets and forced a smiled. And the next time he ran down the field he clipped the trash talker's heel with his foot. Splat. There was snow in the kid's hair, down his sweats. He had no clue what had happened.

'Cut it out,' I snarled the next time we were close.

'It was an accident,' he said.

'Bullshit,' I said, as the ball sailed toward us and we jockeyed for position.

'What do you know?' he said, and one of his elbows flashed by my nose and I forgot about the ball. As my feet flew up into the air, I grabbed his arm and took him with me. My head hit the ground. Snow stung my eyes. Complain about this, I thought, as my first punch glanced off his shoulder. The second dented the grass. The third ended with my hand tangled in his jersey. The game stopped. I pulled off my glove and looked with a demented kind of pride at my bent, already swelling finger. It hurt like hell, even more when I yanked on the thing to straighten it out. Sam puked.

Eight

Shawna Brophy had become a folk hero. When one of us would say 'I'm having such a bad day I'm thinking of brophying it,' we'd remember our poor Math intern. The students had also added brophyisms to their vocabulary. They were saying things like, 'Hodge pulled a brophy on his History test, and Davis wouldn't give him a make-up' or 'Cass is going all brophy in the dorm because she got an extra day of restriction.'

The parents of our Asian students must've wondered why their children were now honoring this shy young woman? I'm sure they even considered buying more current dictionaries to keep abreast of the hectic, overzealous language their kids were learning. It was rumored that the seminal phrase, pull a brophy, had even crossed the international dateline and found a home in North Korea, where it was now airdropped in leaflets encouraging Communists soldiers to throw down their weapons and pull a heroic brophy.

Our Shawna Brophy rose to fame when she packed up her apartment and ran away less than two weeks after the students arrived. No one chased Shawna to find out why she left and, sadly, no one actually noticed she was gone. Two full days after her escape I was sitting at the teachers' table in the cafeteria when a student walked up and asked where his tutor was. Even though Ms. Brophy was supposed to be living in my basement, I was stumped; Kara was stumped, and Sam, who was whining about his salty Goulash, had never said boo to the girl.

'She took off,' said Candy. 'Got a good look at you guys and freaked.'

'For real?' said the student, and within seconds the news spreading from table to delighted table and the phrase 'pull a brophy' had been coined.

'She complained to Ichabob that we were cold to her,' added

Candy.

'What a freak,' said Roger Day, shoveling macaroni and cheese into his mouth.

'I said hi once while I was cleaning the laundry room,' I said, remembering that one of the few kids I'd seen her interact with her was Joe Causeway, who after ten minutes was begging for a piggyback ride.

'I went through orientation with her,' said Sam. 'Goldie asked me to be nice, but I never got the chance.'

A few weeks later, a student pulled the second documented Brophy. Billy Drexler, nicknamed 'The Worm' by his own mother, refused to make his bed, so I had no choice but to give him a dorm violation. It was his second. Eighteen more and he'd have to do an unsavory dorm job. No big deal. But Billy had skipped his meds that day—actually, he'd been skipping them all week—and he overreacted. So it's raining hippos and hyenas, tree limbs are falling everywhere, the soccer fields are lakes, kids are mudsliding down the nicest grassy hill on campus and Billy The Worm is nowhere to be found. He misses our Tuesday night sit-down dinner. He's not in the dorm. He's nowhere.

'He pulled a brophy,' said Kwame Aziz. 'I saw him riding his bike down the low road. You going after him?'

I dropped my napkin next to my plate. Outside the trees bucked wildly. Rain was pounding the roof. 'Yeah, I'll take my skateboard.'

As I walked to Ichabob's table, whispers darted about the cafeteria. By the time I returned to my seat, half the room knew of The Worm's brophy.

A state trooper, actually a friend of the officer Kara still couldn't dump, found him riding his mountain bike down Route 22. For twenty minutes Billy the Worm screamed that he wasn't getting the patrol car, but finally he got off his bike and allowed the officer to put it in his trunk. At school, Ichabob greeted Billy with a towel and the news he was being sent home. Billy the Worm was soaked to the bone, but happy. Ichabob, as I would learn time and time again, was no fool.

We teachers also needed to pull brophys now and then, but since we obviously relied on our paychecks more than Shawna, we usually didn't run away. That's why some got stoned, some ran in the woods, some fantasized about sleeping with students, some resorted to treachery, and few of us, I guess, punched things and polished our resumes.

After a trip to the emergency room for an X-ray and a splint, I channeled my anger into a plan and stopped by Don DeWillum's house. He led me to his kitchen, where he started making a cup of tea. His house had been the original Shaker Meeting House and was one of the few on campus with a modern kitchen. I liked how his wife had decorated it with blue cafe curtains and paper maché sunflowers.

'I've got no excuse,' I said, folding my coat and using it as a pillow for my hand.

'Art told me about the black eye you got courtesy Sam's elbow,' said Don, 'and I hear he may have hit you again today, accidentally. Was that it? Just a sports thing? Or does it have anything to do with what Gunnar's report that he's got a defiant streak?'

I love you Gunnar, I thought, and said I wasn't sure. 'I'd prefer like to think our dustup was just a sports thing,' I said, 'but I Sam doesn't share a lot with me. Maybe he thinks I'm a little reckless with commas.'

Don smiled. There was some powdered sugar stuck to his cheek. 'When in doubt, leave it out is my favorite rule. If you ever write a textbook, it'd make a great footnote. But seriously, what's going to happen with you guys?'

I held up my injured finger. 'Maybe this'll ease the tension.'

'Or on Monday I'll find Sam hiding in the apple orchard.'

We laughed and I stood to leave. Don DeWillum said the right things sometimes, but I still didn't trust him.

An hour or two later, I was nursing my worries with a pint of coffee ice cream when Candy called with a threat: either I put on a clean shirt and get my ass to Kara's, or she'd drag me off the sofa by my busted digit. I protested, told her Kara was in league with the

Devil, but Candy didn't care. She thought a swing at Sam might be good for my love life. How, she didn't know, but the party had started and I was on the clock.

Wearing black jeans and a brown cable-knit sweater, Kara gave me a hug when I walked through the door and asked if I'd share my painkillers. Scanning the room, I saw Roger Day, a beer in one hand, a bowl of chili in the other, holding court.

'People need to be reminded we can do room searches,' he said.

'We can't afford to be complacent,' said Kyle Searcy, who was usually a listless administrator and a yes-man.

'How about we just scrap the handbook,' said Gunnar. 'Institute an honor code and give ourselves the freedom to make up rules as we go along?'

Candy, wearing a green T-shirt with her old rugby team's name, The Steel Maidens, and the slogan Hit 'Em High, Hit 'Em Low, Tag The Bitches On The Toe, was annoyed. 'Say that to the lawyer who doesn't want little Johnny kicked out.'

'We just need to scare 'em,' said Rog, 'with consistency, like Don said or by putting pressure on them. Kids need to fear messing up or they'll do whatever they want.'

'There's a creative interpretation of what Don said,' said Gunnar.

'They're kids. This is a private school,' countered Rog. 'What rights do they actually have?'

'If you ever have kids, they're going to kill you in your sleep,' said Candy, sucking salsa off her thumb. 'I bet you'll have a paddle a home.'

'Almost as good as hitting them with an eraser,' he said, and he imagined how smoothly classes would run if we had paddles at our desks and weren't afraid to use them. Because no one had the right to be that confident, Kara took away his untouched chili. Then she stood in front of me and looked again at my bandaged finger.

'You talk to him yet?' she asked.

'I told Don I would.'

'I don't care what's happened with you two,' she whispered, putting me in a headlock, 'but you better say you're sorry.'

'I'm sorry.'

'To him,' she said. Then she pinched the tip of my nose and told me she had to take care of something in the kitchen. Meanwhile, Goldie and Art clamored into the room. He was wearing his drinking shoes, a pair of Timberland boots a student had left behind. She was squeezed into a pair of old Levis—they came out only on weekends now—and some mules with pointy toes. Once through the door, she said, 'What a crew, my word,' and she did a shot with Rog and whispered something naughty into his ear.

After three drinks, Goldie used to name students she wouldn't kick out of bed. After five, she'd start naming teachers. After seven, she might, with more than a hint of disgust and a strange degree of admiration, tell the story about how her father, a sergeant in the Army, had impersonated a captain in order to trick her mother into bed.

'Where'd Sam get such a cute bee-hind?' she asked, as young Mr. Iafrati skirted past her outstretched hand and she followed him into the kitchen for a powwow.

By ten-thirty the coffee table was littered with bottle caps and I had a good buzz. Rog was slouched into a big chair next to me scrutinizing Candy's shot pouring technique. Gunnar and his posse were smoking on the fire escape. Rog, Art, Sam and I—proof we'd put aside our differences—were sitting inside talking about Rog's lacrosse team. I was talking sports, but really I was waiting for everyone to leave so I could clear the air with Kara and ask for a real date. Yeah, she still had a boyfriend, but I'd decided to apologize first and worry about that later.

'I saw two tenth-graders tossing a ball around,' said Art. 'They seemed pretty coordinated. Miles Twohig even looks like he's played lacrosse before.'

'I could knock 'em both over with a good fart,' said Rog. 'Besides, I talked to him and the little fag wants to do theater in the spring?'

'What'd you call him?' demanded Kara, who'd been talking out the window to the smokers.

'It's just a figure of speech, like 'rump ranger' or 'turd burglar.''

'He's cute, but he's sure dumb,' said Goldie, climbing in the window.

'I heard how you meant it,' snapped Kara.

'Is this what happens when women go to college? They start reading minds?'

'Do you enjoy sounding like an asshole?' said Kara.

'Come on, we're at a party and I'm playing with you. Can't you just pretend I'm a Parisian or something?'

Kara scowled. 'How can you take yourself seriously?'

'I don't,' said Rog, 'and neither should you.'

'Straighten him out,' goaded Candy.

If she'd been a man, Rog would've stuck his chest out and stared her down. But when he looked at her angry mouth, he couldn't resist.

'I guess I don't get along with artsy little fruits. Maybe it has something to do with my latent homosexuality.'

While Kara and Rog endured a few insults from the peanut gallery, she circled the room and sat on the arm of his chair. I expected her to tear into him, but her eyes tiptoed over his face as he pretended she wasn't there. And when they finally talked—about candle making or sewing or something—the moony look on her face made my stomach rise. She'll wake up tomorrow and feel stupid, I thought. But then she laughed, with her chest and shoulders, and he rested a hand on her arm and left it there.

Someone cried that were out of beer and Sam volunteered to run down to the valley. Trying to mend fences, Art suggested I go with him, but I couldn't move. I just gave Sam thirty bucks, muttered my apology, and told him to buy whatever.

'Then I'm copilot,' said Art. 'Don't expect any change, Greenie.'

Goldie stood next to me but didn't sit down on the couch.

'If it isn't Ms. Teen Interim Department Head?'

'Who's got the big mouth?' I asked, as Kara fiddled with the buttons on her shirt. Then, because I had nothing to lose, I asked Goldie to do a shot. She gave me this why-not expression to show how cool she was and found two glasses. I grabbed a bottle and poured. We raised our glasses. The lemon-flavored vodka sat on my tongue for a second and made a bitter trail to my stomach. Goldie smacked her lips and turned her glass over on the coffee table.

'Art told me about your display of bad sportsmanship. How does it feel to be off the pedestal? Losing your cool, disorder in the classroom.'

'What have you heard about my classes?'

'That your sophomores are wild. But don't sweat it. I'm sure you'll reel them back in with a little charm.'

It was Sam's fairy tale. Or maybe it was hers. Regardless, it was the kind of talk Goldie loved to share. I spent the next five minutes telling her fun my class was and the five after that wondering why she'd deigned to talk with me in the first place. Talking faster and faster, I was about to call her for manipulating Sam, but just as the words 'conniving' and 'diva' coiled up on my tongue, The Girlfriend, Mary knocked lightly on the door and stepped into the room.

Candy threw her arms around her and said she looked great. Kissing her cheek, Mary Katherine waved to Kara and gave my busted finger a glance. I felt guilty for not going on the beer run. Sam and I could've come back reconciled, and I would've had an excuse to say hello. Now she was turning her back on me because what else do you do when a guy takes a swing at your boyfriend?

'Booty Boy is buying more beer,' said Kara.

'He's Booty Boy now?' asked Mary Katherine.

'You have some catching up to do,' chimed Candy. 'Tequila or vodka?'

'Nothing for me,' she said. I noticed the skin on her fingers was peeling and wondered if I had anything to do with it. Then I realized she was hiding something.

Growing up, Mary Katherine had a choirboy little brother, a tight-assed older sister, and conservative parents who prayed their middle child wouldn't turn out liberal. But their prayers failed, she put her faith in birth control, pushed against their version of the church and became a quiet Democrat who didn't fight. When her father would wave his dinner fork and curse the new president, she'd think about how they used to play catch in the backyard. The softball moving back and forth between them—smacking into worn leather as they backed up to the fences—made it easier to be his daughter, easier to keep a few things to herself. To get closer to her mom, she learned quilting. When she was home from college, they'd listen to oldies and make samples, their hands moving up and down like dolphins, another game of catch, another way to hide the fact that she'd become a grown up.

When Art and Sam paraded into the apartment with two cases of beer, Mary Katherine gave Booty Boy a big kiss.

'How many have you had?' she asked.

'Just one,' he said. 'I was waiting for you.'

She put her mouth close to his ear. No one could hear what she said, but we knew the words exactly. Sam's frozen manner. His glazed eyes. Mary Katherine had no choice but to drag him out into the hall.

They were gone for an hour, his blood pressure soaring, her stories of morning sickness and four home pregnancy tests delighting only the Shaker ghosts. Inside the apartment the tension was delicious, but no one dared say the words out loud. Even when the music stopped and Candy took ten minutes to find a CD, we just bit our tongues and made faces at each other.

'Have a drink for both of us,' said Mary Katherine, when they came back, 'I'll make sure you get home.' But Sam, coiled tighter than a titanium slinky, didn't know what to do.

'What's the matter, Butt Boy?' asked Roger. 'She just said the nicest thing a woman could ever say?'

'I'm tired,' he said, and five minutes later he pulled a brophy.

'What a baby,' exclaimed Goldie. 'Good riddance.'

Mary Katherine let out a breath she'd been holding for five hours. Her eyes seemed bigger, her mouth relaxed.

I joined Gunnar on the fire escape, where he was spinning a yarn about a yacht-racing brother-in-law with a cocaine habit. Looking down, we noticed a kid shuffling in the darkness below.

'What the hell is he doing?' asked Kyle, as a Korean boy named Seung Koo—for six months we thought his name was 'Some Goo'— shuffled toward Rog's dorm.

'Cooking, laundry, beer run, beats me?' said Gunnar, and he

cleared his throat. 'Seung Koo.' The boy ducked as if someone were throwing rocks at him.

'Up here,' I said loudly, and the boy figured out where we were.

'Go back to your dorm,' said Gunnar.

'Can I give something to Tae Hee?' he asked with a straight face. It was one in the morning and he was already breaking a major school rule.

'Go to bed,' said Gunnar.

'Can I get a soda first?' he asked, pointing in the wrong direction.

'No,' we said in unison, and Seung Koo dropped his head.

Was the kid in trouble? Sure, but not really. He'd get the week of restriction he deserved, but the fact that he'd left the dorm only because an older Korean boy had told him to made us forgiving.

'You look terrible.' said Gunnar, lighting a cigarette.

'I just feel like shit. I think it's the chili.'

'It's Goldie,' he said, rubbing my shoulder. 'But, don't worry, we'll figure something out. In the meantime, don't break any more fingers, okay?'

I was watering the ground behind a tree, listing from the chemicals in my bloodstream, but somehow I had enough coordination to follow Per as he circled behind the apple orchard, the Assistant Headmaster's house and the two dorms in the center of campus. A minute later the little idiot scurried across the road just as a car rounded the corner. Dropping to the ground, he became invisible. The lights passed, the thump of a radio playing REO Speedwagon faded into the night and he was on the move again, slipping from tree to tree, hoping over a stream and avoiding the glow of lights from the apartment at the west end of Meacham Dorm. Once in the shadow of the building, Per grabbed onto a window ledge and pulled himself up. Since the window was already ajar, one good push was all it took to get in. I walked around to the faculty apartment at the other end of the building, and five minutes later—because he was brave and stupid but not nearly sneaky enough—Per was being escorted out of the dorm and the term 'brophy' had garnered yet another definition.

Nine

The day after Kara's party the temperature shot up to sixty-five, so I went with Gunnar, Art and a cook we called Scorch to the local public golf course. With my finger splinted all I could do was putt, but I needed to get off campus.

Elsewhere, before any of us had gotten out of bed, Kara's man showed up with a beeper and a gun. Finding her asleep, he made coffee and went to the valley for a newspaper. When she woke, her apartment was cleaner and Handsome Pete was napping on the sofa. She touched his toes, but he didn't move. So she poured a cup of coffee, took her birth control pill and picked up the Saturday Times, which he bought in favor of the Berkshire Eagle because she liked the crossword puzzle. Grabbing a pencil, she sat by the window and was just finishing a corner the puzzle when Pete began to stir.

Roger's 'friend' Theresa—yes, he was seeing someone else—also arrived before breakfast. I'd seen her a bunch of times over the last two or three years, and she always struck me as a woman I'd find lying on a beach in Nevis or working in a twenty-seventh floor midtown office. When he was with her, I'm sure Rog considered leaving The Mount, taking over his dad's textiles business and buying a house in the suburbs. And as he slid his manly feet into wool socks, I bet she looked with contempt at the Shaker boxes, bluebird houses and empty seed packets littering his apartment.

Kara and Pete walked single file down the Chapel Trail. When he was in uniform, women occasionally slipped him phone numbers. Once while returning a lost wallet, he was mistaken for a stripper. Pete looked legit to me though, and as far as I could tell he was a standup guy. You could tell he trusted Kara even more than she trusted herself, and although he was an quiet optimist, he was no fool.

When Kara and Pete approached, Mary Katherine put a finger to her lips.

'Six turkeys. They're huge.' The birds, hunchbacked old men in shimmering brown coats, were shuffling in the underbrush.

Pete shook Sam's hand. 'You hungover too?'

'A vicious rumor,' he whispered.

'Maybe we could all have dinner tonight?' suggested Pete.

Sam made sure his feet were planted firmly on the trail and said maybe. Kara nudged her guy and made him stumble. The birds went crashing through the brush.

'What's with them?' he asked, once the others were out of earshot.

'She's pregnant.'

'I didn't see a ring,' said Pete. 'Do they have plans?'

Kara sighed as the words 'I have to tell you something' began to gather steam.

Roger and Theresa drank from his wine sack he brazenly carried over his shoulder. He showed her the locations of some old ponds, all of them empty except for the one next to the old tannery. He explained that there had been a series of five millponds the Shakers harnessed to power their workshops. Then he pulled a hunk of cheddar out of his pocket and squirted wine at her.

'We're building a log cabin about over there,' he said, handing her the wine sack and pointing at a cluster of trees. 'It'll be a great place for kids to smoke.'

'It's in the middle of nowhere,' said Theresa. 'At least they'll get exercise.'

'If we didn't hide it out here, we'd need a permit to build it.'

Voices drifted through the trees as Peter and Kara came round a bend in the path. As the couples exchanged pleasantries, Roger was jealous that Kara's man carried a gun for a living. Theresa, who was jealous of few women, wished for a second she weren't so fair. Kara, looking at Theresa's chest, which seemed to be staring back at her, felt short and boyish. Pete saw everything and felt like an outsider.

'Did she show you the bridge she worked on?' asked Rog.

'She painted half my house last summer,' said Pete.

Kara didn't like his standing up for her. 'It's over there,' she said brushing by him and leading the way. But she didn't take him to the bridge. She took him off the path, past the clearing where Rog's crew had been building its cabin and into a stand of pines. There she pushed Pete against a tree and put her hands inside his jacket.

'What's up?' he said, peering around for the bridge.

'Will you drop these for ten dollars,' she said, sticking her fingers in his pocket and feeling his wallet.

'Miss,' he replied, 'for you I'd do it for nothing, but...'

'Shut up,' she said, tugging at his belt. And when she was done, she ran her fingers through his hair and broke up with him.

Mary Katherine took Sam's hand and asked if he'd provoked me.

'I didn't do anything,' he said. 'He pulled me down and started swinging.'

'You didn't bump him first or anything?'

Sam was trying not to make excuses. 'I clipped a kid's heel. I shouldn't have, but he was talking trash. But it looked like a total mistake.'

'You're better than that. Did Jeff Green see it?'

'Maybe, but I still don't trust him. Did I tell you he suggested I teach like I was at a cocktail party? There's a good way to win me over.'

'It's not the worst advice I've ever heard,' she said, as they came out of the woods onto a field dotted with greenish brown cornstalks that had escaped the combine.

Now was the time, not the only time but a good one. I'm sure Sam felt safer away from the rutted trail and the overgrown Shaker foundations that so intrigued his girlfriend. But the ground was too wet, the light made him squint, and he had serious doubts about his ability to make it through the school year.

If Sam had paid attention while we were teaching *Romeo and Juliet*, he would've remembered how the young lovers married quickly and without fanfare. They married to sanction their love, steal power from their parents, justify the ladder outside her window and, of course, because they were crazy for each other. Hasty perhaps, but they also felt marriage should be exalted, celebrated, and mourned before being embraced. That's why Juliet scolded Romeo before the ceremony when he offered her poetry and asked for poetry in return. Words, words, words. She wanted something more, something higher to guide her through the wilderness ahead.

'How big is it?' he asked. She told him it was the size of a fig, and Sam, who had two older sisters with kids, nervously asked if she was taking prenatal vitamins. She told him they looked like horse pills and tasted like crap. Otherwise she was feeling good, no morning sickness yet.

'Maybe we should get married,' he finally said. 'This isn't the way I envisioned asking, but it's beautiful out here and...or maybe we should just get engaged.'

She'd predicted it, knew he'd find a way to both circumvent and overstate his feelings. She also knew she was going to turn him down, so she put her arms around him, felt the fig growing between them and apologized.

During my second year on The Mount, when I still believed in love, I took a walk on a frost-covered golf course and talked about the noisy geese on the ninth fairway. I talked about my new job, the price of coffee, the size of The Boston Sunday Globe and that I'd shaved on my day off. Then I took my barely pregnant girlfriend to the clinic. Six years later I gave into temptation. I borrowed Art's driver, swung hard, and the pain shot from my hand up to my elbow. The ball sliced into the woods and a clot of grass sailed through the air. Scorch and Gunnar thought it was hilarious until I began beating a ball washer with a branch.

All morning, they guys had been calling me lefty, but now that I was attacking a defenseless ball washer, they didn't know what to say. There was an understanding though: I'd fallen into a rough spell.

Jesus Demaquina, Cassandra Diaz's twenty-two-year old boyfriend, was frustrated too. Straight out of Brooklyn, three hours of parkway and a country road behind him, Jesus wanted to take Cass out for lunch, so he was not pleased to find out she was on restriction and he was going to be treated like a teenager.

'He's an adult,' she complained, resisting the urge to say that he was her uncle, 'and he's up here with my parents' permission.'

The adult on duty happened to be Goldie Remlap, and she did not want Jesus take the girl out—for food and who knows what else. So she checked in with Icabob, who validated her opinion and broke the news to Cass.

'I got blanket permission,' the girl pleaded into the phone. 'You have to let me.'

Since her parents' letter was, in fact, on file in his office, Ichabob had to think fast. 'But you're not in good standing right now,' he said. 'I need to hear it directly from your mom if she wants you going off campus with him.'

'That's not fair,' whined Cass, whose parents had no idea how often Jesus drove upstate in his Monte Carlo. 'I've got blanket permission.'

'I can make the call for you if you want,' he said. 'Otherwise, Mr. Demaquina will have to leave.'

The next morning, Ichabob told us over hard-boiled eggs and burnt coffee just how difficult it had been to keep a straight face while Cassandra kept insisting over and over that she was a senior with blanket permission.

Ten

Feeling like Mr. Rodgers with a scorpion in his brain and a tent in his pants, I sat at the bar with a cheeseburger, a book and a whiskey sour. The Green Hat in Pittsfield was a stupid place to be on a school night, and I was about to leave when Grace started talking.

'Hey, Mr. Cardigan with the bad hand, you gonna to tell me about that black cloud?'

Yes, I was wearing a cardigan. She was in blue heels and a black skirt two stools away. Looking up at her dark hair and pale face, I saw that she really was gazing over my head. I invited her to guess.

'Dumped, I'd say. Got the crap beat out of you.' She looked at the cover of my book, A Catcher in the Rye, and gave it a nod of approval.

'I got the crap beat out of me at work,' I said.

'Almost as bad,' she said.

I liked that skirt of hers. Just a little slutty, but not over the top. Candy liked girls who were a little slutty, too, laughed when I tried to sound ethical, taught me it was okay to be a slut once in a while, and did her best to beat the 1950s out of me.

Anyway, as I got a little drunk, I told Grace about Goldie and Kara and Sam and his baby and about how horny I was. I couldn't decide whether I was jealous of Sam or scared for him, but the real reason for my cloud was a girl I used to date. It always worked like that, crap happened and I stepped into the time machine.

When I finished telling Grace that she was right about me, she told me she waited tables at a restaurant where they let monkeys run the show but they gave her health insurance. She drummed her fingernails on the bar, smoothed her skit just like Goldie and tapped my elbow.

'So why's the old girlfriend still haunting you now?' she asked.

She was a fledgling lawyer. If we'd gotten married, I would've followed her paycheck, but when she chose a five-year plan over motherhood, I put on a brave face and stayed at The Mount.'

'You put on brave face?' said Grace. 'Who says shit like that?'

'You're right, that sounds dumb.'

'Keep it raw. Some people get scared of baggage, run for the hills when they find out you see a shrink, but I'd don't trust anyone who hasn't been kicked around a little. You need to find someone sweet though. No barracudas or train wrecks like me. And don't hit things'

She pointed a cautionary finger at my hand and I caught a glimpse of a snake tattoo on her upper arm. She also had a rose on her ankle.

'You need to toughen up,' she continued. 'I was pregnant once with a guy named Patrick. When we met he was so cool: vegan, intense. My friends thought I was an idiot going out with a guy who'd been living in some commune, but before I even told him I was gonna have the baby, he changed. He completely started gobbling down deli platters and partying all the time. And he stopped worshiping me, so there was no way I was gonna to tell him I was having his kid.'

She squeezed my arm.

'It's okay, sugar, she's with my mother in Great Barrington.'

'Does he know?' I asked.

'Yeah, and I'm so glad he isn't in the picture.'

For a second I fantasized that I'd been lied to, that there was a six-year-old somewhere with my annoying habits, but I really had driven her to the clinic, received her after and taken her back to the world.

Grace and I were groping each other in my truck. I didn't have any condoms, but she wanted me inside her anyway. I told her I didn't have to cum. She said, 'Please don't' and hiked up her skirt. My legs had been trembling all week, but suddenly they didn't bother me. I also didn't worry when my ass hit the radio and we were blasted with country music. Grace didn't mind either, didn't even blink when she kicked the horn and I started laughing like a madman. At some point the wipers began squeaking across the windshield and the dome light flicked on.

Eleven

The Shakers had a credo, 'Hands-to-Work, Hearts-to-God.' Our kids knew it well, but while we didn't ask for their hearts, we did require their hands, backs and short attention spans every Wednesday morning. For me Hands-to-Work meant skipping a shower, throwing on a sweatshirt, and wolfing down a hot breakfast. For the students, it meant streaming into the cafeteria at the last minute and clogging the food line.

'My first girlfriend's dad was a square dance caller,' said Roland Meadows, the art teaching lay preaching libertarian who lived in the dorm where I worked. 'Guess what we did on dates?'

Candy, who had a new girlfriend with a pet chinchilla and a pickup truck, drained her coffee and dropped her mug on my tray. 'You dated a strange woman there.'

Rolly spread butter on his waffles. 'She seemed normal at the time.'

'Can you top that one Greenie?' asked Candy.

I'd dated a girl who made me listen to her sister's demo tape when we do-si-doed. Bad disco. Okay sex. Maybe not so strange, but I was too miserable to share the story. My talk with Don had become a gadfly. For a week now I'd been standing in front of my sophomores wondering if one of them really became uncomfortable when I told them a girlfriend liked my earring. When I said she was persuasive, was I really talking about sex? I talked Gunnar and Candy and they told me I was being silly. Candy called it a spider bite—Goldie being the spider, of course—and said I should watch what I said around Sam.

'Attention,' said Rog, flapping his arms, 'no one's getting switched to an indoor crew until the new sign-ups after Christmas Break. Is that clear? So let's have announcements and we'll get out there.' A dozen kids with cramps and headaches started begging Ichabob for permission to go to the nurse. Gunnar's crew began throwing cereal. The Japanese table erupted in laughter. Roger Day, who had his own table because he was always under siege on Wednesdays, looked quite manly in his big boots and worn jeans, but at this hour even he had little clout.

'Okay, let's start with the people who are missing,' he bellowed.

I sat with my crew, The Tree People, and as usual called out Josh's name.

'Who's the prefect in Henderson's dorm?' asked Rog, and a Saudi boy with bedhead worse than Sam's trudged off amid a barrage of hoots. Meanwhile Cassandra Diaz, having discovered that the Business Office no longer needed her envelope-stuffing prowess, tugged at Rog's sleeve and begged to join the handicrafts crew. He decided she needed to do real work though and directed her to my table. Then, after Per had asked the seniors to give him forty dollars each for a class trip, the kids raced to the tool room, where they signed out rakes, saws, hammers, paintbrushes and the like.

With the wind whipping up clouds and pinning leaves in the corners of the buildings, we trudged off to our projects. Gunnar's crew, the Donner Party, headed for the woods with axes and saws. A girl named Elizabeth Perkins, carrying a can of orange spray paint and wearing an enormous parka she'd borrowed from the tool room, was whining about the weather.

'How can you be cold in that Eskimo jacket?' chided her crewmates.

'Groucho, stop moaning or I'll nominate you for a Shining Shaker Award,' said Gunnar. Loathing the attention the nomination and a prize cookie might bring her, Elizabeth smacked him with a mitten and demanded to be left alone. Of course, Gunnar chanted Groucho wants a cookie until she started chasing him down the trail.

In my crew Josh Henderson showed up in vinyl pants he'd purchased during his drug suspension, his Rocky Horror Picture Show sweatshirt and combat boots two sizes too big. Holding up a twenty-four ounce plastic mug, he asked if he could run inside and get more coffee.

'No,' I said, 'you've probably had enough coffee already to kill a horse.'

'It's why he's such a freak,' said Harriet Barth, a melodramatic D student and a critic of everything. I'd sent her back to her dorm for showing up in roller skates.

'At least I don't spend my whole life stretching,' he said.

'You stretch. I know you do,' she said. Her pockets were full of apples she'd taken from the cafeteria.

'You're right,' said Josh, pretending to be embarrassed, 'I stretch all the time, night and day, day and night.'

'What's stretching?' I asked, as one of our chickens, a crazed Polish Bantam, began scratching near my feet.

'It's what guys do every night before they go to bed,' said Josh. Harriet laughed through her nose and started eating a bruised apple. She'd washed her hair this week and was wearing a little makeup.

'It's why bathrooms have shades,' she said, as the chicken started staring at her. Because the girl had already been pecked—we had five roosters and two terrified hens—she jumped behind Josh.

'Do I have to remind you that you're talking to a teacher?' I said, throwing a weed at them and shooing the chicken. 'Now get to work, you little turds.'

'They pulled the same routine on Mr. Davis at breakfast,' said Cass, who by now had read *Leaves of Grass* cover to cover.

Today my crew had the thankless task of weeding an orchard of tiny Christmas trees. Some of the kids got down on hands and knees and started pulling. Others, like Harriet and Cass, spent their time chatting. I was mildly annoyed, but—contrary to their industrious stereotype—the Shakers probably wouldn't have cared. Walking The Holy Mount a hundred and forty years earlier, visitors would have discovered a relaxed air about the communal village. And no one was embarrassed when a hired man did the work of two, sometimes three Shakers.

As the day warmed up, my back and my newly mended hand grew sore and sweat soaked my collar. The kids never stopped complaining, but I reminded them that we didn't have the worst job. That distinction belonged to Sam's crew, the Handy People Eaters, who were investigating the stench in Wickersham's cupola.

Sam climbed up a ladder and unlatched the trapdoor to the cupola. Dirt, plaster and pigeon droppings rained down on him and the kids below leaped out of the way. He slowly stuck his head into the cupola. A few feet above him loomed the bell and chicken wire that needed to be repaired. In front of him, he saw the dim outline of a half dozen pigeons in various states of decay. I've wondered what he imagined up there: his girlfriend breaking up with him, a child he might not raise, or just a bird? Maybe he'd have to borrow money, find another job, another mountain to climb. A baby. Dead birds. His parents' disappointment. Maybe in a selfish instant he wished it all away and now he felt God's hot stare on the back of his head.

'Can I pull the rope?' joked Miles Twohig, looking up at Sam's backside. The teacher gagged and the boy, as punishment, was forced to hold the garbage bag. The kids started when the body a pigeon fell out of the darkness. A few feathers and more turd followed. They put their shirts over their mouths as three more adult birds, light and crunchy, dropped out of the ceiling.

Outside was cold and bright. Slivers of light pierced the stale, dusty air of the cupola. Sam's skin was crawling. He felt the body of yet another dead pigeon through the leather of his glove, dirt working its way into his pores, his chest tightening. One step up on a ledge was something he didn't want to touch. He grabbed it though and pried it away from the wood. His stomach rose up and he had to climb down. Taking the garbage bag, he pushed Miles up the ladder to gather the last of the birds, said he was too large for the job. The boy didn't want to go but a teacher was telling him. Miles bit into the collar of his shirt and climbed up. Two dead chicks, feeble and pale, were curled up in the bottom of the nest. He lifted one. Its mouth was slightly open, almost smiling. Then the same force that gripped the teacher got hold of Miles and he dropped the bird and nest. They hit Sam in the shoulder. Then a larger object, Mile Twohig himself, fell out of the cupola.

'You effing retard!' yelled Sam, when the boy came crashing down on his head. 'Can't you stand on a stupid ladder?'

In shock, his leg stuck in the ladder, Miles couldn't have understood what the teacher was saying. In his hand was the second dead chick. Sam rubbed the angry welt forming on his head and screamed, 'It's just a bird.' Miles freed his leg and sat against the wall, his heart pounding. Sam leaned against the other wall. 'It's just a bird,' he said quietly, and finally, when it was too late, he asked Miles if he was all right.

Candy roared across campus on the tractor. Children were sprawled atop the flatbed she was pulling. Among them was Joe, his feet dangling off the side and a stocking cap on his head. In work boots and gloves that gave him back his missing finger he looked quite the man.

'I dig those booty huggers, Mr. Day,' he shouted to Rog, who was out checking on crews. The kids on the flatbed laughed. Rog had no clue what Joe was talking about.

At the woodpile, Kara was splitting stovepipe lengths of birch. Before her dad died, he taught her how to swing an axe, so she loved the sight of firewood on chopping block. Raw fingers and hard palms gave her pleasure.

'Calabria, can I stack this?' asked one of the mud-covered boys in her crew. Kara helped him pile the wood and set up a piece of soggy pine to split just as Rog stopped in her field of vision. He checked out her leather gloves with a black seventeen on each wrist and her beat up work boots. He also took in her hair, pulled back into an industrious ponytail, her jeans and her oversized flannel shirt. Kara swung the ax, but it sank just a few inches into the wet wood. After levering it out, she gritted her teeth and the blade bounced off the side of the log. Kara swore. A few heads turned, and with murder in her eyes, she repositioned the offending piece of wood.

Josh and I had wandered over from our weeding to get hot chocolate from the school pick-up truck. He'd was telling me how he'd actually enjoyed his previous night's homework when noticed Kara and her insolent log. Thwack. The ax stuck again. To free it,

Kara smacked the bottom of the log into the block, but she jammed her wrist and let go of the handle.

On any other day, Rog might have called her a fool for trying to split bad wood. Today he smirked at Josh. 'Your pants might crack in this weather.'

'You'd look good in vinyl pants. They're muy macho.'

A hen ran by Roger. The spastic rooster chasing it raced right through his legs. 'Those birds aren't going to be around much longer,' he said casually. 'The hens are too spooked to lay because they keep getting raped.'

'You're twisted, Mr. Day,' said Josh.

'I'm going to give them to Scorch,' said Rog. 'You think you'd notice if we put a Polish Bantam in your barbecue?'

'I'm never eating chicken again,' said Josh.

Kara finally made it through the log. Josh gave her a mock cheer and ran off to join a crabapple fight. When I went back to the little trees, I saw that everyone except Cass had deserted to the herb garden.

'Mr. Green, I need your help,' said Cass. 'I think I might have broken a rib.'

I told her she'd be in more pain and suggested she go to the nurse. Cass gazed at the at the infirmary door fifty yards away and said it was too far.

'Just tell me if something looks funny,' she said.

Was she making a joke? Cass opened her jacket. I could hear the tractor and the occasional thump of an axe. The wind picked up. I put my back to it as she lifted her shirt over her light brown belly. When I saw her navel peeking over the top of her pants, I felt the insatiable urge to poke my finger in it.

'It looks like a scratch,' I said, nodding at a small mark on her ribcage. Your lips, that reddish-brown, I thought. They should name that color after you, Cassandra Diaz.

'But it hurts.' The fabric of her bra was pink. Her skin was Fair Latina, really Puerto Rican or Dominican depending on which parent she liked better at the moment. She playfully dropped her shoulder. 'My word, the bottoms match,' she said, thinking she was being funny, and she tugged at the top of her jeans and showed me a couple inches of her thong. I should've jumped like a scared rabbit and run, but for some reason all I could do was enjoy her skin and think how nice. A second later she tucked in her shirt and skipped off for a smoke on the Chapel Trail.

Twelve

Did Cass really say My Word? Damn, Goldie was everywhere. She may have even been peeking over Candy's shoulder when she busted one of my advisees.

There were clothes on all the floors and not a bed was made, but on Hands-To-Work Wednesday Candy had a lenient pen. She was also lenient on Mondays and Fridays and on weekends there were inspections, so her dorm was the most popular on campus. In the land of clogged toilets and shaving cream fights, however, there was one fastidious exception: Kwame. Candy saw shoes lined up under the bed, CDs alphabetized, crackers, Pop Tarts and a box of brownie mix like soldiers on the windowsill. She checked out his closet of Hilfiger, Kani, Carhart, Timberland, Spoof and Urban Dingo, shirts all facing the same direction, even his jeans on hangers. No wonder the boys called him George Armando. In the desk, which she wasn't supposed to look in, Candy found three-dozen pens still in their packages, a box of condoms and a roll of stamps. The condoms he'd use; the stamps, never. Finally, she followed her nose to a jacket on the back of the door and found a baggy full of pot.

Brownie mix, smoke on his jacket. Ichabob, our Dean of Students, hated to see any kid busted, but Kwame was a shrewd child and a dose of humility might do some good. Don DeWillum let out a big, conflicted sigh because Kwame had already been suspended once for dropping his drawers in public. This time was his first for drugs.

'Can we even do this kind of search?' asked Don.

Ichabob pushed his dirty glasses up his nose. 'It's not in the handbook, but we have the right to search a kid or his stuff if it smells funny.'

My leader was looking for an option other than suspension. He could've pretended we'd never found the pot, but then the kids would've been checking our eyes and calling us thieves. Don sighed again. He also saw Kwame as two children. The first was promise: piano lessons survived, siblings doted over when they visited, an essay in which Kwame turned his careless world into a poem and exploited it shamelessly. 'I'm afraid to reach twenty,' he'd written, 'afraid I'll look around and find all my friends in jail, afraid I'll lose the only hope I have, my education.' But the other Kwame loved temptation and had begun to believe his own stories.

When the boy in question stormed into Ichabob's office, he threw himself into a chair right on top of a stuffed penguin and a stack of year-old Christmas cards. Don and I were parked on a ratty sofa, riffling through a candy dish.

'I don't keep weed in my room. Besides, I ain't smoked in that jacket. I wear that home to my mom's.'

'Do you want to face a Disciplinary Committee?' asked Ichabob.

'But I didn't do anything!' complained my advisee, mad because someone had dropped off the bag that morning and since he'd never seen it, he felt innocent.

So Kwame faced the six members D.C. and asked us to sniff his jacket. The kids on the committee, three upperclassmen who'd been elected in September, were confused. 'You can't tell me this thing smells,' he said. 'So why would she go into it? And y'all know she hates me, right? She's the one busted me for tucking in my shirt on the road.'

Art Remlap, the chair of this particular DC, began to squirm.

'You're saying Ms. Dafoe planted the marijuana?'

Kwame looked to me for support, found none and pointed out that he never let his key out, and the brownie mix was for, guess what, making brownies. 'Can you see me eating space cakes and wearing palooka oil? I look like a damn hippie? Everyone knows teachers party the most around here.'

The kids wanted to follow his logic and throw a cloud over the search. But when Kwame began padding his story with half-truths, they changed their minds. Besides, some of them had actually seen him waving his bum-bum at the girlies. So after ten minutes of deliberation, he was found guilty.

'That's right, nail the city kid who don't pay full tuition,' he said, as I drove him to the Pittsfield bus station for a week at home. 'Hey, why you all so strict now? Even Calabria made me spit out my gum.'

'She doesn't think you can speak Spanish with gum in your mouth?'

'I can't speak Spanish anyway,' said Kwame, as we passed the local pig farm. It was dark and the windows were up, but we could still smell it. 'Come on, Mister, ain't you ever done anything wrong?'

'Yeah, but I owned up to it when I got caught.'

'When you got caught?' he said. 'How often did that happen?'

'My mom had a sixth sense. I always got caught.'

'That means you're a bad liar. So what did your mom do?'

'Grounded me. Took away the car.'

'All you guys act like you never done stuff. Come on, wouldn't you like to party with us like they did in the olden days?'

Kwame was right: there was a time when students and teachers socialized together and most schools had one or two hooking up. Hell, back in the '70s they were doing it with parents' permission. What a life, I thought, knowing I could never be one of those hip teachers—Santana on the turntable, peach wine coolers in the fridge, girl on my sofa waiting for a professorial kiss.

I asked Kwame if he needed any money, and he said Ichabob had given him enough for his ticket. I gave him ten dollars in case he got hungry and asked what he was going to do when he got home.

Kwame shrugged. 'Smoke crack, slap hos.'

'Give me my ten dollars back.'

'Greenie, DeWillum acted like he wanted me to confess, said it would be between me and him, and God. Even invited me to church with him. Is that dude a Mormon?'

'I don't think so.'

'Good, I don't like those guys. They dress like lawyers, sound faker than Mrs. Remlap. But, man, Dafoe was sneaky. You all got no trust.'

A mist was falling. Challenging people to believe in him and letting them down didn't bother Kwame. If I were his dad, I would've cracked a college catalog off of his skull and hit him even harder with a curfew. I would've told him how frustrating it was to have a stereotype for a son. Church might've helped him out, too. But I wasn't his dad. I was just a hypocrite, who wasn't crazy about the search but had absolutely no problem sending him home.

'You try to have fun at this place, they send you home. You try to stand up for yourself, they send you home. And if someone's got it out for you, forget it. Know what would happen to me if I went and tried to punch Iafrati in the head?'

'I could've lost my job.'

'No way,' he said calmly. 'Not you, not when you're the attraction and Iafrati's just some punk you got to watch your back around.'

He sounded so wise and so world weary, all at the age of seventeen. But truth be told, he was just a smart kid with good bullshit. Most adults I know treat city kids like raw chicken. They spend way too much time worrying about what to touch or the harm they might do when it shouldn't be that hard.

Kwame's comments about Don DeWillum and church got me thinking about Bobby Doherty and Joey Salerno, a pair of fourth-grade buddies who taught me the finer points of confession. Ah yes, the dark box, the dusty clergy, the spiders that invariably crawled across the grille: it was clear at a very young age where their troublemaking would lead them. Yet despite their concern that hell really was littered with the wrappers of stolen chocolate bunnies, they enjoyed confessing, enjoyed it so much they made up extra sins to go along with the ones they'd actually committed. Bobby bragged about stomping on snowmen that had never been built, and Joey, the imp, cursed his grandfather's tomatoes by pretending to spit on them.

Confused as to whether their lies made matters better or worse, I asked my mother about their sacrament. But she just patted me on the head and told me smart Jewish boys had to own up to their sins, too. I was doubly confused. Was there some part of the synagogue I didn't know about, some nook where rabbis dispensed wisdom and pondered the souls of wicked boys? I asked and my mom laughed. No Jefferson, she said, dooming me to almost thirty-five years of misery, you take your misdeeds to God directly.

According to Mary Katherine, Sam was a lot like Joey and Bobby. First, he rarely confessed the truth. No way. If he'd mentioned the dirty magazine he'd seen, the kids he'd tripped, or the candy bar he'd slipped into his gym bag at Dison's Pharmacy, he would've been a goner, for Father Trumble was a righteous windbag. So for slightly different reasons that my buddies he resorted to the time-honored practice of making up transgressions. I fought with my brother. I didn't do all my homework. I teased Lorena Huey. Then he'd mumble his Hail Marys and run away.

Was Father Trumble a fool? Did he believe all the boys in his parish were so unimaginative? While sitting outside Don DeWillum's office, the answer may have come to Sam. If he was worth his salt as a priest, Father Trumble would've cared more that they were in church in the first place. A well-intended lie is better than being absent, and on some occasions even better than the truth. Ten Hail Marys and four Our Fathers.

Sitting behind his desk as the sun set on a chaotic day, Don told Sam that Miles Twohig's parents were unclear how their tree-climbing son had fallen off a ladder. Eager for Sam's story, Don leaned back in his creaky leather chair and listened to an explanation of digestive maladies and the events leading up to the accident.

'Are you surprised they took him home?' asked Don.

'In my family a bump on the head didn't mean much,' said Sam, 'And if we had a run in with a teacher, it was our fault, no matter what. There were a lot us.'

'A more traditional upbringing.'

Sam didn't know whom he was being compared to—Miles, Don or all the little Americans with one sibling and between one and four parental figures—but he agreed anyway. 'I was the youngest, so it was pretty easy.'

'About Miles,' said Don. 'The family says you've brought the boy to tears twice. And you've pelted Steven Hodge with an eraser.'

Sam rolled with the punch and offered to call the parents, said he'd like to know why the boy cried over not having his paper graded and why he fell out of the ceiling. That conversation made Don nervous. He said a quick pat on the back when the boy came back would be sufficient. Sam called it a good idea. He liked the kid, wanted the family to know his response wasn't personal.

'Look,' said Don, picking up a red ballpoint pen and doing my dirty work for me. 'You're here on a one-year position and I know you'd like to be in the classroom next year. Well, there may be openings in your department, but I don't feel comfortable offering you anything right now. Maybe in June, after I see your evaluation and how you finish the year. In the meantime, you'd be wise to keep your options open.'

Sam wanted to hide his trembling hands from Don, but Goldie had coached him to keep them in sight. Be confident and win his sympathy. Let your voice crack if you can. Don't hesitate to bite your lip: it's how you look scared.

'There's something else I need to tell you, sir,' Sam said hoarsely.

Over time Don had come to think of Sam as an overly serious boy with a father complex. He thought Sam lacked both confidence and maturity. The nice girlfriend, Don feared, was going to disappear in a few months.

'What are your plans?' asked Don, aroused by consequence, paternal instinct and possibly the image of The Girlfriend Mary with a large belly. Sam realized Goldie had given him a lot of good advice, but he hadn't thought through the entire confession.

'I'm not sure at this time, sir,' he said. 'But I have a few ideas.'

Daggers in Men's Smiles

Thirteen

Gunnar and Candy knocked once and barged in before I answered. I was lying on the living room floor with the remote on my stomach. I hadn't run the vacuum in a few weeks and there was a stack of unopened mail spilling off the bookcase.

'This is your intervention, dude,' said Gunnar. 'We know you've taken a few hits lately, but we're here to save you.'

'We bring alcohol, weed if you want it,' added Candy, 'and we're willing to spring for a hooker.'

'You guys are the salt of the earth,' I said, reaching for Candy's six-pack.

Gunnar popped the top off my beer with the opener on his key ring. 'We want you to see that you can still kick some ass.'

Candy rubbed my head. 'But first the bad news. Oscar's definitely not coming back. Gunnar begged him to stay for just one more bloody semester, but he said he'd just bought a new fedora and he'd rather pluck out his eyes.'

'So Goldie's just biding her time?' I said, not bothering to sit up.

Gunnar grabbed my remote and turned of the television. 'We've got a solution. You go ahead and tell Don your leaving. Tell him you need the title while you interview so it'll look good on your resume. It's brilliant, right? I mean, who'd change department heads in the middle of the year and make you look bad?'

'You want me to tell Don I'm leaving but then stay once he does me a favor? Oh, and am I supposed to take personal days for fake interviews or can I do some real ones?'

I was wearing a big smile and they had no clue why.

'People change their minds all the time,' said Candy. 'At the end of the year, tell Don his good work's the reason you're staying.'

'Then he'll know I'm lying,' I said.

'Probably, but in the meantime you also need Sam out of your class,' said Gunnar. 'Try to do it gracefully and let Mr. Tiebreaker know he cannot trust Goldie.'

'I did and he hit me in the eye,' I said. 'But, tell me, sweetie, why do you hate that woman so much?'

'Hate?' said Candy. 'I use hate for runny eggs, student musicals and when I go to the beach and get sand up my ass. No, that self-serving, gold digger inhabits the ninth circle of some foul place I can't even imagine. If I had to write a poem about her, I'd take a piece of paper and hack up something green and runny onto it. And if you told me it was the most disgusting thing you'd ever seen, well, then I'd know I was getting close. And, by the way, you will know what I mean. Just wait.'

I told Candy she should join the poetry club and she drained my beer.

'How's that for a poem, Greenie? But seriously, what do you think of her touching up the Hodges for, what, twenty-five grand for that writing center?'

'They might've given ten times that. But that's Don's bad judgment not hers.'

'True,' said Gunnar. 'The guy's got no vision, she oversteps and he just rubberstamps the bad idea? It's obvious the dude needs us.'

'So how do I get Sam out my class without me looking like the fuck up?' I asked.

'You should've thrown that boy under the bus a long time ago,' said Gunnar.

'Evaluate him,' said Candy. 'Let his performance sink him. Then throw your weight around and don't let him vote for the next department head.'

Gunnar clinked his now empty bottle against mine. 'How you like them balls?'

I told them they were definitely turning me into a dick.

Miles' desk was empty. Sam was at the board for the first time in two weeks, but even though his prep was solid and his delivery was clear, the kids just shut down. In the halls they'd started calling each other 'retard.' During pickup basketball games the ball was now the eraser and an errant pass was a Bammy. In the cafeteria Iafrati was filleted and flambéed at every meal.

One afternoon I took my creaky finger to the weigh room below the gym. While I was debating whether to bench sixty or seventy pounds, Cass appeared in the doorway with a prospective student.

'This is the fitness room,' she said to the slack-jawed teen. 'And that's Mr. Green down there doing weighty things, like contemplating a new tie and a haircut.'

We hadn't talked since the peep show. I'd glanced across the room at morning meeting and smiled innocently in the cafeteria, but as she teased me, all I could think about was her hideous flannel shirt and how I wouldn't mind seeing her in something tighter. But then my arms began wobbling and I got scared the weights were about to crash down on my neck.

After my workout, I shot baskets in the gym until my team arrived. We'd been destroyed in our last two game, mostly because we stunk but in part because we were trying too hard, so I let them play H-O-R-S-E and ran a silent scrimmage: no calling for the ball, no complaining and bad passes—turnovers, not Bammys—cost you push-ups. Finally, instead of wind sprints, we ran to the cafeteria for Scorch's stir-fry. Then I proctored a study hall. Then I busted two smokers behind the tool shed. Then I settled into my second home, the tiny room on the second floor of Ann Lee.

This cozy space didn't have a TV or a wood-burning stove, but because it had a enormous hissing radiator, it was always loud and warm. Usually, I'd strip down to a T-shirt while I graded and during breaks I'd strum a beat-up guitar Gunnar had lent me. When I ventured into the dorm, I'd harass kids while they cooked Ramen or borrow CDs. More often than not though, the boys sought my company.

Josh Henderson, in flip-flops and his grandfather's bathrobe, otherwise know as The Arnold Palmer Shave Coat, caught me yawning and told me I partied too much.

'Who has the time?' I said.

'Come on, your work doesn't start until finals. We're the ones freaking out.' I waved a slab of unmarked papers under his nose and asked why he was anxious.

'Your essay,' he said, 'and I keep having this dream I'm being chased by dogs.'

'Are they trying to steal your homework?'

Hodge leapt down the stairs and crashed outside my room. I yelled at him so Roland Meadows in the adjacent faculty apartment would know I was doing my job.

'Why are you in such a crappy mood, Greenie?' he said. 'Hey, is it true Calabria's pissed at Day for some video he took of her?'

'She's not in it,' said Josh. 'It was his Secret Santa present.'

'It's a video on how to chop wood,' explained Joe, poking his shirtless somewhat hair torso into the room. 'I saw her with it, complaining to Dafoe with her ears all red. And she's his Secret Santa'

Looking lost without his lacrosse stick, Hodge wondered how chopping wood would make her angry. Joe didn't know but he'd heard Kara retaliated.

'How do you know this if it's supposed to be secret?' I asked, glad they weren't gossiping about my pathetic love life. I'd already given Art a sleeve of golf balls and some chocolate cherries.

'Ms. Remlap tells us. Says Calabria got him flowers and a bottle of white wine, a zin, whatever that is. Remlap says it's sweet and fruity.' Hodge was proud of himself for remembering. 'And the flowers she put on his desk were so big he couldn't see over.'

'Why did he come back and give her nail polish?' asked Joe, scratching himself then holding his package. 'She can use that?'

'It's a diss,' replied Josh, ''cause she likes to get dirty. We're betting he gives her a real gift though, eventually.'

The radiator started banging, distracting Joe for a second, but he remembered we were talking about burgeoning relationships. 'Hodge has got it going on for Harriet Barth. He wants to get busy with her. That's why he takes showers now.'

Hodge punched him in the middle of his pointy chest.

'Hopefully horny Hodge can make Harriet happy?' laughed Josh, hitting his H's hard but from a safe distance.

'Fuck you,' said Hodge.

Joe rubbed his chest, but I didn't stick up for him: this was the dorm and the rules were a little different.

'Miles and Kwame are back tomorrow,' said Josh, after Hodge stopped denying he had the hots for Harriet and her roller skates. 'I bet Miles' parents won't let him climb ladders anymore.'

'They might stay and chew his food for him,' added Hodge.

'Don't be mean,' I said.

Joe put a hand on my shoulder and looked at the guitar in the corner. 'Greenie, will you play us one of your love songs?'

I was flattered. I'd wasted entire evenings making up ditties about insensate women, but I'd never realized anyone listened to them.

'Not when you should be getting ready for bed. And, Joe, don't touch me when you're half-naked. It makes me nauseous.'

'Gonzaga, Greenie, I know what it does to you.'

Josh asked for late lights. I gave him thirty minutes and I told him to turn it off himself or it was a DV. He didn't know whether to thank me or ask for more time. After he left to brush his teeth, I asked Joe if he and Josh were getting along; earlier I'd seen them doing Geometry proofs together.

'We've always been friends,' he said. 'Hey, Mr. G, play the song about Josh.'

I told him it was too late, but when Josh protested from his room down the hall, I had no choice but to grab the guitar and play my three favorite chords: G, C and F. *Hey, hey, hey. Ha, ha, ha. Josh the Hendu had a pony, fed it lots of old baloney, but it wanted macaroni, so Joshie had an unhappy pony.* The subject of my song ran in wielding a pillow, and Joe, who'd been trying to sing along, threw his arms around my neck. I was yelling for him to release me when Hodge jumped on my desk in his boxers. Someone slammed a door and Roland Meadows shot out of his apartment holing a little paintbrush and wearing red and white stripe pajamas. I peeled Joe off me as Josh hid his pillow behind his back.

'Sorry Rolly, the show's over,' I said, hopping out of my chair. Then roared, 'Gentlemen, it's time for your beauty sleep,' and ushered Hodge up the stairs.

After giving late lights to half the dorm, I returned to the out-of-dorm-dorm parent room and found Sammy the Eraser sitting on the bed. Next to him were a few delinquent papers my juniors had completed during study hall. I added them to my pile as he eyed my guitar, the dorm parent log, the peeling walls.

I asked about Mary Katherine. He said she was fine and asked if Miles would be okay. I cracked the window, yes, and Sam held his hand up to the air.

'I just can't see what good will come out of my teaching him.'

I didn't know what idea he'd come in with, but I told him to put together a second semester elective and submit it to Gunnar. I'd help him recruit some students. Sam was speechless, probably torn between the certainty that I was out to get him and the suspicion that maybe I wasn't. Feeling as if God was patting me on the head, I asked how old he was.

'Twenty-four,' he said.

'Did you ever take any time off from school?' I imagined him being hazed out of a military academy or selling encyclopedias for a year.

'Why do you ask?'

'Just curious.' I touched my temple on the same spot where he already had a little gray. 'The salt and pepper makes you look older, almost ready to be a daddy.'

'I'm old for my age because I repeated a grade. I got sick with something like arthritis for half a year when I was eight. I got chicken pox and measles, too, so it made sense to do third grade over.'

His story made me think of barefoot children and bed sheets hanging in a backyard. 'I'll tell Gunnar and Don you have my support,' I said. 'Also, and I mean this with good intentions. Trust yourself, Sam. Don't let anyone get in your head, okay?' He flashed an uneasy smile and looked at my broken hand, which was healing quite nicely.

'Hey, I was wondering. Did you say anything to Don about me tripping that kid? I mean, I wouldn't be mad if you did but...'

'I told him I reacted without thinking. That was it.'

'Thanks,' he said, stretching his back and acting as if he wasn't thinking a mile a minute. 'Okay, I'm off to work. I owe you one.'

Not really, I thought, and I discovered Joe standing in the doorway with his hand on his crotch. He couldn't sleep because someone was fixing a car under his bed.

'Why now?' I asked, as Sam made his escape. 'The radiators clang every night.'

'I don't know,' said Joe, trying to put an arm around me. 'Everything's just so crazy this time of the year. Calabria's acting weird. Day doesn't talk to me. I miss soccer.' Soccer doesn't miss you, I thought, recalling the hours I'd spent reattaching the rubber nosepiece on his sports goggles. 'I suck at Geometry. Henderson teaches me everything. And the Shaker pegs! I count the ones in Wickersham, but every day another's broken. Sometimes they get fixed at Hands-To-Work, but they're not the same. The old ones screwed in. The new ones are longer but they break easier.'

'I can't do anything about the pegs, Joe,' I said.

'What about the radiators? They drive me nuts everywhere, even in class. I mean, this place is nothin' but Shaker pegs and radiators.'

I knew what he meant. Before the end of the year, homework was going to wear him out and loneliness was going to bury him. I put a hand on his shoulder for a change and suggested he sleep with music on. He said he'd lent his headphones to Hodge, who'd broken his with his ass. I pointed out that Hodge wasn't a real friend and he shouldn't lend him anything.

'How do you know?' asked Joe.

I saw a chance to be good. 'Let's play our game,' I said, crossing my arms and narrowing my eyes. 'You're my best friend.'

'You didn't mean that.'

'Here's another.' I flashed my teeth and said I was going to kick his ass.

'In your dreams, monkey face.'

I lowered my voice and clamped my hand into fists. 'Don't talk to me now.'

'Sorry, I'll find you later.'

'Good.' I asked what Hodge was like when he talked to Joe.

'He promises to hang with me, but maybe he doesn't mean it. I also know the headphones he sat on didn't belong to him either. He's a piker.'

'Where did you learn that word?' I asked.

Joe fidgeted. 'I dunno.'

'Okay, I'll tell you what, if you can get to sleep, I'll buy you a two liter bottle of soda tomorrow. If you can't, you have my permission to turn your light on in fifteen minutes, no sooner, and read as long as you want.'

Joe blurted 'Gonzaga,' hugged me and went back to his room.

Fourteen

Roger Day was staring into his mailbox. Inside, dressed up with a pretty red bow and a card that read From Santa, was a blue cardigan. It looked expensive, scholarly and wildly un-Rog. He picked up the sweater as if it were a bag of dog shit. But when it unfolded and one of the sleeves grazed the floor, he jerked it into the air and jammed it under his arm. Twenty minutes later he was modeling it at morning meeting and graciously accepting compliments.

At lunch Kara chewed with pleasure on a coffee stirrer, oblivious to the fact that she was entertaining a table of teenage boys. That afternoon she became the owner of a pair of fuzzy slippers and a box of Belgian chocolates.

'What the hell are these?' she fumed, using a slipper as a hand puppet. 'Hi, my name is Buffy and the thing I most like to put behind my ears is my ankles.' There was a small crowd in the Teachers' Room, including Sam who couldn't hide his smile. 'Tell that bastard this hasn't even begun.'

Rolly walked in, saw the slippers and forgot what he was looking for. By the end of classes there were a half dozen pairs of women's undies—a queen-sized rainbow of colors—lounging in Rog's box. Myriad styles and infinite smiles! exclaimed the card. Because Santa knows how you like to pull the curtains and prance. A pair of shiny handcuffs, with a key, sat proudly atop the underpants. At dinner we were too smug to sit with, so like Wednesday mornings Rog—who'd actually been working nights to make Kara a real present—sat by himself.

'His face,' laughed Goldie Remlap, sitting three seats away next to Art as innocent as can be. 'I bet that jackass had no clue what 'myriad' meant.'

It means too many to count, I thought, like Goldie Remlap has myriad schemes to make herself queen of the universe.

Goldie stuck her spoon in her mouth and licked it clean. 'If he screws this up...'

'Do you think they were Pete's handcuffs?' asked Candy.

Then Goldie whispered something across the table that I know was a lie.

'All I know is she had the hots for handsome Roger from the second she laid eyes on him. She'd cut off her left arm to do him, but don't tell anyone. That's supposed to be...you know.'

I was lingering after dinner, staring at the glowing drink dispensers and student self-portraits, when Cass plopped down beside me. She was wearing a loose shirt and her hair was pushed behind her ears, clipped in place with two red barrettes.

'You got a haircut while you were avoiding me,' she said, scanning the back of my head and possibly wondering at the red creeping up my neck.

'I needed one.'

She shot me a sly look. 'My parents are still buggin' out. They still don't believe I'm doing well.'

I asked what she was talking about.

Cass had returned from Thanksgiving break in a Toyota with the Virgin Mary on the dashboard and two little sisters riding shotgun. It was a fine day, but then her stepfather—a thin man with a mustache and a tattoo of the cross on his arm—saw the condoms in her dresser. The door closed and Cass got angry. No one had the right to criticize her about sex, especially when her mother had gotten married in high school and her real father had disappeared two stepfathers ago.

'My stepfather thinks I ought to be celibate,' she complained. 'I don't get that guy. He gives my mom money, but he doesn't own me. My mom and him are upset for other reasons, too. They still think I'm with my old boyfriend. You know, she used to like him, but since my dad got mad at her for letting Jesus visit, she thinks like him now.'

I traced the scratches in the table with my finger, and asked how she'd ended things with her folks. She said, get this, that she didn't want to talk about it. Then why'd she bring it up?

'Okay fine, she didn't say anything, but he said they'd make me finish school down there if I was messing around.'

'Maybe you should listen to him,' I said.

'Or not get caught,' she replied, pushing back from the table and squeaking her chair on the linoleum. 'So, Mr. Green, you gonna be here next year?'

Her question caught me off guard. But I wiped the surprise of my face and told her I wasn't going anywhere. If I did, I might give a few lectures at Harvard or MIT. Cass said she was thinking about becoming the Queen of Hispaniola. Then she turned her face to the light. The cafeteria was empty except for us. A radio was playing in the kitchen.

'Let me ask you something. What made you get back into shape?'

'I was looking old,' I said, trying not to sound old.

It was her turn to be smug. 'You know, we thought you were seeing Calabria for a while. Me, I don't know what she sees in Mr. Day. He's attractive and all, but he makes my dad look liberal. I hear she's gonna buy him jeans for Secret Santa, not tight ones like he wears to Hands-To-Work, but ones that fit. Then he's buying her perfume?'

'Mrs. Remlap tell you guys this?' I asked, as Per poked his head into the cafeteria.

'We got fifteen minutes,' he said. I noticed his scowl was gone. Even if he'd gotten restriction for it, slipping into a girl's window had given him bounce.

'My word,' said Cass, who grinned with pleasure when I laughed, and once again our conversation ended by going off for a smoke

Three days later I received a note via the U.S. mail. Written in purple pen and smelling faintly of a perfume I knew by the name of

Cassandra Diaz, it praised me for being easy to talk to and ended with a flourish, *I am she who walks with the tender and growing night. It took me an hour to find the reference. I am he, the stanza began, I call to the earth and the sea half-held by the night./ Press close bare-bosom'd night—press close magnetic nourishing night!/ Still nodding night—mad naked summer night.* And far down at the bottom of the page, after Cass had resurrected a lost summer in New Hampshire, I saw Walt Whitman's proclamation, *Smile, for your lover comes.*

I fondled the note, inhaled its ink and tasted its letters. Then, full of shame, I placed it in the kitchen trash under a burrito wrapper and backed away slowly. Meanwhile, a door closed in another part of the building. I crept into the unused part of the dorm—six rooms on two levels—and down the back stairs. More doors closed, shades were pulled. Sam uttered the word 'disgusting' and left.

He was disgusted again later that week when I took the basketball team to Albany and he had the sophomores alone. He didn't want to be there without me, but getting someone else to babysit his own class would've been embarrassing. So he marched in and...well, let me relate the tale as I came from the reliable mouth of Josh Henderson.

Sam wasn't hungover. He wasn't angry at Josh's smartass comments or annoyed with Joe's non-stop hip-hop lyrics. The kids just assumed he was. They were reading Catcher in the Rye but too apathetic and disillusioned to like it. I'd waved my arms and yelled like a madman that they were missing out on a great piece of American literature because they had no appreciation of rebellion or true profanity, and they simply agreed. Yawn. Fuck yeah. Anyway, I'd asked Sam to go over the last twenty pages of the book and give out review questions. The kids would work in groups and create study sheets for an exam. In case there was confusion, I also gave Elizabeth Perkins an overview of the lesson and the instructions that everyone was supposed to behave for Mr. Iafrati.

'Okay, I've pulled some quotations from the novel,' said Sam, excited because he'd put together a promising lesson. 'Working alone at first, I want you to figure out who said them and why they're important. Then we'll set up a study guide.'

Joe stared at the fluffy yellow cat outside the window. Josh pulled his hat down over his eyes. Miles, who'd found a nice deep rut, was too depressed to work. Sam started passing out the sheet he'd worked two hours on, and Josh held his at arm's length like a fish.

'Where are Greenie's review questions?' asked Elizabeth.

'Don't you have the questions?' asked Josh.

'If you have questions, why do you want us to find quotes?' asked another kid. 'Isn't that just busy work?'

'It's quotations,' replied Sam, 'quotes is...

'...it's a verb, we know,' interrupted Elizabeth. 'God, adults are so...'

'...phony,' said Josh.

Recognizing Holden Caulfield's catchphrase and the start of another shadow lesson, the kids grinned at each other. As they waited for Josh to tell them how he was twice as sensitive as a toilet seat, the cat pawed silently at the window. Miles put his head down. One of Sam's sheets, along with his spirits, drifted to the floor.

'Why are you even here?' exclaimed someone—Josh wouldn't tell me who said it—and Sam turned red. Before he lost it though, he excused himself and stepped out of the room. Unfortunately, he literally stepped onto Don DeWillum's foot.

'Is everything okay?' he asked.

Sam spun around as if to go back into the class but then looked his boss in the eye. 'I'm getting some water, seeing if they can work independently.'

Don poked his head into the room and found the kids making airplanes out of Sam's worksheet while they were, in fact, engaged in a lively debate about the book.

That same week Ichabob took a professional day to learn about drug enforcement programs in private schools and asked me to cover his Honors English class. They were reading The Lover by Marguerite Duras, a novella I liked but never brought to the classroom because it was too racy for most of the idiots I taught. Anyway, Bob left me with the skimpiest of lesson plans, including the option of doing whatever I wanted, so I asked everyone to take out piece of paper and draw a picture of his or her life: families, major events, favorite toys, triumphs, and defeats. Soon, we were lost in our drawings, and the clock spinning.

I drew a picture that showed me in tennis shorts. In one hand I held my racket, in the other a book. Around me were my laptop, my mother, my two fat fathers, and the house I grew up in. Above me the sun. To my left a few women wearing puzzled expressions with their hands on their hips. One was separate from the rest. And finally, mountains, a Shaker Peg, a skyscraper, a child, a key and a road to the horizon.

'Tell me about yours, Per,' I said, folding mine into quarters.

'It's a window,' he began. 'See the frame? There's some books, so I guess it's a college room, but I also see my bear, so it's my room at home, too.'

'You have a teddy?' teased Cassandra.

'Is that a corpse in the bed?' asked one of the boys.

'It's not made. Except for when I'm here, I never make it.'

To me it seemed that there was a girl under the sheets, warm and cozy. Perhaps Per, like us, was also looking in the window. Was he going to climb in? Slip in beside her? Or just watch her sleep?

'You've avoided chronology, or rather, you've blurred it,' I said.

'It's the way I think,' he replied. 'It's like the book's set up.'

I nodded approval, and Cassandra held up her picture. She'd drawn a girl in flowered dress with smallish breasts, full lips, hair pulled back into a bun. In her hand was a telephone. By her side was a car full of family, driving past a river, a city and a cross. Floating above her where the sun might have been was a man with strong arms, a lattice of stomach muscles and flames for hair. The class was smiling.

'Where's the bed?' asked one of the girls.

'And the video camera?' smirked Hodge.

'Jerks,' replied Cass.

'See me after class, Hodge,' I said, noticing that she'd drawn buttonholes on the man's open shirt, hair on his chest, the creases in his pants. Her family, like the family of any girl dying to break free, was secure in that car and moving in the opposite direction.

'Okay, our lives usually seem to unfold in time, but when you look at these pictures, what do you think?'

'The memories aren't linear,' Per offered.

'Exactly, now what was the central image in the novel?'

'The girl taking the boat across the river to get it on with her lover,' said Cass.

Just because the words had come from her mouth, the class teased her again. But then because I'm good at my job, they got serious and we had a great discussion.

Fifteen

I pointed out that the class would be small and Sam was desperate to put some meat into his resume. Don said he'd think about it and told me he'd been impressed by the drawings the kids had done while I was covering for Ichabob. Then he leaned back in his chair and gave me one of his scary big grins.

'Oscar informed me that he's contemplating not coming back. Either way I think it'll be good for your department to have a permanent chair in January.'

'Doesn't June seem like a more natural time to change heads?'

'I'm not inclined to leave such an important position vacant for that long,' he said.

I waited until he was embarrassed by the silence; then I put our plan into action. Gunnar and Candy called it The Cipher Deep Six—I referred to it as the Anna Karenina Option—and we all agreed that it was the best way to deal with a man terrified of his own large shadow and obsessed with picking up garbage.

'I don't mean to sound rude,' I said calmly, 'but the position isn't vacant right now. And I'm doing a lot more than just holding down the fort.'

Don looked for a little confidence in his desk drawer.

'That's true,' he said, finding his favorite pen, 'but I'm not fully convinced anyone's as totally committed when the job's not permanent.' Our man in full tapped his pen. 'It just sort of feels like we need more stability down in your neck of the woods.'

He sounded like Goldie, but because he was the one person I didn't mind lying to, I held my tongue.

'I appreciate your candor,' I said. 'And I invite you sit in on some of our department meetings so you'd get a little more insight into our unique dynamic.'

Don tapped his pen two more times, and for an instant he was blurry, edges shimmering, features melting. But he became solid again and stepped into the trap.

'You're alluding to Goldie? I know she has a strong personality.'

'She's definitely hard to supervise.' Don stopped tapping and started playing with his tie. 'I hate saying anything negative about a colleague, but to put it bluntly, she's not just frustrating, she's divisive.' For a full five seconds Don was transparent. But he failed to make himself disappear and had no choice but to listen. 'She often acts as if she's a department of one, and I've addressed this tendency in a very professional manner and she's been unresponsive.'

'What do you want me to do?' he asked.

A week earlier, I wouldn't have say it, but now I was playing with house money. Prior to my sit down with Don, Gunnar had blamed Goldie for Oscar's taking a sabbatical. The man should've been enjoying his last year on The Mount, for God's sake, not costing us money. My friend had also protested that the pittance the Hodge's donated to the secret writing lab exonerated the family far too easily for the sins of the child. More money down the drain. He'd added that Goldie was the most brazen drunk he knew and he wouldn't let her within a mile of a randy trustee. In short, she was another costly embarrassment just waiting to happen.

'I'm torn,' I said, in the most sincere, collegial manner possible. 'I adore Art, but there have been a few student complaints.'

'I thought she was popular?'

'The kids say she's condescending and plays favorites. But they're just kids and you have to take what they say with a grain of salt. I doubt they've hired any lawyers.'

It was Gunnar's idea to mention lawyers. He also told me to look in Don's eyes when I said the word, then I'd really see the fear.

'I'm also concerned with her treatment of younger faculty. Goldie might think her teasing and her suggestive comments are playful, but it's uninvited bordering on unprofessional. Kara's described her as intrusive and shared the opinion that Goldie's done a number of Sam's confidence.'

Securely wedged between my assertion that Goldie was a castrating narcissist and his tangible fear of her indignation, Don's face took on a purplish hue.

'What do you want me to do?' he asked again.

'I honestly don't know,' I said. 'I just wanted to give you a heads up, and give you some context in case somebody comes to you with a complaint.'

He thanked me. I thanked him. He didn't know what else to say. Gunnar and Candy were going to be thrilled. Don tried one last time to disappear. No luck. I played my last card.

'But I agree with you, let's throw open the competition for department head and see what happens. If we believe in the democratic process, then a vote of the permanent faculty is the best way to show it.'

'That's great,' said Don, putting on the same awkward grin he'd started with and sticking out his hand. As I shook Don's hand, I took a hard look at him. There's a way you regard a person when his actions fill you with utter contempt. I'd never been so close to that look before, not even with Goldie. Yet somehow I left Don's office feeling both dirty and elated. I felt even more dirty and elated when I looked in mailbox and found a postcard from Graceland addressed to Jeff Gray.

Dear Jeff,

I doubt you think of me often — if at all — even though we shared a glorious evening together last July. I'm sure you weren't expecting to hear from me again, but you did tell me where you worked, and even though I think you're perfectly capable of taking care of yourself, I still wanted to check on you. Doing better, I hope. Oh well, I don't expect to be friends or anything, but please reply so I know you got this musing.

Yours, Willow.

Wrong color, but obviously for me. She worked for the Registry of Motor Vehicles in Watertown, Massachusetts, a pint-sized redhead with a potty mouth. We'd talked on the deck of the tennis center and then we met up for drinks at the Flying Squirrel Inn. I wasn't planning on sleeping with her — I was just tired of watching television by myself. She was the one who dropped the words 'consenting' and 'adult' into the same sentence.

Stuffing the postcard into my pocket, I stepped outside and discovered white stuff in the air for real this time. The campus was buzzing; brown-gray autumn was officially over. The first snowball flew. By sports time the nurse had treated two bloody noses and a jammed wrist. A snowman with a large carrot in the middle of his face was built in front of Wickersham. By dinnertime the carrot had been moved to just below his waist.

And magically, just as the snow began painting The Mount a million shades of white, the photographer for our viewbook arrived on campus. In minutes releases were being tossed around and our kids were being turning into models. As expected, the camera avoided unsightly grime, body piercing, tattoos and boys, like me, with earrings. Lana Wilson-Wade, bald, black and out of the closet, was not photographed. Hodge, who lived in a down jacket and plaid scarf, was. Harriet Barth, who'd been cultivating the disheveled look since she was nine, was asked to step out of frame. Meanwhile, Per's pretty new girlfriend, Debbie Tremont, was told to stand straighter and show just a little bit less of her teeth.

At dinner Ichabob handed out a few restriction letters in the cafeteria.

'In all my years,' he said for the millionth time, 'I've never put anyone on restriction.' He was right, kids put themselves on restriction, but the end of any semester was still the cruelest, most absurd time of the year. Speaking of absurd, I was eating dessert when Josh waltzed into the cafeteria with strawberry-colored hair. Within seconds Goldie reminded Don we had a rule that no one was allowed to have an unnatural hair color. You could be a bleached blond, a raven-haired vampire, or even dabble in the oranges, but red, even Josh's yummy berry hue, was a no-no. Don, however, had a unique way of explaining rules.

'Some of the trustees are coming this week,' he said, leaning over the boy's shoulder. Trustees? Hair color? Josh pulled a rolled up student handbook out of his back pocket and argued that strawberry was a natural color. 'A natural color for hair,' explained Don, 'and even if we had no rule, it would still be inappropriate for you to parade around with a head like that.'

The handbook fluttered through the air and landed in the middle of the cafeteria. And in the blink of an eye we were having an all school assembly to discuss hair color and the suspension Josh would get if he refused to change it. In the Winter Meeting Room we pushed the chairs and tables to the walls and sprawled on the floor. Per displayed a petition started by Harriet, and the kids talked about rules, individuality, hair color and the school's new golden calf, the viewbook.

'His hair makes us unique, we should celebrate it,' exclaimed Lana, who had a big pacifier around her neck and pierced eyebrow. The kids clapped.

'It doesn't bother me,' added Hodge, happily holding Harriet's hand.

'My parents wouldn't mind,' said another, and Don was forced to talk about the tender relationship between image—looking attractive to outsiders—and the school's survival. But with every word he uttered the kids smoldered. He looked around for help, but even if they understood the power of a tuition check, the students would never side with a man who could speak of order and unity with such a crooked face.

Later as we ate Pop Tarts in the dorm, I'd told Josh his new coiffure was a sign of laziness. I explained how getting work done and following rules was like a punishment from the gods. Being good was like pushing a rock up a steep hill. Every day he had to do the 'right' thing and push that rock, even though it was going to roll back down every night and force him to start over.

'Man, you're worse than my mom. Look, I've been a good bee up to now.'

'It's not enough to be good for a few days or a couple of weeks,' I said. 'You got to do it every day for life, and you don't get any sympathy if you take a vacation. But why do you hate your mom so much?'

Josh threw his pillow at me and quoted Salinger. 'Because all mothers are insane? Besides, she's always right and I can't win a fight with her. Do you know how annoying that is? C'mon, Greenie, why can't you just think of my hair as a personal statement?'

'It doesn't work that way,' I said, thinking Josh trusted me a little too much, and in the end I had no choice but to yank the pillow from his hands and whack him with it. That night he washed his hair seventeen times. The resulting hue was a dusty rose, twice as hideous as the strawberry, but because he'd made an effort, Don put his inane objections aside and Josh's fame, like that evening's study hall, evaporated. And I—because I was a fool and I liked the kid—agreed to take him and a bunch of his misfit friends to a concert on a school night.

Cass walked into the Winter Meeting Room five minutes late and smelling of cigarettes. Feeling like a big, powerful dog, I was amused by the idea that she might sit near me. But the girl was determined to ace her exams, so she picked up her test and went to a seat at the far end of the room.

That afternoon, however, I was making a grilled cheese sandwich and wondering how to make Goldie Remlap miserable when there was a knock. Next thing I knew Cass was in my kitchen handing me a box wrapped with Christmas paper.

'It's paisley 'cause I know you like that style, and it'll go with your blue shirt. And you have to take it. You gave me a book; it's only fair.'

'You shouldn't be here,' I said. The tie was crimson, brown and dark green.

'Calabria lets me visit her at home,' she replied, poking through a stash of Time Magazines on the table. 'Are you busy?'

I turned off the gas and sucked on my fingers. 'It's not the same and always.'

'Did you get my note?' she asked. 'I've been afraid to ask.'

'I did,' I said, checking to see how much time I had before basketball practice.

Cass sat in a Shaker chair I'd built from a kit. 'Man, these things are so uncomfortable. What were the Shakers thinking?'

The peculiar grace of a Shaker chair is due to the fact that it was made by someone capable of believing that an angel might come and sit on it. The quotation and an image of its author, Thomas Merton, hung near the entrance to our library. The words had inspired me to make my chair, to sand for three hours, to weave the seat as if it were the last thing I'd ever do, to look for tired angels just in case they needed a place to sit.

'The Shakers thought an angel might sit on one of these things,' I said. 'That's why they put so much love into making them.'

'So it isn't made for people? That explains a lot,' said Cass, putting down the magazine. 'My mom wants me to read even more.'

'Nothing wrong with that.' I put my sandwich on a plate and moved the skillet to the sink. While my back was turned, she took a bite of my lunch. I noticed—just as the phone rang—that she'd unzipped her fleece and was wearing a low-cut shirt underneath.

'Don gave me Sam's proposal for The Literature of War,' said Gunnar. 'He's giving him the course, dog, but it's totally over the top.' The elective had too much reading and a ten-page research paper. Sam also intended to show movies during the kids' free time. I suggested tossing half the readings and having them write shorter papers. The movies should be optional as well. As I talked, I tried to shoo Cass, but she started wandering around until she found a list of the schools I wanted to send my resume to that I'd left out.

'Tell Don he'll be fine.' Cass pretended to pinch me and I pointed at the door. 'And, let Sam know we're doing him a huge favor. Right now he's stuck in the spider wed, but if we take a broom to it, maybe he'll come around to our side.'

'You free in about fifteen minutes?' asked Gunnar. 'I've got a million things to do and I need to talk with you and Candy. You know, about Plan B.'

'Fifteen? Yeah, I'll be there,' I said, and I hung up.

'Mr. Green, you lied to me,' said Cass. She was holding up my list as if she'd found stolen jewels. 'You're looking for another job *and* giving Mr. Iafrati a class?'

'I don't know what I'm doing next year, but you have to do me a favor and keep it a secret. There is not a single person at this school I want knowing this.'

'Why?'

'Because Mr. Lazarus is about to retire and I want to hold on to his chair.'

'Why would you lose it in the middle of the year?'

'Don't ask, just promise.'

Cass walked across my living room, glanced into the wood box behind the stove and got an idea. 'But why does Mr. Lazarus have to retire? You know, I got this cousin who was about to get laid off, but between taking every sick day in the book and filing for workman's compensation, he got paid for like six more months. Can't Mr. Lazarus do something like that?'

'Wow, you're the sneaky one,' I said.

'My family's got a gene for it,' she said, leaning against the bookcase, too. 'So how are you going to thank me?'

Shortly after college I got a lap dance at a bachelor party from a woman wearing work boots and a tool belt. She also had a website, an armed escort and a talent for separating boys from their money. Straddling me, she called me 'Sweetie' and I started dreaming about saving her from a world that was so wiling to exploit her. After I'd deposited a few dozen bills into her panties, she nodded to her bodyguard and said I could touch her breasts. When she whispered, 'Honey, I can feel you,' I almost came in my pants.

In that same voice Cass said she knew exactly what she wanted: me to wear my new tie to the holiday program. Then we did one of the most terrifying things I'd ever done. We walked out the front door together.

Sixteen

I slid down to the apple orchard from my house. Cass circled through the woods behind the Assistant Headmaster's house with an unlit cigarette in her hand. If someone came upon us, I'd give her a fake smoking point.

'You know,' she said, 'I don't really trust people. It's probably 'cause I crept on most of my boyfriends.'

'You cheated on them?'

'Jefferson, rules are made to be broken' she said. There was a small metal shed in the back of the orchard. The sun was reflecting off its roof; the grass had been trampled flat by the door. 'So how do you feel about me?'

'You're bright and pretty.'

'And eighteen,' she said, playfully touching my ear. That summer she'd told a friend that an older man could keep her sane. Boys had acne on their backs, talked with their mouths full and laughed at farts. Men gave real back rubs and had cleaner sheets.

'Hey, I gotta be straight with you,' she said. 'My guy, the one you've seen before, he doesn't quite understand we're over, so I'm gonna have to talk to him over break.'

'Fine, but if you really want him gone, you should be clear.'

'Clear like you,' she said, nudging me, letting her hand linger on my arm.

I glanced at the shed and raised an eyebrow. Without a word, she led the way, lifting the edge of the metal door so it wouldn't stick and telling me to watch out for the rusty rake inside. As I pulled the door shut, slats of light cut across our bodies.

'Don't you dare bite me,' I said. 'At least not anywhere that shows.'

She went after my belt and I knew I was a bad man. But not a monster, not a guy who craved nymphets, searched them on the Internet and cruised the Greasy-Mart where they ate slushies and smuggled raisins under their tank tops. My eyes adjusted and I saw cigarette butts, an empty bottle of juice and the corpse of a lighter.

'Are you going to let me complete it for you?' she asked, but before the sentence was even out of her mouth, I hushed her. Cass got to her feet and looked through the chinks in the door. I jumped to the back of the shed and kicked the juice bottle against the wall.

'It's Hodge,' she whispered. 'He wants to smoke.'

Her fingers closed around the door handle. I could hear his footsteps. My pants were around my ankles and the temperature was near freezing. Beads of sweat ran down my face and hit the dirt floor. Hodge paused. Something held him back.

'What are you doing?' someone said loudly. The voice wasn't Hodge's. It was adult, serious, annoyed. It was Sam, prowling around, trying to bust kids.

Cassandra gasped and I yanked up my pants.

'Stay against the wall and don't make a sound.' I took a deep breath and flung open the door. 'Damn you, I had him so busted.'

In my hand were some butts I'd picked up off the ground.

'I thought something fishy was going on,' said Sam, blinking and looking at the shed. He took a step toward me and put his hands in his pockets.

'I've been trying to catch him all semester,' I replied. Sam eyed the butts in my hand. I wiped my sleeve across my face again, told Hodge to go away and started back to my apartment. Nodding, Sam headed in the opposite direction, and I counted my blessings. Inside the shed…

Well, there was no inside the shed. I was at morning meeting, slouching in a Windsor chair, oblivious everything until just as we were excused, Harriet Barth jumped up and shrieked, 'Stop staring at me.'

Joe was picking his nose about four feet away from her. 'I'm not talking to you, Hairy Beast.'

'Do you even know what personal space is?' she yelled.

'How can I answer without looking?' He tried to touch her arm.

Harriet shrieked again and looked to Roger Day for help. 'Every time I look he's staring at me. Make him go away, Mr. Day.'

By now it was impossible for Joe not to stare. 'I look maybe once every few minutes,' he said. 'She's looking at me every ten seconds to see if I'm looking at her. Maybe you should make Harriet—I mean, Mrs. Hodge—go away. Gonzaga. I think she kisses him in her roller skates.'

'You're both freaks as far as I'm concerned,' said Rog. 'Why don't you both act a little more normal? And Joe, get a box of Kleenex. Someone might actually want to talk to you if they weren't worried about being smeared with mucus.'

Kara angrily pushed in her chair. 'If he says one more obnoxious thing.'

Of course, Rog chimed, 'Godzilla, Joe. Go stick a handkerchief in your brown booty huggers?'

Kara walked over to Rog and pulled a little Shaker chair from her jacket pocket. It was a replica of a ladder back chair, a miniature version of the kind once made on The Mount, and he'd taken great care to stain its wood evenly and weave its tiny seat. Well, Kara placed that little chair on the floor, raised her foot and turned her Secret Santa present into matchsticks.

The sight of one teacher screaming at another usually has students wide eyed, cringing and inching toward the exits. But our kids, hoping public scorn would soon transform into public love, moved to the edge of their seats and imagined Rog and Kara floating above the tables in a featherbed of erotic apologies.

'Are you done?' he asked, when she finally took a breath.

She told him to shove a rake up his ass and someone in the back of the room whistled.

Before the kids took off, we celebrated in the Tannery with our Festival of Lights. The program began with the faculty children marching into the building in white gowns with candles in their hands and illuminated wreaths on their heads. After the little ones placed their tapers into a candelabra on stage, our lay preacher Roland Meadows ascended to the podium and invoked Jesus, Gandhi, Moses, Mohammed, Chief Seattle and a slew of other prophets. The choir sang songs in English and Spanish, and Candy's History class presented a mock debate on the meaning of Christmas.

Cass had scored the seat directly across the aisle. She looked cute in a satiny red dress with thin straps under a jean jacket. She had on makeup and she'd done her nails. For a fleeting second she caught my eye—I couldn't quite figure out the semaphore of her blinks—before she turned toward the stage, which was set up for the singing part of the pageant.

Candy slipped up behind me.

'You, my little genius, owe Oscar a box of cigars. I turned into her enormous grin and she told me Oscar was grandfathered. Unless he had children we didn't know about, she was talking about his contract. In this case, he discovered that, unlike everyone else on staff, he'd been rolling over sick days for close to fifteen years.

'What does it mean?' I asked.

She moved to my side and blocked y view of Cass. 'It's top secret, but Gunnar suggested that instead of retiring, Oscar take a medical leave to help his because the old lumbago's acting up. Well, Oscar liked the idea so much he called Don and told him he'd decided to come back, but first he was going to use about sixteen weeks of sick days and get paid his full salary.'

I felt wicked, like dancing, like telling Cass.

'Don probably won't poop for a month,' I said. 'How's he take it?'

'Oscar didn't say. He just called me Rocky and said he was negotiating a buyout for the rest of his sick days, says could be on the dole for two years if he felt like it.' Goldie, her face glowing in candlelight, was at the front of the room helping a singer with her costume. Art was sitting near her in his Christmas sweater. 'Don will probably be out, what, at least thirty grand? Can we blame Goldie for that, too?'

'No, but it's still poetic,' I said, feeling like a king, and Candy moved out of the aisle so Roger Day, dressed as a cowboy Santa, could jangle by with some goodies.

'Santa's got a little Reindeer jerky and some homemade fudge for y'all,' he chortled from under a ten-gallon hat.

The kids clamored for smoked turkey and grainy fudge. Then they found their seats and the last part of the program began. After a half hour of singing, we ended the evening with the song Simple Gifts and dispersed into the night with candles. As always I was surprised to see how manners and nice clothes transformed our kids. Cass, of course, looked old enough to date. Freshman Debbie in her mom's silk blouse and slacks could've been hosting a cocktail party. Per, decked out in a school blazer (not ours; we didn't have one), still looked like a high school student, but he was a civilized one for a change. Even Josh was wearing a tie. But then I scanned the crowd for Kwame. My fashion plate of an advisee should have been sitting near me or at least have checked in, but alas he was nowhere to be seen. At the door I informed Ichabob, who said Kwame was sick and had actually gone to the trouble of telling him. Happy again, I strolled past the pond, looked back at the Tannery and noticed a pleasant murmur of voices. The Mount could be so fickle, so dysfunctional, and so petty. But during Molier plays and concerts, on Wednesday mornings when we gathered for Hands-To-Work, and especially when we'd finished exams and were singing in the Tannery, it was no less than sublime.

'Happy Holidays,' said Cass, blowing out her candle. 'Nice tie.'

'Thank you,' I said. 'I like it.'

'So...you guys going to start your celebration tonight?'

'I'm going to save myself for the faculty party tomorrow.'

'We'll be in the dorm, fighting over the vacuum cleaner and making popcorn.'

'Sounds like fun.'

'There are a lot of other things I'd rather do,' she said, as we passed from the light of the Tannery onto the shadowy path leading to Wickersham. 'You going to be alone?'

'Looks that way,' I said.

'Dorm parents usually go away around eleven fifteen. Could I bring anything?'

'Nope,' I said.

'Just me?' she replied, making sure.

'Just you,' I said, a split second before Goldie bounded over from out of nowhere and pinched the girl.

'Yo, frisky woman,' said Cass.

'First and middle name,' replied Goldie, not looking at me. I wondered how long she'd been behind us. 'So how's my favorite student? Are the boys being nice to you?'

'Why you always asking about my love life?' asked Cass.

'Because you're a catch and I'm the insatiable Miss Want-to-Know.'

'My word,' said Cass.

'Too cute,' laughed Goldie, hugging the girl, and after walking a few yards, she asked if she'd like the pageant costumes she'd made for the children.

'They were beautiful,' said Cass. 'Did you make Mr. Day's outfit, too?'

Goldie noticed me smiling and got this little whirlpool of disdain between her eyes. 'That getup was his own creation. So when do you think he and Calabria are gonna get their blood test?'

'I don't know,' said Cass. 'Maybe Mr. Green does.'

Even if it was just a dig, I was happy Cass made her acknowledge me.

'On no, faculty romances are Ms. Remlap's specialty,' I said.

'That's right, Mr. Green doesn't know anything about romance,' replied Goldie.

'I'm just a sad old bachelor,' I said.

Goldie smacked her lips. 'And enjoying every minute of it I'd say.'

'You make him sound like Mr. Lazarus,' said Cass.

Goldie winked at the girls. Okay, she didn't really wink. And she's not really a cartoon character who rubs her hands together when she's about to perpetrate evil. But she still gave Cass a mischievous look, the girl blushed—even in the low light I could see that much—and I knew at least one of my secret had been given away.

More annoyed than worried, I said goodnight and started walking ahead toward my apartment. But when I heard Cass tell Goldie that she'd changed her mind about getting hot chocolate in the Student Center, I ducked into the main building and doubled back past the still-glowing Tannery and the old metal shop.

There, beyond Cass's dorm, welcoming visitors at the foot of the campus was the dark shell of an old stone barn. It had once been the largest stone barn in America, but twenty-five years earlier a disgruntled student had destroyed it with a single match. When it burned, the heat was so intense it was felt a half-mile away. The solid oak beams and wood stables abutting the structure were all gone. The forty-foot walls, now black, were left for the tourists and half-wild cats.

Eight years later a former teacher overheard the arsonist bragging in a Florida bar. Phone calls were made, a police report was faxed and big mouth got arrested. There was a lesson there about staying ahead of your fuck ups and keeping your mouth shut, about the dangers of curses, dark stares and piles of rocks.

Darkness hid the skeleton of the barn, but I could feel it looming. The top, some forty feet above us, met the high road. The bottom had greeted the cattle. Hay was loaded up top. Animals were herded below. The building had been a magnificent example of Shaker economy, but the Shakers weren't as smart as fire.

Cass came out of the dorm without her jacket and put a cigarette between her lips.

'You know that's bad for your health.'

She jumped and I loved it. 'Shit, you scared me! How'd you know I'd be here?'

'When my crew was on trash patrol, I saw a dozen butts with lipstick on them.'

'You know my color?'

'Aren't you the only smoker in your dorm?' Her teeth started chattering because she didn't want her jacket to smell. No wonder she was always in the nurse's office.

'Hardly,' she replied. 'So why are you creeping up on me?'

I'd been so calm, but now brain was galloping. I don't know why I felt the urge, but I wanted to tell her I hated lying. I was sick of doing sit-ups and watching what I ate. Sure, I had a woodstove and a truck and a tiara of my own, but I just wanted to be with someone who didn't care about this crap then get the hell off The Mount.

'You told Remlap that I was thinking of leaving?'

'I didn't tell her I went up to your apartment. I said I overheard you whispering to Ms. Dafoe. You guys do that all the time. Are you mad at me?' Cass wrapped her arms around her sides. 'I'm sorry. I guess I wasn't thinking. If it makes you feel any better, Ms. Remlap wasn't happy or anything. At least she didn't look happy.'

'Believe me, she was happy. You tell her anything else?'

'No.' She dug her toe into the ground and her voice became tight. 'You still want company?'

I wanted to comfort her, but I didn't know what to say. I just thought of Goldie and Kara and how wonderful it felt to be stupid, and I told her I'd leave the door open.

There was knock, quiet at first but then louder. I woke confused, wondering why Cass was banging when I'd told her just to come in. I sat up just as Gunnar and Candy danced in with a bottle of tequila. They didn't seem surprised to find me napping on the sofa. They just shoved a shot glass under my nose and told me a diamond had popped out of Goldie's ass when she heard that Oscar was cashing in on his sick pay and not retiring.

Taking the glass, I looked behind them fully expecting to see Cassandra with a box of condoms. But instead of freaking out, I drank a shot, then another. Gunnar pulled out a bag of chips, turned on some music, and we celebrated the long rein of Ms. Teen Interim Department Head. Lame duck, my ass, they kept singing. Gunnar made me another tiara out of tin foil and Candy drank us both under the table.

Seventeen

In our first hours of freedom all we wanted to do was act like imbeciles. And once we got a little momentum, watch out. I'd seen Gunnar dive off the science building into a snow bank. I'd seen Rolly eat a live bee. I'd seen Rog and Candy wrestle in long underwear. Aware of our dark potential, Don sent his wife and children away. Then, so we'd be less likely to hurt ourselves, he opened his doors and hosted our holiday party.

Walking into Don's house, I felt like the Jew sneaking into Santa's Kingdom. There were little reindeer hanging from the ceiling. The Christmas tree was overloaded with ornaments, tinsel, candy canes and flickering lights. Presents wrapped in green or red, but never both, were piled beneath. On the mantle above the stockings was a Bible, as if someone had put it there for a moment and gotten distracted.

This year's party promised to be especially jovial. Candy was bringing her new girlfriend Lauralee, who'd she met in Northampton and who taught film at SUNY Albany. Gunnar was flying off to Hawaii in the morning to eat poi with college buddies. Goldie, who was taking her disappointment gracefully, looked cute in a Santa hat. Kara was decked out in a tarty black dress. And Sam would soon be shitfaced and sporting a welt the size of Texas on his head.

At first things the administrative staff and their spouses politely nibbled on appetizers and the housekeeping staff and maintenance guys migrated to a far corner of Don's living room, but after a few trips to the keg, the old-timers got loud and told us anything we wanted to know about anyone who'd ever worked on The Mount. Say a name, like Chester Reinheimer, History teacher 1996-1998, and someone would spin a tale about a hairy truck driver, a pickle jar of vodka and the school tractor. Lou Toro, Latin and Spanish 1981-1983, and someone would tell you about the summer night when Lou walked his afghan hound wearing nothing but a fishing hat. (I assumed Lou was wearing the hat, not the dog.)

I was on my third beer when Don joined Gunnar and me at the keg.

'I've got news. Oscar not coming back from Sarasota next month. He's not retiring either.'

'He's extending his sabbatical?'

'We're calling it a medical leave so he can take care of his bunions and spend time with his sick sister.'

'I think she's got a condo near the racetrack,' said Gunnar.

'That explains why he told me to bet on a gelding named Mr. Mumbles in the third.' Don turned to me. 'So it looks like we're going to keep our interim chair a while longer. I hope you don't mind.'

'I'd rather bet on Mr. Mumbles,' I said, 'but okay.'

Gunnar poked me in the ribs just as Sam and Roger waltzed through the door with red cheeks and snowflakes in their hair. Despite a vow of temperance, Sam had been doing shots of Becherovka because this was a big night for him. We'd soon learn, when we raised our glasses to a semester survived, that Mary Katherine would be joining us to start a tutoring gig. So this, we assumed, was a sort of bachelor party for Sam. How close the baby? How far off the wedding? I wondered if they'd get married over break so they could live together and remembered Sam's look of disgust as he prowled around my basement. Please no, not my house, I thought, and I chugged my beer.

After the toasts, Kara toured the room and handed out anatomically correct chocolate Santas. Giving one to Don, she asked how he liked having three floors seven bedrooms and a flagstone patio that backed onto Tanner's Pond.

'The house makes noises,' he said. 'I tell my kids that's what old houses do, but they think we have ghosts.'

'Here?' said Gunnar, looking at the beamed ceiling and the Shaker cabinets. 'I've never heard of ghosts here.' Gunnar told him about the usual spooks: Sherman in Hinckley, who liked to try on people's shoes; the woman who walked through snow on the high road but didn't leave footprints; the boy who'd been crushed by a wagon; and a journaling Shaker teacher I was also fond of, Sister Emily Danbridge. Meanwhile, Don sipped on a second adult beverage and nibbled the leg off his Santa.

Shortly after eleven, the full-time staff left. An hour later, the clouds parted on an enormous moon and we ran out into the night. Fresh snow crunched under our feet. Someone pulled a twelve-pack of Bud in cans from their car and we tromped to the softball field to make angels and write our names.

'Go out,' yelled Gunnar, holding a can of beer at his shoulder and patting it with his free hand like a football. Sam was off like a shot.

'Throw it,' he yelled when he was about ten yards away.

When Sam was about fifteen yards further, Gunnar hurled the beer high into the night. We lost sight of it but heard the thud and saw Sam fall into the snow. He howled like he was dying, but when Rog saw he was okay, just a big red mark on his forehead and a dented sputtering beer as a trophy, he popped the can and handed it to him.

'You'll be fine,' said Kara, pressing snow to his head. She was wearing boots now and a long down coat over her dress. Feeling manly, Rog dumped a load of snow on her. She called him a prick, tripped him and the rest of us whitewashed them both. And when Gunnar and Candy were satisfied that they had snow down their shirts and pants, they whitewashed me, started singing Hail to the Chief and carried me inside by the arms and legs. I ended up on Don's kitchen floor, knocking over a chair in the process. Goldie and Don didn't know whether to help me up or get out of the way. And when Candy started quacking—because I was no longer a lame duck?— Don ran upstairs for some towels. Meanwhile, Goldie found some ice for Sam, who was now straggling through the door and falling down as well.

Then we killed the keg and devoured the rest of the cake.

'Where's the big guy?' asked Candy, licking her fingers.

On cue, our headmaster popped his head into the room.

'I think I'm going to go upstairs for a minute,' he said. 'Stay as long as you like. Just don't break anything.' He stepped back and bumped into the wall. I got up in case he needed help and took his arm.

'I'm glad Oscar's being a pain,' he said. 'It makes my life easier. But I want you to know I respect your honesty, Jeff. You help everyone and you always have something nice to say about students.' He steadied himself on the banister. 'Jeff, I don't usually tell people this, but my father was a strict man who didn't always have something nice to say. He was a scold. Well, that's an understatement. One time my mother brought home some grapes from the market, dark purple grapes with drops of water clinging to them. My father though, he got it into his head that we had to save them for a guest. He was like that with thank you notes and handshakes, too. But I ate some of those grapes—heck, I ate them all—and it earned me a good trashing.'

'But do you know what I did when he sent me to my room? I was so mad I climbed out my window, went to the kitchen and made myself a sandwich. Then, I went and proudly confessed to him.' Don sat on the steps. His face was flushed. 'I'm not sure what I was trying to accomplish. But that's when he locked me in a closet for two hours.'

'My step-father tried to be a scold too,' I said.

'Now that I'm an administrator, I know I've gone over to the dark side,' said Don, 'but I know for a fact I've never been a scold.'

'You do a good job,' I said, helping my headmaster to his feet.

'Really?' he said, and he grabbed the banister, almost ripping it out of the wall. 'My wife's going to murder me if she hears about this party.'

When he disappeared upstairs, Gunnar quacked and fell out of his seat, his face bright red, tears in his eyes. Candy quacked, too and we were so inspired that we hauled the empty keg out to the Pond, where Candy and Lauralee, wearing pink corduroy pants and her beloved biker jacket, counted to three and bent their knees. The aluminum keg sailed through the air and embedded itself in the thin layer of ice.

'It's wedged in pretty good,' said Candy, tossing an arm around her honey and giving her a sloppy kiss. I put my foot on the edge of the pond. The ice broke under my weight and my foot sank into the freezing muddy water.

'O, my Oscar,' shouted Gunnar. There was a boat upside-down

next to the patio, but before I could put it to use, Gunnar got down on all fours, pressed his belly to the ground and inched out on the ice like a giant insect. 'I'll save him,' he yelled. There was more cracking and we held our breath. 'I'm coming,' he gasped, as he grabbed the keg with his superhuman fingertips and dragged it back to shore.

'And you thought you were the only one who walked on water,' said Candy, once we were back inside and Sam was passing out the last of the beer, three bottles he'd found in the fridge. Grabbing one, I snuck away to Don's living room to think about my foolishness for a few minutes, but when I got there, I found Goldie on the sofa. She was gazing into the fire with a poetry anthology open but face down in her lap.

'They're pretty drunk,' I said.

'It's okay, Greenie,' she replied. 'It's late. We're all toasted. Kara and Rog are off bumping uglies. Let them quack. It's time to confess though. You see, I heard a little rumor. Actually, I'm lying. I was sorting mail last week when I ran across a postcard to you from an amorous lady?'

'Isn't reading mail a federal crime?'

'Handcuff me now,' she chided. 'But even the way you say that, so casual I should pat you on the back, serious enough to make me think you have a conscience.'

'I'd rather have a girlfriend, but, I'm sorry, it's not going to be Miss Postcard.'

'Too bad. But you know what scares me about you? No matter how many you put back, and sometimes I count, you always look sober.'

'You think I'm hiding something?'

'Everybody's hiding something.' She stretched her neck and gazed at the empty beer cups on the mantle. The Bible was still there. One of the Christmas stockings had fallen. A little plastic robot was lying face down on the hearth. 'But there's another side to you though. It's creepy and you don't understand it. I might be the only one who does.'

'You scare me, Goldie.'

'This place eats at you, underpays you and craps on your good intentions.'

'I love it, too, Goldie.'

'But differently,' she said, trying to sit and kicking the coffee table. A few cups fell over and she flopped into the armrest. I hadn't seen her drink all night, but unlike her, I didn't count. 'Okay, where were we?'

'We were going to bury the hatchet.'

'Greenie, why do they keep telling me to wait in line? Why don't they...' As she was talking, Sam stumbled into the room and sank into a chair. In less than five seconds his eyes closed and he was breathing heavily. 'I swear that child has no idea what he's in for,' she said. 'When he wakes up, the party's going to be over. He may not even have a job because of you. Come on, how about we keep him for one more year?'

'I make the recommendation, not the decision. And June is a long way away.'

'Fine, let him dangle. But let me in on one of your dark secrets then. A hook up, a crush, anything. Don't your secrets get to you, Greenie?'

'How about a ghost story?'

'No thanks,' she said, closing her eyes a little. 'Is it okay if I hate you, pretty boy?' Then she leaned into me with her lips parted, and I turned my head away from her.

'Stop it,' I said, and she sank her forearm into my chest. Gunnar and Candy stumbled in to find us at opposite ends of the sofa. Candy was one of Don's blue curtains as a toga, and Gunnar, who had turkey grease all over his shirt, had another wrapped around his head like a turban.

'I didn't think anyone was still here,' he said.

'Only a couple of sinners,' replied Goldie, with no irony whatsoever, and the semester ended with the three of us loading Sam into Goldie's car and throwing him onto the couch in his dorm's common room.

Eighteen

Mary Katherine was going to miss St. Agnes'—every mass, every class, every chatty nun, like Sister Courtney who had a PhD in Education; Sister Amanda who had an MBA from Dartmouth; and Sister Mary Katherine—the other Mary Katherine, the socialist with the hairy mole on her earlobe. And they loved their Social Studies teacher, would've kept her through the pregnancy if she'd been married. But Mary Katherine wasn't even engaged.

In the reception area there was a wooden statue of Jesus. Earlier in the year his right hand, the one raised to his chest with fingers extended, had fallen off. Dryness and then humidity had been the culprits, but how do you mend the hand of Jesus? Mary Katherine thought about this while she took her pregnancy test. The beautiful hand with tapered fingers and a delicate wrist. Blue cross means you're pregnant. A lifetime of wishes spun like a coin. It lands and you've forgotten to call heads or tails, but you take a chance anyway. You leave behind the only real job you've ever had, your family and a roommate you actually like. You leave them all for a desert island and a guy you've already said no to. And no matter how right it feels, it still feels like a mistake.

Vacation, she thought, sitting on the toilet and looking at the blue X. Vacation, is when the joints and tissue of the world become invisible. When the workmen take Jesus' hand from the bookcase and apply a thin coat of glue. Hold in place for five minutes. Time enough to gaze at His young face and think about bigger things. Time to clear your mind and put your scruples aside. Time to pray you've done a good job.

When the children return from holiday, few will remember the hand had come off. Something seems different. Something is missing, but now something is whole again. Where's Ms. Kimball? She's elsewhere, walking through a dream world, looking at fine architecture, caring for a sick relative, taking care of family business, living closer to her fiancé, maybe even looking after herself for a change.

The day after the Christmas party, I threw my bag into my truck and drove through a desolate campus and past the shell of the stone barn. Slipping back into time, I motored down a two-lane highway, looking at bare trees and ground covered with old snow. A deer carcass was frozen into one black snowbank. On the pavement were pieces of broken headlights. I popped in a Ska CD I'd borrowed from Josh, and two hours later, I was pulling into the driveway of the house I'd grown up in.

In the front door I pictured my mother wearing an apron and holding cookies. In life, she'd never made anything as mundane as cookies, but that's how I wanted to see her—in the doorway in a yellow apron, the sash tied loosely behind her back. I put the cookies and a wooden spoon in her hand to complete the picture and remembered the morning after my fourteenth birthday, when I slid down to the living room in my socks to discover my stepfather reading the paper and eating the remnants of my cake.

'Can I have the Sports Section?' I asked. He pushed it in my direction without looking up, and for the third or fourth time that week I told him to go screw himself.

'I'm going to tell your mother you said that.'

'Go ahead,' I scowled, and the dance began. But this time, instead of retreating to my room, I hung on tight. I had the grades, the Boy Scout badges and a Little League All-Star trophy. I was a man now, and he was just a freeloader who left spots on the newspaper because he kept taking it to the bathroom.

'You're a brat,' he said, shooting me a lazy glare.

I don't remember what I said next—maybe I blacked out—but I'm told I threw houseplants. I do remember my mother coming in from the kitchen, wearing the same frown that had been on her face for almost three years, but also a glimmer. Yes, a glimmer, because beneath the broken jade, the wandering Jew and all the potting soil, was my first victory.

My mother was Juliet Green, and although she excelled at making people happy, she loved only me. Growing up, I had sugared cereal whenever I wanted it, an 8-track tape player that ate the soundtrack to Saturday Night Fever twice, and I always seemed to be falling off a new bike. Unlike my friends' flashy suburban supermoms, mine had real flair. She couldn't cook dinner to save her life, but she made museum quality hors d'oeuvres. She couldn't sing, but when she'd warble along with the Patsy Cline in the kitchen, her voice was a change purse full of silver dollars. You'd just have to watch as she those butchered lyrics, kicked off her shoes and did a slow twist on the linoleum. Sometimes, I'd have to look away, but there was something about her that was impossible to resist. If she'd worked, I'm certain she could've been a real estate mogul, the owner of a swank restaurant or, at the very least, a TV meteorologists who made men swoon every time she said things like 'high pressure' or 'mixed precipitation.'

But she also could be ruthless. When I was seven, she critiqued my homework in front of my second grade teacher, the ravishing Ms. Wonderchuck, (a name that was a fantasy all by itself) and proclaimed I was an ignoramus no girl would ever date. It took me three years to recover. But then she scared me for life when she told my two best friends in the world that she was no longer doing my laundry because I'd clearly forgotten how to use toilet paper.

A father might have saved me. But my first dad, Stan 'Little Man' Feinberg, died a few months before I turned two. Based on his jaunty presence in photographs and a few artifacts I'd found around the house (moustache comb, sliver business card case, shoe trees), he'd had more looks than character and a tragic dose of pride. Legend has it he refused to go to the hospital when his mouth dried up and his fingertips went numb. Mom wasn't even allowed to call a doctor; instead, she was ordered to phone her brother, who made it just in time to see the ambulance roll away.

Six years after Stan's exit, my mother found another handsome man with a time bomb in his chest. Brock Winston (née Bernard Weinstein) could do fifty push-ups and lug an air-conditioner up three flights of steps without breaking a sweat, but Mom had bad luck when it came it marriage—that or a sixth sense for wealthy men with bum tickers. Anyway, even though I was out of diapers and already playing football, Brock wasn't interested in me. We could've been tossing a baseball in the yard, but he spent most of his time soiling the newspaper before I could get to it or entertaining buddies he referred to as 'boss' or 'general.'

When his friends came over, I'd pass through the smoky living room in my pajamas as my mom served mushroom caps. After a few patronizing but somehow sympathetic salutations, I'd go to my bedroom and gaze at the dark sedans out in the street. My dad's friends had money, too—the light glinting off their polished fenders told me as much—but no loyalty. Some days, when I'd come home early, I'd see one of those cars parked in front of a neighbor's house or around the corner. Coming in the back door, I'd stamp my feet and announce myself, and sometimes I'd hear a murmur of voices and a door close on the other side of the house. Then my mom would saunter into the kitchen, always dressed, but somehow not together.

Filled with rage, I started dawdling after school, coming home later and later. But one afternoon I got so sick of being her accomplice that I ran home, slammed the back door and threw my book bag into the wall.

'How's my boy?' asked my mom, putting a glass into the dishwasher and starting on the breakfast plates that were still in the sink.

'Fine,' I said, and I noticed the scrapings from my dad's burnt toast in the breakfast nook. His plate was gone, but there was a Santorini-shaped pattern on the table beside the heavy ashtray that contained the butt of his morning cigarette. I could still see the foul thing pinched between his fingers, his big black shoes, trim haircut and striped tie. It was 1976 for Pete's sake: my male teachers wore bushy sideburns and listened to the Alman Brothers, but this asshole dressed like a Cold War spy.

'Just fine?' my mom asked, stepping over my book bag.

'Mrs. Jasper caught Joey Salerno cheating on a vocabulary quiz.' I pronounced the word 'cheating' so slowly and so clearly.

'I thought Joey was smarter than that,' said my mom, picking up a sponge and wiping down the table. When she finished, I kicked my book bag a few times. Crunch went my lunchbox. That snap must've been my three-ring binder. My mom stared at me for a few seconds before she told me to stop. And I did. And while I was looking around the house at all the things we both hated, I swallowed my anger and decided I didn't have the right to judge anyone.

My mother was brazen and sometimes I hated her, too, but she did have a conscience. One day when I was sixteen, she yanked me out of Spanish class and took me to the hospital. There, I saw my stepfather's body in a bed with all the tubes and wires removed. We pulled up chairs and she made me sit. I took her hand.

'Jeff,' she said, 'we need to do this. And, you, my little knight, even when you're right, you need to know…' Her voice trailed off, but then she found the words, '…it's not the same thing as being good. Not even close.'

She wasn't holding my hand anymore. She was on her own.

Juliet did well as a widow—two houses and two insurance policies made her comfortable—and in time we settled into a routine. I went to school, played sports and lost sleep over girls. She delivered meals to sick people, stopped voting Republican and lost sleep over the B's on my report cards. I worked harder until I got A's, but her love was always tough to understand. Sometimes her attentions seemed downright bizarre. Once she showed my baby pictures to a girl I'd just brought home. Another time she chased a girl away by asking to check her teeth. From then on I kept my social life secret. I even made up an imaginary friend named Leo Cox, who loved video games, too, but didn't do all of his homework. And just about the time my mom started asking for his parents' names, so she could find out whether Leo was as cruel to his mother as I was to mine, he moved to Ann Arbor.

My first night back at my mom's, I raided the pantry, found dried pasta, a jar of sauce, some jam, and crackers that weren't too stale. I'd brought dirty laundry just so I could sit on the dryer. The next day I ran the vacuum and dusted. I turned on the radio and cleaned the kitchen. I watched football and ate the last of her food.

The supermarket was full of green and red displays. I bought a box of half-price Hanukkah candles, a steak, cereal, milk and some puff pastries. In a trailer out back I found the stock boys cursing the cold. After a double take and a what-the-hell-are-you-doing here, they let me climb onto the loading dock and grab all the boxes I could stuff into my car. While I worked, I remembered being seventeen and taking my mother's Buick out in the snow in that same parking lot. With her blessing I practiced skidding. For an hour I spun in circles, faster, tighter, backward, forward, until I had mastery of the car, the slick surface, and my own fear. At seventeen, I also learned how to cut the engine a block from her house and to coast into the driveway. By then, I was fixing everything that broke, setting up her computer, installing an icemaker in her freezer.

I'd even realized what I wanted to do with my life, when on a sad but somehow fortunate Monday, my high school math teacher had a nervous breakdown in front of our class. Mrs. Bright had been talking about linear equations when some figure on the blackboard changed her. Who knows what it was, but like a dry leaf under a car wheel she crumbled into her desk chair and buried her head in her hands. We sat there staring—all of us too young to understand how bleak math could be when you had fibroids—until I picked up her textbook. I didn't think I could do it, but all eyes fixed on me, confusion was assuaged and I read the answers to our homework in a voice I hardly recognized. The next day we had a sub and the boys were calling me 'professor.'

That same year I lost my virginity, but it wasn't until my freshman year in college that I fell for a girl. Sarah Masters was funny, the center of any party, and she hit a tennis ball good enough to get games off me. But she also had a mean streak I didn't understand or, perhaps, didn't want to understand. No wonder we had five amazing months and ten absolutely miserable ones. After college I met a girl with manners. We dated for more than two years and never fought. I thought it was the real thing, so when she got pregnant, I took a knee. But when I got up, we were no longer dating. No problem, I thought, you're a man. You've got a wood burning stove and bottomless bag of tricks. You'll be fine.

When my mom's cancer was diagnosed, she refused to give me details because she was afraid I'd become an expert on her illness. I was irate, but when I met her seventy-year old Romanian oncologist, Martina Crinescu, I knew my mother was in good hands. The doctor's face, like my mother's, was a feast of beautiful lines. And when she attended the funeral, in a vintage black hat that made her hair look silvery and magical, she was one of the few in a parade of strangers who knew what to say.

'You've gained weight,' she told me. 'Your mom would like that.'

I had a brave mother who in many ways kept me, like all the men in her life, at a distance. And when I did show interest in her, she'd tell me a mother complex scared girls away faster than pimples and sloppy skivvies. I learned to teach differently, but I liked her style: how she cut me down to build me up, how she'd curse a girl who wronged me and then slap me around a little herself.

'If you stick that spoon back in that jar of peanut butter, I'm going charge you for it' was her last scolding. Amused, I pretended to dip it back in until she threw her hands up. 'Oh, go ahead, you never listen anyway.'

'I've always listened,' I replied, and I put the jar away and washed my spoon.

After piling my boxes, newspaper, rolls of tape and markers on the living room floor, I packed a suitcase with things I wanted. The next day I put the picture I'd drawn in honors English on the fridge. I left my earring in the soap dish in the downstairs bathroom and finished packing. By the end of the month, the house had been sold. When I went back to take a last look around, my drawing was in the living room. Although the child floating above the crowd was still a loose end, I put it back on the fridge and locked the door behind me.

Nineteen

I drove slowly to a wooden village where ghosts rattled windowpanes. In the rearview mirror were two houses—one going, one gone. But maybe I saw a fort of blankets propped on dining room chairs. Me crawling around on the oriental, late morning murmurs, filtered light, stirring dust. Me catching the motes, releasing them before the castle was torn down, folded and put back in the linen closet.

I drove the speed limit because I'd decided that time travel in either direction is impossible. I had to stick with the facts. I was sliding through space, from a box no longer mine to another that never was. A school was waiting for me, ticking as always like an antique watch, a weak heart, or a bomb.

It was definitely time to say goodbye, again.

A few days after I returned to The Mount, I hiked down to the valley for a bagel and a cup of coffee at Little Sandy's. At the next table was the forty-year-old woman with the nose ring and a Celtic love knot tattooed on her neck. She was talking with the Sufi massage therapist who lived up the road and lead-footed it through campus in a rusty Pontiac. A few old men, tobacco-stained regulars in baseball caps read the paper and nodded at everyone walking in the door. In one of the three booths the 'church ladies' held court, complaining about their children and their neighbors' children before they migrated to Reverend Brown's rectory for more coffee.

When I got home, I an email from Cass was waiting:

Hi mr, green,

I just wanted to say hi and ask how things are going. how was the teacher party? did everybody get crazy? How's the weather up there? You watch a few college football games? My New years resolution is to be less sarcastic and more practical. What's yours?

I gotta tell you though. I had this Gatsby moment the night when...you know. Well, first I got stuck in the dorm because we were having this fashion show. All the girls were trying on each others dresses. And Sally even had this green bridesmaid dress since her older sister got married in October, and we all tried that on too and took turns looking like an avocado.

But then things finally cooled down and I was able to step out for a few. Well, I was very careful to avoid the road and the snow was mostly gone so I could cut behind a few houses. But when I got to yours I saw that the lights were on and there was loud music coming out. (I thought you were going to save yourself for the big party, but when I climbed up the hill a little behind your place, I saw you laughing with mr. Davis and ms. Dafoe. I was sort of standing next to a tree getting poked by all these bushes I couldn't see, but I could see you guys inside passing around a bottle. Ms. Dafoe was really loud. What was she yelling about ducks?

Well, I was about to go home cuz it was really cold out there, but then I couldn't because who else is looking at you guys but Mrs. Remlap. I got really worried because she was wearing her winter coat and all and might be there for a while. I was afraid she was going to come up on the hill and find me too, cuz I was at the only place where you could see inside, but she just sort of snuck up to the windows and started listening. I guess she was having her own Gatsby moment. You know when he's outside of Daisy and Tom's house—I don't remember the page number—and he's gazing at the lights as they drink a beer and make all these shifty plans? Only you guys were being a lot louder.

Well, lucky for me Mrs. Remlap didn't stay too long. I was hoping Davis and Dafoe—when I say it that way they sound like a law firm—would go too but I could kind of tell those two like to have a good time. Anyway, I made it back to my dorm okay and now I can't believe it but I kind of miss school. Hope you're doing ok.

Cassie.

P. S. Get this. I need an extra English credit, and I can't take Ms. Remlap's Famous Heroines again. The only course I can take is Mr. Iafrati's. Uggghhhh!

I wrote back and said I was having a restful vacation. I hoped she was reading some good books. Then I crossed my fingers and prayed she wouldn't write anymore.

A few days later I was manning the waffle iron at Don's—everyone still on campus had been invited to brunch—when he noticed I'd taken out my earring. He called the change 'an improvement.' But Gunnar and Candy looked at me suspiciously.

Later, after I went snowshoeing with Art for two extremely quiet hours. Then I went over to Gunnar's apartment in the building we called Ministry.

'We dodged a bullet,' said Gunnar offering me a Coke.

Candy slid her feet out of her boots and curled up in the window seat. 'Goldie's got a reason to kiss your ass now. Who knows you could be evaluating her soon.'

'I heard she's advising a new club,' said Gunnar, 'something called the Twenty-First Century Coalition?'

Even though Goldie's invention sounded like some kind of a corporate think tank, Gunnar explained that our blonde-haired blue-eyed spider was going to become the diva of diversity, a beacon for all 'historically marginalized' students and adults on campus. On the surface, it actually sounded like a good idea. We already had a club called Students and World Recognition. But the SWR's idea of celebrating was to eat junk food and blast hip-hop for forty-minutes. And despite the fact that we had students from five continents on The Mount, the members of the SWR—more commonly known as Students with Rhythm—were mostly Black or Latino and from New York. The only non-American was Hip-Hip Hideo Tanaka, who sometimes sprang for pizza.

'What the hell is she doing now?' asked Gunnar.

'I don't care,' I said. 'You know, she was a mess at the holiday party. At one point I actually had to push her off me?'

'She try to scratch your eyes out?' asked Gunnar.

'No, no, no, no, no, she tried to kiss me,' I said. 'I swear.'

Candy sat up. 'That woman's a freak. What is wrong with her?'

'I said I don't care,' I said. 'And, guys, this shit is getting to me.'

'But you're just getting good at it?' said Gunnar.

'My soul hurts,' I said. 'I just want to be nice to people and take care of myself.'

Candy suggested I see her therapist. She'd helped with her anger and was cool weed. Still intrigued by Goldie's behavior, Gunnar wondered if we should tell folks how she attacked me since nothing gets more people riled up that an aspiring adulteress. I groaned and told them to leave me alone before I hurt myself.

It was a frigid day, but as I swung the axe, my shirt soaked through and I started feeling saner. I was halfway back to myself when Kara walked by carrying a few bills and an L.L. Bean catalogue in her bare hands. She was wearing a baseball cap, but there was no hiding the long face and despondent hair. According to the grapevine, Rog hadn't disappointed in bed. His buns were perfect and he'd let her insult him. He'd also confessed that he 'liked' her, but now he was skiing in Utah with another woman.

'Hey,' I said, propping my axe against my block.

'What's going on, G?'

'I'm trying to get good at this.'

'You could try some of the other axes. They're lighter.'

As I eyed the piece of wood I'd set up, Kara dropped onto a stump and tugged on her scarf. She'd made it herself, her first one. I swung the axe and the blade slipped through the log. Gaining momentum, I hacked my way through a few knotty pieces of pine while Kara turned her face toward the sun. She wasn't as pretty now, but a month of worry had made her a more attractive.

'You hear from him?' I asked.

Her eyes opened wide. 'What does it matter to you?'

'I'm not allowed to ask?'

'Greenie, you and I...let's not have this conversation.'

I leaned the axe against the stump. 'I'm just trying to be nice.'

'I can take care of myself,' she said. 'You may think my life is a disaster, but you don't see me cruising the bars in Pittsfield.'

'I forgot, when you get lonely, the circus comes to your house.'

She told me to fuck myself. Sick of ending conversations like that, I told her Rog had a thing for sheep and wiped my nose on my sleeve.

Just before the end of break Mary Katherine Kimball pulled up outside my house in a Ford Country Squire station wagon. The car had three or four good dents in it, one of the windows didn't open and the entire tailgate sported a few bumper stickers, like I'd Rather Be Ice Fishing and the logo of a minor league hockey team called the Albany River Rats.

Wanting an up-close of the brave mother-to-be, I greeted her on the back steps. With a quick smile, she allowed me to hold the door but said 'no thanks' when I asked if I could carry anything. She must've been about five months along, but with her parka and her gloves zipped up I couldn't see much in the way of a bump or an engagement ring.

'Suit yourself,' I said, nodding at the icy stalactites above us 'but I'm going to leave some salt. When the water comes off the roof, the steps freeze.'

'Wait,' she said, as I turned to go, 'I've wanted to hit Sam a few times myself. But I still wanted to thank you for getting him get a class.'

'Just giving him a little rope,' I said.

'Well, he appreciates it,' she said, enjoying my joke, and she thanked me again.

Soon Shawna Brophy's old apartment began to buzz. I heard a vacuum, a radio and even Mary Katherine shouting over the music that Sam was hanging a picture too high. By the end of the day, she'd settled in. Through the window—she was in the basement common room, so her place was easy to spy on—I saw a makeshift kitchen with little more than an electric teakettle, a microwave and a hot plate. She also had a sofa with a quilt over it, a small television with a wire hanger for an antenna, and a canvas bag full of sewing material.

That afternoon I made a fire and dug into a novel. I was putting code in the margins—V's for vocabulary words, Q's for questions, stars for passages that turned me on—when I heard Mary Katherine drive off.

In the unused part of the dorm, I'd stored some stuff I needed to get rid of before I moved, including a toaster oven that had become redundant when my mother died and left me one with a bake timer, non-stick broiling pan and the ability to toast on one side if I wanted to pretend I was English. I shouldn't have, but I penned Mary Katherine a note welcoming her to my corner of the campus, dusted off the toaster oven and left it outside her door.

At the start of our January meeting, Don introduced Mary Katherine and told everyone who wasn't in the know that she'd be working in a dorm, tutoring and doing activities. Then, as folks took note of the fact that she was not wearing a diamond, he announced that Oscar had extended his leave and I was still interim chair of the English Department. Except for Kara and Rog, who were busy glowering on opposite sides of the room, everyone yawned, and then we went over new duty schedules, second semester electives, and board updates. Finally, Don waved to a shady figure who'd appeared in the doorway and said, 'Okay, let's get to the matter at hand so we can do this right.'

A white-haired man in his sixties limped into the room with a big black case and set it on the table in front of us. He was retired police detective J.J. MacFarlane, and he began showing us samples of the drugs our kids might use. Next he showed us where they'd hide them in their luggage and led us through a role-play so we'd know how to act while we searched them. Art and Candy had the honor of busting Roland Meadows.

'This is something we're doing to everyone,' joked Art, even though he thought a search was probably the worst idea in the history of the school. Rolly clutched his little blue suitcase and stared wide eyed at Candy. When she took his bag, he started drumming his fingers and stammering.

'I don't know why you're doing this. It's such a, such a stupid thing. I really don't like other people touching my stuff.'

'We're only looking for drugs and alcohol,' she said. 'Anything else you're not supposed to have like knives and lighters will be taken, but they're not going to get you in trouble. I'm going to check the clothes you're wearing, too.'

'Look inside his socks,' said detective MacFarlane. 'The ones in the bag, too.'

'I don't want to touch his socks,' replied Candy.

'Rubber gloves,' suggested the detective, and he informed Ichabob someone should be stationed on the road to make sure kids we'd already searched didn't tip off their arriving friends.

'This isn't fair. It can't be legal,' stuttered Rolly. 'My dad's a lawyer and my mom knows someone at the UCLA.'

With a grin that was far from sympathetic, Candy opened the little suitcase and took out a can of shaving cream, a dictionary and some clothing. She also found a jar of honey labeled 'The Good Stuff.'

'Was that it?' asked Candy. Detective MacFarlane shook his head, so she checked the lining of the case, while Art thumbed through a book. In time, he took the top off of the shaving cream and found a baggy full of suspicious leaves.

'I don't know how that got there,' Rolly howled. 'Why are you doing this? I thought you liked me. I thought you trusted us.'

Rolly pretended to hyperventilate. Folks laughed, but as I scanned the room, I could see on people's faces that this was a horrible thing we were about to do.

'It's okay, son,' said Art, gently patting him on the back, 'I'll just hang on to your toiletries while you have a talk with Mr. Driscoll.'

That night Mary Katherine's radio grew silent and I heard her crunching off to Sam's through the snow. The next morning, she returned as I was pulling on sweatpants and figuring out what to have for breakfast. Her steps were light and happy, but I had no clue what she was doing on The Mount without a ring. She flicked on her radio and I heard water running. Later, when I opened my door and started down the stairs to get another bagel at Little Sandy's, I almost tripped over my toaster oven. A message was scribbled below the one I'd left. Thanks, but I was planning on buying my own.

Twenty

The kids were intercepted on the road and told to report to Wickersham. And whether they were nefarious pot smokers or honor role goodie goodies, as they presented their luggage to be searched, they all looked guilty of something. It was a bad day for the school, one of its worst I'm sure, but there were a few moments of comic relief. One involved the expandable suitcase of a Korean boy. The bag held nothing illegal—the child was a bookworm with a Pez dispenser collection and a golf fetish—but with every zipper, every stray golf tee, every moldy quadruple-bogey-plagued scorecard, the boy's face became redder and redder. Eventually, the nylon monstrosity accordioned out to the size of a body bag and the amiable kid was in a kind of embarrassed heaven.

'Please me, I close,' he exclaimed, bowing and starting on the zippers as my customs partner, the one and only Mary Katherine Kimball, sniffed at a package of dried squid and turned green. Ichabob had put us together—a cruel welcome if ever there was one—for the simple reason that I was a guy, she was a girl, and our last names were close in the alphabet.

'What are the odds of us finding anything?' she asked.

'Zero,' I said, picking up a golf tee from the carpet, but of course the next kid we patted down had rolling papers. The one after that had a pipe stem covered with pot resin. The one after six little bottles of Vodka. And, to cap things off, I found a small crocheted pouch, a dope bag if ever there was one. There was no pot inside—the boy probably slipped it to his parents—but, alas, there was paraphernalia, an alligator clip my nose told me had been used to hold roaches.

I apologized for the fourth time in two hours and directed the catatonic junior to Ichabob, who was arranging for no less than eleven students to be drug tested.

Mary Katherine stared wearily out the window. She was sporting cotton chinos with an elastic panel in the front and her hair was pushed hastily behind one ear as if she'd gotten up late. I caught myself looking at her naked finger and wondering what had changed about her. The buoyancy that won me over was still there, along with the grandeur of her being pregnant, but now, in addition to fatigue, there was a sad air of resignation about her eyes.

She was still gazing out the window when Cass strolled and noticed my missing earring. In a pale yellow cardigan over a white turtleneck and with her hair in barrettes, the girl could've been working in a dentist's office or selling muffins for the PTA. I got the feeling the outfit was actually a costume worn for me.

'I'm sorry, but I have to check your pockets,' said Mary Katherine. 'I'm Miss Kimball, by the way.'

'I know who you are, but I won't hold it against you,' replied Cass. 'Should I put my hands against the wall?'

'If you want,' said Mary Katherine.

'Which bag do you want me to check?' I asked.

Cass dumped her backpack in front of Mary Katherine and left me to rummage through a suitcase that contained, among other things, a bra with a cleavage dial, two pairs of flesh-colored stockings, and a few loose snapshots. In the pictures she was posing with a champagne flute and dressed to the nines. She and a girlfriend, both of whom could've passed for twenty-five, were waving at the camera. Jutting into the frame was a man's leg and a tan love seat.

'Our chaperone took those on New Year's,' said Cass. 'It was a somber occasion.'

Mary Katherine glanced over as she thumbed through a few books, including *Leaves of Grass*. I found myself peeking at Cass, peeking at Mary Katherine, peeking at the girl—shamed by both and certain they were exchanging some kind of intelligence. He saw my underpants Cass said with a subtle nod. He busted a finger trying to hit my boyfriend nodded the other. He's scared of me, they both said.

'Hey, I think I have the same sweater,' said Mary Katherine.

Cass gazed at Mary Katherine's belly. 'You know, my cousin got huge ankles when she was pregnant. They never went back.'

'I feel for her. But I'm thinking I'll get new shoes out of this thing.'

'It was my cousin's ankles,' said Cass, without blinking.

'I think my feet and my ankles are connected,' said Mary Katherine.

'You should tell your boyfriend if a girl's sprinting to the bathroom in the middle of class, he should know better than to demand a pass.'

'Cass,' I said. 'It's Miss Kimball's first day. You can complain about Iafrati tomorrow, okay?'

She turned on me. 'What happened to your earring?'

'It was time,' I mumbled, zipping up her bag and pushing it back to her.

'Mr. Green, why are you guys treating us like such criminals?'

'I'm not a fan of this,' I said. 'I'm sorry, but it's part of the job.'

Cass turned to Mary Katherine and sighed. 'I got this sweater in Greenwich Village,' she said. 'I think it's kinda fun. And I'm sorry for being obnoxious.'

Mary Katherine smiled at both of us and said she hadn't noticed. Liking the sarcasm, Cass dragged her shit out of the room just as Sam dragged his shit in. Actually, I take it back. Not shit there. Sam looked like a new man. I guess it was nice to have Mary Katherine close, to know how many steps and not miles it took to find her. Leaning against my desk, he gleefully recounted his search of Joe Causeway.

Before leaving for vacation, Joe had loaded a suitcase with wet clothes and left it in his room. Normally, even he would've opened the bag when he returned, taken a whiff and tossed everything in the dumpster. Hearing his belongings were going to be inspected, however, he was gripped by the need to comply.

'His stuff was rancid,' said Sam. 'And he kept trying to help me.'

'What's the kid's story?' asked Mary Katherine, her shoulder brushing against his. Outnumbered, I moved to the back row.

'He's just weird,' said Sam. 'Jeff's good with him though.'

Mary Katherine turned to me for an explanation.

'He's part teenager, part octopus, and he wants everyone to be his friend,' I said, tracing a pencil mark on the desk with my finger. 'But he's missing the social piece and he drives people nuts. Some days you want to run away from him. But I swear, you'll never stop talking about him.'

'Is he autistic?' asked Mary Katherine.

'Probably, but his parents refuse to get him evaluated, so we treat him like any other eighteen-year-old sophomore with OCD.'

As we talked, the dulcimer voice of per Rothstein wafted into the room.

'That gorilla checked under the cap of my shaving cream,' he said loudly. 'Inside my socks, too. Figures she'd know where to look.' Happy to bail on the lovebirds, I stepped into the hall and found him bitching to Harriet and Hodge.

'Was I being loud?' he replied.

'Is it true you're giving us cavity searches later?' asked Hodge.

Harriet had her hands in her pockets, her back against the wall. She'd gotten her hair done over break and looked like a different kid— not happier, just different. Hodge was sporting a new earring.

'You're funny,' I said, as Per pulled a slab of bills from his pocket and said he thinking of playing tennis for me in the spring. I told him I couldn't wait and suggested he put the cash in the Business Office.

'I'm gonna buy a soda,' he said, and the little shit winked at me. 'Hey, I just got a load of Iafrati's woman. Is it true she's living in your apartment?'

I corrected him and he asked if Sam was really the father of the baby. The boy needed punishing, so in great detail I began explaining the importance of manners and how a class leader should set a better example. About the time I transitioned from respect to integrity, Sam strolled out of the room and shouldered his way past the kid.

Per played dumb. 'I didn't know he was in there. Besides, he didn't hear me.'

I wagged a finger at him and went inside to find Mary Katherine reading.

'This *Romeo and Juliet* is abridged,' she said, holding up the textbook.

'How'd you know?'

'It says so in the table of contents.'

'I thought maybe you read a few scenes while I was out in the hall,' I said, as I rearranged furniture. Mary Katherine put the book down and began to help.

'Don't give me too much...' She didn't finish because she—to put it delicately—passed gas. 'Don't ever get pregnant, Jeff. Your body turns into a tuba.'

I liked the image of a woman with a musical body. And because I'm an over-confessor, I apologized for being a five year old and told her a story.

'When I was little, I pooted in front of my mom. Just once, mind you, and she decided without consulting a single doctor that I had an allergy to wheat. So no more bread, no more bagels and, here's the best part, she insisted that we drive around with the car windows down all winter just in case.'

'Does that mean I have your sympathy?' asked Mary Katherine, finding another golf tee on the floor. This one said *Saint Andrews* on it.

'It means I have the right to make fun of you.'

'As long as that's clear,' she said, reshelving my book, and I decided that even if she was going to marry Sam, Mary Katherine was still good people.

'So you're teach French?' I asked.

'Social Studies.'

'Why'd I think you were a French teacher?'

'That's Sam's other girlfriend,' she said. 'My kids, I mean, my former students, are learning about the Constitution as we speak.'

'U. S. History?'

'From the Big Bang through The Reconstruction. And I'm about to get a crash course on the Shakers.'

For a second I thought I'd get to talk about my second favorite religious sect—behind Reformed Jews, of course—but Mary Katherine slumped onto a desk and moaned. 'You know, I'm so glad the search is over. I hate having to find a new bank and a new doctor. I don't even know where to buy deodorant. And as far as the kids are concerned, I'm just Iafrati's girlfriend. What's his nickname again?'

'Turtle is the least offensive.'

'Great, and I get to greet them by rifling through their stuff.'

'It's not the kind of memory you'd like to leave them with.'

'You can say that again,' she chimed.

Art begged me to come over, and since I was trying to mend fences, I couldn't say no. I arrived with an open but cautious mind to find a house full of belated holiday cheer. I looked for signs of discord, repaired vases, bedding by the sofa, divorce papers pinned to the refrigerator, but when I scanned the corners of their tidy cottage, I saw only Art's slippers and Goldie's needlepoint pillows. The sole source of darkness in the room was Roger Day, who'd searched kids with an air of indulgence, intimidated them with formality, and avoided small talk.

'She had it in this plastic make-up case,' he said, sitting backwards on a Shaker chair. 'I knew the second I picked it up I was going to nail her.' He'd added a bohemian air to his manly appearance by letting his sideburns grow. He was also wearing a new shirt, red chamois with a factory crease on the pocket. Maybe he'd been expecting Kara to be there, but at the moment she just wanted to hit him with a baseball bat.

'She called him a fascist,' said Sam, all cozy on the sofa next to his girlfriend.

'She's on the Dean's List,' I added.

'She does well here, but at the next level?' asked Rog. 'I mean what's going to happen to a kid like that? Carrying drugs and dressing like a freak.'

'She dresses like a college student,' said Goldie.

Rog scratched his sideburn. 'Still, I think we caught enough to send our message.'

'What message is that?' asked Mary Katherine.

'The quiet one speaks,' he said. 'Well, as far as I'm concerned the message is we're not going to look the other way anymore.'

'I don't know if they care,' she said. 'One boy, Hip-Hop Hideo, actually bowed to Jeff when he found rolling papers in his luggage. He didn't look very deterred to me.'

'Greenie should be meaner,' said Rog.

Goldie was leaning forward in her seat, perhaps a little torn between cheering on Roger and backing Mary Katherine.

'But then I wouldn't get any presents,' I said. 'Besides, I like most of them.'

'I don't think Roger worries about presents,' said Goldie, and she told Mary Katherine that in the last five years Rog had received only one gift from a student, soap from a Taiwanese girl. Rog endured more teasing—despite adoring his manly ways Goldie had a few things to say about his wardrobe and the state of his apartment—then he thanked her for the cookies and got up. The second the door closed behind him, our hostess grabbed the chair he'd been sitting on and tipped it over.

'He didn't call her once over break, and when they finally talked, he acted like he was doing her a favor.'

Sam picked up the chair. 'She could've called him.'

'No excuse,' cried Goldie. 'Honestly, why do men play such stupid games? Can you tell me that, Greenie?'

'I'm staying out of this,' I said. Art was already hiding behind the piano.

Sam was the only one brave enough to speak.

'I don't know really what happened between Roger and Kara, but with him what you see is what you get.'

Goldie raised an index finger, but Mary Katherine got in the way.

'Why don't we just let them work it out?'

'Roger Day may know what's good for this school,' she said, surveying the men in the room. 'But maybe Kara should've stayed with Pete or set her sights a little higher.'

Sam realized it was pointless to argue. In her own house and with the wrath of a million sisters on her side, Goldie was always going to be right. He tried to make a joke.

'He can tell you the sex of a turkey just by looking at its poop.'

'Now there's a keeper,' said Mary Katherine, slipping her hand into his.

'I'm just saying he knows a few things.'

Mary Katherine glanced at me and stumbled. I thought I was wearing a smile, but who knows what else she saw: my hatred of Goldie, my wavering opinion of Sam, or maybe even the fact that I liked her? She recovered though, messed up Sam's hair and announced that she was tired. Goldie settled back into the sofa and watched the youngsters squirm.

'Amen,' said Sam, as Goldie picked up the plate of Christmas cookies and passed it to me. Her smile could've almost passed for sincere.

'Bygones?' she said.

'Definitely,' I said, and I grabbed a cookie and took a friendly bite.

Twenty-One

At our first assembly of the New Year, Goldie stood up in a yellow and green sari she may have made out of an old curtain and pitched her new club. Some kids yawned at the prospect of celebrating the school's diversity, but there were a few nods of approval when she announced she'd be making cookies. There were more nods of approval when my sophomores walked into class after the assembly and discovered that Sam had vacated the back row. There were even more nods in the dorm when I played Solomon over remote controls and lost CDs. And finally there were nods from Gunnar and Candy, when they spotted me chastising booksellers and calling parents from the antique chair behind Oscar's desk.

I also started visiting classrooms, but not Sam's, not yet.

Meanwhile, Cassandra Diaz was ringing up friends just before lights out and commiserating late into the night. She was mad that everyone but her was sneaking around. Debbie was now kissing Kwame, but Per was none the wiser. Hodge and Harriet, who no longer liked each other, were still groping in sheds. And a few other couples, neophytes and horny old pros alike, were stealing off to do the Shaker Shuffle. But when she'd tried to do a little sneaking, a party had gotten in the way, and now it seemed like I was never in the cafeteria, never in my classroom, never where she could find me. I guess other people's happiness became too much to endure, for one Thursday night there was a knock on the door separating my apartment from the rest of the dorm. Assuming it was my downstairs neighbor, I turned down my music and checked my fly only to find Cass holding two slices of pizza.

'Don't flip, Mrs. Remlap thought we should give you these,' she said. 'She dropped me off out front, but those steps are too icy, so I had to go around.'

'She really drove you up here?' I asked.

'Yeah, she spent half the night complaining about department heads who think they're God. Then she begged us to join her club. Then she tells us this story about picking up a guy named Denny at a Denny's in Cincinnati back when she was single. And then when she's done with that, she gets all silly and suggests you need pizza. Seriously, I don't think that woman can help herself. One minute she's a prude. The next she's crazy.'

'I leaned against the wall and sighed. 'Thanks for the food.'

'Are you tired? Normally, you would've noticed I'm depressed and I wouldn't have to come out and tell you how much I hate Iafrati's class.' As she talked, she walked into my apartment and, of course, found all the cover letters and resumes I was about to stuff in envelopes and send out. 'The guy talks too much, and when we talk, he gets lost thinking about the next thing he wants to say. So no matter what we do, everything's just 'valid' or 'interesting' or 'astute.' And, get this, he grades super easy.'

'Just show him how smart you are and he'll shut up.'

She read the first line of a cover letter and chuckled. If she'd found a typo, I would have kicked her out.

'Man, I wish I could drop his course. So...you run the English Department now?'

'What are you getting at?'

'Nothing yet,' she replied. 'Well, some army guys are trying to blow up some other army guys, and I gotta go read about it.'

'Wait,' I said. She stopped in her tracks and I started the slow process of breaking her heart. 'Cass, I shouldn't have been flirting with you before break.'

'Don't you like hanging with me and letting me in on secrets?'

'A little,' I said, 'but you really shouldn't be in my apartment.'

She grabbed my sleeve. 'What are you saying?'

'I'm saying I don't want to have a fling with a student. I shouldn't and I can't cross that line.'

She started to cry—not bawling, just water at the corners of her eyes as if she'd been walking into a cold wind. She wiped them with the backs of her hands and took a deep breath. 'Okay, fine, I hear you. You want to hit the brakes,' she said. 'But there's something. You, you may not believe this, but you're like the only one around here who gets me. If you just shut me down and stop talking to me, I don't know what I'll do.' I handed her a tissue and she blew her nose. 'I know I've been playing you a little, so I understand your being cold now, but I've got no friends here.'

'I'm not planning on being cold, Cassie.'

'That's all I want, and I don't have to come up to your apartment or anything.'

I pushed my fists into my pockets and put my outgoing mail in a safer place. 'Good, I can't do secrets.'

She tried to be playful again. 'I know that's not true.'

'Seriously,' I said, 'I'll be friendly, but, please, no inside jokes and absolutely no surprise visits, okay?'

She zipped up her coat to go and started pulling on her gloves. 'When we talk, it'll look all proper and I will act totally bored.'

'That would make me so happy,' I said, and waited until she'd descended a few steps before closing the door. Less than a minute later though, there was another knock. Prepared to shoo Cass away, I opened the door and found another curious woman.

It all started with a bump overhead, then another. It was Sam's fault, too. Since the very beginning he'd been complaining about me. But when we spent a morning searching kids' bags, I seemed perfectly normal, nice even. I'd clearly gotten into Sam's head. And now I was creeping into hers, for as much as she tried to focus on her reasons for being there, she couldn't stop thinking about appliances. In Sam's Spartan tree house lived a toaster and a wheezy coffee maker, in hers a hotplate and a teakettle. But in the upstairs apartment of Medicine

Shop she imagined not just a surplus of toaster ovens, but waffle irons, stand up mixers, and a self-cleaning espresso machine that spoke three languages and gave massages.

To her the basement was a third world country. Every morning she expected to find chickens in the hallway, rabbit hutches by the laundry room, giant insects in the showers. If she kept a diary and hung prayer flags from the pipes, she could pretend she was in the Peace Corps, roughing it with a purpose. She could turn the banging pipes into exotic animals and her cheap window sheers into mosquito netting. For a while she even imagined that her belly had been invaded by a parasite and with the right medicine she could just walk away from this place. Later she turned the parasite into a child and Sam into a brown-skinned man or a hunky Scandinavian medical student.

And then there was Goldie's bizarre performance. The woman hadn't said much of anything to Roger Day, but the second he left she knocked over his chair. Same thing with Jeff Green. Not a peep to his face, but the second he walked out the door, she threw herself onto the sofa and told everyone he was a creep.

Her second cousin, some shy girl named Shawna Brophy, had told her that he'd lurked outside her apartment, lurked in their laundry room, and made it impossible for her to even use her own bathroom. He let students humiliate her when she tried to say hello and play some pool, and then he followed her home—heavy footsteps fifty yards behind all the way up to her apartment. She heard them all the time. And that lock on her bedroom door was so cheap. Anyone could force it open. And his cold smile, his talk of thermostats. It made her skin crawl. So she told her cousin, but before Goldie could help the poor new math intern, she'd packed her stuff and run away.

Mary Katherine squeezed Sam's hand during her story. Later she asked if Goldie had said anything to Jeff or, more importantly, to Don DeWillum? Sam had no clue, and reluctantly admitted that he too was confused as to why Goldie would be railing now, *after* Mary Katherine had moved into his basement?

For a few days Mary Katherine tried out the idea that I really was a creep. But then she heard a car in the driveway, Goldie's voice and a girl's voice. The car idled for a minute, its lights painting squares on the wall above her small television. There were purposeful footsteps on the back walk, someone pushing through the door. The car pulled away and the squares slid off the wall. With only a flight of stairs between Mary Katherine and my side door, the knocking was downright intrusive. And when Cass told me not to flip because 'Mrs. Remlap thought we should give you these,' Mary Katherine knew exactly who was talking. She didn't know what 'these' were or why Goldie would have a pretty girl deliver them, but she was intrigued enough to knock on my door.

'I hope I'm not bothering you,' she said, biting her lip, 'but I was wondering if you had an extra cookie sheet. I can get one at my parents in a few weeks, and I'd hate to buy another.'

Cass's visit made sense. Mary Katherine's caught me by surprise. With a mouth full of pizza I invited her in and offered her the other slice.

'I wish I could handle tomatoes, but still you've got a nice perk there.'

She slipped out of her clogs, padded down the hall behind me and we rounded the staircase. Without a winter coat on her belly seemed smaller. The baby, she'd later tell me, was now the size of a grapefruit. I offered her a seat, but she didn't seem to hear me.

'There's the wood stove I've been smelling,' she said. 'You've got it all: real furniture, rugs, a fireplace. Me, I'm still trying to figure out what I left behind.'

As she walked around my living room, I got the feeling she was measuring me, especially when she paused in front of a black and white photograph of my mother on the Atlantic City boardwalk in 1963. For a second I wondered if she'd heard everything Cass had said. Then I wondered if she was cold.

'Do you know there's a thermostat for your place in the hall above you?'

'Yeah, someone told me about it,' she said, giving me an odd little smile and playing with the New York Rangers medallion on her key chain. Her yellow socks were big for her feet. Maybe they were Sam's.

I invited her to sit again, but she followed me to the kitchen, where I dug through a drawer of brackets, adapters and power cords. If she was disappointed I didn't have a talking espresso machine, she kept it to herself.

I put a white extension cord into her hand and she started for the door.

'Wait, is this what I asked you for?'

'I...I don't remember,' I said. 'Do you need an extension cord?'

'Not really,' she replied, giving it back and trying to figure out what she'd asked for. 'But there is a window that doesn't close between the bathroom and the laundry room. Sam was going to get it, but we both forgot. It must be the building.'

'I know that window. Is it okay if I give it a try?'

'Be my guest,' she said, and we walked through the vacant dorm and descended the stairs to the basement. Mary Katherine's two rooms abutted a bathroom with two showers, two sinks and two stalls. Beyond the bathroom was the laundry room and its insolent window.

While I tugged on the sash, she asked if I minded her stuff in the laundry room. Not at all. I did laundry on weekends. I leaned back for leverage. Also, if I ever heard the shower or sink going, I'd make a u-turn. She thanked me and moved to the side because I was putting my full weight into the window.

'Hey, kids are calling me Miss Kimball. I thought they dropped the 'Miss' here?'

'It means they like you. But don't be surprised if they call you misses or man.'

Out the corner of my eye, I saw her pull a handful of almonds from her pocket and start popping them into her mouth. I told her when my mom was pregnant, she loved blueberry blintzes, strawberry milk, and she couldn't get near a cup of coffee. Mary Katherine said she craved cheese and beer. Then, just as she remembered that she'd asked for a cookie sheet earlier, the window broke free and slammed down on my hand.

'Oh my Gosh,' she blurted, as my face became crimson and my eyes welled up. She motioned for me to show her my hand. The thumb was red and starting to throb. A trickle of blood slid across the knuckle toward the nail.

'You know you can swear. It's okay.'

'Fudge cake,' I said, heading upstairs. 'I need ice.'

Feeling a little guilty, Mary Katherine concluded that Shawna Brophy had to be one strange bird, and Goldie, despite her noble aspirations, was a menace to sisters everywhere.

Twenty-Two

Offering her condolences to my bandaged thumb—just a bruise and a cut—she handed me a plate of peanut butter cookies. I put my beer down to sample one.

'Beer smells so good now,' she said, scratching her belly, and I asked if she was having a boy or a girl. 'Ask Sam. We had an ultrasound three days ago, but I covered my ears when the nurse told us.'

She started to giggle because the baby was moving—not real kicking but enough to surprise her. I caught her looking around again, checking out the fire irons, the vase behind the sofa, the cast iron train bank on the windowsill and the picture of my mother. In the photo my mom was leaning against a metal railing as the surf broke behind her. My mother's face, framed by dark shoulder length hair, lighting up the image.

'That's my mom,' I said. 'She died last year.'

'I'm sorry, how old was she?'

'I think sixty-seven, but no one really knows.'

'That's a pretty dress,' said Mary Katherine, looking at the dress's simple neckline and the neat bow on my mother's waist.

'She had closets of dresses like that. She had a thing for Jackie O.'

Mary Katherine wondered if I'd kept any. It seemed an odd question, but I'd soon realize it wasn't, not for a woman who made quilts. I told her I had a few in mothballs and added that I was a mamma's boy. She was still gazing at the photo, so I told her it was taken by my grandfather on Thanksgiving Day and that despite my mother's warm smile it was fifteen degrees outside. Then I asked how she was settling in.

'I could grow mushrooms down there, but in Sam's place I feel like an elf.'

'You and your fiancé are rookies, what do you expect?'

'It's a little too early to call him that,' she said.

'Really? Well, I won't make that mistake again,' I said, a little surprised by the enthusiasm in her voice, and I offered her a seat.

'If there were a hockey game on, but I'm beat. I can't believe you guys start classes before eight.'

'Sounds like you've been spoiled, Kimball.'

'Not anymore,' she replied. 'Not anymore.'

The class looked at my thumb and asked if I'd tried to hit Iafrati again. They doubled over when I told them his girlfriend's window had done the deed. Elizabeth Perkins suggested I avoid the pair altogether.

'Okay, open up your books to page...' I said.

'Come on, Greenie,' begged Josh, 'could we not talk about literature for once?'

Sensing weakness, the rest jumped in. Voices assailed me from all sides. We talk about books every single day. Can't we do something fun? I begged them to cut me some slack because I was injured, but Miles suggested we meditate. Josh looked at him like he was crazy, and Elizabeth asked to look at an art book. Now there was an idea, so I left determined to find the most painful art book imaginable. Folk, Abstract Neo-Impressionism, Grecian urns—they'd pay for their insolence. By the time I'd trotted across the walk from Wickersham to the library, however, my need for revenge had dissipated. I went for Picasso. We'd look at his blue period. I'd tell them about the women in the asylum. Then I'd assign a few short stories I usually saved for juniors to make them stop complaining.

Returning to class, I pushed through the door and the hair went up on the back of my neck. Too quiet. They must have left, run off to share some stupid joke on me. I was prepared to stomp off to the teachers' room and write cut slips for the whole lot, but, no, they were in their seats. Perfect little children trying not to smile, they'd polished their halos just for me. In front of each were a clean piece of paper and a ready pencil.

'Miracles happen,' I said, putting the book on a desk and going to the board. When I turned my back, I heard the rustle of papers, the shuffle of mischievous feet and a few thumps. I didn't turn around. I wrote Picasso's Blue Period in chalk. What do you see going on in these pictures? How do they make you feel?

When I turned around—kids slumped, papers and pens on the floor, feet up. Some feigned sleep. Others had pulled their hoods over their heads. Josh had even emptied his book bag onto the floor. But they were all peeking to see how I'd respond to the birthday card they'd spent most of a study hall making.

'Aw, you guys suck,' I said, and the room erupted into a raucous *Happy Birthday to Greenie. He's such a meanie. His homework's obscenie. Happy Birthday to Greenie.* I didn't have the heart to tell them my birthday wasn't for another week.

After class I detoured past the new writing lab to make sure the door was locked. It had been left open a few times, and if I didn't find students playing games on the computers or changing desktop images, I'd find candy wrappers and soda bottles. Today the door was open, but the room was empty and, most importantly, odor free.

Our head of maintenance, Dorsey Lefevre, had overseen the conversion of the former staff lounge in the basement of Wickersham—not to be confused with the faculty room where we received our mail and drank burnt coffee—into our new writing lab. He'd wanted to gut the room before installing the counters, cabinets and computers. But Don didn't have the money for new walls, and when he found out the carpet was only two years old, he decided it was good enough, too.

In the gruff matter-of-fact style of a six-foot-five prematurely gray but undeniably rugged former Technical Sergeant in the Air Force, Dorsey informed him that the lounge had been a smoker's den for more than thirty years. But Don hemmed and hawed because he was determined to stay on budget.

So Dorsey outfitted the new lab, and on they day it opened, Goldie took her class there to work on essays. Within ten minutes, however, two boys had begged out to see the nurse because their eyes were watering. Sure, they were exaggerating, but how could She call them fakers when half the class had pulled their shirts over their mouths and the room really did smell like an ashtray. Determined to triumph over all unsavory odors, Goldie dragged out her steam cleaner—Art had found it at church flea market—and went over the rug for two hours that night. The room still smelled though, so she opened the windows and ran a giant fan for three days straight while her class worked in winter coats. When the room continued to smell like an old man bar, she tried baking soda, saucers full of vinegar, kitty litter and bags of charcoal, which she hung like piñatas in every corner.

Meanwhile, Gunnar, still desperate for dirt on the woman he'd dubbed the Diva of Diversity, and Candy were sneaking into the lab each night for a smoke. Neither of them actually liked cigarettes—Gunnar only lit up when he was drinking—but hearing Goldie complain at meals, made them giggle like little kids. Yes, enjoyed her indignant scowl as she indicted Don for his cheapness, but I still threatened to rat out my buddies if they didn't stop their subterfuge. Then I went to Don and offered up part of my department's discretionary budget to save us all a headache and get the stinky carpet out of the writing lab. Two weeks and a third coat of paint later, Goldie stopped whining and Gunnar and Goldie were calling me a traitor. I wonder what they would have called me if they knew how many resumes and cover letters I'd sent out.

Mary Katherine liked playing backgammon with Candy in the faculty room. Sitting in the big chairs with the board on the coffee table, they did not look like overworked teachers. Candy taught Health—she spent a lot of time teaching kids about the dangers of tobacco—and chased down receipts as the Director of Student Activities, so her afternoons often took on a leisurely appearance. Mary Katherine, tutoring and working in the dorm, had more free time on her hands than she knew what to do with. To stay busy, she was helping Gunnar. His European History class had finished studying The Russian Revolution and now were writing and producing a musical about Lenin, Stalin, and Trotsky. Mary Katherine thought Gunnar had gone off the deep when she heard about the chorus line of dancing assassins, but she agreed to help each student keep a journal analyzing the facts behind their play. The show was going to be performed as dinner theater on the Ides of March. Gunnar had already started to make ice axes out of cardboard and tinfoil for his dancers, and the entire school was buzzing in anticipation.

Unlike his girlfriend, Sam had very little free time. He did, however, carve out space for Date Night. At Forno Famiglia they sat in a booth and read their menus by candlelight. She was tempted by the wild mushroom raviolis and the hangar steak, the sparkling water and the fizzy lemonade, the key lime pie and the bread pudding. And the wine list, of course, for she coveted a glass of pinot, which for propriety's sake Sam would have to order.

The meal was a success. Mary Katherine uttered the words 'hate' and 'apartment' only seven or eight times each, and Sam's garlic-fueled indigestion abated by the time his entrée arrived. Afterward, happily full and genuinely excited, he took her hand while his fork hovered over a piece of tiramisu and he told her a story about Roger's yellow lab eating a candy bar wrapper and all. Half listening but relieved he wasn't talking about drugs, diversity, discipline or dress codes, she shot him a sly smile to let him know he might get lucky. She felt guilty changing the subject.

'So did you ask for a letter?'

'Not yet,' he said. 'But I've got others.'

'You need something from this year and he's your department head.' Sam started scratching the tablecloth with his fork. 'You can also invite Don or Gunnar Davis to a class and get a letter from them.'

Sam laid his fork alongside his plate and refolded his napkin.

'Team teaching with Greenie sucked. It magnified every blip in every lesson a thousand times.'

'I wish I hadn't pushed you to take the job,' she said.

'I got off to a bad start. That's not your fault.' Sam was smoothing out his napkin now, fingering his water glass, figuring things out. Mary Katherine felt a pang.

'Ask for the letter and see what comes of it?'

'That I can do,' he said, brushing aside his anxiety, and after they'd polished off two decaf cappuccinos, he dropped his napkin in his chair and said he had to take care of something. Mary Katherine watched him walk away and wondered was he was so focused all of a sudden. And where had that beautiful humility come from? And why was he wearing clean pants and an ironed shirt on a Thursday? And when had the lights dimmed? And why was their waiter lurking behind a wall, peeking into the dining room at them? Her palms became damp—more proof that her body belonged to someone else.

Sam returned to the table with clean hands but no ring. He did have a proposal though. Will you look over some of my preps? My head is so...I just can't tell what's wrong anymore.

Twenty-Three

I was reading in bed when I heard a door close on the other side of the building. The pitched ceiling was bathed in soft light. In the summertime fireflies snuck through the screens and tried to make love to the blue-green display of my stereo. Tonight, except for my neighbor's arrival, there was dead silence, not even the bump of windows shifting in their frames. Beside me was a rotary phone with a broken clapper, so when someone called, I heard the ringing downstairs.

'Hello?' There was a pause, during which I could hear music. I hoped it might be Mary Katherine with a question about the party, but it turned out to be Cass.

'Happy Birthday…again,' she said. 'Is there any way at all I can get out of Iafrati's class? I need the credit, but I figured I can do an independent with you?'

'You'd need permission from the Dean of Studies.'

'Department head first, which is you. Then I go to Mr. Davis.'

'Don't you think it reeks of favoritism?' I asked.

'It's only favoritism if I'm your favorite.'

'That's not what the word means.'

'Look I already asked Mr. Driscoll, but he was too busy. He suggested you.'

'He really said that?' I asked.

'I wish I could get credit for being in Ms. Remlap's justice club. All we do is sit through presentations and read handouts.'

'On diversity?'

'Black Panthers, Stonewall Riots, Gandhi, Dr. King—we've been learning about social movements and what makes them work. Next week we're talking about institutional discrimination and having a debate on affirmative action.'

'Wow, that actually sounds educational.'

'We even got a few teachers doing the work with us. The funniest is Ms. Dafoe, who likes chilling with me in the back of the room. She says she represents all the oppressed lesbians in upstate New York. Anyway, the cookies are good and all, but the whole thing's a little weird coming from a white lady. So are you going to let me do an independent study?'

Maybe I was a fool. Maybe I was a little scared. But I didn't hesitate, not for a second. 'Only if you promise to do the work,' I said, 'and to stop with the jokes.'

'And if I don't?'

'Excellent, you promised. That's my birthday present right there,' I said. 'I'm going to hang up now.' And I did.

The day before my real birthday Mary Katherine knocked on my door as I was running off to basketball practice. Wearing a brown sweater, a brown belt and brown maternity pants, she was carrying a pan of brownies.

'You're turning thirty-five soon?' she asked.

Her sad edge was gone. Her eyes had new light. I checked her hands because, like everyone on The Mount, I kept expecting to find a ring there.

'Tomorrow's my real birthday. Kara's got one this week, too. But she's a baby, just thirty.'

'I'm going to make you guys a cake,' she said. 'The party's Saturday?'

'You don't have to make anything.'

She told me Sam was on duty and she had Saturday to kill. Besides, baking was one of the things that kept her sane. She offered to put little tennis players on the cake.

'If you're up for a challenge,' I said, 'roses, lots so everyone can have one.'

'I like seeing who fights for the roses. Lets you know who the divas are. But there's another reason I came up. The brownies are a bribe. There's a Ranger's game on tomorrow—hockey. I tried to watch in the dorm once, but the girls screamed bloody murder. I could probably go to a boys' dorm, but those guys smell like feet. And Sam would rather have me be a television whore than spring for cable.'

She'd offered me a cake. She needed a place to hang. Who was I to let prudence stand in the way of hockey? So I told her I had duty, but I'd leave the door open, and she and Sam should help themselves to my ice cream.

There was a fine snow falling, just a dusting, but under the light of the Sugar Shack—the only light I could see at five in the morning—it seemed like a blizzard. My bedroom was ice cold. Even in socks my feet were freezing on the wood floor. I felt like the only person in the world, told myself that staring out the window into the darkness while others dreamed of sunshine was the flip side of being cynical. Let Gunnar and Candy scheme. Let Goldie fight for crumbs. And just as that epiphany wandered lonely through my mind, I saw a bundled figure wading through the snowy pool of light by the Sugar Shack.

An hour and a half later I found Goldie's tracks in the snow, heading from her back door down the drive and along the road. Little steps, small feet. Every fourth or fifth step there was an extra divot taken from the now crusty layer of snow. I wasn't much of an outdoorsman, but today I was a tracker. In the gray morning light, I followed the prints past the Sugar Shack and Ann Lee dorm, but at the windiest stretch thirty yards before the road dropped down to the Dairy Barn and Wickersham I lost the trail. But, magically, the little shoeprints reappeared and veered to the left off the road toward an aluminum-sided building where we kept the tractor. Maybe she was dropping off some recycling—the bins were just beyond the garage— but when I followed the tracks, they disappeared into the door at the side of the building. The only other tracks in the snow belonged to a large pair of work boots. The two sets went in. The two sets came out.

That afternoon Art was visiting another school, swapping some unused soccer shorts for some unused lacrosse jerseys, so there was Goldie in a corner of the cafeteria having a private lunch with big rugged Dorsey Lefevre. In the Air Force he'd worked on jets and helicopters, and although I usually saw him in oil-stained overalls, he cleaned up well. We'd talked a bunch of times about snowmobiling and ice fishing and his tricked out pickup truck, which was huge and had a custom exhaust you could hear from a quarter mile away. It made me sad to think he might be dogging my friend's wife, but when I eyed his boots, I was sure, dead sure, it was him.

There was a birthday card in my mailbox from a woman named Zoe, a graduate student I'd met on a tennis court in August. She had a good kick serve, a 3.8 GPA and her own condoms. I think she was Jewish but wasn't a hundred percent sure where to place her aquiline nose, straight brown hair and the seven freckles on her back. After we had dinner together, she gave my favorite bartender flack for not having some crazy French liqueur. She also went through my wallet while I was in the bathroom and lied about it when I caught her.

Five hours after getting my card I felt like a trespasser in my own apartment. In the kitchen I found a single spoon and a bowl in the dish rack. I was glad she'd helped herself to ice cream and not surprised she'd come without Sam. Turning on the TV, I saw she'd been watching the cooking channel. At my bookcase I wondered what she'd looked at and imagined sharing my theory about bookcases. Quite simply, I believe the books you've read tell your story. But it's the ones you haven't read, the unfinished business you keep front and center, that reveals even more about your desires, your dreams, what you feed on when you're alone.

During my first year on at The Mount, I discovered in the librarian's office a barrister bookcase that had been entombed behind a wall of National Geographic magazines. Inside I found an early history of the Shaker community that explained the Articles of Separation that governed the lives of the men and women. I leafed through another book on communist utopias, a treatise on farming by an agriculturally inclined elder named Thomas Dwendle, and a sketchbook left by a visitor in 1907—the same year my grandfather emigrated from Russia. The drawings in this last book were faint and fading, but they'd been reproduced so often I recognized them at once. One was of my house, the Shaker pharmacy, which at the time was connected to a larger, now missing building by a second story bridge. I'd wondered ever since about the people who'd worked there, how they'd combated the lethal drafts, the black flies and the celibacy; if they'd also fallen in love with the meticulous paneling and knotty oak floors?

The last book I found, a slim red journal with frayed edges and an arthritic spine, crackled in protest when I opened it. But then warm yellow paper and neat cursive entries tugged me into the life of a woman named Sister Emily Danbridge, a Shaker who'd lived a hundred and fifty years earlier, and who had known I would some day cross paths with her story.

Year after year, I am amazed by the boys, their heads down and their fingers working intently on their slates. It is so deathly cold. The treacherous snow is always crawling over the windowsills and the wind is always rattling the shutters. However, the boys do not notice. Those small wonders, orphaned, indentured or brought to our Holy Mount by hopeful parents, labor on in the pale winter light.

I imagined her walking from the schoolhouse down the hard-packed dirt roads lined with wheel ruts and iron fences, her footsteps making no sound, her form drawing a clean line through time. Like all Shakers she wore the peasant garb of her ancestors and was careful that every door latch, apron and sewing needle stayed in place. People riding from Boston to Albany—the Post Road ran through the heart of the community—often stopped to admire these pious utopians. Separate from the 'world,' they moved with perpetual Sabbath ease. However, during Emily's short walk down the road, the snow would melt. It would become summer and the boys she'd left behind were now girls. As she walked, she'd pass lilacs that budded and bloomed in a single glance. She'd hear the sound of a wagon become the sound of Candy Dafoe's tractor. She'd see a vapor of people trudging toward the cafeteria.

When she was teaching, there had been no classrooms in

Wickersham. But then again there had never been so many interesting faces on The Holy Mount. She was fascinated by the black kids, thrilled by the Asians, and awed by the tall girls who ran after balls and cursed. She chuckled when they talked about ghosts and imagined noises in their closets. There were no babies in the walls she wanted to tell them. If two Shakers fell from grace, the couple could leave the community and build a family. They would be denounced, as was the custom, but the babies lived.

Mary Katherine, wearing her nice wool pants and one of Sam's shirts, made a beeline for my bookcase.

'You steal this?' she asked, picking up the journal.

'I borrowed it from he library, semi-permanently.'

'You did steal it. So what's the allure of this Sister what's-her-name?'

'Sister Emily, she's my Shaker ghost, and I'm the Winter Shaker she looks after.'

Mary Katherine was confused, so I explained that Winter Shakers were people who arrived with the frost and left when the mud dried in the spring. Usually men, they were some of the best and worst workers in the villages, but they weren't real Shakers and they didn't always fit in. During her life, Sister Emily may have known many of these men, but she'd written only about one.

His name is Owen Warland, and his clothes, which he told the Elders he inherited from an uncle, are far too big for his frame. He also blinks incessantly, a phenomenon that gives us the impression he has difficulty seeing or he is, perhaps, sensitive to light. He is a stooped and homely man, neither confident nor pious in appearance. Being from the world, Mr. Warland should be expected to be a more social creature, but he is a quiet soul who seems to notice very little. He chats with the brethren when addressed, but mostly he keeps to himself. I have overheard that he completes his duties in a melancholy manner and struggles with direction. It is not kind of me to repeat these criticisms and put them in writing, but I do feel sympathy for the man.

'Maybe she had the hots for him?' said Mary Katherine, now snug on my sofa. 'He meant something to her, right? Otherwise, why bother putting him in her journal?'

'Maybe she was bored. As far as I know, she never went anywhere.'

'I don't buy that. Shaker women were still human.'

'The memoir's eight pages and she doesn't say. So we're stuck.'

Mary Katherine ran a finger over the journal but stopped because the cloth cover was old and maybe she'd damage it. Then she surprised even herself when she said, 'Let's finish it then. Doesn't she deserve that?'

'What exactly does she deserve?'

'To get her story right, even if you make it up. Isn't that what fiction is about, Mr. English teacher?'

Cautionary tales, I told her. That's what all fiction was to me. Also, I didn't do stories. I did irony—like how I loved The Mount despite being its prisoner. Stories needed plots, resolutions, and I wanted an open ending. Besides, it was wrong to give anyone homework on his birthday. But then I wondered what it'd be like to work with her on the thing and changed my mind. She complained she didn't know squat about Shakers and Sam said I was horrible to work with, but I fetched her two books—*The Spirit of the Shakers* from the bookcase and *The Shaker Dilemma* from under the side table it kept from wobbling—and I told her to piss or get off the pot.

'Fine, you start, and I'm making no promises,' she said, looking underdressed without a quilt on her lap, and she asked if I was religious. I told her I'd had a Bar Mitzvah and I believed in God, but I hadn't been to temple in years.

'I've fallen away, too,' she said. 'If I'm going to be with Sam, I should be better about going. Think I'll start when I feel less pressure. From myself, by the way. Don't get me wrong, in theory I'm a half-decent Catholic, but too many things are going on right now. So was your Sister Emily a good Shaker?'

'Seems devoted and sober. But at the same time a journal like this was a no-no.'

'No journals?'

'Shakers kind of lived like bees, socially progressive but they were expected to live simply and follow the rules as God had given them to Mother Ann Lee. I always imagined Sister Emily sort of secretly working things out.'

'And what does your ghost think of us?'

'The single mom and the Jew?' I said 'Beats the hell out of me?'

'This is gonna be fun,' she said, and she shook my hand so I'd know she was serious.

Twenty-Four

Wearing a leather football helmet he'd borrowed from a display case outside the headmaster's office, Gunnar asked to be introduced to my date. Our other host, Candy, was decked out in a yellow boa she'd found in her grandmother's attic. Rolly was in spats and a top hat from the student production of *A Christmas Carol* and Kara was wearing the bottom half of a field hockey outfit. Mary Katherine, my date, was clad in second-hand green wool maternity pants with little baby ducks on them.

'Put this on,' said Gunnar, 'I found it in the trunk of my car.' He handed me a hat that made it look like an arrow was going through my head. He also gave me a bottle of Molson's Golden, while Candy adorned me with a strand of love beads.

'Wicked,' I said, inspecting the blue plastic beads and wishing I'd paid more attention to the dress code: used and stolen, the kitschier the better. The theme was Gunnar's idea, and in the spirit of the party his apartment was decorated with a Nixon poster, a disco ball and a sculpture of a cowboy carved out of 'borrowed' Velveeta cheese. For Kara's and my joint thirtieth birthday party, no expense had been spared. Rolly had carted up three cases of good beer. Art had gotten the kitchen to barbecue a tray of ribs. Tiki torches lit the fire escape so the smokers wouldn't fall off. Candy had brought disco CDs. There was even a cake loaded with roses, courtesy of my downstairs neighbor and a TV playing nonstop zombie movies.

'I've got a necklace for you, too, my little love bird,' said Candy dropping beads over Kara's head and giving her a hug. 'You better have fun tonight.'

I hadn't taken a good look at Kara in a while. She looked still skinnier, there were circles under her eyes and her hair was flat. Sure, she strutted around a little and made jokes about being the captain of the field hockey team *and* the Mardi Gras queen. She even tapped the neck of her beer bottle against mine to show me there were no hard feelings, but I still wanted to grab her by the shoulders and shake her.

Mary Katherine congratulated Kara and stole a sip of her beer.

'I won't tell Sam,' said Kara, and she kissed her on the cheek. 'So is it as good as they say when you're preggers?'

'Usually we're too tired from planning Bombs and Books. I feel like I'm teaching that stupid class. I blame Jeff. He gave it to him.'

'Men love things that go boom,' said Kara, poking the cheese cowboy with a Ritz cracker.

At midnight, Kara and I stood on milk crates in the center of the room and received our presents. I got two bottles of maple syrup Gunnar had stolen from the bookcase in Kyle's office. He'd replaced them with empties and assumed the real ones would never be missed. Kara received a book of half-finished pornographic crossword puzzles, a sweatshirt that belonged to an expelled student and a pair of work gloves Goldie borrowed from Roger's classroom.

The room demanded speeches. Kara said no fucking way, but I stood atop my milk crate and told them I'd been thinking about this day for six months. Thirty-five. It was the number that had inspired me to take out my earring. Thirty-five. A bell ringing for the demise of my mythical sports careers. In the NFL I'd have been on the junk heap long ago. In the NBA I'd have been a grizzled vet. In baseball I might've been okay for a few years, but baseball wasn't my thing. And tennis, my favorite, was dominated by teenagers, so I'd be toast. However, this was a mythical career, so I was entitled to this day of appreciation, columns in the local papers and, of course, this wonderful farewell banquet as I embarked upon a new mythical career as a jazz musician. I'd play the trumpet, wear sunglasses everywhere and barely exercise. I'd also have a cool name—Commodeus Pantz— and I'd be the slickest horn player on the east coast. Thank you. Thank you all.

When I was done, Gunnar snatched my beer and Candy wrestled me to the floor. (I'll never understand their need to beat me up.) Then she sat on me and wished me a Happy Birthday.

'I think thirty-five is going to be your year, Greenie.'

'I think you're right,' I said, and we looked over at Mary Katherine who was cutting her cake.

'Check out that woman,' said Candy. 'There's something about her that doesn't make sense to me. It's like sometimes I totally forget she's with Sam. I said that to her, too, and she thanked me like it was a compliment.'

'She's smart,' I said.

'She's got us pegged. She called Gunnar the brains. Me the muscle, and guess what you are?'

'The spleen?'

'To her, my friend, you're our conscience, our heart, our man of faith.'

'Isn't that Sam's gig?'

'According to her he's the worrier. So, dude, what do you two do up there when Sam's on duty?'

'Hey, I am Switzerland. I got no stake, so don't start any rumors.'

Mary Katherine was coming over, so we shut up.

'You're in shape, Greenie,' she teased, handing me a piece of cake. 'Even with a bad thumb, you should have held out a little longer.'

Candy scoffed. 'I was about to take that thumb as a trophy. Well, maybe on his birthday I'll let him keep it.'

'This is why the Shakers didn't celebrate birthdays,' I said, as Mary Katherine, nibbled on a rose and pushed around some icing with a plastic fork.

While I was polishing off my birthday cake, Kara brought over a pair of mittens she'd made. I apologized for not getting her anything. She asked for my truck and I offered her the keys, which she took but then shoved back into my shirt pocket. By now the disco ball was spinning and Gunnar was projecting art slides he'd borrowed from a mouse-infested closet on the fifth floor of Wickersham. Mary Katherine glanced at Botticelli's *The Birth of Venus*, which Gunnar referred to as the most pretentious piece of hooey ever painted, and tapped me on the arm.

'There are a few nice people at this place,' she said, 'and some of them actually like you.'

'Yeah, they deserve their roses,' I replied.

On cue, Kara told me to shut up and try on my mittens. Candy called me a pussy for wanting a cake with so many flowers. Gunnar told Kara with a truly horrible Spanish accent that she was the real Diva of Diversity and everyone started dancing.

The second Meeting House was an elegant white building with an arched roof and three wide doors in front—one for men, one for women, one for Elders. Like most Shaker buildings, it was designed with the Separation Acts in mind. Mother Ann Lee had believed a division of the sexes would help Shakers flourish. She thought the sexes, like Adam and Eve, were disparate life forces that created havoc when allowed to mingle, so many of the buildings had separate entrances and dual staircases. The world might need the union of men and women, but The Holy Mount was not the world but a haven where men and women adored God and worked apart as Brothers and Sisters.

For this reason, the building—like the wild poppies growing in our fields—had become a strange symbol to Sister Emily. A library now, it was still a vibrant sanctuary, but the books it contained had brought the outside world onto sacred ground. Many of the stories made her blush. The pictures were too private. Yet she understood their necessity, for these children would not be spending their lives on The Mount.

That Sunday night, someone crept to the upper level of the library and slipped through a propped open door. On the dark mezzanine he groped around until he felt the hand of the girl who'd snuck up after study hall. Above the wind made a hollow sound over the bowed roof. The pair lay some cushions on the floor. The girl's top came off. The boy's pants were undone. But then an arm of light slashed across their bodies, and the forms of Gunnar and Candy filled the doorway. The boy pulled up his pants and ran downstairs. Cass turned her back on the flashlight.

'Who was that?' asked Candy, as a door shut in the lower library.

'Nobody,' said Cass. 'Can you guys give me a few seconds?'

That same night I was walking across campus when I ran into Kwame ten minutes after check-in. I would've given him a hard time, but he would've started a twenty-minute conversation and then had a legitimate excuse.

'Hurry,' I said. 'Maybe you'll get lucky.'

'Already did,' he replied, not smiling, just stating a fact so I'd know what he was up to. Candy, who knew all the kids' business, told me he'd been creeping with Debbie Tremont. The girl was still with Per, officially, but that didn't stop them. But why brag? With his secret a secret, he could pretend he wasn't hurting anyone. He could keep his friendships and his aura of apathy. With it out, he'd be just another dog.

The next day I found my Gunnar alone in the cafeteria after dinner and sat with a cup of coffee. I thanked him for my birthday party. He shoveled a forkful of cold Chicken ala King into his mouth and said he'd had a good time. He also told me Kyle had discovered his maple syrup missing.

'I'm not telling him where it went,' he said, poking a butter pat with a plastic stirrer. 'You keeping up with the talk in the girls' dorms?'

'They figure out who Cass's mystery date was?'

'It changes every fifteen minutes. Last I heard it was a guy from the Greasy Mart. Before that it was you.'

'Oh great,' I said, 'that's all I need. But hey, I got a story you're going to like it.'

A few nights earlier I'd been walking home past the sugar shack after putting my dorm to bed when Cassandra stepped out from behind a woodpile. She was wearing a bulky sweater and a dark skirt. I told her to go back to the dorm as she reached into her pocket and absentmindedly pulled out a plastic cigarette lighter. Without thinking, I took it from her. I wasn't about to give her a smoking point though, so I gave it back. By then my stomach was on fire and my feet were ice. I asked if she was cold.

'Only when the wind blows,' she said, and she started lifting the hem of her skirt.

'Don't,' I said, looking away. It wasn't a request. It was a plea.

Gunnar was, indeed, thrilled. 'You gotta like that kid. Huge balls, ready for college two years ago. Seriously, if you guaranteed I wouldn't get caught, I'd sneak around the mezzanine with her. So, is that the end of the story?'

'I made her go back to the dorm. But she did write me an interesting email over break.'

'Before the woodpile thing? So there's a history?'

'She told me she snuck up to my place the night before the kids went home. She was going to knock on my door, but you and Candy and your bottle of tequila beat her there. But, get this, as she's hiding in the shadows on the hill behind my house, guess who she sees lurking under the window?'

'I don't know, Mary Poppins?'

'No, Goldie.'

Gunnar howled. 'She really is a spider. Man, do you know her social justice club is writing an open letter to the headmaster? The kids have discovered, all by themselves, of course, that we've never had a department head or upper level administrator who was a person of color or a woman.'

'Scandal,' I said.

'Candy says they're lobbying to publish it in the alumni magazine, but it's probably just going to be a broadsheet they post around campus.'

'I'll bet you anything a copy finds its say to the board,' I said. 'I should write my own broadsheet, tell everyone about the trials and tribulations of being a Jewish department head?'

'That'll win hearts and minds. Goldie didn't see Cass at your place, did she?'

'I don't think so, but since you love dirt, you're going to love this. Mind you, I've got no real proof, but I think Goldie might be banging

Dorsey Lefevre.'

Ah, the things power makes one do. Gunnar's vibrated like a little kid who just got out of a bouncy castle. I reminded him I was just following footprints in the snow and Art Remlap was our buddy.

'Of course,' said Gunnar, sliding his mug around his tray. 'We don't make any wild accusations. But if we catch her...' He rubbed his hands together and licked his lips. 'So if you knew you weren't going to get caught, would you rather do lusty young Cassandra or brazen Goldie?'

'Cass is a kid.'

'She's eighteen, man. But, you know, you could just wait a few months and visit her in college.'

'You done that?'

'No, so who would you do?'

'Goldie would be an adventure, but she'd have way too many rules.'

'And your buddy Mary Katherine? You dig that bump of hers?'

'I don't think I could get past the he's-not-my-fiancé.'

'You liar, the woman digs sports, bakes better than Goldie, knows the Cold War, and she's hooking me up with some girl at a conference next week. Oh, and don't forget she's got the stones to quit a job, move here and kick it with Sammy? That puts her at the top of my list. So who rounds out your top five?'

'I'd need to think about it.'

'You loser,' said Gunnar. 'To be murdered in my sleep, I'd go with Kara at two. To be driven insane, Goldie's next, but I'd bump her up if I could slap a muzzle on her. To lose my job, Cass, because she can't keep her mouth shut. Speaking of big mouths, Goldie's been talking about Cass visiting your place with pizza?'

'That's because Miss Goldie drove her right to my front door.'

'The foxy feminist left that part out.'

'Does that surprise you?'

'Man, I'd shit my pants if Cass showed up at my apartment with a couple slices of pepperoni,' replied Gunnar.

'I gave her another pep talk and sent her home.'

'You're a good man, Jeff Green.'

'Not as good as I'd like to be.'

'Do you know how many lonely teachers dream about that scenario?'

'At least two,' I said, and I put my empty coffee mug on his tray.

'You know, you have to tell Don about her. Just clean up the story a little.'

'The kid's harmless.'

'You got to get out in front of this thing, man, before there's more talk. Besides, if you don't tell him, I will. In the meantime, stay away from woodpiles.'

I told him I was doing my best.

Twenty-Five

A t 4:09 in the morning, Gunnar was roused from a sound sleep by the deep growl of a muffler. Dorsey Lefevre's truck. It had to be. In seconds Gunnar was out of bed, pulling on winter boots on and scurrying up to the garage. He'd seen Dorsey and Goldie after lunch, and they looked suspicious as all hell, but when Gunnar crept up to the garage, no luck. The spot where Dorsey parked was empty. The next night Gunnar bolted out of bed at 4:27 certain he'd heard the big bad truck cruising up the road. But once again, the spot was empty and the garage was dark.

This is stupid, he thought, and he decided it was time to get sneaky. So he bought himself a spotlight with a motion sensor and a pair of walkie-talkies, combined them using a soldering iron and duct tape and hid the sensor near the garage. That way when Dorsey pulled into his spot and tripped the sensor—the light bulb was no longer part of the equation—the second walkie-talkie would start chirping next to Gunnar's pillow. He was determined to catch the tricky vixen and get some sleep, but two nights later he raced up to the garage at 3:31 to find a windblown plastic bag stuck to his motion sensor. One night later at a few ticks before five he scared the shit out of a coyote that had been sniffing around the henhouse.

Two weeks of poor sleep were getting to Gunnar. His head hurt, his eyes were bloodshot, and he was starting to get mad that I wasn't helping.

Hanging out with Gunnar was making me feel extra dirty, so I was extra nice to everyone. I took Joe on my Hands-to-Work crew, drove Josh to a fast food restaurant for a cheeseburger and a chili-filled baked potato, and introduced Mary Katherine to Lana Wilson-Wade, who was sewing her family history into a quilt and needed help. And while I was banking as much goodwill as possible—and enjoying myself immensely—the snow returned to cover the brown patches that had appeared like a pox all over campus. With the snow came a photographer, who took pictures of photogenic students playing in the white stuff. Because I'd taken out my earring, she asked me to pose with Hodge. For the photo, Candy parked the tractor by the hen house, and Hodge and I sat on the end of the flatbed with cups of hot chocolate. Hodge was wearing a ski parka. I was decked out in a school sweatshirt and a green stocking cap.

'Look collegiate,' I said.

'Cheers, loverboy,' he replied, blowing into his cup.

'Neither of you guys is smiling,' exclaimed the photographer. 'Come on, act like you've been working hard and you're enjoying a well-deserved break.'

I was able to force a grin, but Hodge noticed Harriet Barth down the road. I should've have asked why they weren't talking, but the shutter began clicking and the photographer kept cajoling us until Hodge finally showed some teeth.

'Okay, now I've got to find two boys with funny names,' said the photographer. 'Pear and the other's Kiwi or something.'

'Kwame,' replied Hodge, 'and they're both fruits.'

The woman with the camera thanked him and went off to shoot Kwame and Per in the gym. Neither of them had stuck it out on the basketball team, but they put on uniforms and ran around anyway. The light in the gym was so bad though the photographer couldn't shoot there. Instead, she put the two back in street clothes and stationed them behind sewing machines. Unaware of what his friend was doing with his girlfriend, Per joked he was going to make me some suede underpants for the next time I visited Cass. Kwame, annoyed that Per was making fun of his advisor, bet him five bucks he couldn't sew a straight line. Later, Per denied having taken the challenge, but there was no denying the fact that he'd sewn his hand to the fabric and got dizzy at the sight of his own blood. That night, kids began peeking at me at the teachers' table. They'd lean close to each other, peek again and burst out laughing. I heard the nicknames *G Spot* and *Groinie*, and was forced to ignore them.

When Don finally asked me to stop by his office, I peed three times in ten minutes and walked over with a dry mouth. The door was closed because he was talking with Danny Lemansky and his parents. The kid had a history of drugs and cutting—arms and classes—but now he was just failing his courses. Don wanted to let him finish the year and spare him the stigma of being kicked out, but after a little push from his manly Science teacher and a little shove from his persuasive female English teacher, the boy's fate was sealed. Besides, Danny had piled up more than forty dorm violations and he'd forgotten how to do laundry. I guess it was time for him to go.

By the time the Lemankys filed out of the office, I had hives on my chest. Don asked me to sit, closed the door, and moved behind his unusually messy desk.

'Something has come to my attention,' he said, pulling an envelope from under his blotter. My name was written on the envelop in block letters. I turned it over and saw that it was sealed. 'I expected you to say something. How did you think you could get away with it?' Don raised an eyebrow and cocked his head. I wanted to tear my shirt off and start scratching.

'If I'd known,' he continued, pulling another envelope out of his jacket pocket, 'I would have liked to have been there.' Now I had two envelopes and no clue what he was talking about. 'The first is a note, a little serendipity from the Board. Since you're interim for the entire year now, they approved a modest raise. The other is from me. I know you're pretty health conscious, but I figured you wouldn't turn down ice cream. I just wanted to show my appreciation and wish you a Happy Birthday.'

I graciously accepted my gift and because he knew nothing about nothing and less about me and Cassandra, I said goodbye without making anyone look like a fool.

The next time she popped in to watch my television, Mary Katherine programmed her favorite channels into my remote control.

She came over a week or so after that, discovered faceoff wasn't for half an hour, and explained the difference between Jesuits and Franciscans. On her next free night she went to Gunnar's to watch a documentary on the French-Indian War. Having written her college thesis on Washington and Fort Necessity, the film was old news, but it gave her the chance to eat popcorn and drink half a beer. A few days later, she returned to my place, made raviolis in my kitchen and didn't give me any. But fours nights later she dropped off oatmeal cookies and chided me for not having made up a story about Sister Emily.

Instead of a Shaker tale, I told her about my walks home with my fourth-grade heroes, Bobby Doherty and Joey Salerno, and how every day after football practice, they'd mesmerize me with stories. Bobby, blessed with impeccable timing and an irresistible smirk, loved to act out all the racy scenes in his sister's diary. In a pint-sized falsetto, he'd swoon, he'd coo, he'd close his eyes and flutter his long pale lashes while a half dozen of us hung on every desperate sigh. And by the time he'd finally embraced his sweetie pie, we were rolling around on someone's immaculate lawn in our practice uniforms and humping their bushes. Not to be outdone, Joey became a master of the prank phone call. Born with an uncanny ear and absolutely no shame, he'd once rung up Bobby's mother—always his favorite target—and in a stumbling voice that was a dead ringer for our principal's set up an entire morning of emergency parent-teacher conferences.

My friends clearly had the gift, that gather-round-and-listen confidence that made every walk home a grand occasion. My mother, another lover of grand occasions, fully understood why they were so important to me. She used to tell me about seeing Maria Callas and Pablo Casals on a snowy December night in Washington D.C. This was back in the 60s when mom was just getting into Chanel dresses and pillbox hats. Anyway, as she was taking her seat in the National Theater, Mom heard excited whispers that Jackie Kennedy was in the house. Where? Where? No one seemed to know, but magically just as the music began, there she was on high in one of the boxes, beyond beautiful, beyond dignified. My mom couldn't have asked for more (oh, it was her honeymoon, too, but she usually left that part out, so it was easy to forget), but then there was a flutter of curtains, more movement in the box, and John F. Kennedy slid into a seat beside his regal wife. Then Maria Callas opened her glorious mouth, and my mother was lifted out of her seat. Yup, walking home with Bobby and Joey was like that, maybe better.

When I finished my tale, Mary Katherine was holding her face in her hands and beaming. She loved a quilt—a couple of nine-year old boys, my mom in an expensive dress, an opera star, the First Lady and her man. It didn't matter that it was really Bobby's cousin's diary or it was really Margot Fonteyn in the blizzard, she, too, loved stitching things together until they were greater than the sum of their parts, until they covered her legs and spread like an ocean across the sofa.

'You still in touch with those guys?'

'Bobby died in a boating accident when we were in grade school. I ran into Joey a while ago at the supermarket, but we didn't talk much.'

'That is so not fair,' said Mary Katherine. Then she looked away and fiddled with the remote control because I'd been looking at her too long. For a second I was embarrassed.

A different kind of specter emerged from the mist the next morning. Bundled against the cold, my scarf trailing behind me, I made out the forms of two spirits coming down the road. It was a gray, gusty day, the wind sending a fine spray of ice crystals across the mountainside. Sam was wearing a plaid cap with earflaps. My buddy was huddled in a long wool coat, wearing red mittens and a big red hat. I expected little more than a grunt before they disappeared back into the gray, but Sam flagged me down.

'What's up?' I asked, nodding to Mary Katherine, who smiled only when she saw a green glove on my left hand and a blue mitten on my right.

'How's the class?' he asked.

I told him it wasn't the same without him and I'd heard he was having fun with his elective. Mary Katherine was pushing snow around with her foot and pretending not to listen. Like a gentleman, Sam said he was enjoying himself. Then he thanked me for letting

Kimball use my place.

'You should join the party,' I said.

'I might have to do that,' he replied.

'See you, Greenie,' said Mary Katherine, tugging Sam's elbow, and they walked gingerly back into the mist.

Sam was less civil when he accosted me in the faculty room that afternoon.

'Are you doing some sort of independent study with Cassandra?'.

'She was taking two lit classes and worried about the reading, so I'm letting her write stories.' I stuck my nose in my mailbox and fished out a credit card application. While I feigned interest in my mail, Sam asked if Cass was a good writer.

'She's not bad,' I said, 'but I sort of wish I hadn't agreed to do it. The kid's a pain sometimes.'

'She acts like school is the last thing on her mind.'

'Her transcript says she thinks about it a little,' I said, wishing I hadn't called her a pain because, in truth, it felt like I was betraying her.

The next time Mary Katherine came over, I joked that Sam was getting jealous and made a point of asking how they'd met. She responded by telling me she started almost all their arguments and they usually argued about the stupidest things: vacations, movies, phone bills—it didn't matter. During one phone call, he complained about driving underage students to see the R-rated movies they snuck into. She asked if there were seatbelts in the school vans, and before they knew it, they were arguing the merits of shopping malls. One compared them to town squares, the other to negligent foster parents. Now she couldn't even remember which side she'd taken. Then she told me they met in college through friends. She was seeing someone else, but when she became single, she invited him out for a bucket of fries. About four dates later, she figured out he was a virgin. He'd had willing girlfriends, but he was clearly daunted by the prospect of having sex and having to face his family afterward. One look at his face and his mother would be devastated, his father would shake his head, and his sisters would burst into uncontrollable laughter. There'd be a painful session with Father Trumble, and he'd be talked about as if he were a dog that had bitten the neighbor's kid.

In time Mary Katherine went to Sam's house and discovered that Barbara and Michael Iafrati were far more liberal than their youngest son. Experienced Catholics, they expected him to sleep on the sofa bed in the basement while she took his room, but they understood the allure of sneaking around a dark house. There were no shenanigans at the Iafrati residence though. Sam was too honorable, too disciplined. All she got was instant coffee, a blueberry muffin and a slew of introductions at a high school basketball game.

She'd seen enough, so at a party the next weekend, she waited for Sam to get tipsy and said she had a headache. While they walked to her dorm, she took his arm at the elbow and told him he needed to loosen up a little. Afraid to protest, he agreed with her, and when they stepped into her room, she took him by the lapels and kissed him. As much as she wanted to pull him under the covers, she also wanted to freeze and admire that glorious startled look on his face. Sam just wanted his legs to stop shaking.

'It's okay,' she said, pulling him close, and she told him how frustrated she'd been at his parents' house, how she'd hoped for quiet laughter and light footsteps. And then he stopped shaking, stopped covering himself, stopped worrying about his parents, and they whispered until his heart stopped racing.

Twenty-Six

Curled up in Sam's bed at 5:30 in the morning, she'd been gazing at the pale light outside the window. It was freaking cold in his place. When she exhaled, she could see her breath. Sam's nose wouldn't warm up, and neither of them had slept well.

'Forget about the lesson for a minute,' she said for the third time. 'I want to share a little pearl Sister Mary Katherine once gave me. She said, 'Mary Buttercup, there are two types of successful teachers.'' She felt Sam's body tense, but she kept on going. ''There are teachers that come across as scholars. They're all about the academics and they don't care what their students think of them. Then there are the teachers that become popular because they let kids in and enjoy sharing a little bit of their lives.''

Sam took some of the covers. 'You know which kind I want to be.'

'Well, I've got news for you. You don't look the part of the scholar. You got the penny loafers and the sweaters and you're smart, but you're too young and sporty. These kids may be obnoxious and apathetic, but if you showed them a little love, I'm sure they'd fall all over themselves trying to please you. They'd at least cut you some slack.'

'Roger knows how to be tough.'

'He's full of himself and he's big,' she said. 'He also knows how to disengage after he squashes a kid. But you take things too personally and it's easy for them to dislike you back.'

She stole back the covers and asked if he was listening. He said he was upset with Don DeWillum for holding his contract. First year teachers deserved more slack. She agreed, but only in theory, and pointed out that it might be nice to live someplace a little warmer.

The girls in Watervliet spoke with angels and that began the revival. Emily soon saw their spirit first hand, men and women receiving gifts then banging their palms against the furniture until they were tender and swollen. Another time, Sister Miranda Barber spoke the voice of Holy Mother Wisdom and marked every brother and sister at meeting so they could receive salvation when the hour came.

Some of The Mount's current residents searched for joy, insight, even divinity in artificial clouds. It was easy to frown on them—to point out that prayer was a better way to converse with God—but weren't poppies still blooming in the fields from the time when Shakers used opium as a ladder? *My Lord.* The cry rang out like a great bell. *My Lord.* It welled up and the body went limp. *My Lord.* And the spirit, the frenzy and the reverence would burst from hearts of Believers.

Emily's life was also shaped by confession, a mandate that tore down privacy and made every life on The Holy Mount a public one. Along with a workday practically devoid of personal time, confession protected the community against the sins of the individual. It was a way to ensure consensus and remove 'uncongenial' elements without mystery, rebellion or, God forbid, force.

I often wondered if confession was truly good for her. *I did not do my chores well. I passed a brother on the stairs. I desired to shake a man's hand.* One entry shared her concern about the gifts some of the brothers and sisters had been receiving. *I fear that their passions and incantations lack sincerity. I wonder if their vision has actually been obscured. Perhaps I should confess these doubts before I attend meeting on Sunday, but I do not have the courage and am afraid my feelings are a sign that I am lacking faith.*

'Finally, a story,' said Mary Katherine. 'But you really don't like plot, do you?'

Her Rangers were pounding the Boston Bruins, and tonight, for the first time, she'd brought her cell phone as a chaperone. On her lap was a growing quilt, yellow and blue with patches of green and little red flowers. The fabric came mostly from dresses, shirts, curtains and tablecloths she'd grown up with. But one section, gray with blue vines, was from the shirt of a cousin who'd died in a car crash.

'I wanted backstory so I'd know what she's pushing against, so shut up.'

Brother Gideon Halberd, the Elder who first interviewed the Winter Shaker named Owen Warland, couldn't discern the man's age. Once Owen removed his hat, however, the Brother must have noted the fair complexion and thick dark hair of a man not yet thirty. Then Brother Gideon explained the rules of occupancy and Owen disclosed his possessions: a broken watch, a sketch journal, and the ragged note that had accompanied his inheritance. He also produced one thing that would have alarmed Emily: four yellowing paper envelopes containing seeds. The Elder asked what purpose they served, and a noise more bird than human escaped from Owen's mouth. Brother Gideon was perplexed. At first, he thought the man might be ailing, so he repeated the question more slowly.

'They will be flowers,' said Owen.

'Are they flowers that produce medicines?'

Owen glimpsed into Brother Gideon's earnest eyes and wet his lips.

'Not that I know of, sir. They lift only the spirit.'

'You may keep them, but they cannot be planted here.'

The Elder returned the envelopes to Owen, who realized the Elder was far too staunch for reason. Besides, the younger man was following an empty stomach, and he owed The Holy Mount his respect.

Mary Katherine scratched her armpit. 'If you won't put in some sex, how about a little swordplay or an earthquake?'

'They're Shakers, not Knights of the Round Table.'

She made like she was going to nail me with a pillow but put it behind her head, and I told her of Brother Gideon's concern. Over time, he decided that Owen Warland may have been an honest man, but he clearly marched out of time. To all who'd listen, he talked of flowers, planting, hybridization and his dream of tending blooms.

Wary, the elders paid a visit to Brother Owen's room and rummaged through his belongings until they found a moist piece of cloth. Unfolding it, they discovered a dozen seeds that had just begun to germinate.

Elder Hunter examined the tiny roots. 'Have not you realized this is frivolous?' He spread his arms to emphasize the fact that chaos grew from small seeds. 'We have opened our eyes anew to Mother's words. Our lives must be simple.'

'I mean no disrespect,' said Owen in a faltering voice. 'I am grateful for what you have given me, but these seeds are not destructive. I have reconsidered: these blooms bring joy, so in a sense, sir, they are medicinal flowers.'

But the elders saw indulgence, and since Owen's spirit was obviously different from any they had known before, they concluded that he needed to converse with someone who could correct him in a gentle manner.

'I am not a 'sir,'' scolded Elder Halberd. 'You should not use that haughty word if you desire to live among us. Now, tell me, what work are you doing at present?'

'I am in the fields, spreading manure. I am told I will soon be hauling wood and preparing the orchards for winter.'

'Your work is good, Brother,' the elder said calmly, 'but I believe it is time for you to participate in a union meeting.'

As the second period of the hockey game ended, Mary Katherine sank into the sofa and said she liked messes. I told her I hated them with a passion and asked when Sam was going to propose.

'He tried but I didn't let him. Actually, he didn't really ask,' she said. 'He sort of suggested we get married after he found out I was pregnant, but it was totally lame. He needs to do it the right way.'

'Would you say yes if he got cable?'

'For three months?' she said, putting the remote down and toying with her phone. 'He has this theory that only settled people have nice stuff like cable television. I just think he's jealous of your rugs.'

'I told you he was jealous. But at least I know what to get you as a wedding present now.'

She looked at me a little funny, as if she knew the reason behind my jokes.

'We'll probably be living out of a van. Just give us some gas money.'

'You'll need food, too. Maybe Goldie will give you some cookies?'

'That woman's idea of generosity,' she said. 'You know, when she found out you used English money to carpet her glorious writing lab, she jumped up on a soapbox and turned it into you making her look bad. I can so imagine her in a bunker somewhere having little powwows with Roger and Sam. I see her at a big conference table, stroking a fluffy white cat and plotting world domination.'

I suggested we call their gang *The Spidermen*. Mary Katherine liked *The Gold Diggers*, but decided that would be a better name for my gang. Then she came up with *The Golden Asses*.

'Weirdest thing is,' she said, 'Goldie keeps saying nice things about you. The other day while Kara and her were killing a bottle of wine, they decided you'd be the most interesting lay on campus. Then she changed her mind and started arguing for Dorsey in maintenance because he's got big feet. I picked you, too, to avoid a three-way tie, and Goldie threatened to tell Sam I was a whore unless I handed over my recipe for peanut butter fudge.'

Mary Katherine pushed her quilt aside as I slipped in and out of a daydream. 'Christ, the whole discussion was bizarre. This is such a weird school. And I've been in such a mood lately—punchy, obnoxious, horny. You know my trip to the doctor yesterday was my first time off campus in two weeks?'

'Welcome to the island. The only new bodies you'll see are the ones that wash up on shore.'

'That's how I got here. Ugh, I could be sleeping in a big soft bed, eating breakfast in my pajamas in a nice kitchen. My mom said she'd even do my laundry. But, no, I decided to live in a basement and help The Turtle teach literature and war.'

'Wasn't that the plan?' I asked.

She glanced at my mom's picture. 'Greenie, you seem like the only girl around here who can keep a secret.'

'These things always get me in trouble.'

'I have to tell someone,' she said. 'After I jumped Sam in the woods, he changed—his voice got this weird edge, he started walking like his pants are too tight, and I have no clue know where his confidence went. You think you've done a number on him? You think Goldie has him confused. That's nothing compared to what I've done. Now I just want him to get out of here so he can start over.'

Twenty-Seven

When Per and Debbie broke up, he raged from dorm to dorm filling the air with profanity. She, apologetic at first and then indignant, followed him into the near empty cafeteria and declared as a lone black fly buzzed overhead that she was an entirely different person now. Yes, to go along with all the drama, we had black flies in the middle of winter. In my apartment almost every day one would launch itself from the crevice where it had been hibernating for a hundred years to make a slow, pointless journey across my living room. When I smashed it with a rolled up magazine, the lumbering monster left a gruesome smear.

Mary Katherine covered her head as I leaped from the arm of the sofa. I missed the fly just as her phone rang. She let it ring twice before answering, covered the receiver and asked if Sam could stop in. And by the time I'd squashed my diminutive nemesis, he was walking in my door for the second time in his life.

After a cursory but somehow awkward hello, they snuggled up beneath her quilt. Tonight she'd brought peach cobbler. The dishes were on my bookcase, and a homey smell lingered in the air. If I'd been him, I would've bought a satellite dish the next day. I would've blanketed the country with resumes, too. Who cares if you spent only one year at The Mount? At interviews, you feign respect, drop buzzwords like collegiality, school culture and isolation, and they're impressed you left so quickly. Spend four, five, eight years wrestling with underachievers, and they begin to wonder what's wrong with you.

'There's a car outside,' he said. 'The woman in it asked if you lived here, but she wouldn't come in or give her name.'

I asked what she looked like, but Sam just shrugged. So I pulled back the plastic from my window and saw a dark Minivan idling next to my car.

'I'll be right back' I said, and I grabbed my coat. On my way out I saw a set of footprints both coming from and going to the car. The car window glided down. I half-expected to see the barrel of a gun, but all I found was a familiar woman biting her lip and furiously twisting a paper clip.

'Remember me?' she asked.

I remembered her shoving my license back into my wallet after I came out of the bathroom six months earlier. She said she'd knocked it by accident onto the floor, but she was a shitty liar.

'It's Zoe, right?'

'Gold star for you.'

'Sorry, it's dark. Aren't you from Rhode Island?'

'Central Mass, but I'm in grad school in Rhode Island.'

I scanned the interior of the minivan. Except for an angel dangling from the rearview, it looked like a rental. I asked why she'd made the trip. She fiddled with the rearview mirror and said she was hoping to see me.

'I thought we were just having fun?'

'We sure did, two times, but while I was driving around in my real car the other day—I borrowed this monster from my sister in case you're thinking I'm some crazed soccer mom—I realized I wanted to see you, to see if you were still single.'

'I'm not,' I stammered, knowing I was a shitty liar, too.

The lights were glowing in my house. It was a cold night and the windows were shut, but I could hear my phone ringing. Zoe thrust an ATM receipt at me.

'Just stop, here's my number—I hope you'll want it when you get over the surprise of seeing me—and I have one more tiny thought I want to share.'

'I really have to go.'

'Jefferson, that pregnant woman lives in your basement apartment. If I had to put money on it, I'd sat the guy who checked her windows before heading up to your place—that guy right there—he's the boyfriend, so she's not going to miss you for the thirty seconds this is going to take.'

Sam was indeed walking back down the road. Without thinking, I told Zoe she was really creepy and reminded her she'd rifled through my wallet. She urged me not to say anything I might regret and explained how patient she was. That was it, patient. Like being patient was the key to a relationship. Well, to prove I could be patient, I waited until she pulled out of the driveway before I tore up her number.

Mary Katherine was waiting when I got inside. 'Your machine picked up a call while you were out.' She rose from the sofa, picked up the dishes from my bookcase and carried them to the kitchen. I pushed the button on my answering machine.

Hi, it's me. I thought I'd try to get you a little earlier since you've been so tired. Well, I'm sorry I've been asking for so many favors, taking advantage of our friendship. But, I promise, I'll work hard to make you proud. No more games. Well, I gotta go now. Calabria's being super mean. I guess she doesn't like being over thirty either.

Mary Katherine came out of the kitchen rubbing lotion into her hands.

'Who was outside?'

'Some woman I met last summer.'

'A stalker in a minivan? Was she telling you about her STDs or were you really that good?'

'Neither,' I said, following her to the sofa. 'Did Sam leave for a reason?'

'You really should get normal voicemail.'

'Did he run off to Goldie's lair?'

'I don't know, maybe,' she replied, 'but I do remember looking through that book you gave Cass and seeing your dedication. I thought it was kind of nice, even if it was Whitman. And now she's leaving voicemails like you're her best friend in the world.'

'Something almost happened,' I said, as her phone rang again.

'Hello?' she answered. 'Yes, I'm downstairs now. What do you want?'

I noticed her quilting was gone, as if she'd left and come back.

'Wait a second, I'm making tea.' She put her phone against her shirt. 'Something almost happened? What does that mean?'

All I had was the truth. 'I told her I wasn't interested, but she still begged me to be friendly, said she had no friends.'

Mary Katherine put to phone back up to her ear. 'No, no, he's upstairs. He probably thinks we had another fight. I doubt he's even listened to the message yet.' She rolled her eyes. I walked into the kitchen and washed a few cups. She told Sam not to overreact and her voice became a little strained. I could hear his shrill voice on the other end but couldn't make out his words. I was about to wave goodbye and send her back to her place when she pulled the phone away from her ear and said, 'Crap, I just spilled tea on my pants. Ouch, ouch, it's hot. I've got to call you back. Five minutes, okay?'

'You,' said Mary Katherine, after she hung up, 'should've told her not to call ever and changed your phone number. So what does almost happened really mean?'

'It means I thought about it.'

'You lead her on?'

'A tiny bit,' I said. 'Now I avoid her, but she sort of makes that impossible.'

'No, you've made it impossible.'

'I was pretty mean. And I shared everything with Gunnar.'

'Gunnar,' she said, with a snort. 'He's probably bummed you didn't screw her.'

'He told me to go to Don and get ahead of any story.'

'And did you?'

'Talking to him going to help anything.'

Mary Katherine shook her head. 'You're so stupid to let this get so messy.'

'Look who's talking,' I said, and she shook her head in disgust and told me she had to go call Sam.

That Monday Per was kicked out of the health club for beating up a vending machine. On Tuesday, he got his third smoking point of the semester and landed on restriction. On Wednesday, he lashed out at a pay phone and Ichabob suggest he go home for a few days. And as he was doing his impersonation of Mount Vesuvius, Debbie was back in her dorm complaining that he made her look bad. Meanwhile, Cass was losing sleep and turning in sloppy homework. Talking to distant friends after lights out made her lonely. Being on restriction made her surly, and she'd started gnawing on the back of her thumb. There was something boyish in her behavior. Boys, I'd thought, were the ones who clung to threads until they unraveled. Girls, especially smart ones like Cass, knew how to let go. They didn't write painful emails, stare at you across busy rooms, or walk up to your front door and start banging.

'Sorry I'm here, but I showed Kimball these.' Cass waved some marked papers, part of our independent study, I assumed, and begged me to let her in.

'Kimball and Iafrati were here when you called the other night.'

'Why didn't you pick up?' she asked as she sat down.

'I was getting some books from my car.'

She thought about it. 'Okay, so what? I told all the idiots in my dorm it wasn't you in the library.' Cass folded her papers. 'But, wait, I didn't leave my name or say anything that sounded weird.'

'It was you,' I replied. 'That's weird enough for a guy like Iafrati. But I'm sorry you're getting teased.'

'So what are you going to do?'

'Maybe talk with DeWillum before he does.'

'You going to tell him I got some kind of mad crush on you and I leave you weird phone messages? That is so humiliating. I'm going to die. But go ahead and tell him what you need to tell him. Just take this first.'

Cass unzipped her coat and pulled out a small volume of poetry she'd found in Northampton. I took it and asked her not to buy me any more gifts. I also asked her to do some writing, so I wouldn't have to lie about her grade. She said she would and thanked me for talking with her.

Twenty-Eight

Gunnar slept over on Friday because we were going out later, around four-thirty or so, to catch Goldie. I told him there was no way I was staying up, so he brought along his walkie-talkie and put in on the windowsill behind the couch. When I sat next to him with a few papers and a copy of *Frankenstein*, he told me to put that shit away and watch a movie with him.

'I've got a class to prep,' I said.

'You prep for Saturdays?' he said. 'Damn, got any scotch?'

'I'm Jewish, how about Sambuca?'

'You're fucking kidding,' he said, and he went into my kitchen, where he found some Jack Daniels and a warm can of ginger ale, both left over from a party I'd hosted more than a year earlier.

'Do you know how tired you look?' I asked, when he came back.

'Stalking Goldie is killing me,' he said. 'I've also been running over to Albany a couple nights a week.'

'What's her name?'

'Agnaldi Dorgo. She's the one Mary Katherine hooked me up with.'

'What kind of a name is that?'

'She's Romanian, Greek, Filipino and a little Indian. And, man, is she smart.'

'What does she do again?'

'Interim Dean of Studies at Miss Posey's School for Pampered Young Ladies. You'd like her. She was an English teacher but she majored in Economics.'

'And you've been seeing her a couple nights a week?' I asked.

'Sometimes I carpool with Candy. She's got needs, too, you

know.'

'More power to you guys,' I said, and I stuck my nose into Frankenstein.

Gunnar ended up having a few Jack and ginger ales. I graded a set of outlines; then we watched Animal House and fell asleep in front of the dying fire. When we woke at 6:30, Gunnar cursed the dead batteries in this walkie-talkie and told me we'd missed a Goldie opportunity.

Sam asked nicely, so she put on a hand-me-down maternity dress—blue with yellow flowers—and they went to church. Arriving a few minutes late, they blessed themselves and found a pew. The priest, with deep pious wrinkles and Brylcreemed black hair, was just finishing his greeting. Mary Katherine noticed a Carolina tinge in his voice and the kind way he connected with the sleepy children and their distracted parents, the smattering of twenty-somethings and the older people who were waiting intently on the Eucharist.

She was glad Sam had asked her to come. The church had lots of stained glass, and the apse was radiant with gold leaf and polished walnut. She wondered if she'd worship there if, by some miracle, she and Sam were still on The Mount in the fall. When it was time to take communion, Sam placed his hands over his diaphragm, bowed his head and shuffled to the front of the church. She hesitated—a few people slipped between them—but she followed with her arms at her sides. Receiving the body of Christ, she felt guilty that she hadn't taken communion since she'd gotten pregnant. Sam chewed quietly and immersed himself in the ritual. Lately this was one of the few times when he didn't worry about what to do next, and this was one of the few places where his worry became small. Sam liked the certainty of church, but when it came to theology, Mary Katherine was more intrigued by riddles. She liked being in this building with other Catholics, but her love of God was both concrete and beyond reason. The rituals were not essential. The Sacrament, which she savored, had always been sweeter than a perfect orange or a good deed, but every once in a while she'd notice it tasting dry and chalky.

In their pew, she knelt and gave thanks for being off The Mount, and she chastised herself for not supporting Sam better, but then she thought of the horrible shower she'd used that morning, the spider she'd squashed and the hollow clang of the metal bedroom door, and she wondered if somehow the basement was God's plan.

After mass, they walked out without greeting anyone. At her old church she'd found kindly Italian women who'd given her cover-and-bake recipes and sewing tips. She'd found girlfriends to start book groups with and to curse the departure of the young priest they sometimes called Father What-A-Waste. Here she would've loved to meet people who didn't work on The Mount, but she dreaded the idea of hiding her empty ring finger or of someone's asking how long she and Sam had been married.

'What did you think?' he asked, as they climbed into his car and he dug his sunglasses out from between the seats.

'It was nice,' she said. 'Do you like it there?'

'I like being in practice,' he said. 'Makes me feel less ragged.'

'Have you met anybody? It looked like there were a few young people.'

'I know a few names but not really.'

In college, Sam's friends teased him mercilessly because he needed it. Alone he was worth seducing. But with the right others in his life he was better. So when he said 'not really?' and put the car in gear, Mary Katherine couldn't help but be disappointed.

'I don't like you hanging out with Jeff Green,' he said, when they pulled into the parking of The Hitching Post. 'That phone message weirded me out. And on top of it, you're the two people on The Mount whose opinions matter most to me.'

'I'm not crazy about your hanging out with Goldie. But you don't hear me saying anything about it. Besides, you're not being judged.'

'You sure about that?' he asked.

She followed him inside, where they found two seats at the counter and busied themselves with menus. When the waitress came over, he ordered a cup of decaf and French toast with strawberries.

Walking on the wild side, she opted for regular coffee and a stack of buttermilk pancakes. While they ate, they talked about the Rangers, his upcoming lessons, and their Spring Break plans, which had been curtailed by a lack of money. Then the baby did a back flip, Mary Katherine's bladder protested, and she quickstepped to the bathroom. After peeing for what seemed like an hour, she promised the baby she'd have tea from then on and felt the impulse that had evaded her in church. Double-checking the lock on the door, she bowed her head in front of the sink.

She told God she was thankful for her friends, her family, the baby and its father. She also admitted that she'd been a flirt and she'd shared a lot of secrets. Then because she was frustrated that a friendship could undermine a love, she prayed for the impossible: to be mindful of Sam and to make sure she kept something for herself. Finally, she was sorry, very sorry, she hadn't been praying. She needed to keep that up.

Returning to the table, she saw that Sam had paid the bill. She also saw, in his tired eyes and tight mouth, that he wanted to ask if she was having second thoughts.

'Sam,' she said, offering him a ten he wouldn't take. 'Maybe you are being judged, but I don't know another way.'

Josh and Joe and a van full of teenage music lovers were going a concert a school night. I might've had fun being the coolest teacher in the universe if not for the fact that Per's ticket was auctioned off at dinner and Cass snapped it up. She probably wished she hadn't come, for the gossip in the van was all about Per and Debbie, Hodge and Harriet, Kara and Rog and, of course, me and my brand new girlfriend, a woman I'd never met but who, according to the kids, hailed from Canada. Serves you right, I thought, checking out Cass's glum face in the rearview mirror.

I can't remember the name of the theater, only that the balcony bounced with the music and the other patrons, all between the ages of nineteen and twenty-two, were high. To tease me, Joe asked if I'd ever smoked pot and Josh imagined me rolling a fatty before a show. I had the last laugh though, for when they tried to smoke in the lobby, a security guard threatened to kick them out if they lit up in the building.

'Awesome,' I gloated, when Josh shared the news. 'Did I tell you how I once confiscated a lighter from someone's twenty-five year old brother?'

'A couple times, Mr. Green,' said Josh. 'It's a great story.'

Before I could ask why he wasn't wearing his vinyl pants, Unicorn ran on stage and launched into a ten-minute ditty about rabid squirrels. The kids went bonkers. The balcony bounced. Josh took out a pen and wrote down the names of the songs. Joe, who spent much of the show trying to pop a lens back into his glasses, danced on his seat and fell only once. The others looked pretty bored. During one epic jam, I discovered that all the rest rooms had been converted into coed lounges. I was washing my hands when Cass coughed behind me.

'Is nothing sacred?' I asked.

'There are three other girls in here and too many guys in the women's room.'

Kids moved about with clove cigarettes behind their ears. There was a girl at the sink. Some guy was guarding a stall door while someone took a leak. I may not have looked like the oldest person at the show, let alone a chaperone, but I felt it.

'Iafrati cornered me today. I was just complaining with some girls in the justice club about how Remlap's bugging us to raise money for some conference when he got in my face. He says I have to fill out some forms to get out of his class. He also wants to know why Mr. Driscoll isn't recording my cuts and putting me on restriction.'

'You didn't do the paperwork to drop his class?'

'I thought it'd come up in one of your meetings. Besides, you didn't say anything.'

I told her Sam was messing with her probably to get at me, but Cass just made a face as if she'd swallowed her gum. Something else was clearly bothering her.

'Is it true?' she blurted. 'Are you seeing someone?'

'No, and it's actually none of your business.'

'I can't help it.'

'Yes, you can. And Cass, be careful what you say to Mrs. Remlap. She may be fun to talk to, but she's a snake.'

'Honestly, I don't see much difference between you guys.'

'Then you're blind.'

'Look, I'm not in the mood to be philosophical. I just want to get your opinion on which school I should go to.'

'So you ask me who I'm seeing? In a bathroom? Why are you being such a spaz?'

She lost it, gave me a big sad look and started blubbering.

'Okay, okay,' I said, inching forward and leaning against the sink. And I spent the next ten minutes explaining how she'd be much happier if she didn't try to be my friend.

Cass seemed to calm down, but on the way home she started sobbing again, quietly at first, but then with more volume. The kids started looking at each other. Harriet reached out a hand to ask what was wrong. But then a deer ran out in front of the van and I hit the breaks. Arms shot out against the backs of seats. Everyone gasped and the unharmed animal raced off into the woods. By the time the commotion died down, Cass was wearing headphones and pretending to sleep.

Back at school, she stumbled through the next two days. Most blamed our weeknight brophy, we hadn't returned until after two, but Goldie was sure there was a man involved. At lunch she saw Cass filling a corner of cafeteria with heavy sighs and asked if everything was okay. Cass told her about trouble at home: a sick aunt, an ex-boyfriend who kept calling, and the stepfather who still didn't get it. Goldie gave her a big hug and told she was always there to talk as the girl's eyes welled up.

In the end, Cass approached one of the few people she could trust. Cloistered in a dorm room, she told of glances held too long, an understanding that grew beyond doubt, a present, her bold move during Hands-To-Work, some deep conversations, another present, the rejection, and finally the childish behavior. At first Harriet didn't believe I'd been Cass's antagonist, but older girl was convincing.

'Was it an actual relationship?' asked Harriet.

'Oh God, I don't know. I don't know anything. But you can't tell anyone. You have to promise.' Harriet promised, and Cass was relieved, relieved enough to gossip about Jesus Demaquina's washboard stomach and the amazing car of another guy, an Assistant District Attorney from Queens, she'd met over the summer.

Twenty-Nine

Sam and Mary Katherine saw me at the teachers' table and found another place to sit. The following day she said hello by the mailboxes but kept looking to see who was coming through the door. The next time Sam was on duty, however, she found me sitting next to a day old cup of tea and doing a crossword at my kitchen table. Coltrane, Radiohead and the Smashing Pumpkins were taking turns in my CD carousel.

'I have news,' she said.

I looked at her finger, still no ring, and asked if she was having twins.

'I walked in on Sam in the bathroom yesterday and he jumped so fast you would've though he was playing with himself. He was writing in a notebook: stuff about you. Like when you tried to punch him, conversations you've had with kids, racy moments in the classroom, even speculations about women.'

'You think Goldie put him up to it?'

'She's too busy raising money for some thing called the Equity Project.'

'What's that?'

'Trips, shindigs with other school. She wants to show equity is profitable and that it's time for the board and headmaster to take it seriously.'

'By appointing an oppressed blonde department head?'

'The kids think the club will look good on their college applications and she brings cookies.'

'Has she recruited Sam? He's oppressed, too, isn't he?'

'I told him to put his energy into teaching.'

'Actually, tell him I've got a book on him, too,' I said, searching the living room for the draft that was freezing my feet. 'It's about how he ripped Miles Twohig a new asshole and was a tourist in my classroom for an entire semester? Tell him goodwill is a two-way street.'

'I'll encourage him to talk to you,' she said. 'But, please, don't let on I said anything and don't do anything crazy.'

In the window by the desk I never used, I discovered that a pane of glass had fallen out. As I was taping a piece of cardboard over the hole, I knocked out a second pane. Putting on my boots to go search for the glass in the snow, I told Mary Katherine her secret was safe with me. I also told her that on principle—yes, I actually had one or two—I had no problem recommending her prick of a boyfriend for a second year if he kept his nose clean.

Mary Katherine stuck her hand up her sleeve and scratched her elbow.

'Have you talked to Don about Cass yet?'

'How about you help me with my crossword puzzle?' I asked, as I headed outside.

She once again told me I was stupid, but there was something about her voice that made me think she wasn't really angry.

In early March, Candy and her girlfriend Lauralee invited everyone to a gay club in Albany. A fan of Candy's, Rog crossed into enemy lines and joined the party, but he also shaved his sideburns and refused to wear his new cardigan because, as Candy surmised, he was scared of being hit on. Goldie, who attended in an official capacity and because she loved all things gay, teased him until he told her she'd make a good fag-hag. And Kara, who'd liked the sideburns, shot a dagger at Rog and found some fans at the bar. That was his first strike. Two more and he was history.

During Hands-to-Work the next week, Rog wore the jeans Kara had given him into a ditch. Clearing a frigid culvert may have saved a road, but it turned him white and covered his pants with oil. They ended up in the trash, strike two.

Meanwhile, the days were too short, nobody slept well, and just when I thought winter couldn't get bleaker, my dorm imploded. We filled meetings with compassion and passed goodwill around like a plate of warm cookies, but the next day someone peed in the laundry room and Joe's favorite boxer shorts were stolen. I threatened to close the dorm to outsiders and the underwear reappeared in the foyer, modeled by a purple teddy bear and bearing a faux poop stain. Joe tore his underpants off the bear; then he tore off the bear's head. Doors began slamming.

This was about when Sammy the Eraser, a charter member of The Golden Asses, foolishly decided it would be best to ignore his girlfriend's advice and bait me.

My boys' basketball season was over. We'd managed a respectable nine and eleven record. Now, as I waited for the snow to melt from the tennis courts, we played sloppy pick-up games during sports time. The games were good therapy. I even got to play with Kwame, who'd grown bored of the health club and, as he put it, wanted some real exercise. But when Sam showed up in his baby blue North Carolina shorts and pristine white sneakers, the hair went up on the back of my neck.

'Well done,' he'd say when I made a basket. 'Nice,' he'd chime when I made an assist. 'Excellent game,' he'd say afterward at the water fountain. On the soccer field, he could run circles around me, but I knew every dead spot in our creaky gym and I'd earned the kids' respect by not calling fouls. Sam, in contrast, was forever stopping play. Reaching in, loose ball fouls, charges: he knew every infraction in the book and made sure the kids did, too. On a playground he would have been removed from the court on a stretcher, but in our games Mr. Iafrati had a license to be a whiner.

'You can't put your hands on me like that,' he said, picking up his dribble and walking to the top of the key.

Kwame was exasperated. He'd already committed a dozen fouls guarding Sam. I whispered that he shouldn't react, pushed a kid out of the lane with my knee (quite illegal) and called out the score. 20-14. One hoop and out. Sixty seconds of effort and we'd be off to diner. It had been a fun afternoon, too, and Sam couldn't take that away from anyone because no matter what he thought, these kids knew the rules.

We didn't pass as much as we should've and some of like to talk trash, but between these lines the order, the unity and the sound of kids complimenting each other after a game made perfect sense.

Lana Wilson-Wade was another child who transformed on a basketball court. In her baggy crimson uniform and black compression shorts, she was no longer a flamboyant young lesbian but the leader of a hardworking basketball team and the only reason they kept their games close, excruciating close, that is, for they'd lost every game that season by less than five points. It had become a curse. But there was always Lana, her hair now grown in and blonde, her long arms spinning like a whirligig as she closed in on five hundred points for her career.

My team was hogging the radiators as the game began. Bundled in my winter coat, I sat on a bench next to Rolly. Roger was standing in the doorway at his first girls' basketball game ever to see Lana score ten points and reach five hundred. Kara spotted him. She also spotted Joe, his finger digging in his nose, going over to greet him.

'Mr. Day,' said Joe, touching Rog's shoulder. 'Think Lana's gonna make it?'

'We'll have to wait and see,' he replied.

Kara fixed her crosshairs on Rog's temple. Her finger trembled, but when Joe turned around and found a spot on the floor, she had to lower her aim. Meanwhile Lana stole the ball and raced toward the basket for an uncontested lay up, but she clanged the ball off the bottom of the rim, fumbled the rebound and lost it. Undaunted, she slung up a three pointer the next time she touched the ball. Her attempt ricocheted off the backboard.

'She's gonna break the glass,' joked one of my players, a Pakistani boy who couldn't dribble without looking down. But Lana was still undaunted. She crouched in her defensive stance, slapped the floor, and a fearful opponent dribbled the ball off her own foot. Scooping it up, Lana scored her first points of the day. We cheered wildly.

On the sidelines Roger sat next to Josh Henderson, who was wearing his vinyl pants and a studded dog collar. Josh wrinkled his nose and asked if Mr. Day had been working in the sheep barn.

'All morning,' said Rog, as Lana pounded the ball into the floor for fifteen second, then banked in a shot from the top of the key.

'Do the sheep ever complain?' asked Josh.

'If you want to help clean the paddock, I'd be more than happy to show you what a shovel looks like.'

'No thanks, three's a crowd, Mr. Day, and I know you're a romantic guy.'

Kara, as if she had a sixth sense, jerked her eyes around. She knew Rog was going to slip. The kid excelled at the insult game, so you had to cut him down when could, and with his crazy haircuts and plastic clothes, it was easy.

'You haven't done a team sport this year, have you?' said Rog. 'Is it going to be baseball or lacrosse?' Josh stared at the court as Lana threw a pass to spectator; then he punched Rog lightly in the arm.

'You're gonna love runnin' my ass up and down the field, aren't you?'

Rog laughed, Kara's brow developed a few new wrinkles, and all eyes returned to the game. At halftime, Lana had six of the ten points she needed and the Lady Mountaineers had jumped out to a nine-point lead. Four more and she'd have five hundred, a game ball signed by the team and an ovation at morning meeting. Looking around, I saw Rog talking to Ichabob about a student he was putting on restriction, and Art at the scorer's table trying to placate Goldie, who looked like something had flown up her ass. Gunnar cruised by on his way to patrol a few dark corners of the campus and asked if I'd gotten any dirt on the diva.

'That's your job,' I said.

He slapped me on the back. 'Sure, who needs sleep?'

When the teams came back onto the floor to warm up, a woman with a bouncy ponytail waved to me. Rolly asked if I knew her. A few seconds later I walked across the court to greet Sylvia Vanderhall. She hugged me, as if we'd actually been friends when we went to college together, and told me she was working in her school's Development Office and helping out the basketball team.

'You're a teacher,' she said. 'I wouldn't have expected that. Well, it's great to see you.' I told her it was great to see her, too, and we chatted about nothing until the horn sounded at the end of halftime. Turning around, I saw that Rolly had given my seat away.

At the start of the second half, Lana raced down the court and threw up a three pointer. The whistle blew, signaling a foul, and the shot rattled in. I jumped to my feet and hugged the kid next to me. Then the gym became silent as Lana strutted to the free-throw line, bent her knees, shot, and raised her arms before the ball even went in the hoop to complete her four-point play. We started screaming. The other team was so shaken by the din that they couldn't score for the next ten minutes. When our lead became insurmountable, the kids broke into a raucous rendition of Simple Gifts.

But Cassandra Diaz was not singing. She'd seen me talking to Sylvia Vanderhall and had worked herself into a sorry state. Walking around the court to the visitors' bench, she approached one of the players and asked if their assistant coach was Canadian. Strange question, but the girl nodded, yes, Ms. Vanderhall was from Toronto.

After the game I felt a tug on my elbow as I was filing out of the gym.

'My left tit you don't have a new girlfriend.' I waited until a few people passed us and told Cass that I hadn't seen Sylvia in nine years. 'You liar, I know she's your Canadian whore.'

Sam, about fifteen yards away, saw the exchange and humbly tracked Cass down in the Student Center.

'We haven't talked about it, but I want you to know I don't mind your dropping my class. Mr. Green's a good teacher.'

'Don't try to play me, Iafrati,' she said, and before he could think of what to say next, she was gone. Sam finally realized this girl was way too savvy. So that Sunday he took a different approach. As part of the activities crew, he'd signed up to transport kids to religious services. Since Harriet was the only one who wanted to go to church, it was an easy duty and the perfect opportunity to help a girl with a secret.

Showered and in a clean shirt, he picked up Harriet outside her dorm. She was bathed too, for the first time in three days, and wearing a red sweater. In church they sat near the front, took communion and followed the service. The sermon spoke to neither of them, but when they left, they did so with a feeling of accomplishment.

'You want to stop for doughnuts? My treat?' asked Sam, and a few minutes later they were at a small pink table with bear claws, honey glazed and cups of hot chocolate. Harriet tore off a piece of doughnut and wiped her sticky fingers on a napkin. To Sam's delight, she started talking about Cass.

'She only talks about her own problems. I don't think she's ever asked anyone else how they feel.'

For a sublime second, Sam must've felt like a priest, or, perhaps, he thought about what he was trying to do and felt more like a vampire hunter. He asked about Cass and me as Harriet sipped her hot chocolate.

'Did something happen?' he asked.

'I wanted to tell her it was wrong,' she said. 'Someone should be told, but it just isn't that easy.' Harriet began to choke up. Sam didn't touch her shoulder or give her any comforting words, but he looked at her so expectantly she had to confess.

'I needed to tell Hodge it wasn't his decision, so we snuck out one last time to talk, and he made me do it. I pushed him as hard as I could and said I didn't want to, but he kept leaning on me until I couldn't breathe. I slapped him, too, but it didn't stop him.'

Sam smiled at the girl. 'I'm glad you told me. That takes courage. And would it be okay if we talked to Mr. Driscoll when we got back to school? He'll know what to do.'

Thirty

There was a buzz at morning assembly. Kids from the Twenty-First Century Coalition were spread throughout the room with index cards. Don started announcements by telling us the local historical society didn't want kids leaving bicycles in front of the dorms. It didn't dawn on him that no one on campus had ridden a bike in the three months. Afterward, there were some announcements, mostly related to sports. And finally, Goldie, wearing a New York Jets jersey and a gold chain, announced that the Twenty-First Century Coalition was hoping to raise money for a multi-school conference followed by a multi-school dance in April. The room went bonkers when they heard Hip-Hop Hideo was going to be the deejay. Don, obviously in on the plans, smiled approvingly, and when things quieted down, the students in the club stood and one by one read from their index cards.

What percentage of African-American teenagers go to college? What percentage of people in Uzbekistan live below the poverty line? How much do women make worldwide compared to men? How many Taiwanese factory workers commit suicide each year? After a few minutes, everyone in the room knew these facts, and then Cassandra Diaz informed us The Mount had never had a department head of color and that we didn't even keep statistics on how many minority candidates had interviewed for teaching positions over the years. Don stopped smiling as the room became solemn. Of course, Goldie was the most solemn of all. But then Gunnar stood and cleared his throat.

'I'd really like to thank the Twenty-First Century Coalition for raising awareness about diversity issues on campus. We certainly have a lot to learn and a long way to go before we can truly say we live in a school that accurately reflects the diversity of our country and our surrounding community.' Our surrounding community was ninety percept white and Christian, but Gunnar had a point to make and he didn't want facts to get in the way. 'I'd like to take a moment though to celebrate a few small triumphs we have had. First, for thousands of years Korean boys have adhered to a system where older boys have special rights and privileges over younger boys. In the past year on The Mount, younger boys did laundry, ran errands, even took physical abuse from older boys simply because they were younger and that's the way things were done. Well, we're committed to stopping that tradition, and I'd like to applaud the efforts by the all Korean boys who are willing to be the change.'

There was a round of applause. The Korean boys in the room looked uncertain. Don was clapping. Goldie looked stunned.

'I'd also like to highlight the work of Ms. Dafoe. When I first came here, lesbian, gay and bisexual students didn't feel safe. And they certainly didn't have a place or a voice on campus. Well, I'm proud to say that is not the case anymore.'

More applause. Goldie brought her palms together once or twice.

'Finally, I was going over old course descriptions the other day, when it dawned on me how much we've changed. For example, under the leadership of Jeff Green, who is by the way the only Jewish department head The Mount has ever seen, we are for the first time teaching literature from culturally significant places such as Columbia, Argentina, Japan, India, Nigeria and Egypt.'

More applause still. And I had to bite my tongue because Goldie was the only one who taught Marquez, Achebe or Rushdie. The kids whopped. Candy pumped a fist. Goldie had no choice but to clap. And Gunnar nodded at me with approval.

Josh Henderson looked aghast at the comingling spaghetti and cabbage on my plate. I was eating with Candy and Ichabob. Sam was there too, but he was so bleary-eyed from prepping he couldn't even smile.

'There was more hazing,' he said, 'after lights out. Joe got picked on, Miles' pillow got totally covered with shaving cream and I got this.' He turned his head and showed me a raspberry just below his ear. No one had hit him, but he'd whacked his head on a doorframe trying to avoid a water-filled condom. 'It soaked my stereo and now it doesn't work.'

'The stereo or the condom?' I asked.

'Funny, Greenie. Seriously, Joe's picked on every night.'

'Who's doing it?' asked Sam.

Josh wouldn't even look at him.

'Call another meeting,' I said. 'Just you guys, no adults. You need to look at each other face to face and say this isn't okay.'

Josh hated the idea, complained that I was being lazy, but I reminded him that I didn't live in his dorm and peer pressure wasn't always a bad thing.

'Fine, I'll do this, but only because you took us to Unicorn,' he said, and he slouch back to his table.

'Why let Josh run the meeting?' asked Sam, skeptical that a small deviant could persuade anyone to follow the rules.

'They don't need me telling them what's right and wrong,' I said. 'Besides, they all respect him. He just doesn't know it yet.'

'That kid who's been on restriction most of the year?'

'Ironic, isn't it?' I said. 'Still, if the dorm can't convince Hodge to toe the line, I'll nail his ass to the wall.'

'There's the Greenie we know and love,' said Candy, taking one of my napkins. Ichabob polished off his tuna melt without comment. Sam looked oddly indignant.

To our dismay, there was another commotion in my dorm that night. But in yet another ironic twist, Sam was its cause. Josh had gone to the library during study hall, but he'd neglected to get a pass. Sam, who was covering for Rolly, could have given him one retroactively. The books, the photocopies and the copious history notes told him Josh had been a good egg. But Sam wrote the cut anyway.

'You know that suspends me?' asked Josh.

Sam calmly insisted it would be unethical to write Josh a pass after he'd already broken a rule. Josh calmly reminded Sam that there was an established precedent for bending this rule. Sam calmly pointed out that the rule was designed to keep students safe. Josh calmly thanked Sam for being so concerned about his safety. Then he called him a 'peckerhead' under his breath. The next day as I drove him to the bus station, I agreed that Mr. Iafrati could be an ugly little fascist but, no, I wasn't about to hit him again. I also made Josh, who was thrilled to be starting Spring Break two days early, promise to fax me his project.

'Forget the high ground, Greenie. Why don't you marry his girlfriend,' he said. 'Name the baby Little Napoleon and put it on the cover of the viewbook while Iafrati's working fast food? I mean, he's not coming back, right? Please tell me I won't see him next year.'

'You're harsh, man.'

'The guy deserves it,' he said. 'Hey, Mr. G, while you're at it, can you suspend Cass for harassing you? Maybe get her some help? She's so bizarre now her dorm won't even tease her anymore.'

'She's not harassing me.'

'That's not what I heard, so did Kwame tell you Iafrati sniffed his hands and patted his pockets yesterday? I swear K wanted to hit him.'

At sit-down dinner I told Kwame once again to ignore Sam. Our best revenge would be his going to college and coming to reunion in an expensive car.

'I ain't never coming back to this place,' he said.

'Don't say that, man. So why'd he give you a hard time anyway?'

'He said I smelled suspicious. I told him it was the lavender and oatmeal hand cream his wife suggested for my flaking. Then I made him give me a pass cause I was late for class. Can I go now?'

I offered him Josh's dessert, but he didn't want it.

I couldn't believe Sam would go so low. Thought it was on purpose and hated him. Thought it was unconscious and hated him even more. Thought for a minute I was overreacting just because they were my advisees, but even if my little miscreants were pathological rule benders, they still didn't deserve to be bullied by Sam.

That night I was sleeping in the dorm parent's room when I heard a slam. It was after one in the morning. I stumbled into the hall and found Joe half naked. Hodge, yet another bully, was standing defiantly in his doorway.

'You're a fucking loser,' yelled Joe, as Hodge stepped back into his room. Joe ran at the closing door and bounced off it. There was something sticky on his shoulder. I ordered him back to bed. Too wound up to be boss around, he flailed at the door until his knuckles were pink. I realized what the sticky stuff was.

'Now that Harriet won't give you happy hand jobs, I should give her a try. Let her see what a real man's like. Not a pencil dick like you...'

Hodge came out of his room. He shouldn't have. When I saw that stupid satisfied bizarrely indignant grin on his face, I slammed my shoulder into him and knocked him back into the wall. Joe finally noticed the cum on his shoulder and started crying.

'I woke up and he was kneeling over me, Greenie. He's an animal. He needs to be put in a cage at the zoo like a fucking monkey.'

Hodge started to say something, but I hit him with an open hand, left a print in the middle of his chest, and told him to get the fuck back in his room.

Hodge, his father, a lawyer and Ichabob met with Don. Because Harriet and her family refused to press charges, the school didn't have a lot to work with. Their lawyer said the words 'assault and battery.' Don replied, 'sexual assault', 'hazing' and 'masturbation.' He also offered a good transfer report, but Hodge's father wanted him to graduate from The Mount. No one blinked until Don started worrying about money, the remote possibility of an assault charge, the ten weeks left in the school year, and the fact that Sam had already pelted the kid with an eraser.

A few hours after Don caved, I had lunch with a table full of happy kids. Smacking Hodge was something they understood. Even Kwame praised me—in his own way, of course—when he said, 'I woulda killed a guy if I woke up and found him rubbin' one out on me.'

In the end the only action taken against Hodge was that he was moved to another dorm and forced to get some counseling. His hazing days were over though. He was the kid who'd jacked off on another guy, gotten slammed through a wall by a teacher, and hadn't gotten kicked out only because the school was afraid of his dad.

When I sat with Don, he wasn't nearly as happy as the kids. I told him I'd wanted to keep Hodge off Joe and send a message. He just thought I'd snapped again. But I didn't snap. I knew what I was doing, and when Don gazed across his desk, I saw all the confusion he was trying to hide.

'I hope you wouldn't do it again,' he said, struggling to look me in the eye. To placate him, I said I wouldn't. Joe's dignity mattered a lot to me, and Hodge had been a shit in the dorm, but, yes, it was a selfish way to react.

'You may be a folk hero now, but you put yourself at risk and you limited my options,' he said. 'All to show up a bully?'

'And protect the kids in my dorm.'

'You're overprotective,' said Don, 'which is another way of being reckless. You need to think about the school and before you put on your white hat.'

'You're right. So what did Mr. Hodge say?'

'He apologized for his son and, get this, he offered to double his gift to the Writing Center.'

'Don't let him,' I said coldly. 'The guy could write a check for two hundred grand and not feel a thing. Show him that old blueprint we have for an arts center and offer to put his name on it.'

If I'd said what I really wanted to say, I would've told Don he was a pussy for not kicking that kid out. But I put my principles aside and tried to speak his language. It was part of my punishment for not listening to Gunnar. The other part was telling Don that Cassandra Diaz had been trying to flirt with me, but when I reviewed my script and thought about the poses I should strike, I lost my nerve.

A night or two later, I saw the lights burning in the gym after check-in. Inside I found Art dust mopping the floor. I took off my boots, found a basketball and started shooting in my socks. Art joined me when he finished mopping, and explained why he was doing housekeeping at ten. He'd busted Elizabeth Perkins for pot earlier. The girl had been behind a maintenance shed with her arm around another girl. There was a burning cigarette on the ground. Not knowing whose it was, he went through both of their pockets. The other girl had the cigarettes, but Elizabeth had some weed. She claimed she hadn't been smoking and held up her fingers for Art to sniff. He believed her but couldn't ignore the bag. Elizabeth didn't protest. She was a good kid, but she'd also come to The Mount on first offense after being kicked out of another school for drinking. This was her second and only strike.

'I wish I could've looked the other way,' said Art, as we started a game of twenty-one. I shot first, missed from the top of the key and handed Art the rebound. He made a short bank shot. 'Then I got into a fight with Goldie. She thinks I'm soft because I don't want to take sides.'

I missed the same shot and flipped the ball to him. 'Nothing good comes from taking sides.'

'Spoken like a single man,' he said.

'You're married to Goldie. Does that mean you have to think like her?'

'I still don't like you guys stealing her thunder.'

'Take it up with Gunnar. I didn't ask to be lauded as a pioneer of diversity. But what does Goldie have against me? I have no clue what it is, but it's clearly personal.'

'What makes you think it's personal?'

'Come on, it's obvious.'

'I don't know,' he said. 'I think it has something to do with her cousin.'

'Who's her cousin?'

'Shawna, the intern that ran away because you made her uncomfortable—looked at her funny, made comments, followed her or something.'

'Harassed her?'

'I don't know what really happened.'

'Art, have you ever heard me tell a dirty joke or even swear?'

'No, but that's not what they're saying.'

'I didn't say more than two words to that woman.'

'Maybe you weren't aware of what you were doing?'

'I unconsciously harass women? Is that what your wife says? I bet she says I screw students, too.'

'Just Cass.' He tried to sound like a joke, but when he sighted the rim and tossed up a wild hook shot, I could tell he half believed it was true. 'But, Greenie,' he said, 'you do make yourself look guilty sometimes.'

'I'm sorry, Art, but your wife's out of control.'

'Are you suggesting I do something about it?'

I looked over at his dust mop and offered him the ball. 'I think you already are,'

He took it and looked up at the rim. 'Goldie wants to have a baby. I've been begging for years, but suddenly now's the time to wear saris and get pregnant? I honestly don't know whether to drop my pants or run away. None of it makes sense.'

'Me either,' I said. Then I apologized, and we shot baskets in silence until Art got his touch back and the ball started going in.

Thirty-One

Catching her breath, Mary Katherine leaned against the counter of Sam's yellow kitchenette. With disdain, she looked at the Toronto Blue Jay's team poster above his kitchen table. Sure, they'd won The World Series, and the poster had been signed by some guy named John Olerude, but what American kid liked the Blue Jays?

'I am being responsible,' he said. 'That guy's attacked two people and he may have had sex with a student.'

'Do I need to remind you that you've assaulted kids, too? And you have no proof he's doing students?'

'I've never pushed one through a wall, and as far as the sex goes, the girl said as much to Goldie. Besides, you were there when she left that message.'

'The whole school knows about her crush. Come on, Sam, consider your sources.'

He looked wounded. 'What if she were your kid?'

Mary Katherine imagined having Cass as a daughter. The girl would do everything she told her not to, and Mary Katherine would pray, even though Cass was too smart to let it happen, that she wouldn't get pregnant before she got married. Pregnant before she got married? That was a good one. Sam saw the amusement on her face and thought she was making fun of him.

'I'd tell her to stay away from Goldie,' she said.

'What do you really know about this guy?' he asked.

'I know he bothers you. But what is the point of attacking him?'

'I'm not saying he's evil.'

'You're pointing a finger and going after his kids. What gives you the right to do that? You know, maybe I should go live with my parents and ask for my old job back.'

Sam was cut to the core. He said he was sorry, but that made him madder, made her madder. And when she took her storm clouds and left, he was glad to see her go.

On a Friday I took a personal day, slipped away from campus and drove to Dunwell Academy, called 'Dun-extremely-well' by its proud alumni. At ten in the morning, two tweedy men and one well-dressed woman lobbed questions at me. There were biscotti, chocolate and almond, and a lot of nodding as I talked about kids and classes. When I said the phrase 'interdisciplinary projects,' one of the guys gave another a little elbow. During a lesson I taught on *Macbeth* to a class of ambitious juniors, a few of them laughed out loud. After my interview, the woman on the hiring committee—Rose Hession, whom I knew through a mutual friend—took me on a tour of the campus and showed me a shiny new gym, a hockey rink, a theater with over four-hundred seats, eight tennis courts with windscreens, a pristine science classroom, a school bus with a television in it, and a lake where I could paddle a canoe all summer. The faculty apartments weren't as charming as the one I'd grown accustomed to, but that seemed a small price to pay for almost doubling my salary. Finally, because the school was loaded, interns put the kids to bed and proctored all the study halls. Full-time teachers worked in the dorms just once a week, leaving them time for tennis matches, magazine reading, even families.

After all of my interviews, Rose walked me to my car and with a big smile on her face. I'd impressed, she said. Folks were already talking about what a great fit I'd be. She even gave me a hug, and although their decision wasn't going to be final for two glacial weeks, I drove home on a cloud, wrote long thank you notes and slept like a log.

The next day I had the pleasure of watching Sam teach. He was good but not great. There were a few things to praise—the most impressive being that he didn't pee down his leg with me in the room—and a few things, such as using students' names more often, that he needed to work on. Nothing I saw screamed get rid of this guy. But nothing told me he was the next Mr. Chips. So I took lots of notes and wrote the most artful, lukewarm evaluation possible.

That night Candy had a party. Sam went because Mary Katherine insisted. Goldie went because our hostess had crashed every meeting of the Twenty-First Century Coalition and she wanted to return the favor. Roger went because Kara was going to be there and he didn't know any better.

The bad guys marched in together, looking as if they were about to repossess the furniture, and camped out in the kitchen. Candy stomped around her living room and debated kicking them out. They were just too fucking rude to endure, but I reminded her she'd be kicking out Mary Katherine, too.

'What shit,' she said, throwing herself onto the sofa.

'I'll take care of it,' I replied, and I went to the kitchen, where I found Mary Katherine perched on a wobbly milk crate—it was either that or the counter since Candy didn't have chairs in her kitchen. Kara was on another milk crate. Sam was standing by the window. Rog and Goldie were on the counters and Kyle Searcy, pink eyed and grumpy because admissions numbers were way down, was propped against the fridge.

'Goldie,' I said, 'we should talk.'

She scanned the faces of her friends. Roger was sneering into a tall glass filled with vodka and cranberry juice. Sam was gazing pensively at a refrigerator magnet. Kara was stranded on planet Ohwoeisme.

'Why?' she asked.

'Because we've got things to talk about.'

'Okay, fine,' she said. 'I'll find you tomorrow.'

Tomorrow? I looked at the drink in her hand and decided, yeah, tomorrow would be better. The second I left Goldie announced she wasn't having any damn meeting with me the guy who put a spy at her club meetings and helped Joe Causeway get permission to take his finals early so he could see a hand specialist in Chicago. The floodgates were open now, she complained. Soon every kid would be demanding early exams.

'This kid's only got four fingers,' said Rog. 'Give him a break.'

'Do you want to make up individual exams for all your students?'

'Joe won't cheat. And he'll be lucky to get a C on my test.'

'That's not the point. The point is we have a policy and Don's too chicken to enforce it. If you can't take the exam on the right day, you take it at *our* convenience, which means when you come back in the fall.'

'Isn't it easier to have them take it early?' asked Mary Katherine.

'If there's a policy, we should enforce it. But some people don't have balls. You know, my cousin Becky—she's teaches high school outside Boston—says it's worse in public schools. You'd think their union would protect them, but their working conditions are a bigger joke than ours. The kids get everything they want. Becky tells me if you're cute or in a wheelchair, at her school you can get anything you want.

I don't know what cute girls in wheelchairs had to do with exams, but Goldie was proud of herself for speaking the truth. Others might not be willing to fight the good fight, but she was brave, capable, and ready to enlighten. And since she was on a roll, she turned to my pregnant friend and asked, 'So, darling, how are things up in Sodom?'

Mary Katherine hoisted herself up. 'Goldie, you're embarrassing.'

Sam's ears began to burn, so he was once again glad when his girlfriend left. Then, for completely different reasons, Kara also put on her coat. Rog been expecting a scene. She'd whack him, tell the world he was a jerk, and he'd take her noise like a man. Kara didn't explode though. Her vigor and violence simply wilted. So he just sat on the counter like a peacock, peeking at her out the corner of his eye.

When Mary Katherine stomped through the living room, I let her go. When Kara breezed through and slammed the door, however, I slipped out after her. She was smoking a cigarette down by the Shaker washhouse, leaning against the building as her boots sank into two inches of mud.

'What the hell are you prowling around for?'

'I want you to start being yourself again.'

'What am I now?'

'According to the kids, you're mean.'

'I'm full of hate. I hate Roger Day, and I hate that Goldie keeps referring to me as a woman of color. It's almost as bad as biracial.'

'Can I share a theory about Roger Day?'

'Knock yourself out.'

'I think he's just waiting for a woman to kick his ass. I don't mean bust up his little Shaker chair; I mean really kick his ass. But, here's the thing, you can't do that by being a bitch. He likes that way too much.'

'You're right,' she said quietly, and she pulled out another cigarette.

Back at the party, Goldie told her buddies I'd seen Cass's underwear and probably done a lot more than that. She'd begged her to keep the secret a secret, but being eighteen, Cass still believed discretion was ninety percent luck. Then Goldie gave her a hug and called me an audiophile.

Hearing the tale, Sam wanted to go to Don and watch me get escorted off campus. But Goldie told him he'd be pissing into the wind. I'd deny it, give Sam shitty evaluations and Don would rubberstamp them. Sam fumed. It wasn't right that he could accidentally hit a student with an eraser and be vilified, while I smacked the same kid, attacked a teacher in front of the varsity soccer team, did who knows what to female students, and was more popular than ever. Shaking his head, Rog offered to change Sam's diaper, but then he shared the reason he was going to help him. He didn't care that I'd belted Hodge or let Cassandra flash me. No, he was annoyed with me for getting too cozy with women who were taken, namely Mary Katherine and Kara, and with Don for caring more about appearance than rules.

'Leave the kids alone,' he said. 'You'll may get to Greenie, but you'll look bad, too. Besides, the little freaks need to be here. And don't go to Don yet. It'll look like a witch-hunt. Besides, why do you think you don't have a job?'

'DeWillum said it'd be wise to start interviewing.'

'Kaiser, a lot can happen between now and June.'

Sam was skeptical, but Rog confided that his contract had been held his first year, too, because our former headmaster found Rog a little combative. By the end of the year, however, he'd changed his mind about the guy who ran the tightest dorm on campus and had fifteen students interested in AP Biology.

'What about a formal sexual harassment complaint?' asked Goldie. 'If we go the extra mile, won't the trustees run from the guy? I'm sure we could encourage Cass?'

'You had your chance with Shawna,' said Rog. 'Cass I wouldn't trust. She might tell you secrets, but she's still one of Greenie's biggest fans.'

'It's not my fault Shawna was too chicken. But what about me filing one?' asked Goldie, 'He's always been creepy to me. What else do I need?'

'Isn't Don getting sick of you by now?' said Rog. 'Besides, you've harassed half the men on campus.'

'Could you imagine if Candy filed the complaint? Don would shit a brick and investigate that thing to death.'

'Why can't we just go to Don with what we actually have?' asked Sam.

'Because the truth's not going to get us what you want,' said Rog, and he and Goldie—who finally decided to get serious—gave Sam a few pointers on bringing down an alpha dog.

Thirty-Two

Mary Katherine spent the morning washing panties and socks. On Saturdays she usually went shopping with Sam, but today she rearranged the damp clothes on her sweater drier, got into her station wagon and drove to the Clark Art Institute in Williamstown by herself. There she squeezed three dollars into a donation box and wandered around. In time she found Degas' statue of a young ballerina, a girl in repose, weight shifted on one leg, head at a casual angle. Often dancers are depicted as birds, ready to take flight, dive or die in a flutter of wings. But this dancer was just a child— true and stark, so honest in form that the moment you realize how beautiful she is, that maybe she can fly, she becomes simple, ordinary, even more exquisite.

Unable to fly but enamored with the idea of balance, Mary Katherine consoled herself with Shakers. From the books I'd given her, she'd learned that in addition to living separately, Shaker men and women worked in separate shops, ate at separate tables and, of course, were not allowed to lodge alone. Many of these rules were obvious; others seemed downright bizarre. Shakers weren't supposed to watch someone of the opposite sex making a bed? How's that a threat to celibacy? Elders read your mail, no open gates, high hats, watches or umbrellas? Also no talking loudly, walking loudly, knocking too hard on or slamming doors? And no wearing spurs, kicking animals or— best of all—watching them hump? Yes, they actually wrote that one down.

She also learned that in a union meeting two rows of chairs were set a half-pace apart so Brothers and Sisters, like Sister Emily and the Winter Shaker Owen Warland, might talk. Elders supervised and conversations were to touch only upon mundane topics. Sister Emily had written about her time with Owen.

He rarely talked of his own life, but he thanked me when I offered to oversee his habits and temporal needs. I will repair his garments if the need arises, and I am certain he will have that need. During our time, I explained the Separation Acts in detail. He now knows that if he desires to have a button sewn, he needs permission from an Elder before he can call upon my services. He also knows that he is required to knock on my door and wait to gain admittance. Since Mr. Warland is shy and generally respectful, our rules should not worry him. However, some he does not understand. He asked why brothers and sisters are not allowed to pet the dogs and cats that wander the village, why we do not give presents and why we expect women to conceal their beauty. In response to his queries, I have tried to persuade him that there is, indeed, much joy in our days. I told him how my spirit is lifted at meetings and suggested he find his amusement there.

That was it. No more Owen in the journal. It was Mary Katherine's turn now, so she put a little dirt under Owen's fingernails and had Sister Emily discover it. Nearby the Elders were dozing in their chairs. Sister Emily could have told them, but she didn't and secrecy made her heart ache. Trying to stifle the feeling, she asked if he had ever sheared a sheep. Owen replied he had, but the sheep had not been pleased with his effort. Then he grew silent as she imagined him toying with pots of dirt—his cheeks smudged, his fingers black, his reckless devotion a thing she'd never understand.

At the end of their silence, Owen Warland told her he was uncomfortable speaking, but that it was not by choice. Emily realized he did not have an ideal disposition for The Holy Mount or, sadly, even for The World. But she was drawn to him, even as she mourned his inward state and his poor decisions.

The next morning, as her girls were doing their exercises, her hands began to tremble. At first it was a slight annoyance, an apparent consequence of the cold, but then Brother Owen took over her thoughts. One moment she imagined being his mother. The next she was a sister. But then she was a wife who wanted nothing more than to gaze into his face and listen to his awkward stories.

The metal door to her bedroom was closed, but when I stopped at the entrance to her living room, a paneled common area she had to herself, I saw a dismantled crib, two piles of baby clothes, and on her sweater dryer some wool socks and a pair of undies with roses on the waistband. This was how the mother-to-be lived. When she came up to my place, she brought the smell of lavender and warm cookies. But down there, even when she was on her school sofa quilting or at the hotplate making soup, it was crowded, ugly and damp, or, to use her words, like being below decks on the Mayflower.

While I was eyeing her stuff, the plastic over the windows stopped rustling and the basement grew so quiet that I had to scurry off to the laundry room. Once there I stuffed the washer with smelly socks and undershirts, fed three quarters into the machine and began to feel reasonably safe. As far as I knew Mary Katherine and Sam were grocery shopping. And because she'd told me she liked to ride on the back of the cart, I imagined her big bellying around the Shop-n-Go, sailing past cans of tomato soup and baked beans, as he pleaded with her to be careful.

Two hours later I was leaning against a dryer and wondering why Dunwell Academy was taking so long to get back to me when she snuck up from behind and pressed her navel right into me. I jumped. She chuckled. And then her hands slid under my arms and the quarters in my pocket started clicking against each other.

By the time she stopped by my apartment to tease me some more and share the story she'd made up, I'd folded and put away my clothes. The last fire of winter sputtered in the woodstove. It was getting dark outside, but there was golf and sunshine on the TV.

'I freak you out?' she asked, settling into her spot on the sofa and fixing a wedgy.

I told her I had work to do. She balanced the remote on the arm of the sofa and told me to go ahead and do it. I wouldn't be bothering her. Besides, I had fancy rugs, two kinds of ice cream in my freezer and my dishes matched. If she had her quilting—and she did—and there were enough hockey games on TV, she could stay for days, weeks, or at least until her water broke.

'So,' she said, tugging her shirt down over her belly. 'Are you going to make out with me some more?' I told her to cut it out, but she just patted the cushion beside her. 'How about we pretend I'm eighteen? Will you help me with an essay, Mr. Green?'

Mary Katherine Kimball had a fair complexion, a small pink nose and blue eyes that looked gray when she teased me. She said she hated her hair—'too dull, just sits there'—and long before she'd started showing, she'd referred to her ass as the Lost Continent. This woman had the ability to make the surliest kids smile and even if she thought it was a good idea to pin me against the washing machine, she was smart. How the hell could I ever resist her?

'Don't you have a wedding to plan or something?' I asked.

She patted the cushion beside her again, but I refused to sit, so she came to me and undid the buttons of her blouse. She let the cotton slide off her shoulders. Her bra was white and satiny. Her skirt zipped on the side.

'How messy is this?' she whispered.

Stark raving, I thought, as I traced a faint blue vein across the curve of her breast, my hands hovering a fraction of an inch above her skin, my limbs rattling. And, just like that, she took me by the wrist and led me upstairs.

I pretended they'd broken up. Mary Katherine was putting away her halo because the Mayflower had run aground. I shut off my brain. I forgot, forgot until I started living through my hands and mouth, the fine hairs on the back of my neck. She pulled down my boxers. She asked if I was ready to do her. I told her I had condoms. She thought that was a good idea, called me a slut, and rolled onto her side. A coy yawn gave the impression she was just waking up, stretching after a nap. I moved behind her. My lips hovered next to her ear. My stomach pressed tight against the small of her back.

While she was in the bathroom, I looked for the frozen pizza I was having for dinner and remembered I'd already eaten it. In the back of the freezer I found a chicken potpie that had been there for over a year, so I turned on the oven and put my icy meal on a cookie sheet. I was debating whether to put it into the oven or wait until the thing preheated when she came in kitchen and adjusted her skirt.

In class when a student flashed me, I'd move off to the side. But Mary Katherine had angled in front of me and was leaning over as if it were the most natural thing to do. Her breasts were admirable. I mean, she'd always had a little cleavage, but now that it was deep and inviting, fair skin disappearing into warm shadow, she didn't mind showing it off. I put the potpie in the oven. Mary Katherine nudged me with her backside and told me not to look so surprised. People rarely live up to their own expectations. Why should we be any different? Then she pulled up her baggy socks and we agreed that some secrets were necessary.

Two days later I found a note taped to my bathroom mirror. *Sam has a coaches' clinic tomorrow, so I'm kidnapping you. Meet you at my car at 3:00. Don't be late.* A few minutes later I watched Sam from across the cafeteria as he wolfed down runny eggs and graded a few papers. I tried feeling sorry for him. I tried hating him. Nothing felt right, so I hustled off to my first period class, where most of my sophomores were struggling through *The Odyssey*. There was no way we were going to finish it by the time break started, so I put the epic on hold and pulled out Seamus Heaney's poem *Blackberry Picking*. To set the mood I'd brought in canned peaches—a far cry from wild blackberries—but the kids slurped them down anyway, licked the syrup out of their paper bowls, and when they were done, they talked and wrote about desire and futility, how the dark juice of the Heaney's berries could become 'summer blood' and how a passion for fruit, August after painful August, could take over a boy's life.

When class ended, I was high—no need for a second cup coffee—but I was brought down by the figure of Sam waiting outside my door.

'You got a minute?' he asked, all serious and scholarly. I invited him to sit, but three seconds after his ass hit the chair, he was standing again.

'I know I've had a bumpy go of it,' he said nervously, 'and we've had our problems. I've definitely found a way to get under your skin. Anyway, I'm here in the hope that you'll be as fair to me with your next evaluation as you were with the first. I think I've grown a lot this year. I'm finding ways to connect with kids and streamline lessons.' His hands were clasped in his lap. 'You probably also know I'm having a rough time with Mary Katherine, and since you guys are friends, I'd appreciate it if you could be on our side. I don't know what that means exactly, but I need all the help I can get.'

Sam had obviously never studied persuasive speeches. Oh, he had some good rhetoric and his premise was solid. I liked the bit about being fair—a nice catchphrase even if it fluttered about without a twig of context to land on. And his use of 'our' to imply to put a wall around his relationship with Mary Katherine was an artful stroke. But he didn't know the first thing about connecting with his audience. He should have greeted me properly, disarmed me with good will and established some credibility before alluding to his struggles. And to tell me he'd gotten under my skin? Sure, he was the subject of the sentence—taking the blame *and* pointing out our connection—but he needed a real proposition—like please don't sleep with my girlfriend—and not some plea for unnecessary plea for fairness that ignored how big an asshole he'd been.

'I care about both of you,' I said, knowing I was full of shit, 'and when I write my summative evaluation at the end of the year, I'll note your strengths and give you a few things to work on. Don and you will get a copy, and I'll remind him that year one is a challenge for all teachers. As far as I'm concerned, the second year is when...'

'...you'd take me out behind the barn and shoot me?'

'I wouldn't phrase it that way, but yes.'

I was patient. I let Sam talk himself dry and I didn't let myself feel too guilty. If I had, I would've promised a job I couldn't promise, given him an oriental rug and a salad spinner, said something stupid and probably pulled a brophy before sunset. Instead I distracted myself by emailing Josh the Heaney poem and telling him he'd missed a good class. He wrote back and said he was enjoying his suspension—he was even getting along with his mom—and that the poem was too sincere but fun to read out loud.

At 2:58 I was looking through her grimy car window at magazines, food wrappers, a few flattened cardboard boxes. She came out, jingling her keys and humming, and I told her we were taking my truck.

'The time machine?' she replied, 'or is it the rolling love palace?'

'I call it cleaner than your piece of shit,' I said, as she climbed into my passenger's seat and slid it back a few inches. 'And you better not make fun of me or I'm not telling you any more stories.'

'So is this where you did the deed, right here?' she asked. She touched the dashboard and moaned as if it was emitting some kind of pheromone. 'Oh, come on, it was a good story. I like accidental comedy.' She fogged the window with her breath and drew a heart, which she erased when I asked where we were going.

'Doctor visit, thirty minutes max. I could have taken myself, but I wanted to see what you looked like off campus.' As we drove away, she scanned windows and doorways, ready to duck if we saw Sam or Goldie.

'To see if my horns are visible?'

'Sam's different when he's out in the world,' she said, pointing right when we reached Route 20. 'He's sillier and not always looking over his shoulder. I have a theory that you don't really know someone until you've seen them in a supermarket or a doctor's office.'

'Or in a bathing suit.'

'That too,' she said, and ten minutes later we arrived at the Berkshire Medical Center. On the way into the brick building, I asked if Sam knew I was there.

'No, I'm a double agent today.' She looped her arm through mine.

'I think that means he knows what you're doing, but you're really loyal to me?'

'What am I if he doesn't know?'

'A tramp.'

'From the expert,' she said.

Our reflection grew as we approached the double glass doors. Opening them, we were greeted by a blast of hot air. Mary Katherine knew I'd say yes when she proposed a kidnapping, but a doctor's appointment was unknown water. She was like that though—the right side of her brain fighting the left. Take your vitamins. Drink a beer. Fall for the quiet guy. Demure for the showoff. Go to church. Go to hell. Tell your dad it was an immaculate conception. Hide in the garage for nine months. Talk about Sam's getting desperate. Take Greenie to an OBGYN appointment and let him wonder why he's there.

In the obstetrics suite, she signed in, grabbed a magazine she had no intention of reading and told me she was itchy. When a nurse finally called her name, I wasn't expecting to go with Mary Katherine, but she tugged on my sleeve and I followed her to the exam room. Climbing onto the exam table, she introduced me to nurse Jules, who gave me a cautious hello and asked how the patient was feeling. Jules then weighed her, took her blood pressure and announced she was going to lift her shirt but just a few inches. She held a fetal heart monitor against Mary Katherine's belly, and I heard the heartbeat, a giant hummingbird fluttering and jumping at 168 beats per minute.

'I'll trade that for swollen ankles any day,' said Mary Katherine, as her doctor, a petite Indian woman with a shoulder length hair, came in, took a quick measurement of her belly and asked her to put her feet into the stirrups.

'I'll meet you in the waiting room,' I said, and the doctor took a good look at me.

'You're not Sam. Are you...' She was trying to pick her words carefully.

'My upstairs neighbor,' said Mary Katherine. 'He's got a nice car.'

'A good neighbor then,' said the doctor. 'So, Mary, are the stool softeners working?'

In the waiting room I played with plastic dinosaurs and was happy. I looked at my watch and heard the heartbeat again. The receptionist smiled at me from a phone call and I thought about that last time I'd been in a place like this.

It was a cold grey day. They told me sitting was the brave thing to do, but I didn't believe them. My mother had always taught me to love God and respect other people's business. I didn't really believe her either. I did listen though when she told me an abortion is the end of a relationship. It's a loss that needs to be grieved, and not just by her or me, by everyone. That was her way of talking my side. She was smart like that, even if I was a silly boy who'd begun to believe in curses.

But who sets the clock on grieving? And who tells you when it's time to stop? At thirty-five, I believed that time couldn't heal all wounds. No, it was the other way around. Wounds messed with time. They could make it stand still, make it jump around. One day you felt terrible. Then you were great. Then you weren't.

Mary Katherine floated into the waiting area and asked for my car keys.

'Sorry it took so long,' she said, as we walked out to my truck. 'Jules asked what was up with Sam. Then we started talking about how crazy I've been feeling. Like the other day I was at the Shop 'n Go when I walked up to a woman who was reading a package of hotdogs and I just grabbed them from her. Luckily, she took one look at my belly and laughed. Anyway Jules told me that kind of thing is normal.'

Mary Katherine pulled out of the parking lot and pointed us home. She was driving slow, checking the mirrors and not looking at me.

'I called Dunwell for an update,' I said.

'What took you so long?' she asked. 'Aren't they your first choice?'

'I've got a few more interviews coming up. Why rush? Anyway, they said I'm their choice, they just haven't met to make the decision formally.'

'That's good news, right?'

'I guess, but there's always something they don't tell you at the interview.'

Mary Katherine was quiet for a minute. We started up a big hill and the engine dropped to a lower gear. I could tell she was about to drop a secret on me, another of her game changers. 'A little over a year and a half ago Sam and I got pregnant. We were using a condom—honest to God we did—and it didn't work.'

I gazed at the bare trees along the side of the road and thought of us on my sofa. Being with me could be such a burden. So much weight and never enough good deeds. Honest to God we did. I heard real fear. Hummingbirds and geese. How could she be scared of me? I wished I'd kept my mouth shut. I wished she'd just drive, far away from any miserable story I'd ever told her, and let me make jokes.

'I just want you to know,' she said, as a car roared past us up the mountain and jostled the truck. The day was overcast but bright. Mary Katherine clicked out of her seatbelt and kissed me. She tested my lips, found them thoroughly confusing and kissed me again. One of my hands found a place on her shoulder. The other landed on the emergency brake so I wouldn't fall into her.

Thirty-Three

For a million reasons, one being that I'm a coward, I never asked Goldie to sit down with me. For Art more than anything, I wish I'd tried, but looking back, I don't think a conversation would have done much good. One conversation I did have was with Don, when I went into his office the day before spring break and told him I couldn't sign my contract just yet. Dunwell Academy was interested in me, and I wanted to wait until they made their decision before I made mine. He was impressed. I could bump up my salary, reduce my workload and, if I wanted, skip from Dunwell to just about any job I desired. He also understood why I wanted to keep my unsettled but status a secret.

And while I was enhancing my reputation with Don, Sam and Goldie went to Little Sandy's to tear it down. They sat in the middle booth with coffee. There was a steady stream of people in and out of the place: construction workers, white-collar types, kids who should've been in school. One regular, who always ordered a decaffeinated coffee and an apple turnover, was Barbara Brown, the minister's wife. Now, Minister Brown had a reputation of being fair-minded and generous. Having a son who'd graduated from The Mount and gone off to the Navy two years earlier, he had nothing but praise for the school. Barbara, however, had not been pleased with her boy's liberal education, in particular the vulgar content of his English classes, our obscene state-mandated Health curriculum and our general indifference toward sexual promiscuity. Through connections at the medical center, she'd heard rumors of pregnancy tests and that our infirmary was distributing birth control. When she'd confronted our old headmaster, the practice was denied, but Barbara Brown's wrath was not assuaged.

When Barbara Brown, referred to her as Beelzebarb by those who dealt with her on a regular basis, sauntered into Little Sandy's, Goldie looked at Sam, who wished he had a fake mustache, and Sam looked at Goldie.

'With a student! I can't believe it!' said Goldie, just loud enough to be overheard. Beelzebarb sat in the next booth, stirred sugar substitute into her coffee and pulled the wax paper off her pastry while Goldie told the story. Sam punctuated it with disbelief and an account of my assault on Hodge. By the end of the day, dozens of outraged women had heard my name for the first time.

Oblivious to Beelzebarb's ire, however, I packed my truck and left campus. The year before I'd spent part of my vacation helping Rog in the sugar shack. But this year I left the mud behind and on short notice visited all the friends I'd been neglecting. In Washington, D.C., I babysat for a two-year-old and played tennis with my doubles partner from college. In Portland, Maine, I hiked around Mackworth Island with a childhood friend and told her I was once again falling for the wrong woman. In New York, I went to the Museum of Modern Art and got lost in a painting by Paul Klee—tiny squares, tones gracefully stepping from light to dark, the childlike face of a man becoming aware of his senility. For a few days I dreamed of moving to the city— I'd applied for three jobs there—but in Burlington, Vermont, I slept under a scratchy blanket in my second cousin's guest room and started thinking about what my world would be like without Sam and Mary Katherine. I'd known him for him for seven months, her for less than three, yet somehow they easily filled up the last two years of my life.

When Sam returned to the mountainside, his shoulders were back and he was wearing expensive leather hiking boots. He walked in them like he was taking a victory lap and I was pretty sure he'd gotten laid. Don, however, took the wind out of his sails when he called him and Goldie into his office to talk about Barbara Brown and the barrage of calls he'd been fielding about the well being of our children.

Goldie wasn't surprised that Beelzebarb had known her name or worried about sitting down with Don. All she had to do was flash her pretty teeth and he'd stammer. Sam, on the other hand, was mortified.

Having underestimated the power of the inveterate lie and the reputation Goldie had earned with her nefarious yet occasionally charitable activities, he'd not expected his name to come up. Now all he could do was put on a concerned face and utter a new mantra, 'I didn't realize anyone was eavesdropping.'

I sat with Don a day later, unaware that he'd already met with Sam and Goldie.

'What's up?' I asked, sinking one of his leather chairs. There were papers scattered atop his desk and the remnant of a sandwich in his wastebasket. Rather than sitting with his belly against the front of his desk, Don seemed to be leaning back in fear.

'I've got Sam and Goldie telling the world you've been having a relationship with Cassie Diaz.'

I stared at him blankly and counted to three.

'What assholes, where'd they come up with that nonsense?'

'From the horse's mouth, they say.' For a second I thought he'd said 'from the whore's mouth,' but it wasn't the time to make jokes.

'That's absolutely crazy.'

'Well, because of them Barbara Brown thinks the sky's falling and that all the girls on The Mount are being deflowered by their teachers. So you're denying everything?'

'Cass had a crush on me a while back. I didn't encourage it and I've had good boundaries with her. She'd be in Sam's class now, and not taking an independent course with me, but she told me she wasn't comfortable around him, in part because he called her princess.'

'Has she been to your apartment? Goldie says...'

'Don, Goldie dropped the girl off at my apartment over a month ago with a couple pieces of pizza to give me. I don't know why she thought that was a good idea, but I sent the girl away...after I took the pizza, of course. You can ask her.'

I could see in his eyes that Don wanted to believe me. But he was also worried about talking to Cass. If she said something happened, he'd have a big pile of shit to deal with. If she said Ms. Remlap got it wrong, he'd have to get a stick and start scraping it off his shoes.

'I talked with Gunnar at length about this,' I said. 'I thought an administrator should know.'

'I wish you'd told me. Can you still teach her or do we need to find someone else to advise her independent course?'

'She owes me some work, but we're fine.' I settled into my chair, eager to give the impression I'd stay as long as he wanted, and he started to relax.

That Saturday, my ninth graders had to spend forty-five minutes with me before they could run off on their weekend trips. I didn't dare make them write, so we slouched at our desks and gossiped about the ending of *The Odyssey*. In February, spurred by boredom and a heroic impulse, I'd pulled eleven copies from a dusty corner of the book room and bragged to Gunnar that not only were my little ones going to finish Homer's epic, they were going to love it. We bet a case of beer on it. I thought I'd win because of Josh. He'd lick his lips over the violence and adultery. Elizabeth, who was still with us at the time, would feast on the poetry and the structure. And the others, they'd succumb to the enthusiasm of my stars and realize the text wasn't so difficult. Besides, we'd already studied myths and gods. Now they could strut their stuff and dazzle me.

'What's up with Odysseus and Athena?' asked Josh. 'Did they ever get it on?'

'She just messes around with him,' said Miles, 'like he's her puppet.'

'She's more like his mother,' added one of the girls. 'Also the goddesses he did sleep with weren't nearly as cool as Athena. Calypso basically enslaved him and that other one, Circus, she'd turned his men into pigs.'

'Yeah, he had to be a gigolo to get them free,' said Josh, 'but it didn't seem like he minded too much.'

Not bad stuff for a Saturday, even if the rest of the class in over their heads and I'd already lost my bet. I asked if anyone wanted to read a passage she liked. Miles raised his hand and directed us to a section where Athena is chiding Odysseus for not trusting her. She tells him she'd never let him be hurt in battle. Fifty bands of armed men could have him surrounded, and he'd still be able to steal their livestock and get away without a scratch. She finishes her admonishment by telling him to go to bed. *This all night vigil wearies the flesh. You'll come out soon enough on the other side of trouble.*

'Just like a mother,' said Josh. 'He's a king, but she's sending him off to bed.'

'What I don't get,' said Miles, wrinkling his brow, 'is why everyone thinks Odysseus is so great. I mean, here's he's getting ready to slaughter all these guys just for hanging out in his house and eating his food. I don't see them as a real threat.'

'They were trying to score with his wife,' said Josh. 'He's got to defend his honor.'

'But he's been gone for twenty years,' offered one of the girls. 'The suitors had a right to court Penelope even if she is holding onto the hope that he'll come back. Somebody needs to be king.'

'They'll never be the real king though,' said Miles. 'That's why Athena backs up Odysseus. But, think about it, he's not just gonna get away with murder. He's going to be praised forever.'

'It doesn't seem fair,' said Josh, 'or like his trouble's really trouble. He could just march in and tell those guys to get out. They'd run if they saw a god at his side. That's why I'm rooting for the suitors.'

'But if Athena's calling the shots,' asked Joe, surprising all of us, 'what choice does Odysseus have? He has to kill.'

'Maybe that's why her words bug me,' replied Miles. 'The way she assures him the killing will be easy makes him seem like a tool.'

'He's still descended from gods,' said Josh, 'he fought for his friends and he's nice to nice people.'

'That don't mean shit,' said Miles.

Josh looked at me with a half smile, hoping—but not really—that I'd scold Miles for swearing. But before I could reprimand, cower or give them my long-winded take on what it meant to be a tarnished hero, class ended and the kids bolted out the door.

Needing a brophy and having a bare cupboard, I went to the Big Y supermarket in Pittsfield. But as I was choosing between creamy and chunky peanut butter, I heard their voices in the next aisle. Not arguing, but having a polite disagreement as any married couple would, they were trying to decide which macaroni and cheese dinner—the three pack or the single meal box—was a better value.

I left my Diet Pepsi and Pop Tarts on the shelf by the peanut butter and started out of the market. At the end of my aisle, I peeked around the corner and saw Sam riding his shopping cart. Mary Katherine had a hand on the front so he wouldn't hit anything. She looked happy.

Five minutes later, I pulled up in front of the movie theater on Route 20 but left without getting out of my car when I saw Goldie and Art heading for the ticket line. I thought about going to Williamstown, but I didn't want to spend the afternoon wondering what Mary Katherine had looked at when she was there. In the end, I went to a diner in Lee and sat at the counter with a cup of coffee and a piece of lemon meringue pie. After scouring a day-old copy of the Berkshire Eagle, I graded a few papers and ordered a second piece of pie. Around five, some older guys and a family with two red-haired boys came in and filled up the booths. I said no to third cup of coffee, left twice my bill on the counter and went back to school.

The mall trip had just returned so center campus was teeming with kids. Amid the bustling, I saw Kwame standing outside the main door with a stricken look on his face. I waved and he flashed a palm. Looking over my shoulder as I passed the side entrance, I saw Barbara Brown bustling into the building. After parking at my house and finding out from my answering machine that Dunwell was finally ready to make me an offer, I went back to see what was up, but Kwame was no longer there. All I could find out was that he'd driven off with Ichabob. I went to his dorm.

'He was so stupid' was the first thing I heard. The boys were gathered around the common room, their feet on the table; a two-liter bottle of Coke was being passed around.

'Could Iafrati and Driscoll just search him like that?'

Apparently, Sam had seen Kwame in the stairwell by the Student Center. He was wearing a backpack, collecting money, and checking off names on a yellow piece of paper. And when Sam had accosted him, not a peep, not a scowl. Almost as if he'd expected it, Kwame followed him to Ichabob's office and opened his backpack. His mother demanded he be sent home right away.

No one believed Kwame had wanted to get caught selling pot. He'd always been so sneaky, so cool. He'd been a good student too, getting B's without any effort. I packed up Kwame's stuff the next day, laying a sheet of tissue paper on top of his clothes and putting all of his shoes in plastic bags. I even boxed his condoms, his unopened food and the brass hooks he'd installed in his closet.

While crating his things, I came across a photograph of Kwame and some white kid. In it they were holding guns and flashing gang signs. Kwame had gotten in trouble for having a gun in July, so at first I thought the picture was old, but there was date in the corner of the picture telling me it had been taken that March. I sent it to his mother and penned a note to him explaining why I'd ratted on him. I had no idea what he'd think of me or if I'd failed him, only that I was never going to hear from the kid again.

Friends in High Places

Thirty-Four

'This is the night,' said Gunnar. 'We're going to catch a bitch.'

'You've said that fifty times in the past two weeks. Why don't you just forget about it and get some sleep?'

'I got real intelligence, the old fashioned way. Art's on duty tonight and he's got no first period class, so he's putting in earplugs and sleeping in the guest bedroom. Don't ask how I know. Anyway, I also saw Goldie and Dorsey laughing it up in the mailroom. She's getting him to help her with this big box and they're looking at each other all sneaky. It was so obvious they were planning something.'

'It's cold out, Dude. I've got half a bottle of port from my birthday and a bag of walnuts. Let's just kick back.'

'I'm sleeping in a black turtleneck. And I'm coming over at four.'

'Gunnar, what are you really going to do if you catch her? You can't get her fired for adultery.'

'I'm going to walk in and act surprised. I'm going to say I thought some kids were sneaking around and I just happened to be out. Then I'm going to tell Candy, and she's going to whisper it to you Kyle, and in about ten minutes every person on campus, except for maybe Art, is going to know that the queen of the justice league is just a spider.' I groaned disapproval, and decided not to tell him—at least not for a while—that I was taking another job she was getting the English chair anyway.

At four Gunnar let himself into my apartment with his master key and woke me. Swearing at him, I pulled snow pants over my pajama bottoms, threw on my winter coat and grabbed a travel mug, which he filled with coffee from the big thermos he'd brought.

'Did the top fall off the sugar?' I asked, as we skirted around the Remlap's house and wedged our bodies into the big evergreen bushes across the drive from the garage.

There was a biting wind and the puddles were all half frozen and on the way to becoming solid ice. Nestled into the branches of the bush, however, I was warm and fairly cozy. Above me the bush was wearing a cap of hard snow and the gap in front of gave me a partial view of the garage and its side door. Gunnar was a few feet away, equally well concealed and about a foot higher because he was standing on a low branch.

We stood there for twenty minutes, chatting softly. Gunnar took a leak in the snow from his perch. He'd already finished two cups of coffee. The garage was dark. The henhouse was dark. The dorms, the mountainside, everything except for the pale light on the Sugar Shack was lifeless. I remembered seeing Sam and Mary Katherine kissing by the Sugar Shack as the moths formed a cloud over their heads.

'You hear about the unhappy justice leaguers?' asked Gunnar. 'Their dance got cancelled.'

'I thought they raised enough money and it was a go.'

'None of the other schools want to stay late, so Goldie's pulled the plug on the dance part.'

'It's just the conference now? Are they even getting pizza?'

'After they take a couple photographs for the alumni magazine, sure.'

Gunnar reached between a few branches and pushed me. I couldn't see anything, but a few seconds later I hear the growl of a big truck with a custom exhaust. I didn't want to believe it was Dorsey. Somehow it was a lot more comforting to think of Gunnar as silly. The truck stopped at the shed and idled. A muffled *Carry on my Wayward Son* wafted over to us. A good song for the guy. Then Dorsey cut the engine, went around to the back of his truck and opened the tailgate. He was pulling a box out of the back when Goldie came up next to him.

Gunnar stumbled in his bush, more surprised than anyone to see them at what must have been about 4:45 in the morning. Dorsey was wearing no hat or gloves, just his work boots and a fleece jacket. He had an old parka in the garage that he wore on cold days. But he the kind of guy cold didn't bother. Goldie, on the other hand, was bundled up—homemade hat with an extra large pompom, mittens from Kara and some big furry snow boots.

'We've got to stop meeting like this,' she said. It sounded like she was being ironic. Gunnar started giggling. Then he clamped a hand over his own mouth, and even though the bush was now shaking, Dorsey and Goldie seemed none the wiser. Dorsey said something I couldn't hear, grabbed the box and she followed him inside.

'Give them a few minutes,' whispered Gunnar excitedly.

'Are you really going to bust in on them?' I asked. I had to pee now. I just wanted to tell Gunnar I was leaving The Mount, so there was no point in spying on Goldie. But he was so excited to catch them pants down, schlong out, that it might not have mattered.

I stepped out of the bush and took a leak. The wind raced into my fly and sent a cruel chill up my spine. I thought of Cass behind the woodpile. At least she had a sense of humor about freezing her tail off. When it was time to move, Gunnar grabbed my shoulder and we snuck up to the garage. Goldie and Dorsey had turned on a light, but since the building had no windows all we could see was a sliver under the side door.

'Let me see it,' we heard her say through the wall.

Gunnar was a four year old with chocolate in each hand.

'Nice?' said Dorsey. His voice was deep and serious as if he was answering his own question.

Goldie complained about being cold, said she could see her breath.

'You want me to take it out now?' he asked.

'Yeah, let me check that thing out,' she said. 'Oh, I like it. I really do. I didn't think I'd be into this. That's what I said to Art when we got married. But I have to admit it's fun.'

Dorsey laughed. By now Gunnar was biting his mitten and jumping up and down with glee. Goldie and Dorsey became quite. Gunnar's eyes became saucers.

'It's perfect,' said Goldie. 'I don't know how to thank you for all of this.'

'I'll think of a way,' replied Dorsey, grunting lightly.

They were quiet again. Gunnar could barely breathe. He got down on his belly and tried to look under the door. He pulled out his keys and found the master. There was a bump against the wall. We both froze.

'I wish there were a way to get warm,' said Goldie.

'This was your idea,' replied Dorsey. 'Hey, let me get this out of your way. You want to use the chair?'

'I'm fine standing,' she said, and she moaned. 'I am something, aren't I?'

'You want to let her rip?' asked Dorsey.

'Can we? Can we?' asked Goldie. 'Then by all means rip it. Rip it.'

Gunnar gaped in amazement. He actually looked scared. It was time to bust in on them, but maybe he was having second thoughts. Still, he pushed his key into the lock and took a deep breath, but just then we heard a gigantic noise, the roar of an engine.

'Oh yeah,' yelled Goldie over the roar.

Gunnar turned the key and discovered that the garage was one of the few places on campus his master key couldn't open.

'Help me,' he said, and he pulled me around to the side of the building. I saw a vent about ten feet off the ground. Light was spilling out of it. After moving a few wooden crates and hopping over a half-frozen puddle, he told me to give him a boost. Inside the engine was roaring. It got louder, quieter and then loader. Goldie's excited voice could barely be heard over the noise.

Gunnar climbed up on my knee, his boot digging in and causing me to wince. Then he leaned against the building a tried to step up onto my shoulders. I didn't quite know what he was trying to do and he slipped off and fell to the ground.

'What the fuck man, hold still,' he said, rubbing his hip.

So we tried again. This time I crouched down so he wouldn't crush my leg, and when he got up to my shoulders, he put his nose up to the vent. Inside over the roaring, we heard Goldie yell 'yes,' and Gunnar once again came crashing down next to me, this time his body smashing into a wooden crate and through the icy puddle.

'Fuck,' he yelled, grabbing his ankle, just as the engine stopped. Then he pulled me behind the shed and bit down on his hand because Goldie and Dorsey were coming out. After the big guy drove away and she shuffled back up to her house with a huge satisfied smile on her face, Gunnar let out a string of foul words and told me to take him to the emergency room.

'Of course it was a motorcycle,' said Mary Katherine. 'The same kind he gave up when he got married, some classic Japanese model, though that sounds like an oxymoron. I can't believe you didn't know? She's been talking about his birthday for months.'

I'd just gotten home after dropping off Gunnar, who now had a cast on his foot, when I'd heard a light knock on the door that separated my apartment from the dorm. Mary Katherine, wearing sweatpants and a baseball cap, had heard me prowling. I leaned against the wall, and after laughing at Gunnar, she told me she was sorry about Kwame.

'If it's any consolation,' she added, 'Sam didn't enjoy catching him.'

'The kid probably needed it. Want a glass of milk?' I asked, and I led her to the kitchen, where I opened the fridge. After pouring the milk, I put some graham crackers on a plate. 'You have a good break?'

'We didn't drive each other crazy if that's what you mean.' She dunked a cracker into her glass. 'But I didn't knock to tell you that.'

Milk and graham crackers. The hum of the fridge. I expected tenderness and we discussed the awkward reality of out 'situation,' but Mary Katherine hadn't come up to let me down easy. No, she ripped into me for playing games with Gunnar while people were screwing with my career.

'I've accepted an offer from Dunwell,' I said. 'You're the second person to know about it. So, I escape, Goldie's dreams come true, and Sam, well, he'll get a fair shake, but I'm not making any promises.'

'You don't think Don's capable of doing something stupid?'

'And keep me from leaving? Never. Besides, I'm done scheming, girl.'

Mary Katherine put her cup in the sink and told me I was being naïve. Don was probably going to spill the beans anyway, but it might be interesting to keep my new job a secret and see just how popular I was before turning over Oscar's keys.

'What are you up to?' I asked.

'Nothing,' she said. 'I swear.'

Patience, iron patience you must show, said Athena—or was it Mary Katherine?—to Odysseus. '*Be silent under all injuries, even blows from men.*' It was advice I was prepared to follow for a while, but sometimes the gods work quickly.

I was watching a documentary on life in the Antarctic when Josh Henderson's mother, Beth Bartkowski, called to ask if I had any open conference slots on Parents' Weekend. Being an English teacher, I didn't, so I invited her to chat with my while I coached my tennis match.

'Won't I be in the way?' she asked.

'Not at all, I'd welcome the distraction.'

'Wonderful. Oh, I don't know if you're the right person to ask, but my husband and I have stumbled into an inheritance and we were thinking of making a gift to the school. I never thought I'd be saying this, but when he was home, Josh was so downright delightful. He actually volunteered to help me soundproof the garage. Anyway, we'd like to give a little something to the school that's giving us our kid back and we were wondering about how to do it. David's interested in a scoreboard or something. I was thinking more along academic lines, something for your department maybe, like an academic chair. Does that sound appropriate?'

I assured her it did, asked her to contact both Don and Scooter Kelly, the Director of the Board of Trustees, and I spent the rest of the afternoon praying to the goddess.

When I walked into my apartment after class the next afternoon, papers rustled. Someone moved across the floor. *Leaves of Grass* was sitting on top of my bookcase. Mary Katherine was sitting in my Shaker Chair waiting for me.

'The dummy didn't want to part with it, but she understood when I explained.'

Cass had been scared to find Sam's big woman standing outside her door, but she let Mary Katherine in and invited her to sit on the bed. The girl was wearing a fishing cap and white jeans that had gotten muddy at the cuffs. Mary Katherine, in faded bib overalls, like someone smuggling a pumpkin out of the patch, asked for help. At first Cass was petulant, but Mary Katherine swore she was going to give the book back to Mr. Green and not to her boyfriend.

'You didn't need to,' I said. 'Really.'

I told her about the possible gift from Josh's mom. Impressed, Mary Katherine stood and rubbed some life back into her thighs. The couch was more comfortable than my Shaker Chair, but the somehow the chair suited her.

'You're something,' she said. 'But Goldie will stoop lower than any of you guys.'

Mary Katherine started stuffing newspaper into the fireplace. I didn't like to see her bending, even though she did it well, but when I tried to help, she told me to get more logs. Outside, the tarp had blown off the pile outside front door and the wood had gotten wet. After loading up, I clomped back into the house and stacked my logs on top of the sputtering stove.

'I've given books to kids before,' I said. 'Doesn't taking it back look fishy?'

Mary Katherine brushed past me and tended to the flames.

'Okay Mr. High Road, how smug are you going to be next time you see Sam?'

'Can I ask how the job search is going?'

'He's had a couple of interviews. No bites yet. If he can't find anything, we can stay here until July. My parents will put us up after that. And if I want my old job, it won't be filled until the summer. That was the nun's going away present.'

'It must be nice to have friends in high places?'

'Or,' she said, with a flourish, 'your tutoring program desperately needs a coordinator and Social Studies is a joke. I could always stay here.'

'You've been talking to Gunnar and Don? They'd actually have you?'

'Why wouldn't they?' She tried to smack me in the head. Then she tried to grab me. 'Come here, I'm not gonna hurt you,' she said. 'Does Dunwell know it's getting a dirty old man?'

'Not yet,' I said.

Don dressed like a used car salesman, talked like a junior priest and walked around campus like he was lost. Sometimes she thought he was a little retarded.

'How are you're classes?' he asked, playing with his pen.

'Good,' she said.

'I asked you to stop by so I can be sure you're going to graduate on time and to make sure you're not having any trouble.'

'My grades have always been good.'

He pulled out a piece of paper covered with dubious scribbles and telephone numbers. 'How about your independent writing class?'

'That's the exception. I owe Mr. Green some work, but I've got a few half-finished pieces,' she replied warily.

'When do you meet with Mr. Green?'

'Mostly during conference period in his classroom with the door open.'

'Have you been up to his apartment or met him outside a classroom?'

'No, like I said, we meet during conference period. He goes over my work while I erase his blackboard. Look, I know there's been some talk about us, but nothing's ever happened, Mr. DeWillum. I was talking with Mrs. Remlap once about guys we both think are cute, and she brought up Mr. Green and Mr. Day. Another time I was upset about some other guy, and she thought for a minute I was talking about a teacher. But that was her mistake. She's kind of got that sort of thing stuck on her brain.'

By the end of the conversation, she'd splayed her fingers atop his desk and begun to slouch. When circumstances demanded it, she knew how to look both disinterested and convincing. Mr. DeWillum might not have believed her, but she'd brought her A game.

That afternoon Josh's parents pledged a large check. Later that week, I learned my tenth graders' poetry would be featured in the alumni magazine. Finally, all of my advisees made the third quarter Dean's List—even Kwame—and one, a Korean boy I rarely spoke to, was slated to be the salutatorian at commencement. Goldie and Sam may have had big dreams and slippery friends. But with Cass blowing smoke rings and The Girlfriend, Mary watching my back, they were still on the outside looking in.

Thirty-Five

Gunnar, Candy, Mary Katherine and Art were crammed into a corner of a bar called The Log Cabin. Gunnar was chasing an itch inside his cast with a chopstick and telling Art, who'd just celebrated his birthday, a slightly sanitized version of the accident.

'There's public enemy number two,' said Art, when I sat. As Art hummed a verse of *Don't Stand So Close to Me*, I blew him a kiss and poured a beer from the pitcher. Secret agent Kimball, a bachelorette for the evening, raised her ginger ale and gave me a nod. Candy asked if she'd thought of any baby names yet.

'Dirk and Fiona are the latest ones,' she said. 'Those were my hamsters.'

Gunnar raised his glass. 'To Dirk or Fiona.'

Art sort of smiled because Goldie, still hoping to get pregnant, was at home with the phone wedged between her shoulder and ear. She'd been having a lot of hushed conversations lately. Tonight when she'd taken the phone to the sewing room, he grabbed his keys and joined us.

'Why don't we talk about Gunnar's burgeoning love life?' said Mary Katherine, who was proud to have been his matchmaker.

'Do you know how big a pain it is to drive with this thing on my foot?'

'He claims he's getting laid by some exotic chick named Mamawaldi,' said Candy, 'but I still think he's gay.'

Gunnar looked sideways at Mary Katherine. 'It's Agnaldi and she's a woman of color. If you call her exotic to her face, she'd punch you. But I just want to know if Greenie's getting any from the upstairs neighbor yet.'

Candy spit beer onto the table and Art almost fell out of his chair. I couldn't tell whether they were laughing because it seemed implausible, absurd, brazen, kinky, possible, or just because it had been a really long winter.

'He's playing hard to get,' said Mary Katherine.

'Does that sound like me?' I replied.

'He only likes whorish teenagers,' she said.

'And she's just a whore,' I replied.

'This is weirder than being home with Goldie,' said Art.

'I'll drink to that,' added Candy, we clanged our glasses together and she blew us away with the announcement that she was moving in with her girlfriend, Lauralee.

'You traitor, where the hell are you going?' I asked.

'Virginia,' said Candy. 'Lauralee's landed an assistance professorship at UVA. She's got an offer here, too, but we didn't think big Don would let us shack up and adopt Chinese babies.'

'Lesbian parents in campus housing? He wouldn't put you in the viewbook, but he'd eat that shit up,' I said. 'But how can you leave us now?'

'Gunnar and you will have to fight the bad guys,' said Candy. 'Lord knows I would love to kick Goldie's ass—no offense, Art—but it'd be hell on my love life.'

I raised my glass. 'Here's to waking up in the same bed as your honey.'

'You know,' said Candy, after we drank, 'I always pictured myself with someone more girly, maybe like Julia Roberts. Never thought I'd get Richard Gere with a pussy and be so happy.'

'How stoned are you?' I asked.

'Not at all,' she replied. 'Gunnar didn't want to drive.'

Some of the students were calling Cass 'Chickenhead'—it meant she like to give blowjobs—and one joker thought it'd be fun to tape kneepads to her door. Cass fended off the insults for a while, but one day she stopped wearing her own clothes—there were still a few closets open to her—and refused to work on her independent project.

Spying an opportunity, Sam led her to an empty tutorial room. For a second Cass thought he was going to make a pass at her and pulled her shirt closed.

'I'm concerned about you,' he said.

'I'll tell Kwame the next time I see him.'

'Look, I like Kwame, too, but Mr. Driscoll and I caught him dealing. But, like I said, I'm concerned about you and it has to do with Mr. Green.'

'Are you so jealous you gotta tear the guy down?'

Sam sighed and was forced to bluff. 'I've got news for you, Cassie. Mr. DeWillum didn't believe you.'

Even though she had a feeling he was lying, Cass blushed.

'What do you want me to do?'

'Just tell Mr. DeWillum the truth. You'll feel better.' Sam softened. 'Cassie, Mr. Green won't get in real trouble. No one will. The school doesn't want that kind of publicity, but don't you think it's time to be honest?'

'I have told the truth, Mr. Iafrati. Why won't you believe me?'

'Mr. DeWillum knows about the phone calls. You may not understand completely, but you are a victim here.' Cass remembered the answering machine fiasco. Sam saw her blink and said, 'You can trust me.' Cass had seen *The Jungle Book*; she remembered the snake and his kaleidoscope eyes. The snake was funny, you liked his singing, but Sam wasn't half as charming.

'Mr. Iafrati,' she said, 'you are one of the biggest assholes I've ever met.'

'I'll pretend I didn't hear that,' he replied, and they both walked out of the room feeling a strange sense of elation.

Saturday morning began with an egg bagel and a cup of hazelnut coffee in the valley. It was one of my last 'free' days of the school year. Between tennis matches, Parents' Weekend and dorm duty I was working thirty of the next thirty-two days. With this in mind, I planned to do as little as possible. I'd take a meal in the real world, teach my

10:30 class and run to the end of Chair Factory Road and most of the way back. At night, I'd prep for the week and watch TV. At Little Sandy's, however, I was driven back to my apartment by the glares of women I didn't know.

Sam's miracle showed up at 10:20 while I was reading The New York Times. Loud, insistent, violent. Through the window I saw a Monte Carlo with smoked windows next to my truck. There were voices—Cass muttering that I wasn't home, some guy swearing under his breath. Then more banging.

'I know he's in there. That guy told me so.'

'He's not in there. He's probably off somewhere getting ready for his class. Come on, Jesus. Let's get outta here. You don't need to beat him up.' She pulled on his arm and he reluctantly went back to his car.

But the little idiot had told him I had a class. Where was all her shrewdness when I really needed it? Cursing all the way, I drove down to the main building, parked by the rear entrance and darted into my class ten seconds before it began. I hardly remember what I made my tenth graders do for forty minutes, only that I felt Jesus Demaquina lurking in the hall and once or twice spotted his shadow behind the white paper I'd put over the window in my door to keep Don DeWillum from looking in.

Bellies rumbling, the students rushed out as soon as I'd assigned their homework. I braced myself for Jesus, but he didn't bust in. Had Cass convinced him to leave? No way, when I walked to my car, I found the Monte Carlo blocking me in. So I scurried back to the teachers' room, where I cleaned out my mailbox and straightened the cushions on the sofa until Rolly came in. We were talking about the money his recycling program had raised, when I saw Cass and Jesus through the window. He was stomping across the gravel drive as if he might plow right through a wall. I jumped away from the window but too late. He'd spotted me and his eyes became saucers.

My instincts took over. When he disappeared in the side door, I pushed up the window and jumped out. Hoping the coast was clear, I started back up to my apartment. But just as I reached the recycling bins at the back of the cafeteria, I heard Cass around the corner.

'Come on, Jesus, I could get in trouble. Let's go to the dorm.' I made a u-turn and cut through the kitchen. On the way I grabbed a BLT and a chocolate chip cookie. As Jesus entered the cafeteria, I bolted down the stairwell to the nurse's office and back outside. Hot on my trail, Jesus asked a kid which direction I'd gone off in. The kid pointed toward the main building.

I stepped into Ichabob's office and found him sitting at his desk.

'Did you know Jesus was on campus?' I asked, closing his door.

'I do now,' he said. 'And I'm guessing he looking for you.'

Jesus stomped by the office. 'People are going crazy with this shit. Will you go out there and tell him I'm gay?'

Ichabob peeked out the window. 'He sounds pretty angry.'

Giving up on my Dean of Students, I made a dash for the woods across the street. If I made it to my house, hopefully Jesus would be gone by dinnertime. When I hit the road though, I saw Mary Katherine in her station wagon. I waved her down, got low in the passenger's seat, and explained my predicament.

'I should make you get out,' she said, slowing to a crawl.

'Who do you think tipped him off?' It was hard to sound indignant from the floor of her car.

'Sam and Goldie are already on Don's radar, so I'd put my money on Roger.'

'If you take me up campus, I'll rub your feet.'

'Just a foot rub?'

'Name your price,' I said. 'Just get me out of here.'

When we got up to our building, she brought me into her apartment and made me a cup of hot chocolate while I looked at all her baby stuff. I was particularly taken with these little socks that were supposed to look like sneakers. Meanwhile, just when Cass thought Jesus was going to start breaking things, he stopped chasing me and started paying attention to her.

'What happened to your hair?' he asked. 'It used to be different.'

'I couldn't control it in winter. There's so much electricity around here I had to cut some off and condition more.'

'Will you let it grow back out?' he asked. 'And why are you

wearing such a huge shirt? You're lost in there.'

Don DeWillum heard Jesus and Cass walking outside his house, but it wasn't until Roger Day called to complain about his chasing me that Don found the courage to investigate. While pulling on his coat, however, he got a call from a reporter at the Berkshire Gazette.

'Have you fired a teacher for having an affair with a student?' she asked.

'No,' said Don. 'Some girls teased another by starting that rumor. I've talked to all the girls and a few teachers, and I'm convinced it was pure fiction.'

'So it was a bullying incident? Was anyone expelled?'

'Barely even hazing,' replied Don, and when he finally made it to the dorm, he found Jesus and Cass and packed a suitcase. If he'd investigated an hour earlier, she would've stuck to her story. If he'd stopped by twenty minutes earlier, he might've suspended her for dry humping Jesus behind a closed door. If he'd come a few minutes later, she might've been gone. But, no, he'd come just when Jesus was easy to shoo and Cass was open to a conversation.

Don sat on Cass's bed. 'Why the luggage?'

'If I left,' she began, 'I could get my GED and be in the city. Away from all this crazy stuff.'

Don picked up a roll of toilet paper Cass had on her dresser and stuck his fingers in the ends. She pulled down a few sheets and tore them off.

'I'd hate not giving you a diploma,' he said, handing her the roll after she blew her nose. 'It'll take you farther than a GED and, besides, you've almost earned it.'

In the end, she shared a few of the details she'd left out before: flashing me, coming up to my apartment uninvited, Goldie's dropping her off, the uneasy truce she'd tried to maintain. She praised me for being generous and told Don that Sam was the one who was bothering her, but not sexually. Then she assured Don the drama was over and apologized for Jesus.

After hot chocolate with Mary Katherine, I went upstairs and pushed the play button on my answering machine. I half expected a death threat from Jesus or a warning from Cass. Instead I heard the voice of Rose Hession from Dunwell Academy.

'Hi Jeff,' she began, 'I've got some really unexpected and unpleasant news for you. It seems that Jeremiah Hart has had second thoughts about retiring. He'd submitted his letter in January and we even planned a party, but when it was time to announce his decision to the faculty this week, he couldn't go through with it. I'm so sorry to be telling you this, especially on your voice mail, but the position we offered you doesn't exist any longer. We'd love so much to have you on board, but Jere has been in our department for so long. Well, if you have any questions, please call. Otherwise, good luck with your search. A teacher of your caliber should have no trouble finding a position. I'm just sad it's not here. Bye.'

Thirty-Six

I held the phone a good ten inches from my ear while Charles Scooter Kelly, Director of the Board of Trustees and Rog's second cousin once removed, informed me that Don had called him about my latest ruckus.

'So you're moving off to Dunwell? I think your timing couldn't be better. And I hope there are no fireworks on Parents' Weekend. It would be very unfortunate if there were. Still, there is a pleasant part to this call: our appreciation for your reaching out to Mrs. Bartkowski. She's obviously pleased by the work you've done with her boy.'

Eat shit, I thought, still smarting that I wasn't going to Dunwell and desperate because I'd cancelled every other interview I'd line up the second I'd accepted the position. And now, now I had squat. I asked how big the gift was.

'Twenty thousand and forty more when John graduates.'

'It's Josh,' I said.

'Are you sure?' asked Scooter.

'Very sure,' I said.

When he heard Don had called Scooter and Scooter had called me, Sam started dancing. Now that Cass had cracked and Rog was feeding sordid details to his second cousin once removed, why not be ecstatic? Why not bounce down the road to the dorm where Mary Katherine was scratching her belly and grab her hand.

The Chapel Trail was muddy and not at all green. The surrounding towns may have been bursting with color, but our flora always waited a cautious week or two longer before gracing the mountainside. Eight months earlier Sam had walked this same trail with Mary Katherine. They'd held hands when the path was wide enough. But when it narrowed, she led him to a secluded stand of birches. Today when they reached the spot where they made a baby, Sam put his hands in his pockets and apologized for being so fanatical, especially about drinking and swearing.

'Do you know where we are?' he asked.

'Of course I do,' she replied looking at the birches. 'Why are you so happy?'

'I'm just happy you're still talking to me.'

'I have no standards.'

'Did you really like me better when I got drunk?'

Not drunk, tipsy. When he'd tease her with French words he couldn't pronounce and intentionally mix up historical figures. Mary Katherine sat on a rock and remembered the dappled late summer light painting a halo above his head.

'Did you know Jesus was coming?' she asked.

'Yes.'

'Did you think for a second about what could happen to Jeff or Cassandra?'

'I'm sorry,' he said, 'but it got her to tell the truth. Now people can sort out the facts and decide for themselves. And maybe I can be judged fairly.'

'Sam, there's something I want to tell you,' she said. 'This shit is none of our business, and it never was. And none of this, by the way, is about the truth.'

Sam heard the words, but he was still stuck on the words *there's something I want to tell you*, still double-checking to make sure she hadn't dumped him.

Per was not cut out to be a jock. It wasn't the occasional pot smoking or the love of rebellion either. No, despite a fair amount of athletic ability, Per just didn't get the 'team' thing. Maybe that's why he decided to play tennis. What he didn't realize is that tennis is a great way to discover that you will always be your own worst enemy.

'Forget about the person on the other side of the court,' I'd said one afternoon when rain forced us inside. I held my hand at my shoulder. 'Now given all the givens, this is how good you are. So what should happen if you play someone this good?' I lowered my hand a few inches.

Harriet, who liked me now that I'd whacked Hodge, spoke up. 'You win.'

'You got it, and what if this is your opponent?' I raised my hand to my ear, but no one answered. 'You're going to get stomped, right?'

'So this is you,' said Per, raising his hand to his shoulder. 'And this is Iafrati.' He lowered his hand to his waist. The kids laughed.

'But what if you lose your cool?' asked Harriet.

'Yeah,' said Per, 'Even pros choke once in a while.'

'That's why they sometimes lose to weaker players and why you have to learn to surrender. Don't worry about the score or the point you just screwed up. Those things will destroy you. Just ignore the competition, or better yet, turn it into fun. Then the wins take care of themselves and the loses...at least you'll know you played to your potential.'

'I'm supposed to have fun when someone's hitting a ball at my head?' asked Harriet. 'No wonder I suck at this.'

We had a chuckle at Harriet's expense, but when my kids stepped on the court, they did have fun. They had fun hitting balls over the fence. They had fun playing in cutoff jeans and black t-shirts. They had fun when I got lost driving to away matches. And after a while, I didn't have to remind them what time practice began. They even started asking for balls so the could play on weekends.

On the Saturday morning of Parents' Weekend, I put on a striped tie my mother had bought me, said a prayer and set up shop in the cafeteria. For the next two hours I impersonated the man behind the deli counter. Number seventy-two, I'd call out, and a parent or two— sometimes more—would plop down across from me. You, tall couple, you guys get a pound of roast beef and a half-pound of imported Swiss. Tell your kid she does good work but her outlines are shoddy. You, the lady in pink whose kid has a D-minus, you get olive loaf, and you might think twice about taking your brat to Aruba while we're in session. You, the man with the bowtie who keeps suggesting books for my classes, you can rest easy, you're kid's getting an A. You, the lady who wants me to talk less about literature and more about current events—like downhill skiing and the plight of dolphins—no offense to our aquatic cousins, but you're kid's getting a D. Next.

Don, wearing an avocado green shirt, made at least three trips through the cafeteria while I talked with parents. No one seemed to notice him though. I could only assume they were deceived by the shirt, which made it seem that he'd accidentally rolled off the salad bar.

When Josh's mother greeted me at the tennis courts as planned, she learned that her boy was getting an A in English. She hugged me. I suggested she dote all over her son and that he'd hate it.

'More than lacrosse?' she asked, and we both chuckled, for lacrosse with Roger and Sam was the bane of his existence. First, he had the palest legs this side of the Arctic Circle. They would not, and apparently could not tan, earning him the nickname Flash. Second, he wasn't bad enough to ride the bench. Every time he sat with me, he'd complain he was allergic to grass, and he wouldn't wear his jersey to class on game days. To his credit though, Josh didn't flinch when seniors tried to run him over and he always came back for more. He didn't realize, however, that his gumption was inspiring Rog to raise the bar.

'Talk it up out there, Flash,' he'd yell from the sideline. 'Be a leader.'

'I tried that in the dorm,' yelled Josh.

'What are you talking about?' asked Rog.

Josh took the opportunity to quote me. 'It means you can't make chicken salad out of chicken shit.'

Miles Twohig, Josh's partner in misery now that Kwame had been kicked out, burst out laughing. Sam was about to make the boys run laps, but Rog was laughing too.

Josh's mom thanked me again, resisted the urge to hug me a second time and watched the tennis matches for a few minutes.

Per, who'd ignored most of my advice and chose to believe that tennis was an abstract form of hand-to-hand combat, was a classic pusher. He was a strong kid who hit the ball beautifully in practice, and he inspired fear during warm-ups with his black sneakers and bandanna. But when he got into a real match, he hit puffballs that landed within two or three feet of the baseline and waited for his opponent to crumble. He'd started the season as the number-four player on the team, but in practice he'd worn everyone down and reached the top of the ladder. In matches against other schools, however, he rarely won.

Today, with his mother and father in attendance, Per came out to the courts early. He was wearing black sweatbands and a T-shirt with a decapitated guitar player on it.

'Greenie,' he said nervously, 'my mom's never seen me play and my dad used to be ranked somewhere. I hit with him once and quit after ten minutes when he tried to give me a lesson.'

'The horror,' I said, and I called the teams together and got the matches underway. As luck would have it, Per was pitted against a kid who hadn't lost a set in two years. The battle was going to be brief.

'Look what he's wearing,' whispered Lily Rosenblum, a rounder and shorter matriarch than I'd expected. Dad was a rail whose pale left hand suggested that he'd switched from tennis to golf.

Per spun his racket and called out 'P or D?' The other boy chose wrong, so Per served first. Over the next ten minutes, he lost twelve of the first thirteen points without making a single unforced error. Good, in a way, but not good enough. Dad twitched at Per's puffballs and groaned with each winner the other boy hit.

'Come up to net,' he muttered, twisting as Per lined up a shot and stroked it softly across the net. Lily hit him in the arm, told him to shush and wondered aloud whether Per would let her buy him some real tennis clothes.

'Good footwork,' said Dad. 'If we can just get him to quit smoking.'

Per, his tongue dragging, looked at his parents and got aced by a serve hit so hard it seemed to hit the court and the fence at the same time. I clapped politely, which my players had come to expect, and Per got aced again. When he'd lost the first set 6-0, I gave him a new water bottle.

'I can't do anything with this guy,' he said, slumping to the court. His parents seemed to be in even more pain than he was. His opponent was joking with some of his teammates, giving off a winning vibe. Per asked if it'd be okay to cheat a little.

'No,' I said. 'But, think about it, you can't push with this guy. He's way too good.' I reminded him we'd been 'hitting out' in practice, but the concept of taking chances in a match was still foreign to him. 'You don't have to go for the lines. Just play to the open court and when you get a short ball, close out the point.'

I walked away with little confidence: Per was many things, but he was not a chameleon. His father asked what I'd told him, and I gave him my report. On cue, Per hit a ball off the back fence and dropped to his knees.

'Praying isn't going to help you,' I said through the fence.

'I know,' he replied picking up a ball and calling out the score. 'Zero-fifteen.'

'Why doesn't he call it love?' asked his mother, as Per hit his best serve of the day. The ball sailed past the kid on the other side of the court and we cheered. At the same time the hotshot's teammates howled. The kid didn't care he'd been aced, but Per took offense to their derision and started playing better.

Per's mother clapped for every point he won. Dad chewed on the knuckle of his index finger. Of course, just as Per got comfortable taking chances, Debbie Tremont strolled by to torment him. Seeing her, he framed a ball into the trees, then picked up a pinecone near the side fence and smacked it with his racket.

Mary Katherine came by with a lawn chair and sat. I told her it was going to be a long day for my team and noticed a little sun block on the side of her nose. I wiped it off and caught Per's mom glancing at us. Per broke a string on the next point and screamed. He was losing four games to one and trying way too hard now.

'How can I play with all this crap going on?' he said, when I came to the rescue and lent him one of my rackets

'Are you kidding? You got your ex-girlfriend checking you out, your parents are here and tonight you're going to eat at the most expensive restaurant in town. What are you stressed about?'

'Winning.'

'Dude, stop thinking and just hit the fuckin' ball,' I said quietly.

With huge eyes, Per sauntered back to the baseline and hit a solid return. After an accidental drop shot and a double fault, he'd broken serve and found some confidence. The rest of his day was glorious. He lost the second set 7-5, but he looked damn good doing it. Afterward dad slapped his son's sweaty back and shook my hand. Then Per's mom asked Mary Katherine when she was due.

'In twenty-seven days,' she said.

Mrs. Rosenblum looked a little concerned. 'Are you guys scheduled?'

'No, that's just my due date.'

'Oh, it's your first,' replied the woman, glancing at me, and Mary Katherine realized she'd been mistaken for my wife.

While my doubles matches were finishing up, the Rosenblums found my boss hiding behind a post at the gazebo and sang my praises. Meanwhile, Rog and Sam were making a very different impression on parents. Motivated by the crowd and frustrated by their team's poor play, they started barking. Some of the kids, like Hodge, fed off their aggression, throwing elbows and making mortal enemies of their opponents. Others, like Miles and Josh, countered rage with finesse, but their coaches didn't see it that way. Sam grabbed Josh by the facemask during a timeout.

'You've got to impede flow through midfield,' he shouted. Spit rained onto the boy's helmet. 'Your teammates are working their tails off and need time to get back.'

If it had been Rog yelling, Josh would've gone back into the game and taken on the biggest kid he could find. Sam, however, hadn't earned the right to get in his face.

'I am playing hard. How do you think I got this?' said Josh.

He showed Sam a purple welt on his alabaster leg.

'You owe me laps Monday,' replied Sam.

The game had started again, but Josh didn't move. He stood for a second with his back to Sam. Finally, he looked over his shoulder and spit on the turf. In seconds, he was poking the ball away from an opponent and advancing it smartly up to Hodge. The spectators, including Mary Katherine, Don and Josh's mom, cheered, but Hodge was dispossessed of the ball by a solid check. He flew threw the air and landed in a heap, tangled with the boy who'd hit him. Instead of jumping to his feet and chasing the play, however, he took a page out of my book and punched his opponent three times. Since they were both wearing protective equipment—gloves, helmets and shoulder pads—no one was hurt.

'That's not supposed to be part of the game, is it?' asked Mary Katherine.

Don dropped his head in embarrassment and waited for a whistle that never came. On the far side of the field Roger and Sam yelled at Miles to chase the play. They'd seen what Hodge had done, but since it was a close game, they weren't going to take him out.

After the game, Miles and Josh, both of whom had played harder and cleaner than anyone, were told to move the goals back to the practice field and carry the water bottles inside. Meanwhile, Hodge limped off into the arms of his adoring family. Looking over from the courts, I saw Sam talking to Mary Katherine. From two hundred yards away, I could see his arms gyrating as he described the game. He was excited and disappointed. The team had won, but it hadn't deserved the victory. Mary Katherine laughed at something. Sam folded up her lawn chair, took her hand, and they walked back to center campus.

Thirty-Seven

The Tannery millpond was covered with thick ice; the sluice running under the building was in danger of freezing. Owen Warland's fingers and toes were stone. His nose and the ears were fire. He wanted to go inside and warm himself, but the salt was an imperative. If the gate froze, the workshop would be inoperable. And if water stopped here, the other mills would become helpless, too.

Owen dug his spade into the barrel of salt then struck a bit of recalcitrant ice. People were surprised he'd volunteered to work on such a night. Perhaps he'd grown fond of prayer meetings, the Shaker life and honest work. In truth, the gesture was made out of respect to the people who'd taken him in, but it was also a way to justify another form of devotion, a devotion to fragile roots and petals.

'Where's your story going?' I asked, staring at the ceiling of my bedroom and holding the phone to my ear.

'You'll like this,' she said, and she told me that four weeks later the outlaw was discovered and told to leave the village.

'Please, it's not an indulgence,' Owen pleaded. 'I can grow flowers where no one but I will see them.' But the Elders, recognizing the threat of Owen's vanity, had already made his sin public. Everyone knew he'd allowed seeds to germinate, cleared a spot behind a shed and stolen manure.

Brother Gideon told Owen he could take the clothes he had acquired on the Holy Mount, including his wool coat. Owen thanked him. The nights in upstate New York were still quite cold. Snow was not out of the question. It would be weeks before there was work for anyone roaming the countryside. Owen didn't seem to care though. He was already lost in the journey ahead and the search for beauty, which he believed came in myriad forms, startling colors, and subtle moments that his hosts failed to comprehend because they were too distracted by simplicity.

So the outsider left with a few shirts and a full stomach, and he headed across the mountains to Albany. There was still snow in shady places, but the sun was gaining strength and any barn would be a warm enough to sleep in.

'You think that's my fate, too?' I asked, switching the phone to my other ear. 'Or do you think Don will keep me? I haven't had the courage to ask.'

'You haven't been able to get more interviews?' she asked.

'My seas have dried up, and to be honest I didn't cast the widest net.'

'Maybe you weren't that serious about leaving after all?'

'I am,' I said. 'But when you get caught up in stuff, cover letters don't seem so urgent. Man, who knows what Don's going to do? You think he's got the nerve to cross Scooter Kelly and the board in his first year?'

'Maybe you can use that gift as leverage. Sixty thousand's a lot of money.'

'Maybe, but what if I take some time off? I could travel?'

'You could just do that?'

'I just sold two houses.'

For a second I thought the line had gone dead.

'Man, I've been dating the wrong guy.'

'Too late now,' I said, and I told her I had to get some sleep.

'I was trying to piss off Iafrati,' said Josh, when he stopped by the out-of-dorm parent's room, 'so I asked what he was doing next year.'

'What did he say?'

'He said he was thinking about working here.'

I tried not to seem incredulous. 'How long before he had you running laps?'

'Didn't do any,' said Josh. 'I had to do pushups instead. He nailed me for goofin' with Miles during a drill.' Miles wasn't thrilled about lacrosse either. He'd wanted to try theater, but the prospect of singing in a pirate costume drove him away. 'And, oh yeah, according to Iafrati, Miles wasn't doing his pushups right, so we both had to do 'em again. That's when Miles called him 'Poofster Napoleon.'

'Did Iafrati even know what he meant?'

'I don't know, but Miles spent the rest of practice running. It was funny. But still, Mr. G, if I hadn't been suspended once, I would've told him what I thought of him.'

'Stay out of trouble, Josh, and don't worry about me.'

'Greenie, wouldn't you be happy if someone found a way to show everyone how big a dick he is?'

'I'm sure that would solve all my problems,' I said.

'Well, I'd be happier if he weren't here next year.'

'But if you did anything stupid, you wouldn't be here,' I said, and I made him promise to be good.

That Friday, Goldie walked into her classroom with a plate of cookies and found it empty. She checked the clock. She looked out in the hall. But the Twenty-First Century Coalition was nowhere to be seen. Walking around the building, she found two of her kids hiding by the soda machines. She ordered them back to the room and kept on searching. In Kara's classroom she found Cass and seven other children of color. They were listening to music on the radio and doing crossword puzzles.

'Let's go, we've got planning to do for tonight?' said Goldie. 'Three schools will be here in a few hours.'

Cass didn't look up. 'I'm not in your club anymore. None of us are.'

'Let's talk about this later,' said Goldie. 'I really need you.'

Kara was behind her desk doing a Sunday New York Times puzzle in ink. On her desk were a small Venezuelan flag and a small Irish flag. There was salsa on the radio, and Goldie may have noticed that the woman who didn't like dancing was bobbing her head with the beat.

'Maybe the other kids will come back and help you,' said Cass. 'I think the Koreans have gone to woodshop.'

Goldie wanted to yell. But we had rules. Kids could leave clubs at anytime, provided there was space in the club they wanted to switch into. This policy was sacred, for it ensured that the interests of students and not those of the adults were the force behind clubs. For a few minutes, Goldie pleaded with Cass. But Cass just apologized, turned to Kara and said something in Spanish that made the woman laugh.

At five-fifteen, Goldie went to Don to tell him her club was boycotting the conference. The guests were going to arrive any minute. The Winter Meeting Room hadn't been set up. And the pizzas hadn't been ordered.

'We're going to look really bad,' said Don. 'You have to give the kids their dance somehow. How long will it take Hideo to set up his gear? Let the kids whoop it up in the Winter Meeting Room. Put some chairs in the hall so they can talk shop. Remember to take a few pictures.'

Goldie ran out of his office and over to Brethren's Dorm, but she couldn't find Hideo. And now she couldn't find Cass either. The student center was empty. It was as if the Twenty-First Century Coalition had pulled a collective brophy and vanished. If she'd looked upstairs, however, she would've found them setting up the Winter Meeting Room under the guidance of Kara Calabria, who was still angry with the Diva of Diversity, but not angry enough to humiliate her.

'They're here,' gasped Don, chugging out the side door of Wickersham and finding Goldie confused and disoriented with her hands on her knees. 'It looks great upstairs, so lead them in and introduce everyone. I've ordered your pizzas.'

If Goldie hadn't believe in miracles before, she did now. And as she led a dozen kids from the Bacon and Meister School into the building, she felt confident that her evening was going to be an overwhelming success. And it was. Except for the fact that every single kid in attendance — including our handsome guests — refused to pose for photographs. The word was out. What word? No one was quite sure, but when Goldie pointed her camera at a kid, the kid stopped smiling and casually turned his back on her. The story ends there. And after a night of pizza, dancing and fellowship, so was the Twenty-First Century Coalition.

That night, while they were having a glass of wine, Kara asked Candy if she knew a twenty-six-letter word for failure.

'I know a six-letter-word for bitch,' said Candy, and she offered to yell it out the window.

The next day the camera crew for the view book came back to campus and the kids remembered how to smile. The crew, however, took pictures of only the pretty kids. They took pictures of my regal tennis team in white shirts. They took a picture of Rog's comely Biology class sitting next to flowers. They put handsome Rolly in a little rowboat and had him paddling around diminutive Tanner's Pond. They showed Gunnar's photogenic Hands-to-Work crew putting up a bat house. They even went to lacrosse practice, where there was plenty to see, but little they wanted to photograph.

At first it seemed a fine afternoon. Rog was in a good mood and Sam was absent, finishing up a phone interview for a job in West Skunk Buttocks, Pennsylvania. But then, just as the players finished stretching, the Asshole With The Whistle jogged out onto the field and mumbled an apology.

'Don't worry about it,' said Rog, and he set up a five-on-five drill and took a knee to watch. 'Game to seven. Losers do an Indian run while winners sit.'

'Come on, Mr. Day,' whined Hodge. 'This is the last week of the season. You can't make us do sprints.'

'Line up,' barked Sam. 'All the seniors on this team.'

In an Indian run a group jogs single file while the person at the back of the line sprints to the front. This is repeated until everyone has gone twice or, in the case of the lacrosse team, the coaches are satisfied that everyone is exhausted and bitter.

'Unfair,' said Josh, circling around the side of the seniors' net with the ball. Miles crossed in front. Josh waited until his teammate found open space and hit him with a pass. Miles scored.

'I'm not running,' yelled Hodge. 'Gimme the ball.'

'Winners out,' said Sam. 'Winners keep possession until the lose it.'

Hodge's eyes blazed as he turned the ball over to an underclassman.

'You're dead,' he said to Miles.

'You gotta catch me, you fat tub,' the boy replied.

Josh almost fell down. Except for the Poofster Napoleon comment, Miles was usually docile—things such as an excess of homework or a lack of pudding at lunch knocked him off stride. Hodge wasn't tickled though. When Josh got the ball, Hodge smacked him from behind with his stick. The ball rolled over to Miles.

'Play on,' yelled Sam.

'That was a foul,' said Josh. He felt like someone had stuck a knife between his shoulder blades and could barely lift his right arm. Hodge was humming to himself.

'I said play on,' repeated Sam. 'You didn't lose possession.'

'That was still a penalty. Why don't you blow the whistle?'

'Do you want to run?'

'The asshole me hit me in the back. Why are you standing there like it's okay?'

'You are so close to being written up for gross disrespect,' said Sam.

His voice may have been calm, but the threat was not. Gross disrespect was a week of restriction and in Josh's case, a black mark he couldn't afford.

To shut his friend up, Miles flipped him the ball, but Josh lost it to the seniors, who passed it around until Hodge took a wild a shot. When he missed, Miles called him fat again and took a swipe at him with his stick. On the sideline Rog was excited to see the Twohig kid standing up for himself.

'Chill out,' whispered Miles, as he coasted by Josh. Then he tapped his buddy on helmet with his stick. Miles also disliked Sam, but not with the same intensity as Josh. True, Sam had forced him to clean dead birds out of the cupola and yelled at him for getting dizzy, but Miles was wise enough to pity the man. He didn't care about taking shit from Sam in practice either. Girls and English papers freaked out Miles. Lacrosse was just a game.

By this time the ring Sam had bought was burning a hole in his pocket, distracting him, making him surly. Then it happened—he yelled at Miles for trying a trick shot and the boy dropped his stick on the ground.

'I'mmmm gonnnnna fuuuckinn' kill you,' screamed Miles, tearing off his helmet and throwing his gloves away. 'You've been picking on me all fuuuckinn' year.'

Everyone was speechless as Miles charged Sam from forty-yards away, his pads flapping in slow motion, his cleats kicking up earth. After what seemed like an hour, he reached Sam and took a wild swing. Sam ducked and Rog stepped in and caught the kid in a bear hug. He saw the tears in Miles's eyes and held him until he stopped squirming. Then Rog pointed toward the woods.

'Take a walk.' Everyone looked into the trees as if they held some new meaning.

'I'm going to tell Don and Bob,' said Sam, patting his pockets to make sure he hadn't dropped his ring.

'No, you're not,' said Rog. 'We're leaving this out here.'

'Does anyone have to run?' asked Hodge.

Rog thought about it for two seconds and ended practice. Sam waited for the team to leave, and asked why he shouldn't do anything about Miles' attack.

'Because this is a sports field and you started it.'

Sam felt betrayed, but Rog didn't care at the moment. He saw a pretty girl riding her bike across the grass, Kara coming to see why the boys were heading back to the dorm early. Since we'd talked, she'd vowed not to let him off the hook too easily. Now she was making his life miserable and enjoying herself. When he was good, she was picking him apart. When he was bad, she ignored him. And when he least expected it, she was screwing him into submission.

'Why does Sam look like he just dropped the soap?' she asked.

'Miles flipped out and took a run at him,' said Rog.

'What will Sam do?'

'If he listens to me, nothing,' he replied, and he picked up a few lacrosse balls and stuffed them into a nylon bag. This was the nicest Kara had been to him in weeks.

'You told him to let it go?' she asked.

'The guy needs thicker skin.'

'Maybe he should stop listening to you then.'

'You know,' he said coldly, 'I've been thinking about us, and maybe we shouldn't go out anymore.' She listened carefully and, to his surprise, she didn't seem upset at all. In fact, while he spoke, she even retrieved a lacrosse ball for him.

'You're trying to dump me?' she said, when he'd finished. Oh yes, she was calm, but Rog could see her gathering momentum. 'You're calling it quits? Well, I've go news for you, Mister man. I am the best mistake you've ever made. And there's no way you're going to break up with me, understand?'

'But I've never fought so much with anyone.'

Kara punched him hard in the chest, and Rog flinched. 'Did that really hurt?' she said. 'You're not dumping me and that's final.' This said, Kara got on her bike and rode away. Rog stood there rubbing his chest and realizing he'd have to work a lot harder if he wanted to get rid of Kara Calabria.

By dinner, The Attack had been mythologized, deconstructed and restaged countless times. There was the comic version, in which the kid goes bonkers and makes funny threats. There was the homoerotic romance, Miles sticking up for the boy he loved. There was the even the cloak and dagger scenario, the boys conspiring to make Sam look like a dick so he wouldn't get a contract, but I kept that one to myself.

Meanwhile Sam visited Mary Katherine in her basement. Don had been on the fence before, but this run-in with the Twohig boy had tipped the scales against him. Don said some kind words. Sam thanked him for giving Mary Katherine a job. Then Don blew young Mr.

Iafrati away. Aware of Sam's penchant for retribution, he told him he was done coaching lacrosse and he'd take back his letter of recommendation if he did anything foolish.

'When that crazy kid came after me,' he said to Mary Katherine, 'I was only afraid that my box was gonna get crushed.'

'What box?' she asked.

'I've forgotten everything I wanted to say,' he replied, placing the ring on the coffee table and dropping down onto one knee.

'Sam, I'm about to explode,' she said, unable to keep from looking at the ring.

'Look, I know things are really messy right now. But I promise I'll have a job in the next sixty days. I'll get some counseling. I'll never talk to Goldie or Roger again.' He gently pushed the ring into her palm. 'Just take it for now.'

He stood tall. The light was dancing on them through the high windows.

'Okay,' she said, slipping the ring over her first knuckle, and shifting her weight forward because the baby was putting pressure on her pelvis. 'I'll take it.'

Thirty-Eight

We'd been sharing a story, but it was my job to finish it.

It was April. Longer days promised summer, but the nights were still harsh. In Emily's classes the boys had finished their studies for the year. Now they were hauling wood, picking up stones and mending fences. Soon there would be corn, potatoes and beets to plant. Her summer students, the girls, were now making soap, tending to the brothers' clothes and preparing to shear sheep. The wool they gathered would keep them busy in the early summer.

Emily rose from bed and put on her long, one-piece dress. Her white collar had become wrinkled, but she had no desire to press it. After donning her bonnet and apron, she hurried outside, holding tight to the iron rail because the wooden steps of her building were covered with dew. A chill lingered in the air, but the day was going to be sunny. She approached the gatepost in front of her residence and noticed the petal of a crocus resting upon it.

Instead of heading for the schoolhouse, she went to the sliver of woods behind the tannery. No one had ever taught her what to look for, but Emily would have been a good tracker. She could identify subtle marks in the earth and tell you whether they'd been made by a deer, a fox or a man's boot. She could also follow them even when they seemed to disappear. To her, tracks were a truth, a story that faded as days wore on and rain washed details from the earth's memory. Emily startled a rabbit. Her skirt became wet. The faint impressions she'd been following, heel marks, a stubbed toe, an occasionally petal, led her to a cluster of outbuildings that housed tools and machinery.

In a shed that had been painted once and left to the elements, she found him curled up and shivering in the remnant of a blanket. At first, the sight of him repulsed her. Flesh had melted from his frame. His clothes were filthy. His mind was addled by hunger. Why had he come back? There was no work for him on the Holy Mount now, not for a man who refused to live simply. But then a wave of sympathy consumed her body. Owen had sat across from her at union meetings. She'd seen lies under his fingernails and had realized he would always be more child than man. In his eyes she saw a dreamer, an artist who would never become a Shaker.

In time, the sheds would topple. Their planks would be taken to build other structures or they'd simply become a feast for termites. By the time I arrived, the shed where she'd found Owen Warland had been gone for over a century, but my ghost would always be able to see its bare walls and feel the cold air inside. By the time I arrived, its dimensions had filled with sapling maples and wild thorns, but I could still feel the anger welling up in Emily as she embraced Owen and his tears soaked her dress.

Dutifully, she brought him food and blankets, but after he'd regained his strength, he hoisted his awkward body off the ground and left, this time forever. I'm sure she never confessed his return or her assistance, for she'd realized disclosure does not always clear the conscience or stanch temptation. Sometimes the truth is a lonely shadow. Sometimes it's more honest to share not what you've done, but what you've learned.

The senior class trip was billed as the Mystery Tour. With great enthusiasm, Per had collected money, scheduled busses and organized an overnight jaunt to a local resort where the seniors could swim, ride go-carts and sleep in motel rooms. It was a great plan except that he'd forgotten to get Don's permission or find teachers willing to chaperone an all-night party. And he hadn't raised nearly enough cash either, so in the end, the class opted to go to an amusement park.

The morning was muggy and gray. The weather forecast didn't look promising, but it was the last possible day for the seniors to have their trip. To make a long story short, half the park's rides were closed for safety violations, three kids got food poisoning, and it started pouring buckets less than an hour after they arrived.

'This isn't a mystery bus,' complained Hodge, when the students gathered to leave the park four hours early. 'It's a misery bus.' But Per was not defeated. There was enough money left over to go bowling and have dinner.

'We're missing two,' announced Rolly, who'd heroically consented to chaperone.

'They went to the emergency room,' said Hodge.

Rolly was stunned. 'When? Why? Which hospital?'

Since no one knew, Rolly had to go back inside. Unfortunately, the information he got from the folks at the ticket office sent him on a wild goose chase, and the misery bus spent the afternoon going from hospital to hospital. When the kids finally got home at eleven o'clock that night—two still suffering the effects of food poisoning—they were so exhausted that no one said a word. They just went to their rooms and collapsed.

My misery came to a head in mid May when the Trustees gathered on campus. Usually our illustrious board took over the Winter Meeting Room, setting up space heaters and cursing the lingering cold just as we cursed the heat of August. But this year, due to the sensitive nature of the business at hand, they met in Don's living room. There, sardined into sofas or perched on folding chairs, they waited for Don to arrive. Waited, that is, until someone noticed him standing by the fireplace and suggested he say something.

'Jeff has a long history at the school,' he said, after he'd shared the confusing stories of what I had and hadn't done with students, 'and even if he's broken rules—going after Sam Iafrati on the soccer field, getting physical with a boy who did something absolutely disgusting in the dorm, no one's ever truly complained about him. You could say Goldie Remlap has complained, but I feel that she's just embellishing hearsay. There's just no smoking gun. Even the girl's reports are inconsistent. She says, for example, that she's never been up to Jeff's apartment. But he freely admits that she has because Goldie Remlap dropped her off. But Goldie doesn't seem to remember where she dropped her off although she remembers taking her out for pizza.'

All eyes were fixed on Don, who despite his magic powers could not escape into the woodwork or hide behind the floor lamp.

'Okay, here's what I know,' he continued, 'Jeff Green seems forthright, but he's stubborn and he doesn't have a deep respect for authority. He has fans—lots of them—but there's no getting around appearances and our enrollment is suffering.'

Scooter Kelly, who'd had a long talk with his second cousin once removed the night before, wanted to know if the girl's family had money.

'She's on scholarship,' replied Don.

'Then maybe we should just cut him loose,' said Scooter. 'I don't care what he's done. The disrespect for authority is enough for me.'

Don knew Scooter Kelly was a hard man and a relative of Roger Day's, but he didn't see this coming. Scared and maybe impressed, he nodded. 'I think that's a wise course of action. I doubt Jeff would make noise. He doesn't seem to be the litigious sort.'

Charles W. Winterhole Jr. had a different opinion. Being the uncle of a child I'd introduced to the novels of Jane Austen, he saw the connection between my helping kids and making money. 'I'm thinking about that gift,' he said. 'If we cut him loose, we jeopardize a substantial amount of money. Besides, he has a bright future in development if we could ever get him out of the classroom. I'd hate to see us make a hasty decision.'

'And he's beloved,' said Don. 'We may not be able to figure out what really happened, but no one can deny that he's popular. Or that Sam and all the kids we've talked about today are leaving in a few weeks.'

Talk of truth and image ricocheted back and forth the entire evening. A small group led by Scooter Kelly were in favor of dismissing me. But Chuck Winterhole's rowdy gang thought my presence was more important than a rumor that'd disappear five minutes after graduation. In the end, after three tedious hours, the board adjourned having agreed upon only one thing: that their next meeting should be shorter.

Time was my ally, for the trustees lacked stamina. They just wanted someone to blame if things got worse, and they wanted cocktails. So the next day, when Scooter tried to rally more support, he couldn't find any. In the end he turned to Don.

'I guess we'll agree,' he said dejectedly, 'that you seem to know the most, so maybe it's best that you use your own judgment on this issue. Maybe that involves firing Jeff Green next year. Actually, that's not a bad idea. You could make it all about job performance and have a year to create a good paper trail. Or you could just fire him now. That'd be okay.'

Hoping to turn to more exciting business, and cocktails, the room agreed with Scooter's idea, and the buck was officially passed to Don, who thanked everyone for their work and finally faded into his sofa.

Around two in the morning, after Scooter had fallen asleep in one of Don's guestrooms, two of the younger trustees crunched up the gravel toward my building. As they settled in, I put my ear to the door separating my apartment from their rooms.

'Scooter's amazing,' said one.

'That's an interesting way to put it,' said the other. 'What did you think of Don's performance?'

'Which one is he again?'

'The dirigible.'

'Moored and bored?'

'Terrified is more like it.'

'That's what happens when you're born without testicles,' laughed the first.

'No, he just passed them along to Goldie Remlap,' joked the other, and they turned in for the night.

Heading back upstairs, I saw a flashing light on my infernal answering machine and I pushed it. I recognized the voice immediately and my spirits soared. But just as fast they came crashing down.

'Hi Jeff, Rose here. Something's come up. I just learned that one of my teachers has gotten pregnant. I didn't even know she had a boyfriend, but to make a long story short, this gives me the chance to shuffle a few things around, and now I have a vacant part-time position that will become slightly less part-time in the spring. It's not permanent, and I know it's not what someone with your experience is looking for, but we both know strange things happen at boarding schools. Anyway, give me a call and I'll fill you in on all the ugly details. Until then, take care.'

I was lying in bed when I heard the tapping. In a pair of boxers I went downstairs and opened the front door. Standing there in her bathrobe was Mary Katherine, who hadn't wanted to bump into the men snoring in the rooms above her. I invited her in and walked toward the living room, but as I rounded the stairs, she started up to my bedroom. I told her to be careful of the pillar and followed her upstairs, where after crawling under my comforter, she tested my pillows and took the one she liked best.

'Sam gave me an engagement ring,' she said, turning out the light. 'He got down on his knee and everything.' In the darkness I couldn't make out her features.

'So you've accepted?'

'I took it from him.'

'Dunwell called back,' I said, putting my arms around her. 'They have a part-time one-year position.'

'Where am I going to watch hockey?' She asked.

I felt her hands. No ring. She wriggled closer and held my arms against her body. Her skin was warm. She smelled of oatmeal and lavender. I kissed the back of her neck.

'Who say's I'm taking it? It'd be like starting over. What do you think I should do? Are you really gonna marry Sam?'

She yawned and pulled on the covers. 'I think I've grown on you.'

'Like a rash.'

'I'm being serious.' She yawned again and her voice became sleepy. 'When are you going to say that you like me, too?'

'Never,' I said, as her breathing grew lighter and lighter. 'Maybe in the morning.'

Classes were ending. Finals were beginning. We were three days away from the school play. Five from graduation. It was getting warmer. Art had already broken out his leather jacket and taken a few spins on his new motorcycle. I didn't know what they hell I was going to do or who would even have me.

'What's wrong with you guys?' I asked my sophomores.

'I'm tired,' said Joe. 'There were some bugs outside my window. They made noise all night.'

'I was eating nachos at eleven,' said Miles. 'They gave me bad dreams.'

'Mr. Meadows let us have a party in the dorm,' said Josh.

'What was the occasion?' I asked.

'We've been good,' said Joe.

'Of course you have,' I said, and I passed out the review sheet for my final exam. The kids whined until I promised to put some bonus points on the test.

That afternoon, my tennis team also complained about being tired.

'It's too cloudy. Why do we have to practice?' moaned Per, who'd won his last three matches. The others were lounging in the shade or swatting pinecones with their rackets. Harriet was wearing her roller skates again.

'Because we have our last match on Wednesday and you guys have a chance at a winning record,' I said. 'Wouldn't that make you proud?'

The kids trudged out to the court and started listlessly hitting balls. I thought about a contest—anyone who could get two points off of me won a sub, or a 'Lefty Challenge'—a round robin with our weaker hands—but my ideas were short circuited by a gust of wind and a sudden downpour.

Everyone except for Per and I scurried under the trees.

'Are the balls gonna be ruined?' he asked.

I hit one out of my hand that skidded past him. 'Don't worry about it.'

After a few strokes, Per got used to the new bounces and a few of the others abandoned the trees to join us. Puddles formed on the court. Our clothes hung off our bodies. Sometimes the balls died with a splash. Sometimes they flew by so fast they were impossible to hit. Soon everyone joined in, and while all the other sports teams ran for cover, we screamed our heads off. Practice eventually deteriorated into a wet tennis ball fight. Then it was a puddle-jumping contest.

While we were playing, Don drove around the back of the cafeteria to dump some cans at the recycling shed. From his car, he watched ten minutes of my practice and listened to Frank Sinatra on the radio. At one point, he noticed Goldie walking toward the courts in a green raincoat. The kids were still jumping in puddles and throwing soggy tennis balls at each other. Harriet was hitting them high into the air so Per could catch them in behind his back. Goldie picked up a ball that had rolled off the court, an extra muddy one, and walked up behind me. In the last twenty-four hours, Sam had stopped talking to her and Rog had invested all of his remaining energy into breaking up with Kara. Her club was gone. She was alone. Even Art was balking at the idea of having a kid just yet. It made sense that she'd wind up and nail me in the back of the head with a wet tennis ball.

It stung like hell. The thing rolled all the way to the side fence. The kids froze and looked in awe at Ms. Remlap. Then she realized that they all had wet tennis balls in their hands and took a step back. There was nothing she could say to stop them. The kids advanced on her and cocked their arms, but I raised my hand.

'No,' I barked above the din of the rain, and knowing exactly what I wanted, Per threw his tennis ball at me instead. Another kid hit Per in he ass with a wet shoe, but then we all wailed because the clouds were starting to break up and the rain had stopped.

By then Don and Goldie were gone.

Thirty-Nine

I'm a skeptical idealist, a view that contributes to a belief in goodness—God in the many—and a somewhat shakier belief in God, the omniscient individual. Growing up, I felt like a heretic, but since my Dads practiced self-absorption and my Mom's Judaism was more social than spiritual, I never felt pressure to attend synagogue. To please my mother and my octogenarian grandparents, I attended services on the High Holy Days and had a Bar Mitzvah. Otherwise, I'd never affiliated myself with any organization (be they Shakers, Jews or Boy Scouts) claiming to have access to the truth.

I do believe in spirit and potential. In my book anyone can become Gandhi, Galileo or Martin Luther King. And I have no problem calling their gifts divinity. I once joked with a more pious girlfriend, one struggling to understand her relationship with God, that I was trying to decide whether I was God. She laughed, but a week later she broke up with me. Maybe she saw goatskin pants and fire dancing in my future. Or maybe she failed to understand that even if I lacked conviction, I couldn't walk away from faith, that power that fills my center and makes me do irrational things.

When I walked into Don's office after lunch, he was wearing a red tie and intently loading a stapler. His desk was spotless for a change. Snapping the stapler closed, he looked up with an efficient gleam in his eye.

'Are you going to be at Dunwell next year?' he asked.

'They offered my a full-time potion, but it disappeared a couple weeks later.'

Don was perplexed. He didn't think things like that happened at schools like Dunwell. His eyes told me he wanted to commiserate, and maybe he realized there was more to my story, but he stuck to his guns.

'I'm not a scold,' he said. 'I feel intense disappointment, but I'm not going to lash out.' He aligned the stapler with the edge of the desk, and I was sure he was about to fire me right then and there. 'With that in mind, you can have a job here, but there will be changes. You're only teaching two classes and no juniors or seniors. You will coach, tutor some and work in the Development Office. I think you'll be good at it.'

'I want a shot at being chair of my Department. That means if they vote me in, I want to know you'll appoint me. Also, when will I get to teach more classes?'

'I don't know, but I could decide by January.'

'Would you mind sharing the thinking behind this unusual decision?' I asked.

'Those are the terms, Jeff. If you don't like them, you can make my life easier and leave. I think I'm doing you a favor here.'

He gave me two days to think about it.

Start over or stay and get bitch slapped? Great. Wonderful. Peachy. I had Don trying to act tough, Gunnar telling me to ride out the storm and Candy saying maybe I was right to follow my heart. Yup, they turned my life into a freaking sonnet. All I wanted to do is lie on the rug and stare at the ceiling, and the world gives me metaphors that make absolutely no sense. And by the time Mary Katherine asked to use my television because it was the payoffs, I was too tired to say no or even ask if Sam knew.

'I don't want you breaking water on my furniture,' I said, as she settled into her spot on the sofa.

'That's pleasant. Do you know how few women actually do that before delivery?'

'Well, if you do, I've got a tarp in my car.'

She gave me the finger and put her hand on her belly.

'What is it?' I asked.

'Just squirming,' she said.

I got up and went to the bathroom. When I came back her face was beaming. I checked the score, but it hadn't changed.

'I just finished this thing,' she said, looking otherworldly. The quilt was like a fantastic skirt, yellows, gold and purple pieced skillfully together, simple yet regal, as sublime as the woman who'd made it. 'This yellow was the drapes in my bedroom at my folks house,' she told me for the third time. 'They were nice drapes until my brother decided to shoot bottle rockets out my window. He almost burnt the place down.'

'Does the baby get a quilt, too?' I asked, forgetting for a moment how miserable I was and how her being there was probably making it worse.

'My mother's making it,' she said. 'That's how we do it in my family.'

'What's your next project?'

'Giving birth. What's yours?'

'I don't know,' I said, but then I was struck by an idea. 'But get your shoes on. I want to show you something.'

Rog once sent my Hands-to-Work crew to clear fallen trees from the iron fence surrounding the Shaker graveyard. With our dull saws and axes, we trudged up to the site ready to work, but when we saw the headstones—some leaning, some toppled, some tall and straight—we started looking at the names and wondering who those people were. One of the kids found the grave of Sister Emily Danbridge, who'd already started to haunt The Holy Mount with me.

I imagine that in death Emily watched everyone she'd known pass away. In time, many of the younger Shakers were enticed into the world and the community shrank to a handful of old believers. A school grew out of their ashes. At first there were only boys, all white and well behaved after a manner. Some even planted flowers in front of the building where Emily had once lived. Years passed and cars with fins and chrome bumpers barreled up and down the main road. Televisions came to The Mount. Eventually, girls arrived and Emily was thrilled, then Blacks and Asians, then gay students, who made perfect sense to a Shaker woman.

'She was loyal,' I said, looking down at her grave, which before the trees had grown up around it, had a lovely view of the valley. 'You think she gave up too much?'

'To be part of a community?' Mary Katherine ran her hand across the headstone. 'You shouldn't think of staying as being loyal. Think of it as love.'

I liked the way that last word came out of her mouth, like she'd been using it her whole life and knew exactly what it meant. I gaze around for more inspiration. The sky had grown dark, and even though it was May, the temperature had dropped into the thirties. Graduation was only a few weeks away, but a few flakes slipped through the sky. They disappeared into the tall grass or melted on the grave markers.

'You'd be okay with me pimping for Don?'

'When do you have to get back to Dunwell?'

'Tonight,' I replied. 'You got a coin?'

She laughed at me, and as we looked around at the gray stones, we laced our fingers together. A snowflake landed on her nose and turned to water. I was jealous of the snowflake. Shivering, far from happy, but not at all unhappy. She didn't have to tell me, but I knew she was going to have a big night, too.

The next morning the sun came out. After an entertaining sophomore class it lured me to the grass across from Wickersham, where I watched a pack of skinny boys slouching down the road. In their dingy ski jackets and oversized sweatshirts they were living proof that adolescence is a form of punishment. I was wondering where they'd be in a few years when Sam saw me on the grass and decided he'd had enough. Madder than the time Miles landed on his head, he wanted a serious piece of me.

'What gives you the right?' he snarled, lowering his shoulder and plowing into me. Flying backwards, I grabbed at his arms, his shirt, anything I could get a hold of. By the time I got my fingers around a handful of collar, his forearm was sliding down on my throat. I flopped on the grass, ducked blows I couldn't feel, saw pretty stars and tracers. I pushed my hands at his face but got scared he might bite me when he let out a growl. I heard shouting. Where'd that come

from? A fist flashed by my ear. Then I rose up into the air. Let go!
More yelling. Let go! Two, three, maybe more, kids and adults. I was
upside down, still clutching at Sam as he called me a few choice
names until someone dragged him back across the road by his orange
sweater vest.

'Greenie, you okay?'

On the ground again, right side up, I gazed at the amused face of
Candy Dafoe. She picked some dead grass out of my hair as the kids
behind her talked excitedly. *He thinks Greenie's doing Kimball. But
she's a house. I know she's a house, but that's what I heard.* When the
world stopped tipping, I wiped my nose on my sleeve. My pants were
stained with grass and my shirt pocket had been ripped off. People had
formed a circle around us. Others were hanging out of windows or
perched atop the dirty remnant of a snow bank. Behind me, some kids
were replaying the fight, showing each other Sam's chokehold and my
silly wrestling moves. It seemed like half the school was there,
including our headmaster who'd heard the commotion all the way
down at his house.

Like a water buffalo in an ugly tie, Don DeWillum pushed through
a wall of kids. The kids, who ignored him, seemed okay, so he
scanned the crowd for a few bewildered seconds until he heard Sam
shouting on the other side of the road.

'How you like that Green?' he yelled. 'I can do it again.'

Don spotted me on the ground, disheveled and missing a pocket,
and the color left his face. Sam was doing an excellent job of
explaining what had happened, so I turned to more important things,
like trying to stand up.

'What'd you do this time?' asked Candy, holding my elbow. Don
took a few steps in our direction, but his instincts took over and he
started directing traffic instead.

'I didn't do anything.'

'I'm supposed to believe that?' she said, as Don waved at cars and
insisted there was nothing to see. Nothing to see, he repeated, his
voice noticeably higher.

'Believe whatever the hell you want,' I said, and I walked past the apple orchard, the Assistant Headmaster's house and back to my apartment.

Looking in the bathroom mirror, I saw a bloodshot left eye and a puffy scratch on my cheek. They told me Sam had been storming all over campus looking for payback, and when he saw me on the grass, he said the hell with a letter of recommendation and came at me fists flying. I just had to smile, and not because of his silly orange sweater vest or the tough decision I'd made the night before either. No, I smiled because Sam Iafrati was the best thing that ever happened to me.

Forty

It was the time of year when cliques broke down. Kids sat at different tables and our school suddenly seemed genteel. All year, we struggled with rules and expectations, but now, tired and comfortable, we were ready for graduation.

In the middle of the night, Mary Katherine went into labor. The next day, with her contractions still twenty minutes apart, Sam brought some lunch to her apartment and they listened to the radio until the midwife arrived. Around two Mary Katherine's mother pulled up the drive with candles and a bag of lemons, and the gang took a slow walk up Chair Factory Road. In the early evening, the contractions became more intense and they drove to the birthing center.

We heard the delivery was long but uncomplicated. The baby puffed up with air and cried like a banshee. It calmed quickly though, and after he'd been weighed, cleaned, probed and tested, he lay quietly with his mother. Candy guessed his eyes were powdery blue. Gunnar bet it had Mary Katherine's mouth and Sam's ears. I was one of the few who already knew his name, Clyde Stephen Kimball. Clyde after a maternal grandfather. Stephen for a favorite cousin and because, like Sam, it started with 'S'.

To the students and their relatives, graduation was a grand occasion, but for those of us who donned cap and gown every year, it was simply an exercise in decorum. I enjoyed the hugging, the tears and the clapping for our newly minted scholars, but the sweetness didn't linger. Soon the throng would be spilling across the lawns. Soon they'd be jamming suitcases into cars and waving. Soon we'd feel the weight of their departure and the void of summer.

I started my day with a trip to the valley. People at Little Sandy's were still staring, but since there wasn't another sesame bagel within ten miles, I had to be stoic. In the dorm, because Rolly had forced everyone to pack two days early, I had nothing to do until the all-school photo and the commencement ceremony.

Sort of proud, sort of sad, sort of scared, I sat on a lawn chair and watched cars. All my students had passed their classes, even Cass, and I hadn't fudged a single grade. Of sixty-four kids, a dozen had been on academic probation for the entire year. Over half took some kind of medication. Twelve had been expelled from other schools because of behavioral problems. None had known what a participial phrase was before they walked through my door, but now they were moving on or moving up, ready for the next grade.

Before I went down campus for the photo, I sealed some papers in a large envelope and put Cass's name on it. On the library steps Goldie Remlap was talking to Kyle Searcy, and when she saw me, she sneered. Kyle, the biggest faker I knew and one of the few people still talking to Goldie, followed her lead and turned up his nose. Art, however, greeted me with a handshake and we climbed to the fourth step together. I caught Goldie staring, mad at Art for liking me, so mad she was probably going to take away his motorcycle again. In front and behind were Rolly, Candy and Kara, whose freckles had returned. Don and some nonpartisans served as a buffer. Kara's sisters and mother were there, too, almost as if it were her graduation, and she was embarrassed to have them watching. She was also reluctant to stand near Rog since she hadn't introduced him to her family yet.

After the picture, which didn't include Sam, we lined up in front of the Tannery for our procession. A few parents pointed cameras at us. Harriet, who was going to a new school in the fall, leaned against the building and watched pensively. She'd wanted to leave early but had stayed to watch Cass graduate. I slipped away from the teachers and wished her luck. She gave me a half smile and a 'thank you'.

The commencement was a blur. Don started things off. Per took over. Cass made a speech. Then Don returned to the podium, thanked everyone and introduced Scooter Kelly, who'd just self-published his memoirs. Scooter talked about the responsibility of having money; then he challenged the students to embrace tradition—family, school, religion, even the Shakers. I saw a few nods of approval from parents as Scooter took his seat beside Don and checked out all the senior girls in the first two rows.

One person I checked out was a brown-skinned woman with perfect teeth and really nice Italian shoes. She was sitting next to Gunnar and holding his hand. Agnaldi Dorgo was the interim Dean of Studies at Miss Posey's School in Albany and because she wanted to go back into the English classroom and be closer to her boyfriend, she was coming to The Mount. Don was ecstatic. He was trading experience for experience, and he'd soon be announcing with great fanfare that we were about to have our first department chair that was both a woman and a woman of color. Gunnar was mad at me for keeping secrets, but he was also over the moon because now he had a brainy girlfriend who ate lightweights like Goldie for breakfast.

When Ichabob and Don handed out the diplomas, the Tannery shook with applause. At most graduations, the crowd is asked not to cheer for individual students. But at a school with fewer than thirty-five seniors enthusiasm is encouraged. When Per rose, wearing only his birthday suit under his robe, his family started stamping on the floor. When Cass accepted her diploma and kissed Don, her stepfather followed her right up the stairs with a video camera and the building lit up with flashbulbs. Finally, we sang Simple Gifts and processed outside. The seniors, now graduates, waited for us to form a reception line.

Hodge, followed by his cautious parents, shook my hand.

'Mr. G,' he said, not wanting or knowing what else to say.

'Be good,' I said. Hodge's mother, a linebacker with big hair, didn't speak. His father, however, lunged over his son's shoulder and grasped my hand. Next, Lana's arms were around my neck. She was going to art school in Rhode Island. Her mother took a picture of us and Lana hugged me again. Caught up in the spirit of the day, Miles, who was just a sophomore, shook the teachers' hands. Since his run-in with Sam, he'd been hanging out with Debbie Tremont. At first she wasn't interested in him as anything other than a friend, but miracles do happen and for the time being they were an item.

Joe also came through with his parents in tow. Joe's pleasure was infectious. Despite all of the fights and failures, he'd actually had the best year of his life. The Mount was the wrong place for him, but it had given him this. To my dismay, however, he was coming back in the fall for more abuse. I hugged him and wished him luck over the summer.

Josh came by and asked if I was really leaving.

'I am,' I said, smiling at his mother, who was waiting at the end of the line. 'The cruelest decision I've ever made. But what about you? You have big summer plans?'

'No, but my mom's playing guitar in a band with a bunch of other moms? They practice in our garage, so I'll get to go out and whale on drums whenever I want.'

'Cool, what kind on music do they play?'

'Beats me, I don't want to listen to them,' said Josh, as Scooter Kelly came over to me in a panic.

'Jeff, I need your help. Is the mother of that kid here? Jason?' He smiled briefly at Josh and tried to be careful with his words. 'The generous parent? Did I get the boy's name wrong again? It's the boy you teach, that rude one who had the funny hair. I just want to greet his mother properly.'

'You're talking about Josh Henderson,' said Josh Henderson.

Scooter's eyes lit up. 'That's it.'

'Yeah, that's her over there in the green dress,' said Josh, nodding in the direction of his mother, 'but he goes by Mr. Tiggy Winkle. No one calls him Josh.'

Scooter thanked us and ran off to put his foot in his mouth.

I wish it had really happened this way. Truth is, when Scooter asked about Josh's mom, Josh identified himself, shook the guy's hand even, and walked him over to his mother for a proper introduction. In the end, Scooter got his money—probably invested it in a hair transplant and a long weekend in Atlantic City—and Josh ended up back home: cutting grass for his neighbors during the day and playing drums with his mom's classic rock cover band at night—until school started, that is, when he worked his ass off to get on the honor roll.

A little ways up the reception line, Cass threw her arms around Kara. Her stepfather had worn out the battery on his camcorder. Her mother, who could smell cigarette smoke a mile away, was searching for her other children behind the building.

'Next stop college,' cheered Kara, whose mother was still just a few steps away.

'I am so ready for it,' said Cass 'And you, congratulations on your engagement. I thought for sure you guys would kill each other.'

Kara's mother turned white.

'You're going to do great in college,' said Kara. Then she hugged the girl and whispered that she'd yet to tell her mother.

Amused, Cass kissed her, moved down the line and extended a cool hand toward me. I gave her a big envelope. She saw her name on it and raised an eyebrow. I told her it was her independent project and she pulled me out of line.

'But I didn't do jack for you. I thought I got a gift for what you put me through.'

I told her to look inside, where she found all the emails she'd sent. I'd removed the background text and the advertising banners and set them up as a series of reflections. She flipped to the last page and saw her A.

'I could blackmail you with this,' she said.

'No you can't.'

On the first letter, I'd substituted Art's name for mine. On the second, I'd used Don's. On the third, Sam's. And so on. Cass gagged when she saw Sam's name. Her stepfather was staring. He didn't look as dangerous as Jesus Demaquina, but it was still time for her to go. I watched as she moved through the rest of the line. At the end, she hugged Don and began to cry. There wasn't any particular reason. It was just the sunshine, the diploma, and the envelope in her hands: a year that was dazzling and implausible, more than she'd hoped for, more than she'd ever feared.

As I was talking to kids and parents, I noticed Goldie glaring at me. It was cruel, but as she sneered in my direction, I slowly, oh so slowly took Oscar's office key out of my pocket and held it up. She may have been confused for a few seconds, but when I turned and tossed the thing into Tanner's Pond, her eyes narrowed and I felt the weight of her miserable ambitions rise off my shoulders. I was free, but as the last few kids worked their way through the reception line, I thought of Bobby Doherty.

A few days before his fifth-grade school year began, my friend went swimming in Buzzards Bay and got hit by a motorboat. By the time they fished his body out of the water he was dead. We learned about it when we went back to school the next week, and no one cried. We were too young. We all remembered though, Bobby standing on top of a desk when he should've been doing something else. Always the entertainer, he'd been disco dancing for us while our teacher implored him to get him down. First she asked nicely. Then she raised her voice. Then she started begging because Bobby Doherty was everyone's favorite, including hers. That's when I stood at my desk and became a game show host. 'Bobby Doherty, Come On Down!' I announced in my biggest booming voice, and the room erupted as Bobby raised his arms above his head, hopped off the desk and circled the teacher. Then as the cheers faded, he settled into his seat and got ready for the lesson.

Six months later he was dead.

Maybe we were too young to cry, but one person, Joey Salerno, took it harder than all of us combined. My guess is that the only reason he played football was the walk home and trade stories with Bobby. Those stories gave Joey something to stand next to. They motivated him to think about what made people tick and even though he weighed only seventy pounds, they turned him into a giant.

I ran into Joey the weekend I packed up my mother's house. On the loading dock behind the supermarket where I got my cardboard boxes, he was wheeling a pallet of canned goods off a truck. He was tall and thin now, mostly skin and bones, and we hugged each other as if we'd been great friends. After a few minutes of catching up, I asked if he still told stories. He said it had been a long time and I remembered. After Bobby died, Joey stopped telling stories and doing impressions. He'd walk home with us just like before. He might even dive over a hedge once in a while or whistle at a girl, but he never told a story again. Once he was a boy who used to look for angels. But now he was stuck. What a lousy way to go.

The Mount became quiet. Just one meeting, which I was going to skip, and a big party, which Don was going to skip. Then the summer would be ours. Mary Katherine was back on campus with Clyde and staying at Don's house since had the space to put up her mom. In addition to helping her daughter, she'd be overseeing her move out of that horrible basement and whisking her back to her real home. In a week Sam would be gone, too. With his pride battered and his anger still very much alive, he was going back to his fancy summer school. After that he wasn't sure. He did, however, have two more interviews and a few letters of recommendation that made him look quite competent. He had Don's because I'd asked the boss not to take back the one he'd written. And he had a beauty from me because it was only fair.

Mary Katherine was the one who stayed. When Don offered her any course she wanted, only one night of duty per week and her pick of apartments, she said she'd think about it. And when Gunnar begged and got her more money, she said yes.

'I can even have your apartment,' she told me when I visited her. She was in Don's house, in a room overlooking Tannery Pond and the playing fields. A breeze was pushing at the curtains. Clyde was fed and half asleep in her arms, wearing secondhand orange pajamas with little bats—Halloween not baseball—on them.

'Take it,' I replied. 'It's quiet.'

'Can you imagine Sam coming back and visiting me there?'

'Surrounded by my furniture? It'd make a good story.'

She didn't realize I was serious, but when I told her about all the crap I had in storage, her eyes got wide.

'The rugs, too? No, you can't do that?'

But I could. She'd be doing me a favor. The image of her on the floor with the baby—fire glowing, windows dark, Shaker ghosts looking after them—convinced me it was right the thing to do. I asked if I could hold Clyde. She nodded, and I slid my hands under his body and held him against my chest. She told me to relax, and soon I found myself rocking as he curled his body into mine. When he started breathing more deeply, his life gently pulsing in my hands, I kissed him lightly on the top of his head.

'Is there anything I'm supposed to be doing?' I asked.

'You could take him when I'm on duty next year.'

'It's only an hour drive,' I replied.

Mary Katherine stood and moved behind me, and when her arms slid around me and her cheek came down on my shoulder, I was ready with a story.

A Reader's Guide to *The Peculiar Grace of a Shaker Chair*

1. Why do most people refer to the adults at The Mountainside School by just their last names? What does this practice reveal about the culture of the school?

2. Is Goldie really a villain? Is she paranoid and dangerous or, considering her circumstances, are her actions justifiable?

3. Are Greenie, Candy and Gunnar models of good leadership? How do the members of this power trio balance their political and romantic goals?

4. Is Cassandra Diaz more than a clever student and an object of desire? How would the story change if she were not in it?

5. What effect has Greenie's mother had on his life? What lessons has she taught him?

6. Does Mary Katherine Kimball make brave or foolish decisions throughout the novel? Ultimately, is she a saint or a sinner?

7. Who were the Shakers and what lessons do they have for the characters in this novel?

8. What's up with the super long title? Are there incidents involving Shaker chairs that shed light on the role of these particular pieces of furniture in the novel?

9. Do Greenie's decisions at the end of his last year on The Mount bring clarity or confusion to the story?

10. What moral questions does this story ask? When all is said and done, which characters seem most conventional and which seem most unconventional?

11. What aspects of life at a small rural boarding school are satirized in the novel? What is the point of this satire?

12. A lot of teaching and storytelling goes on in this novel. What makes a good teacher and a good storyteller, and what do those motifs contribute to the larger tale?

To learn more about these topics, the author and his other writing, visit his website **ianruderman.com**

www.ingramcontent.com/pod-product-compliance
Lightning Source LLC
Chambersburg PA
CBHW022143170626
46807CB00005B/2049